FAIO4FHY

A
SWEETNESS
TO THE SOUL

Other Books
by Jane Kirkpatrick

HOMESTEAD (Nonfiction)

LOVE TO WATER MY SOUL

A GATHERING OF FINCHES

A BURDEN SHARED

MYSTIC SWEET COMMUNION

A
SWEETNESS
TO THE SOUL

JANE KIRKPATRICK

MULTNOMAH BOOKS

A SWEETNESS TO THE SOUL
published by Multnomah Publishers, Inc.

© 1995 by Jane Kirkpatrick
International Standard Book Number: 0-88070-765-8

Cover photograph by Mike Houska
Cover designed by David Carlson
Edited by Rodney L. Morris

Printed in the United States of America

For information:
MULTNOMAH PUBLISHERS, INC.
POST OFFICE BOX 1720
SISTERS, OREGON 97759

99 — 10

"Desire realized is a sweetness to the soul" (Proverbs 13:19).

"For I know the plans I have for you, says the LORD, plans for good and not for evil, to give you a future and a hope" (Jeremiah 29:11).

Round and wrapped in rawhide with a feather hanging from the leather, its center is crisscrossed like a spider web with sinew. A bead or stone symbolizing the mythical goodness of the spider forms the center; the feather represents the eagle, the only bird believed to fly between the dream world and our own. Hung over a child's bed while he sleeps, the spider web catches the child's bad dreams to be burned by the sun in the morning; the good dreams know their way through and wait—to be chased by the child into the future.

DESCRIPTION OF A NORTHWEST INDIAN DREAM CATCHER

This book is dedicated to those who remember:

The People of Sherman and Wasco Counties,

The People
of The Confederated Tribes of
the Warm Springs Reservation in Oregon,

and Jerry.

ACKNOWLEDGMENTS

This work of fiction was inspired by Jane and Joseph Sherar, a remarkable frontier couple. I am deeply indebted to them and the integrity with which they lived their lives. I especially thank the von Borstel family—Donald, Jacque, Carsten and others—for their willingness to share stories, photographs, and artifacts of their ancestors, Jane and Joseph and Carrie Sherar. Their enthusiasm and trust made the Sherar story real. Their encouragement allowed me to speculate and freely weave fact and fiction in relating the Sherar's dream-catching accomplishments.

Special appreciations go to Wendell and Joyce Clodfelter for holding excitement through the years about the Sherars and spending time with me at the falls, pondering and confirming what I thought I knew and correcting what I didn't; to Kathy Conroy of The Dalles who allowed Jerry and me to wander around the sagebrush of her Tygh Valley ranch and photograph the old pack trail and walk the walks and view the views that Jane and Joseph Sherar must have seen more than one hundred years before; and to Patty Moore and Anita Drake for their ideas and insights.

I am also deeply indebted to the People of the Confederated Tribes of the Warm Springs Reservation in Oregon who kept the stories of the Sherar family and their Native American connections alive and willingly shared them with me. Few of their memories have been recorded, yet the Sherars could not have made their mark on history without the Warm Springs people—Sahaptin, Wasco, and Paiute.

Of special note are tribal members Olney Patt and his daughter, Orthelia Miller, and Margaret Charley, descendant of Indian Peter LaHomesh, and her daughter, Rosemary Charley, who shared meals and memories with me. My friends and colleagues at the Warm Springs Early Childhood Education Center believed in my ability to write a story blending the best of both the Indian and non-Indian worlds, fact and fiction. I especially thank my friend and Lummi tribal member Jewell Minnick whose daughter and Warm Springs tribal member, Sunmiet, loaned me her name; and friends Lola Trimble, a Hupa tribal member and Warm Springs tribal members Julie Quaid, Carolyn Strong, Barbara Poncho, Lenora Doney, and Geneva Charley who honored me with gifts of their time, shared experiences, and personal thoughts, feelings, and beliefs as well as the gift of time with their children.

Once I decided to write this book, a variety of people assisted in special ways. People at historical society meetings in both Sherman and Wasco Counties shared ideas of resources and contacts; the librarians at the Wasco County Library located obscure newspaper accounts. The Warm Springs community and the artifacts at the Museum at Warm Springs provided abundant and colorful background information about native life a century ago. The Culture and Heritage Department's work on the grammar of Sahaptin provided authenticity in language, and I am grateful for permission to reproduce several Sahaptin words.

Ruby Kelly, great granddaughter of a family who worked for the Sherars, remembered stories of the dances at the Sherar House. Orville Ruggles and his son, Phil, walked me to a barn built by Joseph Sherar and let me slip my toes in the "green river" of Finnigan, and told me where I could touch the Sherar brand—at the Branding Iron restaurant in Moro, Oregon. A providential phone call—arranged by Dennis and Sherry Gant—from an octogenarian who once stayed at the hotel as a small boy, confirmed the existence of the sweetgrape arbor in the cliff orchard that I had only imagined.

My friends and family, especially Judy and Dave Hurtley, Craig and Barb Rutschow; my son-in-law and step-daughter Joe and Kathleen Larsen; step-son and daughter-in-law, Matt and Melissa Kirkpatrick; our friends Blair and David Fredstrom; and others too numerous to mention who have shared their children with me and supported me in my vision of this book: I thank them.

Previously written works also contributed to this book. Of special significance were articles by Donald von Borstel and Millie Holmes von Borstel and a letter of Wendell Clodfelter's from Jane Herbert's nephew, all printed in the Sherman County *For the Record,* Vol. 3, No. 2, 1985, by the Sherman County Historical Society. The Oregon State Historical Society provided access to Western Publishing Group Publishers book, *An Illustrated History of Central Oregon,* 1905, numerous photographs, and a copy of a letter from the sons of John Todd. Other books I drew upon heavily include Bruce Harris's *The Wasco County History Book,* issues of the Sherman County Historical Society's *For the Record,* William H. McNeal's book *History of Wasco County, Oregon,* and newspaper accounts compiled by the Wasco County Library. LaVelle Underhill's article in *The Dalles Chronicle* and her kind conversations with me provided insights. *Pioneer Roads of Central Oregon* by Lawrence Nielsen, Doug Newman, and George McCart and articles in various works by Giles French and Bertha Belshe were very helpful as was Millie Moore-Voll's book about the Moore home. Several reference works were essential. Marc McCutcheon's *Everyday Life in the 1800s*; J. C. Furnas, *The Americans: A Social History of the United States, 1587-1914;* and Raymond Bial's book *Frontier Home* all made creating life in the 1853 to 1893 era a labor of love. Cynthia Stowell's book, *Faces of a Reservation* was especially helpful for its rich and sensitive rendering of the history of the Warm Springs people and the Confederated Tribes. I am grateful also to her for her recording of the Spokane myth I had Peter share with Joseph Sherar. The myth was originally quoted from *Prophetic Worlds* by Christopher Miller.

I also wish to acknowledge Marilyn Miller for early readings, Carol Tedder for copy editing, my agent Joyce Hart of Hartline Marketing, and Jakasa Promotions for their hard work on my behalf. And I extend a special thanks to Rod Morris, senior editor at Questar Publishers, for his faith and confidence in advance of seeing the finished manuscript and his insightful editing that made this book a richer work. There are others too numerous to mention and I hope my omitting them will be forgiven.

Most of all, I thank my husband, Jerry, for his encouragement, his patience, his suggestions for congruency, and his faith that my writing and this book are part of God's plan for my life. He, more than any other, understands that "desire realized is a sweetness to the soul."

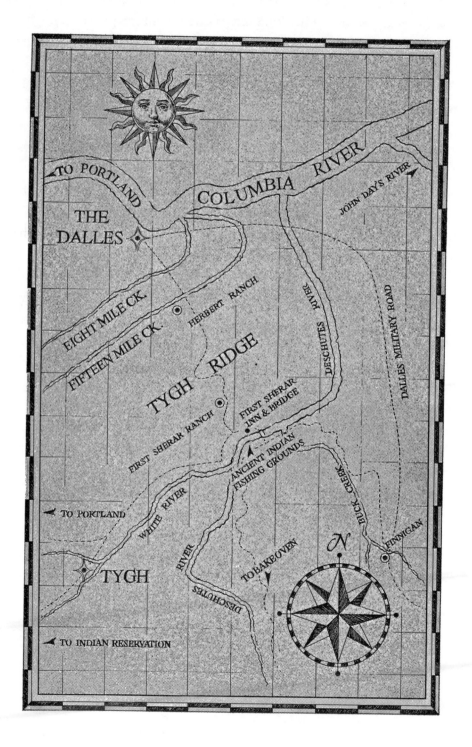

PART I

THE
BEGINNING

CHAPTER 1

CLOSE ENCOUNTERS

LIKE THE SLOW RISING OF THE RIVER after an early snow melt in the mountains, he seeped into my life, unhurried, almost without notice, until the strength and breadth of him covered everything that had once been familiar, made it different, new over old. It was the summer after the tragedy. I date everything from that time, but isn't that often how it is with catastrophes? And I guess, for me, that's when it all began.

I recall little of our initial encounter, really, though in years since he has told me details enough to make me think I remember it well. But I don't. At least not his part in it. Lodenma says I was mourning grievous injustices that summer. At twelve, I doubt I'd have used those words, but Lodenma, my lifelong friend, who is still eight years older than I, had three years of marriage beneath her chemise by that year—1861 it was—so knew first hand about grievous injustices.

No, I would have used words such as "smoking mad" or "hotter than a hijacker's pistol" or just plain "flamin' furious," words that fit my frustration with the mules refusing to enter the pole corral that day. That alone told Lodenma I was grieving or mad, for every Oregon Territory child knows mules will not go where there is danger and attempting to force them is a waste of morning victuals. We should all be so wise.

The milling mules' dust first attracted Mr. Sherar's attention—that and the smoke from my small cooking fire. From a distance (he is fond of relating) he spied the powdery volcanic dust drifting like mist through the pines and firs and junipers. He wondered what created it. He stopped his horse, pulled his telescope from the saddlebags. Through the glass, he eyed a small boy, he thought, waving his arms while mules bolted on either side of the opening to a corral he could barely see for the dust.

"Surprised me," he told me later. "Didn't expect to see anyone so far from settlement, let alone a small boy pushing stock in the shadow of Captain Hood's mountain. Wasn't until I rode closer that I saw you were a little bit of a girl. Still are, just a bit of a thing." He always shakes his head then, eyes a twinkle, and pulls on his grasshay-like beard in wonder, remembering.

That day, I'd pulled my skirt up between my legs and tucked the hem of the homespun into my yarn belt giving me more freedom to move while revealing two bony knees over bare feet.

"But it was your eyes," he said, "that startled me. So dark, like obsidian globes nestled into white porcelain." The Indians named them "huckleberry eyes" promising I'd be fruitful, which I guess I've been in a way.

Of course, I was flamin' furious and I suspect my violet eyes, huckleberry or not, were as hard as black marble. And while I vaguely remember seeing a tall man on horseback off the trail holding a brass glass to his eye, I was more concerned with the mules.

Papa had sent me to fetch them. I was to bring the animals into the shady upper corrals, then ride one home. In the morning, he planned to return with me and push the small herd back to winter nearer our cabin named for the place along the Barlow Trail where those bound for Oregon crossed our creek. Fifteen Mile Crossing we lived at, in the valley of the Tygh people. Our old home is less than a day's ride from this home where we live now, but I have not seen it since the altercation with my mother over Ella all those years ago. It's funny, the pleasures we deprive ourselves of rather than face our fears.

After several disastrous attempts that morning long ago, I stomped again to the corral gate trying to see what would keep the animals from passing through it, wishing just for the moment that I had a herd of horses to contend with. Horses can be convinced to enter in, so willing are they to give up good sense to loyalty and making humans happy. Not so with mules.

I ran my fingers over the poles worn smooth by animal hides rubbing past; couldn't find any slivers or thorns or bees. I looked over the ground just inside the gate but saw nothing but a few pine needles scattered like dead grasshoppers in the dust. Nothing I could see in the corral opening should have bothered them. And beyond, the corral was empty, quiet, cool.

Miss Em, the biggest, darkest mule, stood well beyond the circle of poles, but had not run off. It was as though she wanted to go in but something kept her out. Not unlike some people, I suppose.

"Come on," I pleaded, walking toward her, my palm open in begging. I was getting hungry and she was usually easily caught up. I thought I might tie her to the railing and then gather others up one by one and lead them through. But that day Miss Em jerked back, twisted and bucked her head, kicked out at the hot noon air, snorted, then burst toward an abrupt stop just beyond the gate. Dust spattered like buckshot into the still fall air.

I started around her to herd all seven of them up and try once more to yell them through the gate when I saw movement from the corner of my eye. Just the glimmer of movement, near the center of the corral, almost like a bird's shadow or like the seepage of water from a leather bag left lying in the dirt. But there was no bird, no bag. And no water in the dirt.

I turned slowly. The movement increased, in several directions now, the ooze taking on familiar shape and multiplying. More than one. A den of them, in fact, writhing and turning over each other in the dirt just beyond the gate, making the dust move ever so slowly like the beginnings of an avalanche of snow. The movement formed into diamonds of brown and white and then I recognized them and their hiss.

Their presence incensed me, left me with an exaggerated sense of outrage, of invasion, that they should be there, in *my* corral. Childish fury propelled me toward revenge.

Charging to the fire, I grabbed a limb with flames burning at the end, then jerked the kerosene lamp I'd set quietly beside a sitting log. I gave no thought to the danger. I spun toward the reptile pile, sprayed the kerosene from the lamp over the writhing forms, and dropped the flaming stick.

Rattlesnakes never bothered me after that. At least not the legless kind.

The stench and the black smoke it billowed up into, the braying and snorting of mules, and the scorch of heat at my feet and my face are my strongest memories of that day, not that moments later I met the man sixteen years older than myself who had been staring at me from a distance and whom in less than twenty-four months I'd marry.

CHAPTER 2

FLUFFY MAN

JOSEPH WAS TOTALLY TAKEN with Frederic Tudor, and I suppose that's when the dream really began though it must have been misting up over the lakes of New York long before he met that fluffy man.

I couldn't believe it when Joseph first told me of this fluffy man's wild scheme. We were lying side by side watching the December snow pile up against the isinglass, listening to the wind howl in outrage at our comfort and safety inside our small Oregon home. As the ice formed on the glass, Joseph told me.

"Ice? In the tropics? But how could that be?" I asked, propping myself up on one elbow, sure he was teasing me, something he could easily do with his sixteen years' head start on my experience. But he wasn't. He stretched his muscled arms behind his head. His blue eyes took on a faraway look as he remembered that strange little man who taught him about risk and dreaming.

He met Frederic the day he tried to leave New York, a place Joseph had no reason to desert. At least that's what the family lore is. I've heard wide versions when we've ventured back east to sit around the family table with his brothers and sisters, nieces and nephew. They all say he had no reason to leave.

Joseph's father owned a large farm near Nicholville in upstate New York where Joseph once served as the family expert in stock handling. Though he could match a set of horses to the harness better than most around the county, by the time he was twenty-three he'd settled on his preference for mules over horses "because of their superior intelligence." It's a point he debates still over cards in the saloon.

His father ran a store that offered everything from garlic to harrow plows, pickles to pitchforks. They fed the store from the local produce, imports, and their own millinery and mantua-making operation. Not the flimsy over-garments of the French but American corsets, stiffened with whale bone, sturdy hemp, and flax. Those corsets cinched and shaped the women of an expanding nation. I always felt they cinched more than shaped, but no one ever asked those of us who wore them.

When I visited their store in later years, I was totally taken by the rainbow of colors of calico and the leather boots of Moroccan blue that stretched from counter to rafters. Barrels of pickles floating in salt brine and wire baskets of brown eggs and wheel axles and cooper's rings shrunk the aisles requiring ladies of the day to walk sideways with their wide skirts, their cloth handbags dangling from their wrists rubbing against the bounty as they passed the clerks bent to their work. So much! Such luxuries! And Joseph left it all and had to argue with his father for the privilege.

Joseph says his arguments with his oldest brother James sizzled like any youngster trying to best his older brother. But his arguments with his father burned. "His nostrils flared" with the mere mention of The West. Joseph reminds me that the Hebrew word for "wrath" is translated as "flared nostrils," and I can almost see the old man's outrage rolling up his Irish face, his thick white mustache bobbing as he spoke: "Ye've no need ta go like yer bro," (Joseph could mimic well his father's words). "Ye've all ye need ta here." Then he'd slam his hand on the table and watch the pewter plates rearrange themselves as they often did around Joseph's family table.

"Papa never did understand," Joseph said. And he never crossed the divide to visit us in later years, either. That always bothered Joseph since he saw his father as a kindred spirit having immigrated to the new world from Ireland before Joseph was even born. Joseph saw himself as doing little different.

Maybe if James had not gone west first and done so well, it might have been less troublesome. But Joseph's oldest brother had made the trip around the horn in forty-eight and hit the California gold fields like a hungry coyote in a rabbit warren. He returned four years later laden with a dishpan full of nuggets, treasure enough to last the family a lifetime. After that, his father could never understand why anyone—especially the baby—would want to leave New York.

Of course, my husband sought a different kind of treasure and his father couldn't see the vision. Joseph acknowledges that inexperience hampered his ability to articulate well enough for his father to accept and understand his youngest son's dreams. But I suspect parents never truly accept their children's plans as real until they break out on their own and make them so, regardless of how well they speak their dreams.

Joseph's articulation improved immensely after he met Frederic Tudor. Now there was a visionary! Joseph encountered him the day he walked into a saloon in Albany, New York. Joseph had just missed his intended ship, the ship he planned to take to the Isthmus of Panama on his way west. No reason to have missed it. He just got distracted by the sights and sounds of a strange city. His only regret in missing the boat was that he also missed hearing the calliope. He'd paid extra for that music meant to entertain the deck passengers. He'd wanted to hear the pipe-machine press out happy notes as they sailed across the ocean. An extravagance to be sure. "But what's money for if not to pay passage into interesting," Joseph told me more than once. And then he missed that ship.

Having to wait for later passage, he slipped inside the cool, dark saloon and there met Frederic.

Surrounded by boisterous men with sweat stains streaking their hats, bearing calluses on their hands, Joseph spied that portly man almost as tall as he was wide who "looked like a ball of dough with legs." My friend Sunmiet, a Sahaptin-speaking Indian, would say such a person was a "fluffy man," round like a dandelion fluff, but she never met him. Neither did I though he touched my life.

Frederic impressed Joseph. He wore the finest cashmere suit, hand-tooled boots and a top hat. A red cravat pushed out of his vest like a biscuit pulled from yeast and he talked with his hands, swinging them about in wide arcs, and slapping the side of his head to make a joke referring to himself in German as "dumme Hund," which I've since learned means "dumb dog," a contradiction to be sure. But the most striking feature of the man according to Joseph—

besides his ability to hold the attention of the entire room in the palm of his hand—was his beard. "Two white stripes on either side of his chin with a dark swatch in the center making him appear as the brother of a skunk. Which he wasn't," my husband reminds me, though there are others who might have debated that.

Frederic Tudor had a dream that seemed so bizarre and far-fetched that when Joseph told me of it during the first years we were married, I simply thought he had cogitated on the memory too long and so had fouled it up. But he had actually worked with Frederic and helped him during those months aboard his ship, and so remembered well.

The visionary mind takes many turns before settling on any specific path. It's been the experience of my husband at least and many others who set out to settle in Oregon Territory. Frederic told stories of his own detours into strange investments before he settled into success: selling a salve he acquired from an itinerant photographer said to heal the skin; creating a hotel in the hills near his home of Kerheim-tech in northern Germany, and a summer on a tropical island spent making *Beches-de-mer* for export. Joseph said the latter sounded like some delicacy served in Portland's finest restaurants. To me it sounded like what fills a baby's under napkin in the morning, but that was after Joseph told me that the "delicacy" Frederic shipped came from dried sea slugs sold as aphrodisiacs to the Chinese.

Frederic's strange meanderings into those early ventures were mere side trips along his path, it seems. While the ship's oak creaked, he told Joseph over late-night brandies in the captain's quarters what it was that truly captured him, heart and soul. Frederic shipped ice. From the frozen lakes and streams of New England to the hot ports of New Orleans and across the ocean, to the West Indies, he carried frozen water.

"But how did he keep the ice? Not deliver just puddles of water?" I asked my husband, skeptically.

"Wood chips. And sawdust from the ship yards. And a special cooling system designed by a friend. He had lots of help from friends," Joseph told me.

That a man could see in the familiar and the every day something that could be uniquely rearranged fascinated Joseph, and me, when he told me of it and I finally believed. Frederic had viewed the ordinary and with vision, made it extraordinary! Joseph had seen those same lakes and rivers all his life, thought about them only as they fit into the scenes around him, the way they drained an area, what life teemed within the ponds. In the winter, he thought little of them as frozen except when he brushed snow off a circle to skate about, pulled a fish out through a jagged hole in January, or shortened a trip by horseback because the frozen rivers were easily crossed. It never occurred to him to capture the winter of New England and sell it in the summer. Why, who knew what other sort of ordinary things could be converted into challenges of elements and skill? Who knew how changing the way we see things could also rearrange our lives?

The odds against Frederic's success were enormous! He had to find caves or warehouses close to the ice for storage; locate sawdust to cover the blocks; load the frozen cubes onto the ships and keep them cold while riding the waves through the heat and the humidity. Frederic gambled always with the elements. And people. He had to rely on efficient and expert help at several steps to prevent the precious cargo from perishing before one's eyes. Then arriving in the hot cities of the south, he must have raced the heat, finding buyers quickly enough to outwit the sun. So many things could go wrong! Chance—if you believed in it—had many opportunities to deal the man disaster, but I suspect Frederic liked the challenge most of all.

In its time—the late 1850s—it was a remarkable vision and it doesn't surprise me that Frederic sometimes punctuated his stories with the slap of his head and his deprecating comments that he was a "dumme Hund." Joseph could repeat the gesture, German accent and all. But Frederic's ideas were dogs that did hunt!

"He told me something else that sticks," Joseph said as he relayed their encounter to me years later. "He was a happy man though not so much from the money he made as the effect of his ideas on the folks around him. Said he liked the sparkle in the eyes of children first time they saw ice or the look of surprise when grown men and women felt the cool of another world against the hot skin of their own. He didn't have a family, I guess. At least he never mentioned them, but those kids sure liked him. He warned me not to let little minds or discouragement make my choices. 'Dream,' he said, 'then mit faith, do.'"

Their encounter those years ago impacted Joseph greatly. He was terribly taken with Frederic's mind, the way he converted the ordinary into something extraordinary. Their encounter truly set him to considering his life in a different way. From that moment on, Joseph sought his own ice adventure and stopped looking and started doing the moment he found it those years later at the falls.

CHAPTER 3

SISTERS

JOSEPH HAD A PASSEL of brothers and sisters, all older. I suspect they indulged the child which probably accounts for his belief that he could do anything if he set his mind to it. Initially, he figured his successes were all his, not allowing for any help from heaven.

I relied on heaven earlier. My own childhood began as the second of six born to my mother who did not marry until she was nearly thirty. By the time I was two, I was an only child. My parents kept the memories of their first-born, Ambrose, tightly refuged in their hearts. He lived before me and then died. Ambrose had moved with us to Oregon from Virginia, of course, but before Rachel arrived, he'd already been laid to rest in the Fort Dalles cemetery. "First child buried there," Papa said once then set his jaws whenever anyone mentioned his son's name, and I noticed over time that no one did.

My first memory is that of hearing a baby cry. Flames rippled shadows like water on the cabin walls while I huddled on my bed and watched. Like the call of a distant red-tailed hawk, the crying pierced my thinking, agitated my thumb-sucking. Shriveled and white, my stubby thumb resembled the tapered end of a tallow candle, but it tasted like security to me. I popped it into my five-year-old mouth, but it didn't stop the crying. The harder I sucked, the more that baby cried and there was nothing happening behind that second-room door.

I was hot, though it was cold outside in the April night. Behind me, a hide-covered window kept the night air from slipping like a cold shadow over my shoulders. Pungent resin beaded on the warmed cabin logs. My dark hair stuck to my face and got caught on my thumb, some. Hound moaned under the bed and I knew I'd be in trouble if Mama or anyone else discovered I'd snuck him in for the night.

I needn't have worried over Mama, being she was the one preparing to deliver. But on any other night, I wouldn't have tested her. She was a giving woman, looked often after others, but she rode life with a firm hand on the reins and one didn't consider putting an obstacle in her path lightly. Hound under the bed would have been an obstacle.

Without warning, Lodenma, the midwife, scurried out through Mama's door and into the main room of the log house Papa had built at Fifteen Mile Crossing the second year we homesteaded in Oregon. Lodenma's bending to the fire made the room darker for a minute. She wiped her hands on the long apron and dipped water from the caldron steaming in the fireplace. The water hissed as it hit the colder pan Lodenma came to fill. Her knuckles were large and red; working knuckles.

She turned to me, her thick braid swinging. She said with sternness: "See what you can do about the crying, Jane." It seemed every adult could direct a child in those days, even if the adult was only thirteen which was all Lodenma was.

I felt frozen to the bed. I could smell the dusty corn husks beneath the thin muslin cover I sat on. They scratched my sunburned legs. I could hear the hissing and steaming at the fireplace—but I didn't want to hear Lodenma tell me to stop my sister from crying. I didn't know how!

"How is Mama?" I asked.

"She's doing fine though she thinks not. Wish your Papa was here. Her harsh words are meant for him anyway."

I thought about my Papa riding off on his big mule, dabbing with a blue bandanna at his right eye socket. Water oozed from behind the marble that filled the space in his face that had once held an eye. "I wish Papa was here," I said.

Lodenma grunted and redirected me to my crying little sister. "He's not, so it's up to you. Rachel'll quiet. Just be with her." Lodenma set the pan down for a minute then shooed her hands toward my direction, like clucking chickens into their pen. She watched me until I slid from the cornhusk mattress and began to move across the green and yellow planks of the floor that had once been our wagon bottom. I still sucked my thumb.

The sunburn stung. No one had thought to put bear grease on my legs. I was too tired after grubbing sagebrush all day to even notice that my dress had exposed my skinny legs to the hot Oregon sun. And Mama clearly had other things on her mind.

A little cloud of corn dust stirred around me as I waddled toward the cradle and the now hysterical toddler. Tears squeezed out from her eyes sealed in anger. Her face was chapped almost, from crying. I don't think I ever saw such red, raw pain as I saw in my sister's face, and I felt ashamed for my delay in coming to her aid. I gave her the only thing I could think of that might comfort her: my thumb.

Looking back, I realize Rachel was just then learning to drink cow's milk instead of Mama's which added to her distress. How hard it must have been to have regular suckling suddenly cease.

I bent to Rachel and talked in little sounds she always liked when Mama did it. "It's a-right," I said, "It's a-right." Leaning almost backward, I circled my arms around her, her face to mine. Despair dribbled from her nose. Her dress trailed down and caught between my legs and I barely made it to the bed before flopping her down. That startled her I think because she stopped crying, her brown eyes staring up into my blue ones. I always remembered that: Startling someone could bring them out of their fit.

So Rachel turned quiet when I dropped beside her and put my arm around her shoulder and we both sat staring at the closed door that kept us from our mother.

Lodenma grunted approval then left us girls to return to the matter at hand: My mother, Elizabeth Herbert, was about to give birth to her fourth child in six years.

Sister Pauline was born that April night of my first memory and it was her crying behind that closed door I remember next. I'd just settled one child down and another popped up distressed! When she scurried out of the second-room door, Lodenma told our wondering faces that the baby's crying made good sense, told all of us she was alive.

By then, I wasn't sure if Papa was. He wasn't anywhere around. He said he had to ride to Dalles City, to talk with men about more land and whatnot. Mama said he was "barkin' at a knot" with all that land talk, that he should just take care of the 639 acres we already had. But I suspect hearing her hurtin' in childbirth might have sent him on his way. And he had "interests" he said, giving him an excuse to be gone.

Mama said men always had important, busy things to do and women were to help them, stand behind them. In return, men would provide for them. She said Scripture confirmed that.

I suppose I thought it wise counsel until I learned to read and found all those ads placed by husbands for their run-a-way wives who apparently now resided somewhere in the territory. They offered good money for their return! Some folks even made a living finding and returning them. And I wondered: If they were taking such good care of their women, why'd their women leave?

Mama never left Papa, of course. But he left her that night, though Lodenma said he laid the swaddling clothes out for the newborn just before he rode out, something I think a less loving man would fail to do.

Mama usually had the last word and did that day too before Papa headed out on the mule.

On the morning after Pauline's arrival, Mama sent me out to gather up the milk cow. At dawn, when the earth has that murky underwater look, I headed out. My bare feet left little impressions on the frosty ground. Precious, our old cow, let me catch her up after some deception on my part (I put pebbles in a bucket to let her think it was grain!). As I milked, the sun came up pink over the grasslands and sagebrush, spread like a blush toward the timbered hills behind our farm. I burrowed my head into the warmth of Precious's side. She didn't even kick or dance when I warmed my hands in the clammy space between her udder and her leg.

The rhythm of the liquid with its distinctive scent as it made its way up the sides of the pail almost put me to sleep. I was tired from having Rachel's feet in my back most of the night. Precious woke me up. She swatted her manure-stained tail at my face and dropped a glob of green into the milk. "Precious!" I complained wiping the slime from my cheek, "now I'll have to strain it!"

Whining at the cow about the extra work she'd given me made me miss what Rachel did. That little one slipped from the house in the dawn and headed to the paddock, toward the mules. I heard Miss Em, the big black mule, snort with flared nostrils then move with quick-quick trots across the field, her target sure. Only then did I see Rachel crawling, approaching the split rails. In slow motion I stood, yelled at her, my heart pounding against my ribs. "Rachel! Wait! Please don't go in there!" I shouted. "Please, God, make her stop to think," I prayed. She stopped just long enough to toss her sassy head at me then bent to slip between the rails. Miss Em, true to a mule's nature of disliking little things, came charging toward the small intruder and I saw disaster in the making.

But Providence intervened where my short, skinny legs could not.

Rachel's smock caught on the split rail bark long enough for me to catch her up and launch into a lecture, as I'd seen my mama do often enough, until we heard Papa's mule. Miss Em tipped her ears toward her herd mate, no longer caring about the paddock's threatened invasion by two little girls.

"Papa's home. Maybe he brought us something," I said to distract Rachel, relief gobbling up my scold.

She sniffled and we walked hand in hand to the milk pail and then to Papa as he tied his mule to the post. He didn't ask why we were up so early. He said nothing even when I told him the good news that we had another sister. A funny look crossed his face, like the mule had just stepped on his toe. But he wiped his watery right eye and finally said: "A thorn I am among my roses." He stroked my hair with his wide hands, absently, as though I wasn't there.

That's when Mama appeared in the doorway. She had words with him that made my stomach burn and reminded me he'd brought no present as he'd promised. Cheated out of scolding Rachel, tired with milk left yet to strain, I added my sharp tongue to Mama's. "Only thinking of yourself," I told him and rushed past Mama to the inside, Rachel trailing me.

Lodenma held Pauline, and it was here I found my refuge. Tiny, wrapped in cloth once bathed in sunshine, I fell in love with that small, noisy infant in an instant. She needed me, could not even find her thumb! I stuck my finger into Precious's milk and introduced it to the mouth of the newest child who lay squalling in Lodenma's arms. When she tasted my milk-coated pinkie, she quieted, sucked like a cat's tongue on my finger.

"You've a gift with little ones," Lodenma said. "Not everyone could bring quiet to a toddler or soothe an infant with a milk-dipped finger to her mouth."

I'd done both that first night of my remembrance and felt good about it. I even imagined the kind of mother I'd someday be. All my life I've remembered that night when what I did for the babies worked. I protected them, stopped their crying, and what I had to give, someone wanted.

After the tragedy, I wondered more why the Lord would give me such a wealth of gifts, only to later take them back.

Some questions are hard answered.

CHAPTER 4

PANAMA LOSS

IN THE SULTRY STEAM of Panama's Isthmus, Joseph sweated his way toward me though we didn't either of us know that yet. It was the August following his encounter with Frederic and that fluffy man's ice. Joseph arrived in the Isthmus of Panama in 1855 and could have taken the newly completed railway from the Atlantic to the Pacific—once he gave up the lazy days of New Orleans and the late-night feasts at Frederic's table.

But once in Panama, Joseph found himself drawn to the stock corralled close to the docks and felt he would rather be there with the mules and the Indios than riding the rails with the rich.

Once they began the trek across the narrow strip of land he had second thoughts.

First of all, it was late in the traveling season. (When Joseph told me he arrived "late" in the season, I should have been forewarned. It is an issue we have argued about often as he becomes distracted by whatever passes before his mind, totally forgetting that I might like to arrive someplace on time.) Traveling late meant partaking of a much smaller mule train across the land bridge.

The smallness allowed for better conversation with the natives but opened the group up for bandito attacks.

Joseph said it was also early in Panama's rainy season which meant downpours for several hours each day. In early evening, the rain abruptly stopped revealing steamy forests marked with illusive views of pumas and ocelots and white skies sliced with streaked sunsets and colorful toucans. The mountain trails after the rains were as slick as dog-licked plates and the mud promised to stick tighter than horsehide glue to any traveler straying from the trail. Joseph rode the largest mule, his being such a big man, over six foot plus two.

The Donario family handled the mule string. Stocky Benito Donario moved like an efficient chicken, his head bobbing as he checked here and there for loose packs, frayed ropes, replacing and repairing. Broken teeth flashed a ready smile against a brown face as smooth as a baby's. I don't think I ever saw a wrinkle on his forehead. Even years later only tiny ones finally formed around his eyes. His front teeth were separated by a space wide enough to spit through, a skill that always charmed the children.

The sparkle in Benito's brown eyes defied their droopy appearance. When Joseph met him, Benito wore the bright striped wool serape of his people and a flat-brimmed leather hat that was not. "Gift," he told Joseph when he asked. "Of Californio man." Benito wasn't much younger than Joseph, around twenty or so when they met, but he was three years older than his wife.

After what happened on that trip, I was surprised that Benito made the choice he did, immigrating with Joseph. Benito and his young wife, Maria, had made the trip through the Cotillierra Mountains several times leaving the ocean beaches, rising slowly up through the mangrove thickets into the leafy trees of the mountains.

Joseph thought the Donarios good handlers and after the second day he was surprised when Benito moved Maria into the middle position with her horse leading a string of two mules, allowing the "gringo" to ride drag. Usually, gringo clients rode the safer, center slot in a mule string, where the experienced drag could watch to see that nothing went awry.

Joseph said Maria was exceptionally skilled. Quiet, wearing her long traditional dress and wide-brimmed hat, she carried herself regally, had gentle beauty. Once he started to signal her that a rope had drawn up between one of her mule's legs but she had already noticed. She stopped her string, got off, and wove them into a tight circle that permitted her to untie the rope, pull it through the animal's legs and reattach it, then unwind the string without a single mix-up all done as easily as his mother wound yarn around her peg.

But it seems Maria was with child, a fact Joseph noticed while she sang her quick-paced "Punta" as she and her husband playfully prepared the evening meal. The three were dry inside a stone hut just off the trail the second night out. Mules were staked in the lush foliage close to the trail; the trio prepared for the night.

Flour from the flat pancakes Maria patted out for supper dribbled onto her stomach and as Benito playfully brushed it off, Joseph saw the telltale mound.

It bothered him. "It was no place for a woman and not a pregnant woman surely," he told me. He was always of a mind to protect females and didn't understand that in doing so he sometimes did not act in ways that showed respect for the strengths of the weaker sex. He once told me he could never see any woman he was bound to performing such tasks, a thought which always made me laugh as I remember what we've endured together through the years, and what we would have failed to accomplish if he had "protected" me from what I chose to do instead of learning to respect my wishes.

He dared not discuss his reservations about Maria being on the trail. In those days—and perhaps still—it would be unseemly for a gentleman to broach such a subject with another man, especially one he did not know well. But Benito saw Joseph's look of surprise and told him: "Is better she with me now than to be alone." Benito didn't seem the least bit alarmed that his wife might deliver there in the mountains.

But he had taken the precaution of changing Maria's riding position, moving her and her mules in between the men on the string, a fact he pointed out to Joseph who counted it as wise, but insufficient. "You do well, so we put you last," Benito told him. "I watch Maria. Have delivered many babies. Brothers and sisters," Benito said, his wide-sleeved poncho swinging on his short, stocky arms as he motioned, palms down, "not to worry."

Joseph hadn't expected Maria's time to be close enough to warrant the delivery discussion or consider long the thought that the young adventurer from New York might become a mid-wife! But before he could protest, Benito suggested they head outside where he changed the subject to California.

"Will you look for the gold there?"

"My brother brought home a dish pan of nuggets and it did not bring him peace," Joseph answered indirectly.

"*Las mulas son corrajudas,*" Benito said then translated his Spanish. "'The mules are bad tempered,' but you are happy with them. They like you." And while Joseph agreed with that observation, it seemed not to follow in the discussion until Benito added: "Maria and me, we take mules to California, bring supplies to gold fields. Make good money. Send some home, but have Maria and bambino here," he tapped his heart, "and by side. Like you, seek different treasure."

Joseph said he watched Benito swat at bugs, stunned at the enterprising suggestion just when he'd confined Benito to predictable—and truthfully, maybe a little dull. Benito's simple appearance deceived my Joseph. But to his credit, he let new information in and changed his mind. Joseph heard a mule pawing impatiently near the cabin, just out of reach of the lamp light. Joseph said that was the first time he'd considered combining his interest in the mules with his brother's facts and figures about the gold fields. For Benito was correct: the men in the fields needed everything and would pay top prices for muslin for their tents and baking powder for their biscuits. Better, they would pay to have their gold taken out; but only with a skilled handler willing to take risks. And only with a man of impeccable integrity who would risk himself for their fortunes.

He had decided to explore this idea further when Benito abruptly suggested they retire. He said goodnight and took his leave around the corner of the stone hut.

Joseph lifted his leather-bound sketch book from his vest pocket and made some notes. I have that little book still scribbled full with his thoughts of California, Benito, bambinos, and gold. He brushed the gnats from before his eyes, grateful for the lull in the daily downpour. He smelled damp wool and knew the steamy heat had saturated his red wool vest. He smelled his own scent. Returning his leather book to his pocket, he stood, planning to enter the hut to offer Maria the bed she and Benito had so graciously prepared for him as the "gringo client." Perhaps he was distracted with the innovative thought Benito raised, or perhaps he was just tired—whatever the reason, Joseph didn't notice the restlessness of the animals until later, thinking back. So before he could make his chivalrous offer to Maria, he heard the scream of a woman, a scream that sent him plunging through the hut door to her side.

It was no woman.

Maria stood inside, shaking, but the scream rose again from the far side of the hut, where Benito had gone to relieve himself. "Benito?" she said, her brown eyes full of worry. Joseph said he grabbed his Sharps rifle and ripped a lantern from a post. He headed toward the sound trying to place it. Woman? No. Benito? Not likely. Familiar? Yes.

Then he remembered: Cat! Cougar! Like he'd heard in the mountains of New York in the late winter when food was scarce and the felines slinked their way like fallen women down the ravines to the pastures and corralled cattle.

Joseph raised his rifle to his shoulder when yellow eyes flashed in the lamp light. Too quick for him! As he rounded the hut, cursing Maria's independence and unwillingness to stay inside, he stopped in time to see the dark streak stretch its length toward the back of the smallest mule standing not five feet from Maria. He shot once and the cat skittered into the dark and denseness of the foliage.

Maria did not cry or scream but went immediately to soothe the frightened animals, her eyes searching for Benito who appeared, flushed from his own encounter with the cat. "I smell it, but could not see it," he said, making his way to Maria.

"And I saw it, but could not kill it," Joseph told him. He felt bad about missing the animal or worse, that he might have wounded it and thus would make it more dangerous than it was.

"Hungry. Old and toothless or would not have attacked so close to man-scent," Benito said. "Is too dark to track."

In the morning, the rain had washed any signs of blood away and the trio left early after an uneasy night. Joseph said he did not sleep even when his watch was over and he was pleased that at sunrise, they were all ready to head on down the rain-slicked trail.

What happened next stays with Joseph years later though he is older and has cared for many, is wiser and accepts that he has been forgiven. But he still holds himself at fault.

The first time he told me of it, tears welled into his soft eyes, and I held his broad shoulders in my arms and let the wetness from his eyes dampen the tucks of my calico while I stroked his hair over and over the way a mother does a child she knows has wounds so deep no one can heal them. Of all the gifts he ever gave me, his willingness to share his tears I count most precious. It was a gift I held with tenderness despite how frightened his crying made me. No man had ever laid his feelings on my shoulder. It was only later that I understood how a man of strength must be yielding too or he will surely break. I was pleased to be a person he chose to bend with.

He told me that in the morning, following his missed shot, the trail was slick but the rain had stopped. A blue heron lifted its legs, heavy against the thick morning sky. Joseph said he thought of a hundred things that could go wrong: banditos, slipping on the trail, Maria giving birth, and of course, the return of "el gato," so he kept himself and his Sharps ready and alert.

Maria rode before him wrapped in her bright serape, her wide-brimmed hat pulled down over her dark braid. He thought her a capable and pretty girl, he told me, and Benito a lucky man. Almost before he finished that thought, he saw the form from the corner of his eye and believed at first it might be a bird lifting in flight or a snake dripping from the branch beside him. But the general restlessness of his horse and the mules ahead told him it was not.

In slow motion, into the middle of the string, the cat arched through the green onto Maria and her mule all at once and pulled them over, girl and packs and animal, pulled them as they fell. The soft thud as the fractured three met the rain-soaked earth is louder still in Joseph's mind he tells me, louder than the too-late crack of his rifle; the memory of the cat's attack even more vivid than the despair falling onto Benito's cheeks as he screamed for the life of his lost young wife.

But it was the plaintive look of Maria's eyes as life left them that propels Joseph decades later to give so much of himself, attempting, I think, to seek God's forgiveness for what he could not have caused; wanting to believe, perhaps, there is always good in God's plan for life despite the pain that comes with it; pain enough to make us wonder.

CHAPTER 5

SHYSTERS
AND
SHENANIGANS

BY THE TIME Joseph and Benito set foot on the foggy docks of San Francisco some months after Maria's death, they had weathered serious storms and were a pair; friends. He and Benito had chosen to support each other rather than lay blame, a sure recipe for surviving tragic accidents and forming friendships of enduring strength.

That was perhaps what I had missed the year I faced my own losses.

The men had washed away Maria's wounds and bound the body and returned with it to Panama City, wrapped in a pale-striped serape on a travois of mango branches pulled behind her mule.

Maria's people did not blame Joseph, a fact he found astonishing since he blamed himself. In fact, as was their custom—one shared by the Warm Springs Indians, too—the family gave away their daughter's special things. Joseph found himself a recipient. "Maria's uncle give her this," Benito said. Joseph looked down at him as Benito gently pushed a leather bola toward Joseph, sea green turquoise stones hanging from its leather thongs. "Is yours now. To remember Maria."

Touched both by their generosity and that they held no fists toward God, Joseph filed away their coping for future reference.

The friendship of Joseph and Benito blossomed those weeks and then bore fruit as a result of Maria's death, something good coming from that darkness.

After the mourning, they crossed the Isthmus—Benito for the last time and Joseph for the first. The two docked finally in October in the fastest growing city of the west.

Joseph told people years later that you could see the city building overnight. "In one year," he said, "San Francisco went from eight hundred souls to more than ten thousand. A hotel owner's dream!"

In fact, the hotels and boarding houses bulged with gold mine recruits and every fresh upstart with an idea in his head to make quick money. Even the run-aways: men and women running from family, from responsibility, from their past, all found solace in San Francisco.

Hotels advertised "Beds and Baths, Five Large Cents," but assigned three men to every mattress. One never knew whose stinky feet would greet one's nose each morning—or who would inhale yours! Bedbugs slept without charge. Joseph said he wondered if anyone used the baths. What else could explain the general scent of grime and sweat that swept the rooming houses. So the two new friends decided to sleep in the safety of Adam's Livery not far from Market Street, accompanied by the creaks and stomps of predictable stock rather than share beds with total strangers.

Joseph and Benito took little time before determining that shysters and shenanigans reigned supreme in any booming city, and rather than become unwitting victims, they set their own course with a plan. They would buy mules and head inland, toward the bare hills and then into the mountains on one trip before the snow fell. Weather permitting, they'd make a second trip north into Oregon Country where towns were said to be booming along the Rogue River. Pack supplies north; pack gold back south with the mules they planned to buy from failed miners who only waited the sale of their animals before heading broken, home, back east. They'd winter in California on the spoils of their efforts. It was a good plan, the men agreed; one they could implement quickly.

They were almost not fast enough.

I'm inclined to believe Benito's side of it. Not because my Joseph makes himself a hero in his stories—what man doesn't?—but because of Joseph's tendency, still, to put adventure over prudence, curiosity over common sense.

"We walked through a bawdy circus," Joseph said of that first sunrise after the morning fog lifted over the city. "People washed themselves in the open air, shouting to each other about this and that." Horses and mules and ox carts rattled by as vendors wove their way in and out of gobs of people dotting the cold dirt streets like clumps of yellow jackets, listening, hovering, trying to interpret the latest tidbit of direction.

"Sausages sizzled in pots set up beside the street. And somewhere, I will not forget," Joseph told me, "I smelled the scent of a fresh-baked pumpkin pie!" More than one enterprising widowed woman survived those years by baking pies over open fires, a venture requiring no man to help her, I'm told—nor take the profits.

While Joseph swallowed his saliva and cast his eyes in search of pie, Benito signaled to join him under a small lean-to where two men with bulging muscles slapped dough around chunks of potatoes and onions and wizened carrots before dipping them into the bubbling oil of a huge caldron set over an open fire.

The proprietors, "two mountains of men" (according to Benito), worked under the lean-to. One hummed happily to himself as he bent beneath the center- post of their shelter to fold his pasties. Brown flour stuck to his sweaty face where he brushed straight iron-colored hair from his forehead and pushed it behind ears that stuck out like those of the Yorkshire pigs of Joseph's father's farm. The man smiled and his small eyes seemed to sink into his puffed, reddish face.

The other, who sported a thick dark beard, stood large-armed and stocky as he chopped the onions and shriveled carrots. A sharpening stone lay beside an extra cleaver on the chopping block and he picked it up frequently, sharpening his tool.

Joseph rarely noticed height. Being a tall man himself, he seldom described others by their size. Instead, he said the men looked "Irish" with arms the size for fighting.

Behind the men in the shadow of the shelter, sitting with a second chopping block balanced on her calico-covered knees, was a skinny woman who kept her eyes lowered as she peeled potatoes with an antler-handled knife. Her bony fingers moved slowly around the "taters" as the men called them.

"Hungry?" the pink-faced man asked over the head of his shorter, darker partner. He scratched his nose, leaving a trail of brown flour as a mustache.

"What have ye then, and how much?" Joseph asked.

"Pasties for cuatro reales, friend Irish."

Joseph said, "it's mine," as he pawed through his pile of coins of various sizes looking for reales. He found four in his money belt, not thinking until later that he opened it wide before prying eyes.

"You know I'm Irish?" Joseph asked handing the bits to the dark, big-armed man who slipped them quickly into his own fat purse beneath his white apron. He wore jeans of a nutmeg-color held at the seams and the pockets by brass rivets. In fact, both men wore the heavy jeans and Joseph noted idly that the spitting grease from the cooking pots did not penetrate the material though it did not appear to be oiled.

"Sure," the dark man said, bringing Joseph back to him. "Me name's O'Connor and I recognize a bro." He tapped his ear with his finger acknowledging Joseph's Irish history and his own good ear for dialect. "What be your name, then?" O'Connor continued, turning to dip the pasty into the bubbling pot. A slight breeze lifted the smoke away from them, away from the bay.

"Sherar," Joseph said. "Joseph Sherar."

"Ah, one of the Sherar brothers," the piggish man said, brushing the flour from his hand on his jeans and reaching to shake Joseph's.

"You know James, then?" Joseph asked, surprised, "of New York?" He turned to Benito who had plopped down on one of the upturned powder kegs set around for seats. "He knows my brother! Must have met him in forty-eight! Imagine that!"

Benito looked skeptical, remained silent.

"Sure. We be knowing James Sherar of New York," O'Connor answered, his thin lips formed a smile that disappeared into his thick black beard. "Who made a fortune in the fields?" His last comment was spoken as a slight question as he turned away to check the pasties.

"That he did. That he did," Joseph said, musing. Benito told Joseph later it was lucky probing.

The stocky man smiled expansively and nodded. "And this be me own bro, Paul, though his friends just call him Pinky." O'Connor slapped the taller, pinkish man on the shoulder who raised his eyebrows in acknowledgment. The woman lifted her head and looked through dull dark eyes at Joseph then returned to her chopping when she was not introduced.

For Joseph, the thought of coming upon two men his first morning in San Francisco who knew his brother astounded him more than the quietness of the woman.

"We've a plan, Pinky and me," O'Connor told them their second morning in San Francisco. "Could use some good minds such as yours." O'Connor's flattery tripped easily off his tongue. "James even talked of it before he left, now that I think of it."

Benito was instantly alarmed, thinking it just too strange that James would have talked of some business adventure with these men all those years before. "What adventure?" Benito asked. He rubbed thawed street sand in his hands to clean the grease from them, then gave his full attention to the O'Connors. A sea gull swooped over the roofs of the open-air stalls, settling well beyond the O'Connor stand, picking treasures from the earth.

"It's to be a restaurant. On the wharf," the stocky O'Connor said. Benito noticed the woman who did not speak look up with frightened eyes and glanced at Joseph. O'Connor went on to describe in great detail their plans, his enthusiasm growing. "It'd be a guaranteed success," O'Connor continued. "Just look at all our customers. It's someone like you we'd consider as partners, though. Builders, procurers of supplies. If you go north as planned, think of all you could bring back. We'll be serving them what leaves the gold fields, spreading gold dust like a sneeze. They all have to eat. And they want to eat heartily." He straightened up when he said "heartily" and rubbed his belly as a satisfied man. He stared off, toward the bay, and seemed to be lost for a moment in his vision of the future, built there, settled.

"We got our pocket full of rocks," dark O'Connor said, "but we'd go farther with investors like yourselves. Maybe even open a hotel. What do you say?"

"Your jeans," Joseph said, not interested in restaurants. "What keeps them from burning or staining?"

Pinky startled. "Jeans?" he asked as he looked at his legs as though they'd just appeared beneath his greasy apron. "You want to know about my jeans? I don't know," he said disgusted. "Some German sells them. Eleanor buys them," he said, pointing, making his first indication that he knew the woman who sat behind. "They wear well so we don't buy many. Miners get 'em."

Joseph noted the man's confusion, thrown by his interest in the jeans. Benito was baffled, too, he told me. "I look from him to the surprised faces of O'Connors and wonder what this man thinks of! Before I can ask, the woman makes her eyes look very scared and I wonder more."

"So you be not interested in our restaurant?" the dark O'Connor said. "We're brothers. Irish. Like you. We shake hands. You can trust us."

"We'll consider it," Joseph said, sensing that the man was easily frustrated. "That we will. But now I want to know more about the German and his jeans," Joseph persisted. "Eleanor, can you tell me his name and where I might find—"

"She don't talk," Pinky interrupted, letting his impatient character show openly now as he turned back to Joseph. "And she don't walk neither. Born with club feet and got her tongue cut out after her husband's drunken brawl. Gets carried about, she does." He calmed then and added, "But she writes if you've a need to know the German."

The ease with which the man spoke of the woman's misfortune bothered Joseph, but he reached for a small pad and piece of lead and handed them gently to the woman, his first real contact with her. He noticed a wistfulness in her eyes and a hesitation. She looked at Pinky. Joseph nodded encouragement before she bent for her own little book, ripped a blank page, took Joseph's lead and wrote. Then she pointed, held up two fingers, and wrote "Lexington St."

Joseph read the name but she motioned him to give back the script. She looked warily at the O'Connors who appeared busy with customers and drew a line as though she'd made a mistake. She wrote something else below the word "Lexington."

Joseph read it, a bit confused at first, then told the woman, "Thank you," and tipped his flat-brimmed hat. The woman's eyes smiled now, her face blushed with the gentlemanly gesture.

"You have assisted in what I hope will add to our own grand adventure, ma'am," he said. "Our thanks," he added as he gently tapped her note on his fingers.

"What she write?" Benito asked as the newest emigrants to San Francisco made their way toward Lexington Street.

"This address," Joseph told him, leaving out an important point as they located the small, active German who listened intently to Joseph's request. He nodded, said "Ya, ya," several times, moving his hands in a circular motion as though speeding Joseph's story up, urging him to come to the point. But as always, Joseph was methodical and told the story from beginning to end of what and why he wanted what he wanted.

At last, Joseph finished. The German smiled, nodded his head excitedly, quoted him a price and asked that he give him a day or two.

During their final days in San Francisco, the O'Connors saw Joseph and Benito each morning, still, for pasties, with the restaurant idea never again mentioned. "You've been a help, Eleanor," Joseph told her each morning just to watch her smile.

On the day before they planned to leave, Joseph complimented her again saying they'd soon be picking up their purchase from the German, moving inland. "We leave tomorrow, early," he told her. "So today I'll have my last pasty for a while."

Eleanor's eyes looked worried and she glanced with agitation at the O'Connors who both seemed busy with customers, not noticing their conversation. Her finger against her lips signaled quiet.

"Don't worry about us," Joseph said, thinking her worried eyes were for their travel plans. "We'll pick up our order from the German and be gone and back before Thanksgiving." Her eyes looked painfully at him, pleading, as though attempting to talk with him. "Would you like script?" he asked.

But before she could communicate one way or another Pinky noticed their interchange. Grabbing two handfuls of potatoes he dropped them into her bony lap turned to Joseph and said, "She'll peel extra so ye can have a big pasty this last mornin'. Before you boys move on."

"Fine," Joseph said, anticipating his morning meal.

Perhaps it was Benito's sixth sense or maybe Joseph's love of luxury that protected them that night, for they splurged on their last day and rented a bed and bath at one of the fine hotels on Market Street. So they were not present at Adam's Livery when the fire started.

The owners said it was a miracle they got the stock out and safe and lost so little, really. "Twas a rag-tag boy I said could stay the night for cleaning stalls what saw the flames," the livery operator told Joseph excitedly the next morning when the two men approached the still smoldering pile of boards that was once a section of Adam's Livery. "Claimed he had a dream about big pigs snorting through the stalls upsetting the horses outside and some of yours, in. Thought he might even a seen some dark forms movin' afore the flame started, but prob'ly just dreamin'.'"

Joseph and Benito made their way to what personal supplies they'd kept in the tack room. The sickening smell of old smoke seeped into their bedrolls and blankets tossed around and ripped apart, probably by those who helped to put out the fire. Neither thought much of the disheveled condition of what had been an orderly stacking of their items. When they calmed their sorrels in the adjacent corral and saddled them slowly, they spoke of the fire. When they paid Adam—and ignoring Adam's protest, added extra for his loss—they spoke of it. And as they made their way to Lexington Street to pick up their order from the German, they considered those flames.

But there, with the German, their thoughts changed, moved on to anticipation as the little man rolled the heavy nutmeg-colored material out across the plank floor of his shop. Bits of cloth lay beneath the sewing machines like rocks scattered on a dark beach. Dust drifted past the shafts of light that filtered through the four dirty windows lighting the cavernous building. The women, their young children playing at their feet, stood away from their machines. And at the German's gesture to join him, they smiled in admiration of their work spread out across the floor and formed a circle around it.

They were all seeing for the first time what Joseph had seen those days before: tents. The extraordinary raised from the ordinary. A new line of tents, available for miners ready from the newest pack string to move into the mountains.

"My brother James told me the men are so busy mining, they take no time to build," Joseph told the impromptu audience. "Some just throw their blankets over a buck brush or manzanita and call it home. Lucky ones have muslin to sleep under in their 'muslin towns.' No privacy, though. The muslin may keep some sun off," Joseph continued, "but it's useless in the rains. And in the fighting.

This German, here," he said patting the little man's shoulder, "may have the answer—at least to the prying eyes."

The small group hovered around the cloth as yellow as sandstone except for a patch of natural white. He lifted the tent by the patch of white fabric roof and smiled at the German. "You've made a change," he said. "I like it."

"*Danke, danke,*" the German said, his accent thick. "I tot the roof chud be vite, like is, not dye. And I make pocket, for ridgepole." He glowed over his alterations.

Joseph felt the oiliness of the white patch. "This is good," he said.

"Ya, ya," the German said, his mutton chops moving up and down as he talked. "Paraffin oil. On hemp cloth. Vill kiss da rain goodbye, ya." He kissed his fingers to his lips and threw them out to the admiring women, who giggled.

"It's excellent, Levi. Thank you." Joseph said as the women returned to their machines and he and Benito rolled and tied the blocks of nutmeg canvas. "Perhaps we'll make Strauss tents famous in the mountains."

"Ya," Levi said. "You do that. I make jeans famous myself!" He smiled and waved a quick goodbye before urging his helpers back to work inside his small garment factory where reams of future jeans awaited him.

They rode, then, to the wharf area for one last pasty and to show Eleanor their tents. But they found this last mission thwarted. For the O'Connor lean-to was occupied by others. "What happened?" Joseph asked the new vendor, "to the O'Connors? And the woman?"

The vendor merely shrugged his shoulders. "Some come, some go. Those in this stand only been here for a week or two at most. Prob'ly got too cold fer 'em and they moved on."

Joseph said he suspected otherwise. To Benito he remarked: "Remember you asked what Eleanor wrote besides Levi's address? Well, it was 'Good food, bad plan,'" Joseph told him. "A word to the wise I never even thanked her for." He shook his head. "Maybe fire started by piggish man in boy's dream?" Benito wondered out loud.

The thought unnerved Joseph. Was it coincidence that they'd slept away from the livery that one night? Coincidence that the O'Connors disappeared the morning after? He remembered his mother saying that if you believed in God's plan for your life, there were no coincidences, everything was part of the plan.

But he wasn't at all sure that what he and Benito were entering into in the gold fields with tents and mules was so noble as to be called a part of God's Plan.

Joseph sold his tents and turned his cash into a significant investment of a pack string composed of forty-mules. As they expanded, adding more mules to the string they ran, Benito sent for his brother and some cousins who brought their wives and children and formed a small city of their own with the mules serving as the traveling meeting hall around which all decisions were discussed and made. It made quite an entourage. I never saw it, at least not the string he skinned in California.

But he tells wonderful stories of those years. And once, when we rode to Canyon City the year after we were married, I had the feel of what it must have been like to move always on a mule's back, travel single-file down mountain ridges, listen to the rocks crunch, break loose then bounce down canyon sides as steep as cows' faces, so steep they surely were not meant for men—nor woman—to even see, let alone traverse. On that trip, the sights and sounds and sense of solitude filled me up and then pushed tears of awesome joy onto my cheeks. I think it must have been like that for Joseph in those early days in the mountains outside San Francisco.

The ranch he began in the Hupa Valley in northern California he hoped would be his life's place. In the shadow of Mt. Shasta with the manzanita and laurel to green the brown hills, he brought Benito and his cousins, their families and mules, and several hundred head of cattle who fed on the deep ravines of California's northern country.

Here, Joseph was doing daily what he thought he'd set his heart on doing: making money with integrity and adventure though I do not think he saw his future. That would come later, when he was led north, to Oregon's Valley of the Tyghs. And to me.

CHAPTER 6

TEACHING

WHILE JOSEPH MADE his way in the world of mules and mines in northern California, I gave up baby teeth, added scant few inches to my slender frame, and spent my time looking after Rachel and Pauline and my baby brother, Loyal.

Oh, I pulled weeds from the potato patch we'd planted not far from our Oregon cabin. That was our livelihood those first years, raising and selling potatoes. And I sometimes rode with Papa as he drove freight wagons loaded with the bounty fifteen miles north, to Dalles City and the Columbia River. He made the trip pretty regularly exchanging the loads for necessities that got us through each winter. Together, we cleared more of Papa's acres, bought additional cows, more mules. Mama was with child, often, when she wasn't helping folks coming on the Barlow Cutoff heading for the Willamette Valley, or those coming back, all wet and drenched, looking for a life with less rain.

But it was the looking-after of my brother and sisters that consumed me, filled me up. I never counted it as weight, the older-sister load I carried. No, I counted it as wealth, even when I had to scorch the wheat grain to a dirty brown powder for their wet bottoms or thought to paddle their behinds for being sassy or disobedient or disappearing without warning. Even when I had to pour kerosene over their heads to kill the pesky head lice that they hatched, I counted it as fortunate. For each occasion caulked us tighter than a log chink regardless of their responses to my presence or my scolding.

Sometimes in the night I'd hear Rachel and Pauline awake, chattering like magpies in words I couldn't quite decipher through my sleep, discussing something of great import, enough to wake them up. Beneath a crescent moon casting pale light in the cabin loft, those girls would start to tussle Loyal. Their voices rising, I'd pull myself from sleep enough to counsel quiet, adding with more gentleness, "Itsa-right, itsa-right. Now, find another way to settle, sisters," and so they would, faces buried in the duck-down quilts now shaking with their gentle laughter until they slept again and I returned to my own sweet dreams of babes. So by the time 1859 rolled around, I had my own life sense: to be surrounded by children through a family of my own.

It was the mix of work and care for them that satisfied my days. Especially in the potato patch where left alone, without our parents, we discovered much of who we were.

The potato patch was my classroom until the Walker School was formed. Surrounded by the leafy greens, I sang songs composed with Hound as the subject, or my sisters. Sometimes I talked with rattlesnakes, teaching Rachel and Pauline. "If you speak nice to them, they'll leave you be," I told them. "Just sing, 'I'm too big to eat,' like that, and you won't have to worry about stepping on them even if you see their tracks in tater leaves or tall grass."

I remember in particular the summer I turned eleven. Papa had offered to teach me how to use the Kentucky. It was a huge, long rifle that he'd brought with him from Virginia. Many of the settlers preferred more modern weapons, but Papa liked a rifle he could fix himself if something went wrong with it. He also liked finding flints from the hillsides rather than worrying about spending precious potato money on manufactured percussion caps that the newer rifles required. He was frugal that way.

He'd offered to teach me, said with the Yakimas unsettling up north and our living so close to the reservation, I should learn to help patch at least, in case there was some kind of argument. The Warm Springs Indians, Sahaptin-speaking people, had yet to even disagree about the weather with their neighbors, but one never knows the future. I wanted to shoot more to know I could bring in game if needed or chase off cougars that frequented the timber and terrified the stock. Either reason, Mama had to grant permission for such "unlady-like" lessons.

On the big day, she was mixing up gingerbread cookies, the scent of molasses seeping through the logs to the open air. It was early August and the weeds were coming on thicker than a bee swarm on the lilacs and Mama said I had to work the potatoes before I could shoot.

Then she did the worst: made me choose which of the girls I'd take with me. Rachel could weed good when she wanted but she was a scamp. She usually found something else to do. Once she started digging in some soft dirt near a hole in a hillside, shoveling sand between her legs like Hound would if he'd been with us. It struck me funny until I spied a striped animal with rolling fat moving quickly toward us like he was the landlord and we were about to be visited with an eviction! He stopped and rose up on his toes and I saw that he was huge, weighing more than either Rachel or me. "Rachel," I whispered as loudly as I could. "Back up slowly and stand behind me."

She must have heard the fear in my voice because she actually listened and did just that. I caught a glimpse of her eyes as she turned and saw the animal which we later learned was a badger. It stayed where it was and we backed away. Then Rachel lunged for it, teasing. I could have hit her.

It hissed at us and we took off running like newly weaned puppies until we reached a rock pile. There we sat for a long time, hunkering our feet up, until that badger changed his mind. He headed straight into the hole Rachel'd been invading.

We were late getting home that day and Mama had words for us and Rachel told about the animal and Papa said what it was and shook his head, amazed. Mama said she was glad Hound hadn't been with us as the badger would have sliced him alive with its claws and teeth. Us too, Papa said, if the Lord hadn't provided us with the rock pile.

Mama said the Lord should have provided us with better sense. Mama often brought up the incident to remind us of our foolishness. Mine, mostly, as I was the oldest and responsible and "should have known better."

What I should have known was that Rachel would tell. She was sassy, that girl, and she couldn't keep a secret. But she had a quick mind and the cutest dimples where she wore her charm.

Usually, she had more charm than ambition, though. She'd drift off from the potato patch into the fir trees or she'd stop by the privy on the way to the field and snatch hollyhock blossoms and beg me to make her little dolls from the blossoms and buds. Taking her with me that day would have been interesting; who knows how much work we'd have done.

Pauline on the other hand was still a baby, really, just six, but I confess, she was my favorite. While she cried a lot after she ate it seemed to me, she was generally easy to entertain in the field. Not so at home. Curious, she was always getting into things, wandering too close to the river, pawing at the ashes Mama set aside for soap.

So when Mama made me choose who to take with me that summer day, I chose Pauline. I wanted Mama happy, so she wouldn't change her mind about letting Papa teach me how to shoot.

Papa saw Rachel stick her tongue out at me when I chose Pauline. He didn't say anything, just smiled and patted her head when she weaseled her way around his leg. Mama told her she had to help with the wash and look after Loyal and then Rachel really scowled at me. I didn't care. I took a piece of deer tallow, dipped it in some molasses, grabbed a length of rawhide, filled the water bag from the rain barrel and Pauline and I headed out. Hound lapped water from a mud hole and loped after us. I didn't even feel the heat of Rachel's eyes on my back as we left.

Pauline was especially good. I watched her faded blue bonnet bob up and down in the tall grasses. Later, she sat in the dirt, picked purple phlox and chattered while I was free to pull weeds and dream.

Toward noon, I finished and should have gone home with Pauline. Instead, I rested a bit. Hound sprawled in the grass and even Pauline had curled up sucking on her tallow. I tied the rawhide to it and then to her toe so if she slept with it in her mouth, her foot would jerk the tallow out.

I dreamed of eagles swooping down, dogs barking. A spider crossed my face and I batted at it and felt moisture. Dogs barked louder and suddenly, I woke.

My heart pounded so loudly I thought that Hound could hear it. He stood, barked his deep, warning bark as I reached for the loose flesh behind his neck to push myself away from the horse that stood so close to me I could see the hairs in its nostrils. It snorted. A feather was knotted in the horse's forelock. I couldn't see its rider.

I couldn't see Pauline, either, and my heart raced, half hoping she was nowhere near; the other half praying she was.

The rider had a deep, canyon voice which I heard when he said "*Chchuu txanati!*" Then he said, in English: "Still!" I noticed other sounds I'd heard, sounds of voices, stopped. "She awake," he said and several pairs of painted pony legs came abreast of him and formed a half-circle around me.

"Where's my sister?" I demanded, standing. I hoped my voice was louder than my heartbeat and held more courage than I felt.

The canyon-voice rider backed his horse up. I could see him then but his face was still silhouetted against the noon sun. Long strands of straight black hair hung on either side of his head and flowed onto his shirtless chest. His legs on either side of his pony were bare above moccasins.

He raised his hand and a woman on a horse next to him slid off, her dun buckskin dress sliding up her thighs as she descended. She walked under her horse's neck and reached behind the canyon-voice man and gently pulled something from the seat behind him.

It was precious Pauline!

Settled on the ground, Pauline took her time reaching me. Purple dirt smeared around her mouth. She had the good sense to be still.

"*Nana,*" the canyon-voice man said nodding once toward Pauline. I wasn't sure what it meant but I said thank you and pushed her behind me. Hound had calmed down and in fact had gone sniffing past the ring of riders toward skinny-tailed dogs scrounging behind the circle.

A paper-thin woman wearing faded calico cinched at the waist by a wide, beaded belt, scowled at me. I felt terrible that I'd fallen asleep and left Pauline alone, and it seemed the woman knew of my guilt, made her eyes memorize my thoughtless person.

I'd had some contact with natives, mostly in Dalles City where their blanketed bodies sometimes walked the streets. Papa traded beef with them once or twice. A reservation just a few miles away from us had actually been formed with all kinds of pomp and circumstance four years before. The Indian agent had gathered several bands together including Wascos and Warm Springs or Sahaptin-speaking people and some Indians who had lived along the big river, the Columbia. Later, Paiute people came too. Perhaps the government agents felt the very different tribes would be so busy arguing among themselves they'd have no time to harass settlers moving onto former Indian lands.

I stood now on land that had once been the Indians'. I was still trying to decide how to fill the gaping silence, calm my pounding heart, and break the stare of the old woman when a young girl, about my age, said something in the click-click and swoosh language and the canyon-voice man nodded his head, one quick nod. The girl slipped from her pony in a flash and walked toward me.

In all my born days, I'd never seen a prettier girl. I was conscious for the first time of how skinny and awkward a thing I was. She was slender as a feather and fringe from her buckskin fluttered against her calves as she walked toward me, her hips swaying gently.

The girl blinked long eyelashes at me that seemed to rest for just a second on her high cheekbones.

"Sunmiet," she said tapping herself with her fingers at the center of her chest. "Name. Sunmiet." She pronounced it as three words: "Sun My Et." Her voice was clear, soothing, like spring water. "Means Morning Bird. You?" she asked.

Later I learned she went to boarding school and knew English since the matrons swatted their students' knuckles with a paddle if they heard the click-click swoosh language of the native people. The pain made English easier to learn; but in the summers, away from the school, easier to forget.

"Jane Herbert," I answered with conviction though my name had no special meaning as did hers.

She had trouble pronouncing "Jane," wanted to say "James," and we giggled at that.

She told me they were headed to the mountains, to pick huckleberries and that later, they'd be at the big river the white men called Deschutes. Huge falls pushed through a narrow gorge there and it was where the Chinook returned each year to feed her family. How odd now, it seems to me, that years later that falls should be a part of my existence, too.

Sunmiet stopped suddenly and stared at me. Her look was bold, as though there was something in my eye. Cocking her head from side to side the way Hound does when he hears a sound he cannot place, she moved closer to peer at me. She said something in the click-click swoosh tongue and the people in the circle murmured and nodded agreement.

"Huckleberry eyes," she said. "You," pointing with four fingers toward my eyes, "huckleberry eyes. Black with pools of blue. Fruitful," she finished firmly, nodding her head once.

She reached out as though to touch my eyes. Then coming to her senses, she snatched her hand back. She stared shyly at the beadwork on her moccasined-feet.

I didn't grasp the significance of that statement of my "fruitfulness" until years later. I tried to ask her where they'd found Pauline but she laughed, a tinkling laugh, and said something about huckleberries again and touched her mouth, nodded to my sister. I realized then that Pauline's purple dirt was huckleberry juice. With delayed anxiety, I realized she'd have been deep in the timber to find berries. I swallowed, frightened, knowing she could have encountered a bear there or been easily lost, forever. I was grateful she'd been returned safely, didn't know exactly how to tell them.

We would have talked more, Sunmiet and I, she being the first Indian of any age I'd introduced myself to. But the canyon-voice man spoke, raised his hand and faster than a flick of a fawn's tail, Sunmiet twirled from me. She nodded her head at me once, then grabbed the mane of her pony and leaped onto his back, reins already in her hand.

In seconds, the whole band turned as one and headed out, dust puffing up from their horses' feet. The old woman still scowled as she looked back at me. Sunmiet turned, waved. Her fingers were delicate, like Rachel's.

I waved back and so did Pauline, with a pudgy fist. That's when I noticed Pauline held something. I pried at her tight fingers all the while she was saying, "It's mine!"

"You can have it," I said. "Just let me see."

Her palm opened to reveal a tiny carving no larger than her thumb. Round, like a marble, it bore a painted face of two tiny eyes and a circular mouth that made it look like a hungry baby. "Where'd you get this?" I asked.

She shrugged her shoulders. "She gave it to me," she said.

"Not likely," I said. "Where'd you find it?"

She shrugged her shoulders again, reached for the carving I held beyond her touch. "Did you take it?"

"She gave it to me!" she repeated, pouting at my disbelief. "For my berries."

I turned to call to Sunmiet but she and her family had already disappeared from view.

"Don't tell Mama," Pauline whined as I tied the carving into the hem of my dress.

"Don't worry," I told her, knowing what terse words Mama would have to say about our taking time to talk and trade with Indians.

Mama had words of another kind. I was as sweet as I could be and kept my eyes to the floor as she spoke. "Almost had to send Rachel to fetch you," she snapped.

I swallowed hard, grateful she hadn't as Rachel would have told about the Indians or worse, found me asleep with Pauline in their hands.

Papa waited outside with the Kentucky. Rachel whined that she wanted to go. "My back's aching," Mama said, her hands holding her baby-broadened back. "You'll need to finish hanging laundry. Watch Pauline. Loyal, too," she sighed, pulled her hankie from her sleeve and dabbed her forehead.

Hound paid attention as soon as he saw the Kentucky and headed with us toward the stumps.

I'd never been allowed to touch them, Papa's guns. Mama complained that he had too many though I only saw the Kentucky hung in its place of honor over the fireplace. I could never appreciate the Kentucky as much as Papa wanted me to, but I could try.

"Butt's the shape of a new moon, isn't it?" he said more than asked. "Now run your hand up along the cheek piece," he instructed. "Feel the star there, on the left side? That's strictly American, that brass star. Idea came out of Pennsylvania. Shoulda been named the Pennsylvania but it's always been a Kentucky. Always will be." He smiled, proud. "That box on the other side? Open it."

I remember moving my face from the stock and lifting the hinged brass lid on a box no wider than the palm of my hand attached to the stock. I caught the scent of the tallow-greased buckskin patches resting there.

"Greased patches make for faster reloading," Papa told me. "So you can get more than one shot, maybe, at a buck, four-legged or two. Barrel's got eight sides," he continued. "You can count 'em. Shoots a thirty-six caliber. 'Member that," he said. "There's the rod, for ramming the balls." He dabbed at his watery eye.

"Use both triggers," he continued, stuffing his handkerchief into his pocket. He gave more details, something he was known to do. "The rear one cocks the trigger. When you're ready to fire, you barely touch the first one and it fires. There's the sights you line up. Here, I'll show you."

He held the weapon carefully, lifting the rifle to his shoulder. He kept his only working eye open. "You close your left eye," he said. "Look through at your target and when they line up, you got a good chance to hit what you're aiming at."

He brought the weapon down again, this time carrying it to a stump that seemed to be just the right height to rest the weapon on and still have me look down the sights to the canvas circle he'd placed in the notch of a cottonwood tree.

"Got to make it your friend, feel safe with it. Your mother never has been," he said, wistfully, "but you can, child. Never know what might happen."

I concentrated as he poured a black-powder charge into the barrel, then pulled a patch slightly larger than his thumb from the box. This he laid over the muzzle. From his pouch, he took a lead ball and cradled it like a marble in a hammock over the patch ramming them both down with the brass end of the hickory rod. With precision, he half-cocked the hammer, then lifted the striker exposing a tiny steel pan. Here he tapped a small amount of black powder into the pan and closed the striker. With his thumb, he cocked the hammer to a full cock. He took a deep breath as he pulled the rifle to his face, set the stock on his shoulder, and sighted the target. "Like this, Janie," he said, and he set his feet, bracing himself against the recoil.

I covered my ears and squeezed my eyes shut tight, waiting.

Instead of firing, he turned, saw me with eyes pinched shut against the anticipated crack and brought the weapon down. "Won't learn that way," he said. "Don't get soft on me now, Janie, and close your eyes before you shoot. Won't hit nothin' that way. Got to face what you fear. Here. Put your cheek to it." I could tell that he would have rather shot the rifle himself.

With his arms around me, his bushy beard close to my face, I tried to line the bead at the end of the barrel in the notch closer to my eyes. Papa placed his arm over mine as I stretched my left arm along the barrel and with the right, placed my fingers over the cold metal of the trigger. It felt safe with him there, his wide hands over my smaller ones. He smelled of tobacco and gun powder, friendly scents that even today bring back memories of my childhood and sweet days with Papa and his children. I knew I could please him; I was sure.

In fact, the whole day pleased me. I'd helped Mama and kept her happy. I'd met an Indian named Sunmiet, shared a secret with Pauline, hid a treasured carving we could speak of (and tell Rachel about when she could keep a secret); now I was learning to shoot Papa's Kentucky.

"Take a deep breath, child," Papa said. "Pull the rear trigger till it clicks. Good. When I say so, let out part of your air. On three, stop breathin', hold the rifle as still as a fishing-heron and squeeze the front trigger. Just a whisker of pressure on it now," he said. "Ready?" And when I nodded he added, "All right, child, on three."

Then, just before he began the count he gave me one more instruction, one that distracted me though spoken in his softest voice. "Just pretend it's an Injun's head there in that circle on the tree," he'd said. "When I say 'three' just aim for that Injun's eyes."

I don't begrudge him his jaundiced view. It's doubtful he would even have seen it as such what with Indians uprising, neighbors manning forts. It's just that his image made me think of something I didn't wish to.

I held my breath, blinked away an unplanned wetness in my eyes, let air out. Then with feather-light fingers, I touched the cold trigger.

"Papa! Papa!" Rachel interrupted, shouting, just as I sent an explosion and a cloud of dirt high into the air. Papa cursed. "Get Lodenma!" Rachel said, breathless, pulling at Papa's sleeve. "Baby's coming early!"

My shot ended up far right of the target. Papa jerked the rifle from my arms, turned to run toward the house, leaving me standing with the recoil of the

Kentucky burning in my shoulder and the wonderment of another baby on its way.

I had so wanted to please Papa.

I knew it was not the distraction of Rachel sending Papa for the midwife that had taken my eye from the target. No, it was his last instruction. For the face of the only "Injun" I could imagine when Papa gave his direction was Sunmiet's.

It was a face I simply couldn't shoot at, not on that day, nor any other.

CHAPTER 7

DREADS

THE THING IS, you cannot ease the pain of loss without enormous energy which you have already expended dealing with your grief. Memories flood up from everywhere to overcome you, the new never as good as the old. The smell of hollyhocks, the making of a doll, the sounds of fast-flowing water, none ever arrives from your memory without bringing a bittersweet pain. The pain does not disappear just because you wish it. That was part of the lesson being twelve taught me and I carried it well into my life.

For years I thought about it every day, wondered if the time would ever come when I could roll Pauline's carving between my fingertips or listen to a child catch his breath in his sleep without remembering in great detail the events of one week of that year.

Those events changed my life. But then, it is rarely the event but our reactions to it that change our lives I've found. I know that now. That week changed what I thought I longed for.

Papa said 1860 was the "dawn of a new era" though South Carolina's secession happened later. Of course, our year had already been mightily and irrevocably changed by then.

Mama was busier than ever, I remember. She ministered to the newcomers, helping them find shelter, baking and taking food to them, acting as a midwife when she could. She often dragged us along "to entertain the little ones" while she helped some woman pound laundry on the rocks or skin a hog. I liked what she did to help, but felt green-eyed jealousy, too, over time that others got with her.

Papa, too, was busy and his interests turned to politics. There was war talk among the Paiutes far away but he worried some about "our Injuns" as he called them, wondering if they would shift their peaceful ways.

Papa expressed his views more stridently, getting louder when someone disagreed. Mama never hid the corn liquor when people stopped by but I heard her threaten to a time or two. I can still see them: Papa and Mr. Henderson—with his large stogie bobbing from the corner of his mouth—jawing, they called it, working hard to get the military to release some of their holdings, make them available for sale, so "The Dalles" as Dalles City was being called now, could grow. Settlers needed places to live beside the Columbia. "Why, the army even owns the docks!" Papa'd say, pounding his pipe against his brogans. "How can a river town grow with no right to own its docks?" Henderson and his cronies would murmur their assent while the heat rose from the fireplace and the fervor in their hearts.

Over cups of corn liquor, they talked of Indian uprisings, the unsettled Paiutes, the quiet Sahaptin people, the brassy Wascos who still demanded their fishing sites along the Columbia despite the treaty. "Those Wascos are a trial," Henderson noted. "Acting like worldly traders, flashing their affluence, talking like they know what's what. Even speaking French some of 'em."

"It's Chinookan jargon," Papa told him. "And they know their way around their world; ours too." He relit his pipe and smoked. "Negotiated a pretty fair treaty, you ask me. Got territory south of here not ever a part of their history." He shook his head in a begrudging admiration.

The men spoke of settlement and growth and the need to "take advantage of both."

Mama and Papa were both busy with the Methodist Church where we spent one Sunday in The Dalles each month. Other Sundays, we joined our neighbors at the Walker School for services.

I often watched the little ones while Mama looked after people or spent time with the Methodist Ladies' Aid Society, or if Papa was busy, or when the neighbors came to sit a spell and jaw. Not smart enough, I remember thinking, to listen to the grown-ups, but wise enough to watch after all their children. Seemed a contradiction to me then as I thought the children the greater responsibility. And now, as I watch the mothers send their young daughters off to tend the little ones when they're just little ones themselves. It is one of Sunmiet's family's qualities I most admire, that children are allowed to be a part of learning from adults, challenging themselves by watching and listening instead of being set aside.

I had no memory of Mama's South and didn't know what secession meant so would have stayed to listen and learned about the impending war if they had let me. When Mama and Papa and their friends began their "deliberations" as Mama called them, I rolled my eyes at Rachel knowing we'd soon be asked to step outside.

Often, we two herded Pauline and Loyal out the door before they asked, knowing it would come. Baby George could still sleep through it.

Yes, there were five of us Herbert children in 1860 and doing well. Until that April.

It was Pauline's birthday. Mama and Papa and their neighbors, the prosperous Hendersons, and the up-and-coming Senior Mays sat inside, deliberating.

"Take the little ones with you when you go, will you please, Jane?" Mama said. Rachel and I headed toward the door. Mrs. Henderson fanned herself with a lace hankie and smiled her wooden-tooth smile at me as she sat on the parlor chair, her skirts flounced about her like bloomers on someone standing in a pond. She looked equally as out of place in our small parlor.

"Give Lodenma a break," Mrs. Henderson said as was her way in her high pitched, little girl's voice.

"When you come in later," Mama continued, her voice hurried like she had little time to talk, "we'll have peppermint tea and cut Pauline's day of birth cake. Run along now."

"Yes, run along now," Mrs. Henderson added. She had an annoying habit of repeating what others said, as though to confirm my suspicion that she had not one original thought in her head.

It meant a few more little hands to hold, taking Lodenma's girl, but I truly didn't mind. Lodenma smiled and nodded her concurrence. Her eyes drooped tiredly, a young mother not roused by her children, but wearied.

"Let's play statue," Rachel said as soon as we left our clapboard house and stepped onto the grass lawn sliced out of the rolling hills. "I'll swing first."

It was like Rachel to think of something quickly, something that would put her in charge.

"You're always first," Pauline complained. "You swing too hard. My arm hurts from last time." She rubbed her elbow delicately, her lower lip ready to drop to the ground.

"Baby," Rachel said. Her dark sausage curls flipped as she turned to me. "I want to be first," she said. She always expected me to act as arbiter. The set jaw of stubbornness she was known for was just beginning, and I was deciding whether to let it grow into a full-fledged whine or let Rachel have her way when the Henderson boy interrupted.

He kicked a rock with his foot first. He was taller than me and at fourteen, more than two years older. I only saw him move fast at the butcher shop. On more than one occasion he waltzed into Twin Dika's shop and while Twin's back was bent to some carcass, Luther would grab the end of a spool of string and whiz out the door with it. The trick was to see how long a string he could get before Twin noticed and cut that umbilical cord—and the game—with his knife. It was a favorite competition with the boys and Luther always ended with the longest string. Other than that, he moved slowly, like a summer sunset.

"S'pose Pauline should go first," he offered lazily that day. "It's her birthday." He batted at a gnat before his face.

"Oh, poo," said Rachel, quick to respond. Then, resigned, "Come here, Pauline." She didn't wait for my pronouncement, deciding Luther's words held weight enough. She grabbed Pauline and clasped her hands around the child's pudgy waist and swung her ever so carefully, releasing her arms and tossing her gently onto the grass kept clipped by Papa's sheep. As she should, Pauline lay in a heap, pantaloon-covered bottom stuck up in the air, head and hands helping to balance herself in the bottoms-up position.

"Hurry," Pauline cried out laughing, her voice muffled by the grass. "Before the hogs come round."

"They'll root you, thinking you're a tater," Luther teased as Pauline squealed anew.

Loyal, age two, lined up next and once again, Rachel was gentle, swinging the fragile boy by his bony arm. Giggling, he managed to stay standing when she released him and stood statue-still, one arm up in the air, the other held out behind him. I can see him yet! His effort lasted only a moment once an orange flicker flew by to distract him. He was easily distracted, I remember.

"You're next, Luther," Rachel called. "Come here." She liked to boss the Henderson boy around.

I have never asked him about that afternoon, wondering if he remembered each detail as I, held himself at all accountable, not that he should. It was a subject rarely discussed, in fact, I only discussed it once with my mother, and that was years after.

"Bet you can't toss me at all," Luther said, sticking his stocky arm out for Rachel to grab.

Hound yelped, his long ears flopped joyously as Luther spun Rachel round and round, her pale skirt flying, ribbons slipping from the bow at the back of her dark curls. She squealed. "Told you," Luther said.

Two of the hogs that acted more like pets heard her squealing and joined us, grunting.

"Hurry up!" Pauline wailed. "I can't stay," she added, and dropped to her side, laughing, the pigs getting closer to her tiny face.

Luther finished swirling Rachel, and she let herself be tossed into a half up, half down posture, crossed her eyes and stuck out her tongue. The pigs came running to her. Loyal plunged into her, laughing. Luther shook his head. "Now you," he said to the child sitting next to me on the grass. As he waved his arms, the pigs moved reluctantly off.

Lodenma's little girl was Loyal's age and she had been feeling hot of late, her mother said. Kind of listless and she leaned her head into my side and I felt the warmth and her reluctance to play statue. "Beatrice doesn't want to. I'll just keep her here by me," I told him.

"Let me swing you, then," Luther said to me, prodding. "I bet I can even if you are almost twelve." He smiled his wide smile, his blue eyes twinkling in his mother's horse-like face.

I ignored him. "I'd say you won, Rachel, even if you hadn't planned to be spun."

"I did, didn't I," Rachel said saucily. "I was the most interesting statue, and for the longest, at least 'til Loyal pushed me." She ruffled his blunt cut hair good-naturedly. "Well, that didn't take much time. What should we do now?"

"Jane could shoot for us," Luther said, yawning. "I hear she's a real good shot."

Later, I wished that I had listened to him, done something safe and simple. At the time, I shook my head. "Not today. Besides, I'm only allowed to if Papa says."

"We could take a walk. Go to the creek and look for fish, then," Luther proposed. He sighed and looked around.

"Yuk!" Rachel said, wrinkling her nose.

"Fish?" Loyal asked, interested.

"Papa says no sense fishing when the cows are laying down," I said. We all turned in unison to see if the Herefords Papa had purchased were lying, chewing their cuds. "At least we could walk that way," I said when we noticed none standing.

I wondered idly if Fifteen Mile Creek ran swollen.

It had been a long but open winter and the snow melt might still rush down the mountain keeping the streams muddied though not flooded. A walk, though, was something we all could do, even the little ones. Surely no danger lurked in that.

Loyal reached for my free hand and slipped his stubby fingers around mine and squeezed. I remember his hand felt so warm. So smooth. So trusting.

Beatrice, Lodenma's girl, gripped my other hand and we started off down the path. "Stay close, Pauline," I cautioned as the girl tripped ahead of me, trying to keep up with Luther and Rachel already out of sight down the path.

Papa's holdings had grown over the years so our birthday group walked past two large barns, a smoke house, and corrals holding several mules and horses now, too. The stock would be put on pasture soon. The spring had been late and only recently had the snow melted off the sidehills making room for the shoots of green to push through. Soon Rachel and I would begin taking the cows farther and farther from home each day to graze, watching them and bringing them back again at night. "Yes. Well. Won't be long," Mama'd said, "before Pauline and Rachel should be able to perform that duty, freeing you up to help more with the babies and work at home."

I wish it had all come to pass.

We had more cows, too. Precious had several calves and Papa had traded a month's labor and hard cash for a new, special kind of bull and two cows brought from across the ocean. This new bull we'd named "The Marshall" for his constant guarding look through brooding eyes. He watched us now as we walked past him, eyes following us like we were something good to eat as he chewed his cud and the warm sun beat on our faces. We squinted back at him.

In no time, Beatrice and I caught up with Luther and Rachel. They had already slipped off their Sunday shoes and stockings, and with some alarm I noticed their feet already sloshed in the cold, rushing water. They squealed, jumped back, raced back along the bank, stepping into wild iris and yellow bells that bloomed in a wild bouquet beside the water. The air was crystal clear and their young and chattering voices bounced against the ridge that lined the stream. Pauline took only a moment to join them even though I yelled for her to stop, then thought better of it. What harm could come? And they'd resent my acting like their mama, making them behave. Then Loyal broke free from my hand. Not bothering to unlace his shoes nor wrench free his socks, he simply plunged past them toward the water's edge.

I hadn't thought the creek would be quite so rushing. Now I wondered, too, if the rattlesnakes were out easing their way beside the water.

Branches collected along the edge catching debris, creating mounds of trash beside the banks that seemed perfect places for a small child to explore and that's where Loyal headed.

He was wet from head to toe before I even knew it. I yelled and Luther caught the alarm in my voice and seeing where I looked, headed that way, pulling Loyal farther back from the slick grass beside the banks. Pauline was not much better but at least she sat along the wet bank and darted her feet in and out of the water like dragon flies bouncing off a swirling pond.

I knew I'd best get them all away, take them back, and yelled something about "cake!" hoping they'd come running. And they did, muddy clothes, wet feet, and all.

It was only seconds, really, and away from the water, with the warm sun and grass, we dried their feet quickly. I carried Loyal since even his shoes were wet. I felt his cold feet bob lightly on my hip and rubbed one foot warm with my hand. Luther put Beatrice on his shoulders and we walked back without a care.

I never dreamed as we passed the watchful Marshall bull and ate cake later that I would remember our trip to the stream as my last outing with my sisters and brother.

Loyal began the fever first. Complaining, he pulled away from us while the party still rumbled with the voices of happy children, the men still spoke of politics, and my mother still smiled absently at Mrs. Henderson's repetitions.

Lodenma stroked Beatrice's hair as she curled her in her arms and even commented that she didn't seem as warm as when she'd first gone outside. "Spring fever," Mama said. I could tell as she placed the back of her hand on Loyal's forehead, that she held a worry. She seemed pleased when the Hendersons and Mays took their leave at dusk.

Loyal's voice caught in his throat and he croaked out "porcupine" and with his stubby fingers inside his mouth, he pointed to the pain. Mama put cool rags on his throat and wiped his face of the sweat and gave him juniper berry tea until he shook his head and coughed. He gasped for air each time.

"We'll try garlic and clover honey," Mama said while Papa went for the doctor.

What little memory I had of my older brother Ambrose came visiting that afternoon, and I believe my mother must have relived his dying in those hours with Loyal, wondering if she would ever bring any son of hers to manhood.

The room smelled of sticky bedclothes, garlic and juniper berries boiled in water in the fireplace cauldron. Through the evening, Loyal's breathing became shallower though it seemed he worked harder and his face took on a bluish tint. I put the girls to bed and tucked them in, assuring them that Loyal would be fine by morning. I walked the floor with Baby George, talking softly, murmuring prayers, worrying, too, for him and for my mama.

And then, before Papa and the doctor could return, Loyal's fever deepened and he died.

It was a Monday, early in the morning, before the meadowlarks would sing.

On Tuesday, with Loyal laid in his small bed, all freshly washed by the Ladies' Aid Society women, but not yet put to rest in the ground, Rachel began to rub her throat and complain and Papa, still grieving for a second son, went immediately for the doctor.

A big man who looked always as though he'd slept in his dark brown suit, Dr. Jessup wasn't far away this time and when he arrived, he poured laudanum from a vial dwarfed by his large hands. Rachel opened her mouth like a baby bird and took the stuff, grimacing as the liquid hit her throat and seemed to swell her tongue. Then the doctor conferred with Mama about herbs to ease the throat pain, help the labored breathing that had begun. He said to keep the juniper tea coming. "Think it's the mucous sickness they call diphtheria," he told us. "Keep her swallowing, Elizabeth. That's what matters."

And then he asked what both Loyal and Rachel might have done in recent days together that could have caused the sickness.

I heard that question; knew the answer. The weight of it burned my stomach like a hot poker from the fireplace stabbing me inside: a walk to the water, shoes off, toes dipped inside.

Mama said nothing. She looked at me and I knew we shared the thought.

Then Pauline took ill.

The house became awash with steam and rags and bloody phlegm and sweat; and it was as though I began to die myself watching these little ones I once could comfort without effort slowly slip away. Mama and Papa were tireless at their babies' sides, taking only the short time it took to lay Loyal to rest to leave their bedsides.

At Loyal's funeral, Mama and Lodenma talked of Beatrice's health and Lodenma reported she was fine. I remember feeling both relief and a sense of jealousy all at once and then guilt for having such a thought.

"Why not let me take Baby George with us?" Lodenma offered. "Keep him from harm's way until the girls are better. Free Jane up to help you more and you won't worry so about the baby."

Mama cried, her faced pressed into Papa's chest after she sent Baby George home with Lodenma.

There was never any question that I would stay.

All through the night, whenever I awoke, I saw Mama in the shadows of the oil lamp, leaning over Pauline or wiping Rachel's perspiring brow or heard Papa scrape his chair as he moved closer to the bedside, pulling blankets up, pressing hot rags to their throats to push the swelling down. Their breathing rattled like branches scraping the isinglass windows in a wind storm and while it sounded wretched, I was relieved each time I woke to know they both still breathed.

Pauline did not awake on Wednesday.

She still gripped the tiny carving I had placed inside her hand hoping it would keep her safely. Mama took it from her, saw the baby's face carved with the open mouth, and wept as it dropped from her hands. I put my arms around her and she stiffened, just so slightly before she set her shoulders solid as a granite rock, withdrew, and pulling the hankie from her sleeve, tended next to Rachel.

Mama began dying that day too, I think. What mother wouldn't? She whimpered when she thought me sound asleep and Papa held her till she dozed. Then he'd leave, go out into the cool night, and I could hear him cleaning stalls in the barn by oil light until all hours, then come in, the scent of pain and manure dripping from him as he tried to work his grief out through his pores.

Doctor Jessup returned, exhausted as he went from house to house, an epidemic in the making now, he said. He listened to Rachel's breathing, and we all hovered over her, the sassy one we hoped would spit in the Grim Reaper's eye.

He checked Rachel's wheezing. He told of many children dying. Grownups too, in Fifteen Mile Crossing, some on the reservation. No one seemed to know the reason. Some said once the fever broke, the sickness went away. It was keeping the air open to the lungs that mattered. Said he'd heard of folks sticking reeds down, breathing like a man was underwater, but he didn't hold with that approach. "Have to cut the throat inside and could just bleed to death," he told us. "Best to keep the fever down with cool baths." He felt my cool forehead as he added: "And pray."

Sunmiet told me later that many died on the reservation. More were saved by desperate mothers poking sticks of fat-slicked cockleburs down their children's throats, poking air holes in, pulling the mucous and the breath of death out beyond their children's reach.

Rachel fought hard, she did, but her future lay in the memories of those who loved her, not in the vivid enchantment that had been her promise.

She died on Friday, the third within five days; my mother's fourth. Only Baby George and I remained.

Of course, it was not the creek nor the cold nor the wet that really did it. I know that now. Medical science pushes forward with its explanations I could have used then though it would not have changed the end result. But for years I did not know. I blamed myself, as did another.

Neither did I understand why God spared me. What could be so important that God would let me live?

I consider that dreaded time in 1860 as though preserved in brine—meant to look at every now and then but to never know the sour taste again. Only recently, with the words of Reverend Doctor Thomas Condon of the Congregational Church have I had reprieve.

"Each dark place has God in it," Reverend Condon assured me. "God promised he will never leave us or forsake us no matter how deep we sink or how heavy the burden we are asked to bear. And there is purpose in that darkness, some plan God is working out. We will recognize the light the better for having seen the dark." He patted my shoulder gently as he added, "We must trust his wisdom that when his time is right, the plan will come to light."

I would have gone with them, Loyal, Rachel, and Pauline. Ambrose too— all of them—to the quiet, peaceful place they must still be in, if only to save myself from the hole left in my heart and the guilt I knew would live within my soul, forever.

And so it almost did.

CHAPTER 8

A PLACE
OF
BELONGING

THE MIND SICKNESS MOVED inside of me that summer and into the next. I could not walk or sit or sleep without the feeling that something was amiss, that some part of me no longer wandered on this earth. As I swept the house at Mama's request, I'd turn, thinking I should check on Pauline. When I walked the cows home from the hills with a switch, I'd look ahead, to see if Rachel had opened up the gate, and then with a piercing pain of remembering, make my way through the herd to open it myself. Even Hound who was as old as I, abandoned me it seemed, preferring the quiet of the cabin and the closer huddling that my mother gave to her only surviving son.

Sunmiet and her family rescued me, pulled me from the pool of pain I'd fallen into. I doubt my parents would have noticed my sinking, so involved were they in the depth of their own grief. But nothing puts the salve to sorrow like the presence of an understanding friend, one who does not ask but is simply there. And Sunmiet and her family—all of them I soon considered as family—were there. That's why when I encountered Joseph in the year to come, he saw my spunk and strength and not my sadness.

Sunmiet had risked something of herself to be with me that year. It marked a change in her life as well. I had seen little of her the summer and winter following our losses. Then like the swallows that returned in the spring, she had come to the potato patch where we'd first met. She came alone.

I heard her approach and hid in the tall timber. I didn't want to be seen, even after I recognized her.

Sunmiet stood as still as a blue heron beside the planted patch, her eyes narrow slits scanning the weaving rows of tiny plants poking up through the moist soil. Her slender hand shaded her brown eyes from the hot sun. Above her, wispy clouds streaked the June sky like a finger of vermilion swiped across a blue surface. A light breeze filtered through the junipers and firs, lifted strands of her dark hair which eased like spider webs across her face.

From a distance, I watched her pulling the wispy strands from her eyes. She told me later she felt eyes on her and hoped it wasn't Standing Tall. "Ever since his name-giving, he seemed to think he could 'stand tall' over me whenever he wished, following me, telling me what to do, to think, expecting I will do it as if he were my father or my husband."

She was excited that morning and wondered who was watching at the potato patch beneath the big fir where the *nanas,* "sisters," had scratched the ground like raccoons and raised the big brown roots her ruler-teachers from the school called potatoes.

Sunmiet scowled. I heard her say something in the click-click swoosh language. Then louder so watching eyes could hear her, she spoke. "After all my efforts, my family will arrive and find me alone. Where are those *nanas?*"

Together, we heard the crows call and lift leaving the fir branches bobbing from their flight. Together, we watched *wilalík,* "rabbit," scamper down one row; but she did not see me or my *nanas.*

"What could have happened to them?" she said to her pony but loud enough for me to hear. He shook his head as if he understood her, snot spraying from his nostrils. Sunmiet turned the spotted horse who pulled against his reins. He hopped and bucked once, kicking at the skinny-tailed dog who sniffed too close to his heels. The pony walked slowly along the potato rows while Sunmiet concentrated on the ground. Her long braids hung suspended in the air, away from her as she leaned, looking for tracks or signs that I was near.

"If I do not find any sign," she sang out, "I will follow the road to your house even though I do not wish it. Not without my father or my friend." I think she spoke out loud as much for the courage of hearing her own conviction as to let me know what she had in mind.

She said something to the horse, *k'usi*, in Sahaptin; then to *k'usik'usi*, "dog," who trotted beside them. "We will walk around the plants once more, *k'usik'usi*, and then we will ride to the house of Huckleberry Eyes."

Sunmiet stopped suddenly, noticed the little weeds I'd pulled that morning. They lay still green between the rows, just beginning to wilt. She raised her eyes and looked around again, searching for me, her bare legs exposed beneath her skirt. She sat quietly, her eyes scanning.

I'm not sure why I kept myself hidden from her. It must have been my wish to avoid having to explain why I worked alone now, where the little ones had gone, what had happened to the beings that filled me up, gave me my spunk and spirit.

Sunmiet sat as though she would never move.

With a sigh, I took halting steps out through the buck brush snuggled in among the giant firs. Her horse startled, did not bolt, and Sunmiet turned to see me walking toward her.

"I did not believe it could be you, Huckleberry Eyes," Sunmiet told me later. "That girl with smudges on her face walked slowly, not with the bird-like quick-quick steps of my friend. That girl had heavy shoulders and she was very thin. Almost all bones. Her dark hair hung in clumps that once were braids. Now small sticks and fir needles stuck to them. And that bonnet and dirty string! Not like my friend!" She shook her head amazed.

I wore a faded, dirty dress with a tie belt that exposed my thinness and I did not care.

"And her eyes were dull, not pools of blue. But I knew those eyes," Sunmiet told me nodding her head wisely. "Those eyes had been the watching eyes."

I walked directly toward her and once my exposure was begun, I did not hesitate like most non-Indian children who had never seen a Warm Springs Indian before. Sunmiet's pony flickered his chest to ward off a spring fly and stomped nervously.

On her horse, Sunmiet towered over me. She must have decided it was not wise to challenge an unknown, and so slipped off and stood, waiting to be equal.

I walked close, as we who know no Indians often do, until her moccasined feet stood rounded-toe to the bare toes of my feet. Sunmiet seemed confused by my boldness, standing closely, as family.

"Sunmiet," I said, and then I knew she recognized me.

A gasp escaped her mouth before she could stop it. Her eyelashes fluttered nervously as she reached her slender hand out and touched my face. Her thumb slid across the sharp bones beneath my eyes and she cupped her fingers warmly over my small ear.

"Jane?" she whispered, her eyes searching my face.

I raised my shoulder to hold my friend's hand at my cheek and sighed, the first touch I'd felt in months that did not carry sadness with it.

Sunmiet stepped around me, circling, still running her hand over my head to touch my other cheek, making sense of it. "Are your people gone? Did you not find land animals to eat? You are so thin!"

I shook my head, no.

"My uncles and father have success when they hunt," she said with pride. "I will ask that they bring some meat for you and your family."

Again I shook my head.

"But you cannot have eaten for many weeks," she said, alarm in her voice. She stared at my meatless bones.

"We have venison," I said, looking down. "I haven't felt like eating."

Sunmiet told me later she wondered why I did not wish to eat, but did not want to be rude. She had already been too bold. "I should have waited for Huckleberry Eyes to speak further," she said, though questions filled her. What had happened? Where are the *nanas*? Why is she so thin if they hunted successfully?

I took comfort in the gentleness of her touch and her silence. Crows chattered. Sunmiet looked around.

"Who are you looking for?" I asked, wary. "Did someone come with you?"

"For the *nanas*. And Loyal, the one who looks like all the food he eats is sour."

Tears pooled unbeckoned in my eyes. I blinked them onto my cheeks and looked away, wiping my face with a dirt-streaked hand. Her dog licked at the wetness of my fingers that I let hang loosely at my side. Sunmiet shifted uneasily on her feet. "Loyal did have a pinched look," I said, trying to relieve her discomfort.

"My people come behind me," Sunmiet said, straightening. "We wish you to come to the river, to fish for the Chinook and gather eels. Your *nanas*, too," she added.

Again, my eyes filled with tears and Sunmiet spoke to her breath, as if chiding herself for saying things that distressed.

"We can go to your house," Sunmiet said, motioning me up onto her horse. "I will speak my wish to the mother and the father."

The year before, Sunmiet had ridden with me to our home where Mama nursed Baby George, my sisters and Loyal played, and Papa washed his hands in the store bowl on the plank table beside the house. Sunmiet told me then that she had two brothers, younger, who looked exactly alike. "Same-as-One" she called them though they had their own names. We spoke like older sisters, full of stories of our charges.

Mama and Papa had been wary at first when they met Sunmiet; pulled their children to them. Then, like a dog who sniffs a danger and discovers it of no harm, they lost their alarm. Mama even asked if Sunmiet would like some sweet-smelling tea before she went into the house. Sunmiet had pressed the tin mug to her lips, drinking slowly, looking about.

"We will learn to hold the dip nets and help my uncles and Standing Tall," Sunmiet told me as we approached the house. "Scrape the slimy eels from the rock walls near the falls. Hold the baskets for others at night." Dismounting, we tied her pony. "We will laugh." She looked at me out of the side of her eye. "If you wish it."

A small smile formed on my face. Sunmiet returned it, lifted her eyebrows in a question.

I wondered if I wished it. I had not wished for anything for so long, except to be rid of the large hole in my chest that had once been my heart. For so long, nothing had mattered. Mama and Papa grieved apart from me and kept Baby George in their care and no one else's. They wore black and spoke in whispers when I came into the room. I thought my face would not recognize any creases made in it from laughing.

A long summer of the same seemed overwhelming and I made a decision for myself.

"We can ask," I said. "If you wish it."

I heard the falls some distance from the river before I ever saw it. A roaring like the winter winds that surge through the tall firs filled my ears as the small band made its way over the ridge and began the steep switchback descent down the deer trails toward the white and turquoise water of the Deschutes. Captain Hood's mountain with its south notch gleamed in the late afternoon sunlight.

This country between the mountains and the river, east, is difficult to describe. In tiny script I once read what a Surveyor General had written on a map across this large expanse of land: "Heavily timbered ridges separated by immense ravines," he'd penned. We rode now into one of those "immense ravines." A rock ripped loose from the horses' feet and bounced, bounced, down the rocky ridge as we rode below the crestline.

My knees ached. I tightened them into Puddin' Foot, my mule, as he made his way, far back in the line, in and out of the ravines of the canyon. Sometimes, I could see the wide eyes of a chubby baby looking through the wildrose brace of its cradleboard. It stared at me as it bounced on the side of the saddle of its mother riding several horses ahead and descending. A rawhide circle with a spider web mesh hung from the cradleboard. A feather attached to it shifted violently with the breeze and with each bounce of the board as the horse stepped. "Same-as-One" waddled side-by-side close to the horse of Sunmiet's father, Eagle Speaker.

It surprised me that I rode here among these Indians. That they wanted my presence surprised me. That the old woman with the face of wrinkles did not spit in disgust at my arrival surprised me though I noticed she also did not smile.

But my parents giving permission surprised me most of all. And yet it shouldn't have. My parents had so many things to think about, had Baby George to care for, had other help to handle cattle and then crops. Papa's tolerance for "Injuns" as he called them, had increased what with the calming of hostilities, their help with the harvests. And he sold cattle to the Indians, found several pleasant to deal with. So he'd agreed when Sunmiet's parents caught up with her. If I wished it, I was free to go with her family to the river.

Thinking back, I might even say my parents looked relieved when I left.

Sunmiet looked over her shoulder at me as we rode. She smiled, her teeth displaying dusty grit collected from being close to the back of the line of horses and dogs and people making their way to the summer camp. Though the river was a half-day's ride from our home, I had never seen the rush of white rapids known as "the falls" that raged through the lava rocks.

"You wished this?" I said, permitting my tongue to rearrange my grit, speaking the words loudly to my friend.

Sunmiet laughed. "I wished it! And what I wish the ruler-teachers say happens."

"Then wish us there, quickly," I said tightening my knees into Puddin's withers to keep from sliding forward over his neck. His sure-footed steps slid us down the hill while his round rump seemed to push up against my back. The trail crossed creeks at the end of spring runoff with just enough water to permit the dogs to lap and the horses to splash.

"Look!" Bubbles said, pointing to the silvery ribbon that twisted at the base of the breaks, where the high ridges broke out over the river. A squatty girl, Bubbles belonged to Sunmiet's auntie and uncle. She rode just ahead of Sunmiet She gripped the mane of her horse and slid off to walk beside him, shook her head. "Steeper each year," she said. "I am persuaded to walk."

The pack on her horse slid forward. Her animal hopped and bucked until she pushed the pack, her rearranging causing a delay in the line behind her.

"Hurry up!" a boy yelled from farther back. Bubbles shouted something in Sahaptin to him using the name "Koosh" then gripped her horse's mane and swung up on its back. Sunmiet and Bubbles shared a joke and the girls laughed. Smaller children walked back and forth in the line. Dogs sniffed and darted after rabbits. The boy, Koosh, yelled something about dusty magpies. The girls laughed behind their fingers and I remember I felt something warm and familiar with no name.

Ahead of us, the band of ten or eleven families continued down the ridge, each head lower than the one behind it then higher as they followed the trail up some ravine, back down; to the inside of the ridge, then the outside ledges. Few trees dotted the bare hills. Lava outcroppings, that looked like hog-fat crackling, dribbled at the outside edges of the ridges where the winds and winter snows had exposed then washed away the shallow soil.

The red globe of the sun had already set behind the breaks by the time the band moved through a narrow cut in lava rocks that opened, finally, onto the river. In the pink of the sunset, I caught my breath at what lay before me.

Rusty rimrocks surged up from the water lining the narrow canyon with solid rock. Like blood-red split-rails pushed upright, the lava rocks stood as silent sentinels watching the river roar. Flat rocks resembling hotcakes butted up to the upright rails. The river cut its way noisily through the center of the flat stacks. It surged and twisted like muscle and tendon through a narrow sinew of rock no wider than a Conestoga wagon. All the water of the river rushed through that cut, then plunged into a deep pool that swirled and twisted for hundreds of feet. Rushing again, the water surged on through other, slightly wider wedges of rock, tumbling over and over, twisting at the base of the high ridges and canyons making its way north to the Columbia River and then the sea.

I had seen the high waterfall close to the Columbia River which the Indians called Multnomah. It hung like a bridal veil over a cliff and it was what I thought all waterfalls were like. This falls was different: it was a twisting rope of rushing water that spewed out of the river into a narrow cut then dropped and churned and dropped and twisted, pounding and spraying as it surged for a thousand feet or more.

Nothing green lined the river or the canyon. Only flat rocks—that now our horses stood on—and lava chunks broken up by eons of freezes and thaws dribbled in shades of brown and red toward the water. In the middle of the falls, silver flashes leapt suspended and then plunged back, upstream.

"Chinook!" I heard Koosh shout and opened my mouth in astonishment. The barrenness of the canyon made the brilliance of the water and its bounty all the more astounding, all the more alive.

Across the river, at the narrowest section, toward the end of the roaring cascade of water, lay a single log bridge.

I slid off Puddin' and stood beside him, no longer aware of the soreness in my legs nor how tired and hungry nor how hot and sultry. Instead, the river's power mesmerized me, held me captive in a way I wasn't sure I wanted.

A sea gull swooped, called, and dipped low enough for me to hear it, but no other sounds broke into the roaring of the river. I could feel the power of it through my feet and into my chest as it beat against the rocks. I could smell it, felt the wetness of the spray as the water fought for space in the narrow gorge and splashed like an ocean wave, pounding the rocky bank.

Sunmiet walked softly, stood beside me, said nothing. When I became aware of her, I leaned ever so slightly toward her until I felt the softness of the girl's slender arm press into my own.

In the background, rising above the roaring of the river I heard snatches of conversation. I turned to watch families making fires on the narrow rocky flats. I heard them yelling to their children, being vigilant so close beside the deepness of the river. Hair stood up on the back of my neck. They must be careful with the children.

We walked past the horses stomping in the hastily made hemp corral. I smelled the scent of the first fires. And for the first time in a long time, I felt quiet inside, the beginnings of a bandage forming over my heart.

"In the morning," Sunmiet said, "we will cross the river then gather up our poles to build the fishing platforms." She looked carefully at my face. "You do not need to fear, here," she said softly. "For this is our place of belonging and you are welcome to make it yours."

CHAPTER 9

ON THE
WINGS OF
AN EAGLE

IT WAS HOT at first light. With daylight to guide us, the band crossed the swirling river single file on the narrow log bridge, one animal at a time.

Papa had talked of this bridge built the year before by a man named Todd though Sunmiet said the log had always been here. Papa thought it a waste of time and money since no one but Indians would probably ever use it and "they'd be happier to canoe across upstream."

I'd heard once that twenty years or so before, a wagon train had gotten lost near here and that the Indians had taken settlers across the river in canoes, then helped sling ropes to bridge the narrow gorge and slide their wagons over the water. The Indians had given the travelers wind-dried salmon and berries. Still many settlers had died as they lost their way in the maze of ravines before reaching the Columbia. There had been no bridge—nor even a trail—then.

I did not look down, tried to block out the pounding water rushing beneath me, imagined each step my animal took, setting each foot, safely, firmly. I held my breath and let loose my clamped teeth when Puddin's feet touched the solid rock of the other side.

The band moved downstream, then, along the rocky shore which gave way eventually to a ravine cut down its center by a creek flowing into the Deschutes. "Buck Creek" they called it for the huge mule deer that made their home near the sagebrush and scrubby juniper. It too teemed with fish. We sloshed across the mouth of it to a grassy field. Here the band would camp for the months ahead.

"Come, *páwapaatam*—help us!" Sunmiet shouted. She had already dismounted.

The old wrinkled-face woman said something as she walked purposefully close by me, spurting dust on my bare feet as I stood next to my mule. The woman's thin mouth smirked, looking back over her shoulder as she responded to Sunmiet's request for help.

Sunmiet's mother and several other women worked together to set the ridgepoles for the teepees and I joined them at Sunmiet's direction.

In Sahaptin, the old woman said something directly to me as I stood beside her. I looked at Sunmiet for translation. "'Help here, or go watch those fat, crabby babies','" Sunmiet said.

Sunmiet must have noticed the look of pain that crossed my face for she pulled me away from Kása and into the other side of the circle of women preparing the poles, lacing the ends and standing the bases in a wide circle that would become our home.

"Don't let Kása bring you tears," Sunmiet said under her breath as we spread our hands together over the hide strip being laced to the poles. "Her tongue is sharp but holds no poison."

"She is your grandma?" I asked, recognizing, finally, what *kása* meant.

"Not as with your people," Sunmiet said, pulling on the buckskin to get it centered on the poles. "She is my mother's auntie."

"And her children?" I asked.

"She has no children of her own."

"But you call her *kása*?"

Sunmiet nodded as if to say, "So?"

Confused, I said, teaching, being right, "To be a grandmother, you need to have grandchildren."

"And she has," Sunmiet said. "Me, Same-as-One, Bubbles, to name a few."

The relationships confused me and I changed the subject. "Your *kása* doesn't like me," I noted, wiping sweat from my forehead. I figured she probably remembered the time I lost Pauline to the trees. She would scowl even more if she knew how I had lost Pauline this time, for always.

"She means no harm," Sunmiet assured me.

I shook my head, to dispel the guilt and sadness and looked instead at what happened around me.

Each of the family members seemed to know their parts and perform with a minimum of instruction. Eventually, I gravitated toward the younger children who, like me, seemed to be having difficulty staying out of the way. Kása watched me as I warily played with the children, not sure of my place. Without smiling, she nodded her kerchiefed head. I thought it an approval and was surprised at how warm her nod made me feel. The old woman's beaded earrings bobbed against her lined throat as she sat some distance away working bear grass and corn husks into a basket while her family formed the teepees into a semicircle facing east.

Beyond the camp, Eagle Speaker, a tall Indian, and a broad-shouldered one wearing a white man's hat with an eagle feather in the brim, worked to dig out caches in the rocks. Placed there the year before, they handed more poles and boards to waiting hands of other men who now laced the boards together into platforms that soon jutted out over the river. The pole stilts seemed so spindly I couldn't imagine anyone standing on them let alone leaning out over the water from them with their nets!

Such nets! "These catch the giant fish returning to their place of beginning, upriver," Sunmiet said. She showed me baskets made of similar material, in a tighter weave.

"For the eels my father and uncles gather up at night," she said. "We will hold the baskets," she added proudly stacking several next to the family's large dun-colored lodge.

"We will hold them?" I asked, surprised that girls would be allowed to help.

"You have big hands," she said, pleased.

"What keeps us from slipping into the water?"

"The men tie ropes around their middle and attach it, there." She pointed to rock points. "Sometimes others hold them, to catch them if they slip or if the

Chinook does not wish to be caught. It is the way their fathers and their father's fathers have always netted," she said matter-of-factly, "each in his own place along the river. It is dangerous. We will stay back, away. Everyone keeps his eyes open and his thoughts of only fish and nets and eels. Then few are lost."

I watched as a wide-faced, heavy man moved gingerly down the rocks, closer to the roaring water. He looked a little different than the others, lighter skinned and held a spear instead of a net.

"He is Hupa. Fish Man," Sunmiet said, explaining. "Fish Man travels many days from the giant red bark trees where the Hupas and Euroks argue over land. He leaves the arguments to fish with us each summer."

As we watched, he plunged his spear into the surging water and caught a fish without benefit of platform or the rope. "Ayiee!" he shouted in delight. Others, seeing his success, cheered him on then hurried themselves to the seasonal work necessary to net the big Chinook.

I could have stood for hours, watching, breathing shallow like a watchful deer, listening to the surging falls in the dense heat. It was all so wonderful and strange seeing each do his part to fish and then bring the bounty to the women for skinning and cleaning and forming each into two giant filets. Pink rows soon dried on racks beside each teepee.

The tall, handsome Indian I'd seen earlier walked toward us. "Standing Tall," Sunmiet said as she eased her way closer to the opening of her family's lodge.

Standing Tall derived his name naturally. I imagined he could touch the low branches of the firs when he reached his long brown arms upward so tall was he. He was taller than Sunmiet's father, taller than Fish Man. "His uncles are all tall too, but they are big men, and fluffy," Sunmiet said holding her arms in a circle to mark their round size. We giggled.

"Sometimes Standing Tall lets his height speak too strongly," Sunmiet told me in a whisper. "His smaller mind loses control over his tongue," she added, giggling. "He did not want me to bring you here. He thinks I am too young to be alone with you, a 'non-Indian.' He is a Wasco and thinks himself wiser than me or my family," she said with some disgust.

She mimicked her conversation with him the morning she invited me to spend the summer. "'You should not go beyond the eyes of your father or his friends who wish to protect you' he told me. He smiled his lopsided smile, the left side of his mouth rising higher than the other as it always does, always has since he entered the world that way, contrary and resisting."

As he approached us, I saw that one of his eyes was also more lopsided than the other though one noticed more the strength of his arms, his sure stride moving beneath his buckskin leggings.

"I told him I would speak to my father not a rude boy who does not know when to close his lips to bridle his unruly thoughts," Sunmiet continued. "And my father gave me permission to invite you."

She looked annoyed as the man approached, and something else. "He should not even be here now, bothering our morning fire," she said, and turned her back on him.

Small children scampered about, Sunmiet's little brothers, twins. Their bare bellies pooched out like melons over firm brown legs as they threw sticks for the puppies to chase. Her mother stepped out from the cool of the lodge to stir the embers of the small flames, her body soft, round on thin legs, inviting, like the dough of the fry bread she prepared to drop into the hot pan leaned into the fire.

Sunmiet's father hunched away from the heat then stood to face his guest and future son-in-law.

"I would take your daughter for a ride," Standing Tall said, acting like Sunmiet was not present, "as I am not yet busy with the nets."

I felt Sunmiet stiffen next to me. She wore a dress of tanned buckskin that pulled tightly across her young chest then dropped over her hips and stopped just inches above the already dusty earth and her beaded moccasins. Her eyelashes jumped with irritation on her cheeks, pink now. "I am someone more to be with than merely filling time," she said to her father. "Huckleberry Eyes and I have things to do of value even if some do not."

Standing Tall's face flushed. Eagle Speaker looked at me and coughed and covered his mouth with his hand concealing a smile, eyes flashing quickly over his daughter's head to Standing Tall.

The quick gesture seemed to make the men holders of some secret and I saw Sunmiet's cheeks begin to burn.

"Oh, hayah!" she said, her voice strong, "Come Huckleberry Eyes. Surely my tall friend has more important work to do than ride with a mere girl-child."

"You should not be alone with her," Standing Tall said, moving to stand beside Sunmiet as though that were his right, his place. "The cloud-face children shoot the long rifles," he said, scowling at me.

"Small boys learn to shoot the rifles here," Sunmiet said, "Perhaps that is not so on the Big River where the Wascos live. Do you see her holding a rifle, Father?" She kept her eyes from Standing Tall's. Her words were insults, reminding him he was a Wasco who did not know all the ways of the Warm Springs, Sahaptin-speaking people. "I do not need a boy's protection from a small girl who is my friend."

Sunmiet added: "I am my father's daughter who knows well how to defend herself."

Eagle Speaker smiled openly now as his daughter's long braids bounced on her breasts as she turned. She straightened her shoulders in finality. She pushed herself to full height which still barely reached Standing Tall's shoulder. "Come, Jane," she said, deliberately using my English name, "we have things to do."

Standing Tall seemed to know there was no recourse and he turned abruptly, his moccasins leaving a deep impression where he spun in the dirt. His black hair swung well below his waist as he stomped off. "He is a young eagle harassed by a mere magpie of a girl," I heard Sunmiet's father say to her mother.

"Later, we will clean the fish, roast the eels," Sunmiet said, avoiding the encounter. "Now, the rocks call our name. Come. Put on moccasins I make for you. I show you my place."

While the men set more platforms to jut out over the river, and Fish Man set his feet on solid rock, anticipating his next Chinook, I slipped the soft hide over my bare feet, laced them about my ankles and followed Sunmiet up the rimrocks. "Step carefully," Sunmiet shouted, breathing hard, over her shoulder. "Father rattlesnake likes resting in the sun." She grinned at my wide eyes reminding me, "We make too much noise. He moves."

We climbed for more than an hour with k'usik'usi panting and bounding above us, then below, urging us on until we reached the top of the ridge on the east side of the river. Over rock outcroppings and shale slides of broken lava rocks, and past ravens' nests, we climbed higher and higher until even the birds swooped and dipped below us. "There," Sunmiet pointed. "See where the wagons made tracks in the earth?" Such a steep ridge to bring wagons down! No wonder the settlers were tired and got easily lost.

When we reached a swale near the top of a bare hill, we rested. There we sat, nestled into a hollow depression in the earth, protected from the cooling breezes with Captain Hood's Mountain straight across from us, once again in view. In the quiet, with the river and the world of the band below us, *k'usik'usi* soon fell asleep at our feet.

I watched the men on the platforms, amazed at the streams of water that ran like braids over the rocks and around the stilts they'd lashed to hold them steady. The water poured across the flat rocks, poured back into the river. From our perch, the falls seems not as mighty until I imagined these men leaning out over it to net fish. I could not tell who was who as the tiny dark figures moved below us. I could see them, standing close, the ropes and nets coiled like giant snakes beside them, as each family prepared their platform and planned how they would work together to net the fish, feed their families, stay alive.

For the first time, I let myself feel the sting of Standing Tall's reaction to me. Having never met him, I could think of nothing I had done to upset him. Oh, I knew about people who disliked someone because he or she was Indian. But I didn't think an Indian would see me the same as someone quite so small in their thinking. Even Papa clumped "Injuns" all as one in talking, though it seemed to me he treated several as unique. And here I was, among them, which was, perhaps, Standing Tall's problem.

"Will my being here be bad for you and Standing Tall?" I asked Sunmiet. She lay in the grass beside me, eyes closed.

"He treats me like a child more than a future bride," she said not opening her eyes. "I was promised to him in the month I was born," she said. "So it will be. Do not worry," she told me, turning, resting her head on hands folded beneath her cheek. Her brown eyes sparkled and she smiled. "A little magpie irritating the eagle is good, keeps him quick and alert. Standing Tall will be reminded that he will marry a wife with a mind separate from his own. Give him something to anticipate." She grinned a wide smile that lit up the perfect features of her face.

I watched thin smoke from the family's fires near the lodges rise in a straight line and then disappear into the higher breeze. An eagle screeched and soared out over the place we sat in quiet. Sunmiet seemed to sleep.

I laid back though I wasn't tired. Instead, I felt the scratchy bunch-grass tickle my back as I watched fluffy clouds suspended like dumplings in the deep blue sky. The eagle entered my sight beneath the clouds and I watched him raise and lower his massive wings, pick up the currents from the ravines. The bird screeched again moving out over the river.

"The eagle honors us," Sunmiet said through closed eyes. "He is the only bird to move between the dream world and our own. His presence means he is pleased."

I watched the eagle, his closeness. I could see the ruff of his thick throat, the white of his regal head, the sharpness of his eye. He flew so close above me I heard the mass of his wings cut the wind. But as he soared into the distance, lilting and resting on the currents of wind above the river, I noticed something more: the eagle soared not only by his own efforts but by the strength of something else, by the strength of the wind and his willingness to bend to it.

Something inside me shifted. For the first time in months I spoke a prayer, shared something besides my anger. Thank you, I said. For this place, this friend who sleeps beside me, and for whatever this is I am feeling.

What had once filled me up had been taken in a breath, taken my joy and my confidence with it. But like the eagle, I could rise and rest on the strength of something else. And I could bend to it while anticipation eased back into my life.

CHAPTER 10

A
SEARCH OF
THE HEART

THE 1861 PAPERS were full of it. Joseph had heard rumors beginning two years earlier. Now it seemed the stories were true.

Breaking into Spanish and English with equal ferocity, Benito chattered about it with his cousins and brothers, the younger men talking with their hands marking the air about how they might take advantage of it, whispering a bit when Joseph stepped near. As they rode the fence lines, marking and repairing the sections of land owned by Señor Sherar, they wondered out loud what they'd do if they were one of the lucky ones—to pick up their hat left lying on the ground and under it, discover gold in Eastern Oregon as the paper had reported.

"You could find out," Benito said as he and Joseph walked together to the sheep corrals one July morning. The kelpie dog Joseph had recently purchased from some Australians—along with the Merino sheep—followed closely at their heels.

"Why change things?" Joseph asked. "Aren't you the one who just takes it a day at a time?"

"Is not for me! No, for you!" Benito told him, patting him on the back as they walked. "You get bored here," Benito said. "Lonely. Spend too much time in Yreka. You sleep under stars or maybe have cold feet to truly live. Remember?"

Joseph did remember those years they'd packed into the northern gold fields of California and the southern Oregon Territory. A trial a minute, it seemed, requiring good wits and a strong stomach considering some of the characters and challenges they'd met. Nature, too, seemed less than encouraging those years as they fought their way through slippery thunderstorms, spring floods, and even encounters with Yuroks and Hupas and Klamath natives that were less than friendly. They had always come out on top, no shots ever fired.

But those years were past. He was settled now, mature and so he said: "Just because you're restless doesn't mean I should be." He picked up his pace. "And what makes you think I'm bored? I keep busy enough."

"Your kind of busy is the warts on boring," Benito said, not breathless despite the faster pace required to keep up with his long-legged friend and boss. He spit a stream into the dust. "I know you. You are busy with things others can do. Nothing here makes your heart pound as when we ran the mules. Yes," he said as if to himself, "you are bored." He rolled his ample lower lip over his upper and chewed on it in concentration. "I know you."

"Not so well as you think," Joseph said. A small irritation appeared in his voice. "I have what I wanted. This ranch. Good land, good stock. Even friends, who think they know me better than they do." The last he spoke with finality, a sign he wished to put an end to their conversation.

Benito persisted. "You weary of all this." He scanned the horizon glowing with signs of Joseph's wealth. "You know what will happen next and so, you are bored. You want to be useful. As useful as pockets on longjohns," he added with certainty. He easily climbed the railing when they reached it and sat at the top of the corral, watching Joseph's latest acquisitions rip at the grass.

"Tell me how it happens," Joseph said, his voice directed fully to Benito. "It's acceptable for you to get up every day, see the same scenery, kiss the same woman, ride the same canyons. That's not bad for you. But I'm supposed to find fault with that routine, with all I have?"

"Yes," Benito said, "except for the kissing part. You have not kissed the same woman for four years as I have. You should try it," he added, winking, not in the least distressed by Joseph's irritation. I think he must have understood that this was how Joseph worked things out: talking, arguing some. Instead he said: "The mules, they kept you guessing and so you looked to each day. Saw it different." He grinned. "Now, you see each day the same." He turned his mouth into a frown. "Familiar, like the hair that grows up from your big toe."

Joseph pushed his hand against the air as if to say "enough" and dismissed his friend's suggestions, turning instead to the sheep.

But he remembered Benito's words. That's what he told me. The words worked in his head as the men looked over the two rams and twelve ewes they planned to ship back east. Beyond, dotting the treeless hillsides like cotton fluffs against a homespun quilt, grazed three thousand sheep with their lambs suckling and romping. Prosperity spread before him. "If I'd been honest," Joseph told me, "I'd have agreed with Benito. My life was a little boring."

The man had plenty to do. His ranch had grown dramatically in the six years since they'd first stepped foot in California. The sea of sheep kept them busy along with the more than two hundred head of cow-calf pairs that roamed the redwood and fir trees of the Hupa Valley. Selling his forty mules and the pack string had saddened him at the time, he told me, but he liked not being gone so much despite what Benito thought. Here there were miles of fences that needed daily work, legal issues with neighbors over water and boundaries that needed tending to. Accounting challenges, shipping choices, management decisions about who to hire and who to let go. They all took their toll on his time.

Of course, he hired men, and some women, to do most of the work and even some of his thinking, leaving his task to be making the choices. "That's what prosperity's about. Making decisions that others put into effect. Having time to do the things I wanted. Wasn't that exactly what Frederic had come to?" I don't think either Joseph or that fluffy man of his memory realized until later in their lives what was missing.

Leaning on the corral fence that day, Joseph and Benito discussed their plans, deciding first who would move the sheep to the railway. They'd need to arrange for food for the trip and travel with this investment of Merino sheep.

The shipment was a risk, sending breeding stock back east. They'd travel by rail to San Francisco and then by ship through the Isthmus. Much could happen and Joseph wanted good men with keen judgment and their wits about them to make the trip.

Joseph's first choice had been for Benito to go with Fish Man, the Hupa who worked for them most of the year. But Fish Man had headed north to some river of falls, the Deschutes he called it, for all the white water, near the Cascade Mountains in Oregon. "Fishing good there," Fish Man told him in his slow-talking English. He scratched his muscular arms then spread them wide, to mark the dip net's size. "Dip in once, pull out huge Chinook. Maybe two. Me, I spear the fish." He grinned, his perfect teeth flashing in his wide face. His eyes sparkled as he added, "Nice country to dry fish in. Hot. Women, too. You come see." He'd laughed his infectious belly laugh and Joseph had grinned at the invitation.

Though Joseph tried to talk him out of going, Fish Man would not budge. He could be stubborn that way. His routine just simply included summer fishing on that northern river. "Will be hard winter, this one," he had told Joseph. "Deer already have much fat close to their skin. Maybe next year, rivers too high and muddy, fish slip by. This year, good one." He'd patted his belly approvingly and smiled. "So I will go."

Fish Man told Joseph, too, of the narrow gorge where a massive falls forced the fish to jump above each other in the air making themselves vulnerable to the nets. And he described a log bridge where the white man named Lewis and his friend Clark had crossed it was said, saving days of travel. "Friends cross there, camp," he'd said. "Few white man. If you come sometime, I show you how to fish." He had grinned knowing such an offer would be a real lure for Joseph. "I be back before first snow."

Fish Man left shortly after that and so Benito had arranged for a Eurok who knew the country and two of his own cousins to travel with the sheep as far as San Francisco. His cousins would continue east. It was all arranged. Joseph needed only to nod his approval.

The two men walked back toward the arches of Joseph's stone home, the kelpie at his heels. Benito did not revisit the subject of change. The men walked by bougainvillea blooming profusely hanging from the clay pots and window boxes tended by the housemaids. Benito's new wife managed the household with an iron hand, Joseph noted as they stepped into the cool of the tile entry, stepping around a young girl already scrubbing the floor on her knees. She laughed a tinkling laugh as the kelpie rushed to lick her face. The dog raised its eyebrows, two tan thumbprints above its eyes, delighted to find a human at his height. "Come, Bandit," Joseph said to the kelpie and the dog trotted behind him, his cinnamon-colored coat disappearing into the cool darkness of the dining room.

Between Anna and Benito things were so well organized that despite the usual disasters common to all ranches, things did run smoothly. Joseph could even be gone for days at a time and return with all problems handled. With the government contracts for beef, the war in the east pushing up fleece sales, and now breeding stock being shipped east, he had no financial worries. In fact, he'd successfully shipped an entire shipload of wool around the horn to Boston markets making a killing while helping the north in the war. The only difficulty he'd faced in recent months seemed to be a growing resentment by some of the locals over his good fortune.

The weekly card game at Yreka had become troublesome. Riskier bets seemed to push him, make his heart pound and his face turn hot. He found himself alive in the challenges, reading men's faces, anticipating their cards and their willingness to raise his bets, pushing his own limits to risk even larger sums. "The games really weren't about them; they were about me," he said, "about energy and intensity and taking greater chances." He found himself excited after the games, alive. "I hated taking their money," he told me years later. "But I hated more not playing to win."

Joseph pulled the heavy oak chair from the table and sat his tall frame down on the wide leather strips forming the seat. Bandit slipped beneath the table and lay quietly on the tiles, panting at Joseph's feet.

Benito excused himself, entered laughing to meet with his wife in the kitchen. Before Joseph could even ask, a kitchen maid swooshed out from the carved doors Benito had just gone through. She bent her bare shoulders near him, swishing her full striped skirt near his chair as she placed before him a cool glass of lemonade in a sweating clay mug. He lifted and drank. "I was so totally engaged in thinking about my future," he lied to me years later, "that I was unaware of her sweet perfume."

"Ha!" I said. "How did you know she wore any?"

He returned the subject to his year of change. He said he saw no need to travel into the gold mines of the Powder River country, no need to keep a pack string or to wheel and deal to bring luxuries in and carry gold out. He'd done that. His life was in California, organized, predictable.

Perhaps that was what Benito considered "boring," that everything could be handled without effort.

But it was what he'd worked for all those years.

He pushed himself away from the table, still holding the mug to let a second kitchen maid put before him a platter of steaming huevos rancheros with its reds and greens and yellows. Next to it, she set a platter of tortillas, unfolding the linen that wrapped each one, keeping them hot and soft. She would watch and as he completed his meal, the kitchen maid would bring a hot cup of coffee with three clumps of sugar served in his favorite porcelain cup.

Joseph picked up his fork and began to eat, savoring the scents and aromas and tastes. Yes, this luxury was what it was all about. Hadn't he enjoyed gloating just a bit when he returned to New York last year sharing some of his wealth? He brought with him a full, dark beard, a flat-brimmed leather hat with chin string, and California gifts for everyone. He remembered being a bit surprised when his older brother James, the other bachelor in the family, introduced his wife, Eliza. They beamed over three-year-old Carrie Ann, their pride and joy. He'd known of neither the marriage nor the niece. From a distance, he'd even seen Cherise, a girl he'd once courted, who was now a chubby matron with two tots at her side, and had felt a twinge of something.

But even watching love and family move past him did not cheat him of his moment of pride when he handed James a gold nugget worth several hundred dollars. The sense of delight he had at sharing his bounty with his oldest brother was fleeting. His elderly father had merely snorted and said something about making better use of his time and talents while his mother then herded them into the dining room for a less than jocular meal.

It had been a good decision to go back east for a visit, though the joy of it had not carried him as far as he had hoped. Even the excitement of the train trip across the country had not held the fascination for him it once might have. Oh, he kept notes of interesting sights: roads engineered in difficult places, tunnels bored into mountainsides, bridges over deep gorges, and drawings of unusual gradients in the tracks. Other than that, not much besides his little leather sketch book gave him delight. He didn't call the feelings he had then boredom. A bit fatigued, maybe. And as the housemaids sometimes did, he might have lowered his energy by placing too many hand irons to heat in the fire. But he was almost thirty and a man of means, entitled to be tired. No, Benito had it wrong. He was fine. Not bored. He intended to live out his life in California and be happy.

The kelpie nudged close to his hand he let hang beside him. He scratched between the kelpie's pointed ears, patted the lighter brown spots above the dog's eyes and chest and sighed.

"Maybe you go north, to the Klamath this month?" Benito asked returning from the kitchen.

"I could," Joseph said, though the thought had not crossed his mind before. He stirred his spoon in his coffee idly. "Don't want to make myself a nuisance." He smiled.

He had purchased a ranch in the southern section of Oregon two years earlier, just before he'd sold the string. The small town growing there to serve the miners some 150 miles up the Klamath River seemed to appreciate the supplies freighted from the California coast into the mountains.

The ranch had been an afterthought, really, something to keep him connected to the little valley whose people had seemed so grateful each time he arrived with supplies. It was that part of packing that he liked best, seeing the look of pleasure when his string made it through, brought what was anticipated and needed.

Joseph had hired Philamon Lathrope, the son of a local rancher, to clear ground and build a small house on the donation land claim of 640 acres he'd purchased with a portion of the pack string sale proceeds.

He hadn't seen it since.

"My friend and I could visit his ranch and ride a little farther. To the gold fields," Benito suggested not disguising his interests at all.

Joseph sat quietly, the spoon tapping the side of the porcelain cup until the brown clumps dissolved. The distant chatter of Spanish drifted from the kitchen. "It might be good to check on my investment," he said. "Maybe even go farther, to see about the gold strikes and what settlement they promise. I will go alone." Benito dropped his lower lip in disappointment. "Anna would never forgive me if I took you from her for even a week, let alone several."

"You are wise about this, my friend," Benito sighed, pulling at his long mustache. "But if you like this place, or you have difficulty, you well send for me, yes?" he added hopefully.

"I will send for you. Yes," Joseph said feeling a spark of energy he had not realized he'd been missing.

Joseph sat patiently, gloved hands gently holding the leather reins. He leaned onto the pommel of the saddle, standing in the stirrups for a moment to stretch his legs and still have an eagle's view of the basin. The big roan gelding he rode snorted and stomped his foot impatiently, still full of energy despite the long day's ride through brushy, thick-scrub country. The single pack mule stood head drooped, behind.

Below him, Joseph noted a cleared area not far from the river and knew that would be Philamon's work. "Let's go," he said to the kelpie who had ingratiated himself by being forever present. At the last minute, Joseph had decided to take the dog along. Together, they started down, the gelding stirring up rolls of white lava dust like snow as they walk-slid down the hill.

A young man, nearly ten years younger than Joseph, Philamon had made significant progress in two years. Joseph was pleased that the money he'd sent had not been squandered. A completed two-story house sat at the edge of a huge stand of Ponderosa Pine. Several acres had been cleared and it appeared the timber put to good use as a large barn, corrals, and several out buildings were also complete. Some long-horned cattle tore at grass in a fenced area beyond. Chickens scratched in the garden Joseph rode past, promising a variety of vegetables. Joseph noted with approval that Philamon had ingeniously dug ditches to drain water from a small stream, irrigating the large garden and the cluster of fruit trees planted not far from the house. Even in the August heat with the grasses all around brown from lack of rain, Philamon had created a refuge of green.

Joseph inhaled the strong scent of pine and staying on his horse, listened for Philamon's dogs to start barking his arrival. "Up," he said to the kelpie and the dog leapt into his arms as though shot from his Sharps.

Philamon stepped like a shadow from behind the house at the sound of his dogs. He held a plains rifle loosely but ominously in his muscled arms. "Won't hurt you," he said in a voice surprisingly deep for someone so slender.

"The kelpie can hold his own," Joseph said watching the dog's lips curl back, hearing him clamp his jaws.

Philamon called to the dogs before they bit at the heels of the big roan Joseph rode. They barked louder as they discovered the kelpie, then came to the man who called them.

"Ye've done well, Philamon," Joseph said, removing his leather hat and wiping the dampness from his forehead with the back of his forearm. His Irish accent always seemed to accompany introductory comments.

Philamon squinted. "Who are you, then?" he asked cautiously, adjusting his wire glasses. His hazel eyes quickly took in the size of the man, his expensive leather boots, his chaparejos, his whip coiled on the saddle. He spied the Sharps in the scabbard, an expertly rolled bedroll behind the cannel, a well-stocked pack animal. Philamon stepped closer, eyeing Joseph's bearded face. Looking past the beard to the soft eyes of his landlord a spark of recognition hit him. "Joe?" He asked.

"Aye, 'tis me," Joseph answered.

Philamon's face formed a hesitant smile. "Well knock me flatter than a wallow! What are you doing here?" Then, as if remembering his manners, "No matter. I've just set the Arbuckle coffee on to brew. Down, Brutus! Cassius!" he called to the hounds sniffing at Joseph's boots as he stepped down, still holding the kelpie.

Joseph shifted the dog and the men shook hands. And while each seemed pleased to see that the other had kept their agreements, Joseph sensed a caution from Philamon.

The kelpie pranced behind the men as they walked toward the corral, the larger dogs kept at bay by the smaller dog's snapping jaw. Philamon described the process of planting the fruit trees as they walked.

At the corral, they stripped the gelding of his saddle and bridle and brushed him till he cooled. Joseph hung the blacksnake coiled at his hip and carried the Sharps into the house with him while Philamon pulled the pack box from the mule.

"So," Philamon said clearing his throat, probing, "have you found that California doesn't suit you?" He poured coffee into the porcelain cup he handed to Joseph, some into his own chipped ironstone cup.

"California's chirk," Joseph answered, his glance resting on Philamon's stack of books on the floor.

"Figured by now you'd be wearing a California collar," Philamon joked awkwardly, referring to the popular name for a hangman's noose. "Or aren't you playing cards these days?" Then added quickly, "Not that you didn't always win fairly." He paused before saying, "Some would question your good luck."

"Still playing," Joseph said, "but with less enthusiasm."

"No wedding ring, either," Philamon said. "Should be settled with a growing pack of kids 'stead of just a contrary dog to follow you about." He cleared his throat again and swung a leg over one of several store-bought chairs surrounding the pine table. Sitting, his arms rested on the back of the chair. Joseph felt he was keeping a distance.

"No wedding ring," Joseph said. For just a moment he thought of his brothers and sisters, all married. "But the dog never talks back."

A Seth Thomas clock ticked quietly in the silence.

"Ye've done good work here, Philamon," Joseph said gently leaning into the table, his forearms resting. He was aware that something troubled Philamon. "I've not come to take it away."

Philamon exhaled loudly. He tipped his cup for a drink, sat holding both hands around it as if for warmth. "Didn't think it was so obvious," he said. "I find I like it here, more than I thought I would." He coughed then said, "Hard work, but accomplishments, too. And time to read at night. Think. Even write some with no one to answer to but myself." Philamon stood up, grabbed a section of flour sack he used as a pot holder, and picked up the coffee pot. He refilled his own cup through the speckled spout and turned to fill Joseph's.

"So if you're not here to farm," he said, "what are you doing so far from home?"

"Bringing you more books," Joseph said. I've brought *The Virginians* which should keep you occupied on a cold winter's night. And a copy of Mill's essay on Liberty. Timely, even if it is three years old." Then aware that he wasn't being totally truthful he added, "Not sure why I'm here. Maybe check on market rumors," he finished lamely. He moved to the pack box and began unloading staples and the books.

"Might check out the Powder River country. Hear they're looking for corn freights to supply the mines. Have you heard anything?" Joseph asked.

Philamon sat back down, this time with his feet under the table. "Most of the talk is about the war and if it'll come here. People getting their dander up. Think we were still back in Illinois or New York or Virginia 'stead of out here, making our own country." He reached in his vest pocket for his pouch of tobacco and rolled a cigarette. "Just get the Indians settled and we've a war among our own to deal with." He struck a flint, lit the paper, and inhaled, coughing. "I hear the Canyon City country in the Strawberry Mountains is the real strike. First one was in '59. They're finding more each year."

"Might be something there, then," Joseph said, scratching at his beard.

"Course the Powder River has good promise. But why would you want it, to get back into packing at all, I mean?"

Joseph shrugged. "Not sure I do," he said and took a sip from his cup. "Just not sure what I want to do."

Joseph spent three days with Philamon. They spoke more of books and wars and dogs with Bandit winning Philamon's heart by his cattle-herding abilities and the kelpie's ability to hold its own with the hounds. Then Joseph headed east along the Applegate trail toward Christmas Lake. From the desert lake, Joseph and the kelpie followed an old wagon trail. Vegetation was sparse. Still, he was impressed by a massive granite outcropping that seemed to rise more than a mile up out of the desert, especially as it meant an extra four days of riding to go around it.

When he reached the deep canyons of the Snake River, he headed north toward the Powder River country. Not far from Ft. Boise, he picked up the Northern Immigrant Road and was surprised by the number of wagons he encountered. Prospectors, some; mostly settlers, making their way to the Columbia River and Dalles City, gateway to the Eden they'd all been promised.

He wondered where they would all end up, what dreams they carried with them. He spoke with some: farmers from Indiana; a woman photographer from the Dakota Territory; an investor working for a bank back east. Despite the hardships they all spoke of, there was a hopefulness in their spirit that brought smiles to their faces as they talked of what they'd shared and planned for. It was as though they were rehearsing for the times they'd tell their children and grandchildren of what they'd endured, the fears they'd conquered traveling across the plains, seeking a new and different life.

"And I wished, just for a moment," he told me as we rode together some years later, "that I had someone besides the kelpie who might want to hear my story. Or better, someone to create a story with."

"Well, you *were* almost thirty," I teased, "and had so little to show for your years." He swatted his hat at me.

"Nothing about the Powder River country promised any hope of finding either listener or partner," he remembered. "But neither did the ranch in California."

In the morning, he had rubbed his chilled hands over his fire and speaking with the kelpie, considered the coldness of the sunrise. "Can actually see me breath!" he said. On its belly, the dog eased out of Joseph's bed roll, stretched its short legs, and perked its pointy ears toward his master. "Little too cool for my blood this time of year," he said. When he heard the call of the greater Canada geese and saw above him more than one hundred in formation and it being only September, he was reminded of Fish Man's words. "Looks like it 'twill be an early winter," he said as much to himself as the kelpie.

And having seen enough of high, cold country that turned his thoughts to making memories and relationships he did not have, he turned west, thinking to surprise Fish Man on his way back to California. He'd find the river of the falls, the Deschutes, and perhaps the two could net a fish or two and return together to the Hupa Valley, well before snow fell in the mountains.

Fish Man was a man of vision, after all, though Joseph wondered if he truly could foretell the future or its weather.

CHAPTER 11

CONNECTIONS

᠊᠊᠊᠊᠊᠊᠊᠊᠊᠊

"BE CAREFUL, *NANA,*" Standing Tall said, reaching out to restrain Sunmiet, holding her arm so his fingers pinched into her flesh.

Sunmiet said: "Oh, hayah! This is not my first time."

"The fish make the stand slippery," he warned, treating her as one who did not know anything. "It has turned cold quickly, with frost now. And the wind blows. It could lift a small feather like you, drop you like the eagle drops the remains of his prey into the water." He held her elbow with an owning grip, walked her away from the platform's edge. I trailed after them like a listening shadow. "The rope should be around you, even just to look," Standing Tall chided.

"I am not just small prey," Sunmiet snapped. She pulled against him without success. "My father asked me to bring him the ropes and nets."

"We have been fortunate this year," Standing Tall continued, preaching a bit about the summer's success. "All will return to their families. I would not want your father's daughter to be the spoiler on the last days of the salmon run." His one eye drooped and he squinted at her with the other in the way he had of making his point. Her look seemed to wither him at least and he released her elbow. He said: "*Nana,* you be careful."

"I am not your sister!" She stood a safe distance from his reach. "So do not treat me as one." She stepped gingerly over the coiled ropes that she had readied for transport back to her father's lodge. We were in no danger.

"I will treat you as one I care for," he called to her back, "even if you resist." I could hear true caring for her in his voice.

She spoke to me as we dragged the nets and ropes toward her father's teepee: "I wish we could return to the times when we laughed and played together, instead of stirring the air with our anger."

Since her father had set the time for their marriage—the next summer—after another year at the boarding school, Standing Tall had changed. He had begun teaching Sunmiet when she did not care to be taught, treating her like a small child. "I am neither fragile or a child and sometimes I just want to be away from him as he makes me feel both."

She thought to tell him something, yelled over her shoulder: "It saddens my heart that you see me only as one to be taken care of!" We heard him say something and she whirled to face him. "I have arrived through fourteen summers without your guidance. I can enter this season without your words of wisdom, too." Her hands hugged hips, elbows out. Her teeth held each other to keep from having her tongue say anything more.

"Your father has given me the right to look after you," Standing Tall said, catching us. He touched her gently on the shoulder. "But I will only do it if it pleases you. I do not want a wife who wishes she was somewhere else."

"Then see me as I am," Sunmiet said. Calmer, she added, "for I am my father's daughter, strong. And my mother's daughter, wise. Not one of your little sisters."

The roar of the falls filled the silence as the two stared at each other like dogs with raised hair. I fidgeted, feeling an intruder.

Standing Tall spoke finally. "I will look again at you," he said quietly.

Sunmiet smiled a wary smile at him. I saw her shoulders sink as though relieved they had taken a step to cross a bridge of irritation that seemed to follow them like the swallows to the mud. "Good," Sunmiet said, quick to honor his respect. "We will make a new start."

"But you must still stay off the springboard," Standing Tall added, ruining it all: "It is no place for a small girl."

"Oh, hayah!" Sunmiet stomped purposefully toward the camp leaving him with his eyes full of confusion.

"Let us walk," Sunmiet told me. "I must find a way to bend my thoughts."

"I shouldn't leave sight of the babies," I said, glancing at the row of cradleboards leaning in the shade of the long house lodge. "Even the platform is almost too far away. Kása will have my hide skinned off in a minute if I went out of sight." It had taken me awhile to make my way past the clucking *kása*. Her stares at me from a distance let me know my presence was often not appreciated. When Sunmiet's mother had suggested I look after the babies while the women cleaned fish, cut and dried the salmon, Kása had initially resisted.

"She cannot be trusted to look after so many children," she said in the click-click language. When Sunmiet translated her opinion to me I felt as though she had struck me on the face. Hadn't she nodded her approval that first day? I must have misunderstood.

Sunmiet and Morning Dove had spoken for me in the circle of the women. It had been agreed that I would watch the little ones in the cradleboards. Young married women would take turns being responsible for the more active ones.

The arrangement had succeeded. My tricks to soothe the babies worked and I was diligent, rarely left their sides, never let the sun beat on their faces. When I removed them from their boards to clean their bottoms or let them play, I was careful, lacing the leather, placing a blanket over the empty board to protect it, keep it safe from the spirits the people believed in. I didn't understand their spirits, but I would do nothing to upset Kása. Placing the babies back inside their boards, I swaddled them tightly as they liked, made sure the moss pillow protected their necks and their chubby backs, laced the rawhide with one hand while I gentled them to sleep on my knees. I always tied the rawhide so the brace would protect them should they slip and fall face forward. I kept a cool cloth over the wild rose brace to ward off the flies and the heat and the bright sun from their eyes.

Once I had even startled a toddler turning blue from something she had eaten. Remembering Rachel, in seconds I'd pulled the baby from her board, drummed on her back and a chunk of chewed venison had shot like a spit ball to the ground. I'd savored the murmuring of approval I'd heard for my quick wisdom; looked for Kása's nod and thought I'd found it.

Caring for these little ones was something I could do. I was grateful to feel useful with children again. I touched the dreamcatcher hanging from the brace of Toto as we talked. It moved gracefully back and forth to keep the baby busy.

Sunmiet took notice of the activity in the circle of the lodges, the dogs, the racks of salmon drying, women working, cutting. Babies in their cradleboards leaned against the shady side of the skin lodges. "Yes," she said. "You must stay here. I will walk alone, away from the anger that this man so easily gives me. Still," she said thinking, "your company would please me. The weeks have gone well and as the camp is breaking, there are fewer chores. Maybe Bubbles would watch them."

I was willing to take a chance. "Stay here," I said.

Bubbles lounged in the shade of a juniper not far from the camp. Her round body had expanded like an elk bladder through the summer and I knew she'd be reluctant to move to the cradleboards without incentive.

"Kása put dried choke cherries into the jellied black moss," I told her. "I watched her do it. It will be sweet. I will give you some of my share when it comes out of the fire pit. In return for a few minutes of your time, watching babies."

Bubbles grunted, negotiated. "All of your share?" she said.

I pretended hesitation. The black moss was actually too sweet for my taste so it was easy to give it up. I didn't want to sound too eager. "Well, I like the choke cherries..." I said.

"I will watch," Bubbles said, interested now, "if I have all of it."

"Well..."

"I can be persuaded," she said lazily and grunted as she stood, brushing fry bread crumbs from the folds across her jelly-belly, "for all of it."

I nodded once in agreement. Negotiations completed, she walked with heavy legs, so slowly for one so young, and settled her bulk like a mass of jellied moss next to where the children sat alert in their boards.

"If you hear them crying, you'll come back?" she asked lazily.

"I'll come back," I promised.

"And I get all of your black moss."

"All of it," I said to Bubble's parting grunt.

Sunmiet walked quickly, her long legs taking her swaying away from the river and the camp. I hurried to keep up. The wind blew down the canyon and we made no attempt to talk until we reached the opening where a trail and a stream cut a ravine before pouring itself into the river. In a few steps, the ravine opened up like a lily and a second stream flowed into the first creating a Y, like the crotch of a tree. A cleared area separated the two streams where a choke cherry tree cast an afternoon shadow. We brushed away fallen berries, made sure no stinging nettles lurched in the weeds before we sat. "Wait!" I told Sunmiet. "There!"

A fat snake eased its way into the weeds beside the creek where Sunmiet planned to sit. Its rattles made no noise as it slipped into the cool water, swam across and out of sight on the other side. "I forgot to talk to them," I said, "warn them we were coming. I thought the frost would speak loudest to them."

Sunmiet paid no attention to my attempts at lightness. She plopped down heavily, away from the activity of the camp, out of the wind. We sat a long time just being quiet. I liked that I had learned to let the silence between friends just be, had lost my need to fill it as I often did at home, nervous that the silence would expose my thoughts.

"His words create a fire in me," Sunmiet said finally. She hugged her knees, rested her chin on them. "Because I am not sure I want to leave my father and mother and live with Standing Tall all the rest of my days. Because I am not ready yet to be a wife." She threw a stick at the little stream and we watched it disappear, heading into the folds of the adjoining stream to rush on to the Deschutes.

"Is there someone else you'd rather marry?" I asked.

"No!" she said, surprised at my question. "There is no one." She was thoughtful. "Koosh is kinder to me. At least sometimes. And George thinks better, studies, wants to learn the non-Indian ways, unlike Standing Tall." She sighed. "Trouble seeks him out. He could hide from it and doesn't. Every day at school he did foolish things. He would not wear the shoes without a tussle. When he spoke Sahaptin or Wasco, they finally just cut his braids." She was quiet. "I am glad he will not go back this year, if only so I will not have to worry over his shame."

A meadowlark warbled in the quiet. "My pain comes most with how I feel when he pretends he is my father," she said sadly.

I thought about my own father, his teaching me and his loudness after he returned from his meetings. I thought about the tightness in my stomach when he and Mama argued, when he acted in ways that Mama said were "puffed up." I wondered if that was how Standing Tall was with Sunmiet, changing, sweet then strange.

"Standing Tall will be kind, bring a basket he has traded for, tell me of his efforts and how he battled the disasters, just for me," Sunmiet said.

"To apologize?"

She looked at me, surprised, then remembered I was not of her people. "Oh, no," she said. "He does not apologize." She instructed me then. "The words would be dishonorable. He gives a gift, in hopes he'll be forgiven his shame for having offended. And as a promise he will make efforts to not repeat his offense."

I had to think on that.

"He is sad for his behavior," she continued, "when he brings his gift. I believe his promise." She threw another twig to watch it twirl and swirl in the current. "He can be so gentle. Touch my face and look into my eyes and I feel warm."

She turned to me, her voice lowered. "But sometimes, he takes my arm and does not know his strength. I feel my chest hurt, then, and I cannot breathe. He pulls on me as though only he can keep me from danger." She looked away, embarrassed.

"He hurts you?" I asked, a thought that entered my mind as something new.

She shrugged her shoulders. A curlew pierced the hot stillness with its forlorn call. "He just does not see me as I am," she said, her words thick in her throat. "He thinks I am someone he can weave into a basket of his design. He doesn't know I am my own basket."

"Will you marry him next year?" I asked.

She was quiet. We could hear voices from the camp lifting in the wind, coming to us in drifts and drops. "It is what my family wishes," she said. "And this basket," she touched her heart, "is blended from their material and design so I will do as they wish."

The wind brought louder voices.

"We should go back," she said, standing.

We walked down the steep path following the little stream and entered the cool shadows of the rimrocks beside the river, surprised at the level of activity beyond us at the camp.

People moved frantically near the water, brought ropes toward the scaffoldings rather than away. I heard shouting. My eyes searched for Bubbles. Voices of alarm pierced the wind. I caught a glimpse of someone running toward the water. Bubbles? Was that Bubbles running to the river?

I saw someone in the river, a thin rope stretched taut between the person and a cluster of people on the bank. They pulled on the hemp line, wrestling a man from the depths, like raising an anchor against the raging falls. We picked up our pace, running now too. But I had time to wonder in my racing: was my healing summer now to end with the return of something bad? Something bad I'd caused by my leaving with Sunmiet?

At the very same time, Joseph picked a trail that forked south and he found himself skirting the edge of the Strawberry Mountains, past granite peaks with tints of red topped by snow as white as thick cream. Deep valleys cut up from a river said to be named John Day's. Beautiful country of rushing water and steep, timbered ridges dotted with rock cliffs and slides. "Gold country," he told Bandit, talking with the dog like the companion he was.

A fat deer with a huge rack bounded through the pines while the sun was high overhead and Joseph shot it. It was the first game he'd seen in several days. He spent the next two days, there, in the shade of the pines, drying the meat in the heat of afternoon sun. At his campfire he remembered that the layers of white fat beneath the animal's hide were thicker than any he'd seen in the California country, ever.

He liked the pausing time of drying venison. "More time for thinking," he told the kelpie then pulled one of the books Philamon had exchanged with him from his pack. *The Song of Hiawatha,* he said and began reading out loud to the dog.

He had just finished when he heard the voice.

"Got any extra?"

A man's words, coming from the ravine, materializing so quickly neither Joseph nor the kelpie noticed until he spoke. The kelpie rolled his lips back and emitted a low growl at the voice. Joseph reached for his Sharp's.

The voice was attached to a blond man who reminded Joseph of the milk toast his mother cooked him when he was ill. He wore lightweight pants, a threadbare long-sleeved shirt, and a dirty leather vest. His boots were tied with old rags to keep the soles on. His eyes were two black raisins in a rice-white face dominated by a large nose. Oddly, he carried no weapon, at least none Joseph could see.

"A friend is welcome at the fire," Joseph said, standing, as did the kelpie, both on guard.

"I be that, or would be if you've meat to spare." The blond man eyed the venison hungrily then looked sheepish, embarrassed, or perhaps defeated.

Joseph leaned his Sharp's against the tree and began immediately to lift the strips of venison from his makeshift drying rack, handing several to the man who introduced himself as Archibald Turner. Too busy tearing at the venison, he merely nodded to Joseph's introduction.

"Just had no luck shooting," Archibald Turner said in a pause of chewing. His hunger satisfied, he began packing meat into a small bag he removed from his back. "Think I'd have it down by now living out here for half a year or more." He accepted more venison as he talked. "This'll make quite a difference for me and my wife."

"You've a woman here?" Joseph asked, surprised.

"And our brood," Archibald said. "Two boys and two girls; youngest, Ella, is five. She'd like your dog."

"And children!" Joseph shook his head in wonder as he stacked the strips.

"We're expecting," Archibald said proudly. "We hoped to pan enough by now to trade for ammunition, food at least. Good country for gold. We seen a lot a strikes. Just ain't been a good fall for us, so far." He shifted uneasily as he talked, swallowing. "Don't have much to trade, but could give you shelter for the night. Some dried fruit. Cabin's not far from here, just up that ravine a spell." He pointed toward a timber-covered ridge marred with marble-like rocks.

Joseph shook his head. "No, I'd planned to make a few miles yet today. I was just about to do that when you arrived. I thank you for the offer."

"Little enough for a man who gives up his food," Turner said, eyes shifting downward as he ripped off another hunk of lean meat, chewed.

"Anything else you might need?" Joseph asked, hoping not to compound the man's obvious humiliation. "Some powder, maybe?"

Turner shook his head. "'Less you got a steady hand to loan." He held his hand straight out in front and watched it tremble. "A good meal'll fix that, sure. We'll get by with this," he nodded toward the pack. A smile appeared through his skimpy beard and mustache. "Move into Canyon City for the winter. I got blacksmith work lined up and then head back out to the gold fields next spring. Lots of lucky people in the fields. If you're ever back this way," he said, "consider our home yours. I know Francis would want that."

Joseph wondered if they'd still be here should he ever ride back into these mountains but he didn't say it. Instead he added some baking powder, flour, a small bag of salt, and some brown clump sugar to the pack. "Thank you," Turner said, "God'll bless you, sure."

"And you for your offer," Joseph said as he wished him well. Joseph packed up and headed southwest, never imagining how both would be blessed by the Turner encounter.

After several days of following the now wide and meandering John Day's river, Joseph rode up on the grassy breaks, crossed different country, flats of green, rolling hills of grass. For the past day, he'd ridden over treeless hills covered with grass so high and thick his horse had brushed it with its belly, the feathery strands of green growing from a center clump like a hand-held bouquet. The kelpie tired bounding through it. He finally succumbed by jumping into Joseph's arms to lie across the pommel of the saddle watching hawks and eagles dip over the sea of green. There were few trees on the breaks. Joseph could see the high ridges of what must be a massive canyon some distance ahead. Some snowcapped mountains broke the horizon and he headed west, toward them and the deep canyon he'd have to cross to reach them.

He followed a ridge. "Can see Mt. Hood just beyond," a prospector had told him some miles back. "Looks close but it ain't. Along the top's an old trail. Goes down a steep, rockless slope into a side canyon. Got a spattering of junipers, big pines, some aspens, and a good size stream. Big boulders clumped around like a herd of sheep mark the trail. And a mountain beyond. Once in the canyon, look for the watersnakes eating the fish comin' upstream and you've got Buck Creek. Just follow that stream to a flat flowing falls. Like nothing you ever seen," he'd added, "and you've reached the Deschutes."

Joseph followed that stream now though he saw no watersnakes. He was glad to be at the bottom of the steep point leading off the ridge. Skid marks and juniper logs to hold back wagons marked his descent to the creek which dropped quickly. Joseph found himself soon looking up at tall rocks the color of the kelpie on either side of him with dozens of dry ravines opening into the canyon. The kelpie trotted and chased rabbits but rarely moved beyond Joseph's vision. It was warmer beside the stream, the rocks holding the heat. It felt less like an early winter. But the way was rocky and his horse and the pack mule moved slowly.

Rimrocks shaded the canyon and Joseph considered making an early camp, to take advantage of the trees that seemed to be dribbling away to a sparse few. He rounded a bend looking for a likely tree and was surprised instead by a grassy, treeless flat flooded with sunlight. His eyes adjusted to the glare and then he noticed it: a single tule-covered structure nestled at the edge of the rocks.

This couldn't be the camp Fish Man spoke of! He wasn't that close to the river. At least, he couldn't hear any rushing water. Only wind in the trees. Except there weren't enough trees, he realized. What he heard had to be the music of a larger river, perhaps a pounding falls.

The kelpie whined and Joseph slapped his thigh. The dog joined him at the saddle.

"Hello-o-o-," Joseph called as he neared the lodge, hearing his echo answer. He rode closer, noticing the flattened grass where a ring of several teepees once set. Matted grass, fish bones, and dirt revealed the paths most used. This had been a camp, and recently too. "Hello-o-, Fish Ma-a-n," he yelled, hoping to bring some recognition.

From the corner of his eye he noticed movement and tensed. Two horses with riders approached.

We have spoken often, my husband and I, about that next encounter. That he should have found on the same occasion the falls of his future vision and the man so vital to its fruition seemed providential.

The riders said nothing until they were within speaking distance. "Fish Man goes to The Dalles, north, on *Chewana,* the big river," the taller of the two men said, nodding his head in the direction of the Columbia. Joseph was startled by the correct English of the man riding the spotted horse. He had made a poor judgment based on the darkness of the man's skin.

The speaker was stately, confident. His checked shirt was sweat-stained at the collar as was the rim of his hat that shaded his bronzed face. A necklace of small white shells circled his throat. His hair was cut to the length of Joseph's, black and straight to the collar. An eagle feather stuck out from his hat. "Then Fish Man goes south, to the Hupas," the Indian said. He seemed to bear no question in his voice, about who Joseph was or why he looked for Fish Man.

Joseph reached his hand out then, said his name. The Indian hesitated at first then reached and barely squeezed the fingers of Joseph's hand, lifting his hand once before he released his fingers. "Peter Lahomesh," he said introducing himself. "This is my son, George Peters."

Joseph reached for the younger man's hand and saw the same serious eyes, unflinching gaze. He guessed him to be sixteen or seventeen years old and like his father, he was slender and wore homespun pants and a faded, colored shirt. His handshake, too, barely pressed Joseph's fingers. Joseph has often commented since on the gentleness of Indian handshakes that pay homage but are often seen by non-Indians as "weak"; the strength of a white man's grip given too as homage, most often seen as fierce. So easily our people walk right past each other.

"You can cross," Peter told him that day, and pointed toward the end of the grassy flat. "Upriver is a bridge over the falls. Will find Fish Man after that at The Dalles."

"How far is it to this Dalles?" Joseph asked.

"One day's ride," Peter told him. "Fish Man plans short stay there. Says winter will come early."

"Yes. That's what he told me, too," Joseph chuckled. "He works for me in California. When he's not fishing."

Peter nodded his head once, somber. "He speaks of you, then, you with the many sheep and cattle. Tomorrow we return to the reservation." Peter nodded toward his lodge. "Tonight, you are welcome to share our fire."

The Lahomesh pair proved to be congenial hosts. Their precise English and obvious eagerness to talk moved the evening quickly along. Peter explained how the big wagon train of eight hundred made the skid marks on the hill, how the wagons crossed the river, well above the falls. He spoke of settlers without apparent animosity. He talked of cattle, said he worked for Colonel Fulton some miles beyond and tended the sheep of someone named Chrisaman. Joseph raised an eyebrow, surprised that at a time of Indian uprisings in various places in the west, these two should work for a military man and know of livestock and sheep. It was something to remember.

Mostly, Joseph enjoyed their interest in what he had to say. If Joseph used a word Peter had not heard before, Peter would hold his hand up to stop Joseph from proceeding, consider the word, repeat it as though memorizing it and its use, and then nod to let Joseph continue. He learned *kelpie* that way and *Merino* and words about angles and grades as Joseph talked with him of the terrain.

Joseph learned from them as well. His wife, Sumxseet, had left two days before, returning to Simnasho. "White men call her Mary," Peter said, then told Joseph about the main village of the reservation. Joseph learned Peter and George's Indian names but could not pronounce them. "Call me Indian Peter," he told Joseph, who also learned that some white men called his son George, "Washington." Joseph smiled and with difficulty, attempted to explain who George Washington was in his world.

Joseph's tongue rolled around the Sahaptin language. Slowly, he memorized the phrase for "help me." *Páwapaatam.* "Could save you, any way," Peter said to him, smiling.

"I could be dead before I ever spit it out," Joseph laughed. When Joseph took his leather sketch book from his pack and showed Peter his drawings of the ravines and rivers, of possible dams, railroad grades, how roads might be put in with a little planning and effort, Peter became very still. He looked at the sketches, held the book gingerly touching the raised letters of the embossed title. He paused at each of Joseph's scribblings and designs, running his hands over the thin pages. Joseph said he seemed suddenly sad.

After a time he spoke. "Our books are the rocks and trees and the voices of our ancestors," he said. "My wife's people have an understanding about non-Indian's books. She is of the Spokane, and her mother's father heard this told from someone who was meant to know." Peter tenderly massaged the book as he spoke. "It is said that a different kind of man will come out of the sun. He will bring a different kind of book, to teach us everything. And after that, our world will fall to pieces."

He lifted the thin paper covering a picture in the front of the sketch book. George reached across, turned the book right side up. Peter held it only a moment. Then with just the slightest flicker of emotion crossing his face, handed it back.

Peter said: "It is not so bad a thought, our world ending, if the afterworld is good, as the Eagle tells us as he moves between the dream world and our own. The black robes say this of the afterworld, too. Still," he held Joseph's eyes, "I am hoping you are not this man with a book to change the way the land sits, the rivers run, our world."

Joseph has said since he thought it was the missionaries and perhaps the Bible the Spokane story spoke of. But I wonder if Peter didn't see in Joseph's sketches that it was the land itself that mattered most to Peter's people and so it was the surveyors and engineers who would so profoundly modify their world.

In the morning, a dense fog blanketed the canyon. Chilly and damp, Joseph helped Peter and George break camp at daylight. The men rounded the end of the grassy field dropping quickly to the flat rocks that led to the river where they crossed Buck Creek close to the mouth. The rocks were slick from the fog and the way treacherous. Joseph could hear the falls now, roaring and churning, but he could not see it. He could barely see his hand in front of him. He kept his eyes on Peter whose red-checked shirt sleeves beneath his vest drifted in and out of the muslin mist shrouding the river. George brought up the rear.

With relief, Joseph heard Peter's horses thud-thud on the water-logged timber of the bridge. He soon felt the log beneath his own horse who shied uneasily at the roaring water surging beneath them. The log creaked as they walked, single-file, across.

Peter circled his horses on the far side, waiting.

"We go to the reservation," Peter said moving his hand south as Joseph's pack mule pulled eagerly on the rope. "You will go that way, to The Dalles. Be above this in a little while," he told Joseph. "The trail moves up the Tygh's ridge. On top, you will find sun and trees and look down on this river. Today, it is a long white snake of cloud. But by noon, you will see the river's blue and the white falls, if you wish to return."

"Not likely," Joseph told him. "And Fish Man will have a difficult time convincing me this foggy place is worth leaving California for every year."

Peter laughed. "Who knows what takes a man from California. Everything looks better with the sun, anyway. You will see when you reach the top."

Joseph shook Peter's hand, gently, with the fingertips. He did the same with George, then headed north not imagining he would ever encounter these men again.

The fog lifted while Joseph was only part way out of the canyon and because it did, our lives were changed.

Joseph watched the white haze worm its way away from the rock walls and form a cocoon over the water. The stark and magnificent strength of the canyon walls then stood exposed; the sun shone and Joseph saw the gorge in its fullness. He caught his breath at its immenseness, the flat rocks cut by the twisting river, the deep pools of dark water swirling around rock caverns below the breaking fog. Like my first sight of the canyon, Joseph found the view stunning.

He spied the single log bridge he'd crossed not ten minutes before. It stretched between two rock ledges where the falls roared through a narrow cut below it. "It's the place to build a bridge, all right. Solid foundation." He petted the kelpie absently. "It would need to be wider, for a wagon or two."

He laughed out loud then. "Listen to me," he said. "Where'd a wagon be going in this isolated place?" He chuckled at his foolishness. "I see bridges and roads everywhere." He scratched the kelpie's neck. "Still, this place is an invitation," he said, "moving into me like a prayer as I sit." He shook himself of a prickly, light feeling, the kind experienced under the awesome influence of a measureless land. "Let's head north," he said finally, "see what else this vast country has to teach us." He spurred the roan up the trail.

At the top of the ridge, Joseph rested a moment, stepping off his horse. Here again sprang tall grasses. He could see the mountain now, shining in the sun that was surprisingly hot on his face for September. He checked the pack ropes, tightened his saddle, inhaled air pungent with grasses and sage. He patted the roan's neck and called the kelpie who came bounding through the bunch grass. But he couldn't get the majesty of the canyon from his mind. Finally, feeling the heat of the morning, he told the kelpie: "Let's ride along the edge of the firs. A bit off the trail but surely cooler."

His mind still settled on the canyon, so he didn't at first see the cloud of dust in the timber. When he did, he pulled his brass eyeglass from the pack. Through it, he saw a corral, five or six mules, and a skinny boy chasing them. "What on earth is he doing?" Joseph said out loud to the kelpie who perked his pointy ears toward the voice, not knowing his master was speaking of me.

Joseph stared a bit longer, then corrected himself with a soft whisper of amazement. "No, what on earth is *she* doing, Bandit? That skinny boy is a girl!"

CHAPTER 12

THE
PORCUPINE
DANCE

FOR SOME TIME I wondered what Joseph truly saw that day: a smudged face, pencil-lead straight body, skinny legs; defeat or defiance. The moment changed our lives although we did not look on it as such until much later.

"Sure, and it'll be better without the stench," the man said.

I jumped, startled by the accent and his seasoned voice. I had noticed a rider from a distance, but in my effort and irritation, I thought he'd done the gentlemanly thing and moved on, given a girl some privacy and peace while she watched her reptile pile burn. I guess he didn't like being outside the fire.

I glanced at the smoke drifting away like a bad dream into the cloudless sky and turned to him when he spoke.

"Did I seek the opinion of an old man?" I said. I wanted my words to rip that smirky smile from his bearded face.

He sat up straighter on his horse. "Sassy little thing, aren't you?" His eyes held humor.

I ignored it. "I don't like being bothered, especially by some dandy carrying a slicker and a lunch who probably never dropped his bottom on the back of mule." They were good insults, picked up from a quick survey of his saddle roll, unstained hat, good leather boots, and the coil of the horse-hair McCartys all attesting to a man who knew how to handle stock but liked his comforts, too.

"Whoa now, sister!" he said. He swung his leg over the saddle horn, tipped his hat back, and leaned on the crook of his leg. He was a big man, long-legged straight up to his chest. The accent was gone when he spoke next. "Didn't mean to insult you."

I stepped back as his funny looking dog trotted up beside me and sat down. "What'd you do to your dog's ears to make them stand so straight? Tie them up?"

He let that fall.

"Just wanted to help," he said.

"So does an undertaker but nobody likes to see him coming."

His words had been gentle, like he meant kindness but with frustration dripping along my cheeks, in my face, I didn't care. I could tell by his look that he was wounded, not certain how to respond to me. I noticed I liked the feeling I found in his confusion.

The scent of the kerosene penetrated my senses. I wiped my hands on my skirt hiked up between my legs and stuffed into my belt like pants, and stood, hands on hips, not sure what to do next. I'd worked all morning at this, was hot and tired and didn't really feel like defending my actions to some mail-order cowboy old enough to be my father, judging by some of the flecks of white in his beard, some crows feet near his eyes.

The leather of his fancy saddle creaked. He was moving.

In a moment, he stood quietly beside the gelding and rubbed his thumb smooth on the leather of the reins before he spoke. "Let me try this again," he said politely. He removed his hat, took a deep breath, his blue eyes looking directly into mine. "You did a good job on the snakes. I'm not sure I would have thought of such an ingenious method of eliminating them. Or had the courage to strike the flint." His horse stomped impatiently in the dust behind him. "And I'm sure you know this, but the mules are probably frightened now, by the smell. Which is why they won't go in the corral."

His little dog scurried back to him as he spoke and he squatted down to pet him, looking up at me. "Maybe my horse can calm your stock." He spoke without rushing and stood back up, towering over me like a badger over a mouse.

"Any objections to my pulling up beside that tree beyond, see if your mules will come to him?"

"Go ahead," I said, wishing I had a bell mare to lure them so I wouldn't be relying on this stranger. My spitting-mad was just beginning to lose steam.

"Can you call them? By name?" he asked.

"Course. Think I'm stupid?"

He spoke calmly, carefully. "I think you've worked very hard without much to show for it." He untied his mule from the gelding, and walked with them both slowly toward a fir tree far removed from the corral. He dropped the weight and tether to hold the horse, tied the mule to the tree. "I've known those kinds of days," he said back over his shoulder, "Always wondered if I'd accept the help I was annoyed about not having."

He didn't raise his voice and he didn't take my bait, so I actually heard what he said.

I had nothing to lose by letting him be helpful, except letting go of being right. Besides, Papa had said often enough that only a fool argues with a skunk, a cook, or a mule. And I had already argued most of my morning away.

"The big black one is Bessy," I said, pointing. The man turned and walked back toward me. "The bay is Hard Times, and the one kicking up her heels is Jackson. The little one is Puddin' Foot, though now that she's full grown her feet actually look all right, don't you think?" I didn't wait for his response. "Pepperpot is standing off by himself. If we can get him, the others will follow. I'll call him if you think that will help."

He smiled at me then, a big, accepting smile and I saw his eyes drooped a bit, with a kind of swimming look before easing into crinkles. He flashed a line of straight teeth that looked even whiter in his sun-darkened face. He had thick, brown eyebrows, deep blue eyes, and a nose that had never been broken. I thought at the same time, as I noticed his thin lips, that maybe he wasn't as old as my father.

Pepperpot took some coaxing, but eventually we moved my mule into the pack mule's territory, got a rope on him, and tied him up. The other mules followed suit seemingly both annoyed by the reptile pile stench and by the little dog who backed his way toward the pack mule. The mules nudged toward the dog until they were caught up, just as this savvy man knew they would be. We smiled at each other with each caught-up mule and had seemed to form a wary bond by the time the animals stood grazing near the tree acting like they never did have a better day.

"I'm heading toward The Dalles," he said when we finished tying Puddin' Foot. "I'd be happy to help string them toward where you're headed. Nice animals." He patted Puddin's behind and dust puffed up.

We had walked back to the log where my cooking fire still smoldered, rubbed our hands in the dirt to clean them of the sweaty smell.

I said, "About being so rude earlier—"

"I accept," he interrupted. "It's a sign of good character to welcome help, when needed, and apologize when acknowledging the delay—"

"I wasn't asking *your* forgiveness," I said, cutting him off. His rightness annoyed me. I'd actually been going to comment on *his* rudeness: not introducing himself, talking to a girl in the middle of nowhere. "And I certainly don't welcome your opinion," I said. The man had the power to turn my temperament from kind to cross in seconds. "You've been helpful. Now you'd best be on your way."

He stared for a moment as if considering a response. Then he turned in the dust, walked without talking to his mule, tied it to his horse. He checked his saddle, pulled up the cast iron loop serving as the weight, mounted and patted his lanky leg and the dog jumped up into his lap. He tipped his flat-topped hat at me. "It's been chirk," he said and smiled.

His sarcasm irritated me more because I knew he couldn't have meant he'd had a pleasant time. He pressed the reins against his horse's neck and rode off.

The last thing I saw was the little dog peeking his pointy ears around his master and panting his pink tongue at me in their departure.

Chirk! Not likely. I felt righteously disappointed but not for long. There was always too much to do and I simply set to it.

Joseph said our first encounter stayed with him like a hangover, something he enjoyed getting to then wished would go away. He considered what he'd done to set me off as he rode north toward the big river, the Columbia. He talked to the kelpie about my volatile temperament and said he even commented about some poor soul marrying me someday and having to live with that sassy tongue forever. "Like dancing with a porcupine," he told the kelpie.

Still, the farther away from me he rode, the more he found himself chuckling, about my energy and grit, two qualities he found he appreciated but had never really expected to find in a very small girl he'd first mistaken as a boy.

I put out the fire, tied the mules to my rope, and climbed aboard Jackson, heading home, moving into a world that a summer with Sunmiet had pleasantly interrupted. Riding, I considered the stranger, thought about Sunmiet and Standing Tall, and remembered my last day at the river. Sunmiet and I had been relieved to learn that it was Bubbles who discovered the disaster first. A young man had slipped into the river. The ropes around his middle kept him alive though pounded by the surging water. Because she sat near the babies, Bubbles had an eagle's-eye view of the scaffolding, had seen the young man fall. Bubbles' bulk and surprising quickness saved him as she was the first to shout orders to others, then strain her arms on the rope, dragging him away from the sucking surf. It was Koosh who'd fallen, Standing Tall's younger brother. Sunmiet's intended reminded us that his words of warning had been wise, but then admitted: "One does not need to be a *nana* to be in danger at the river." Sunmiet had nodded her head once in agreement and told me later how good her insides felt to have him hint that she was right.

It was a feeling I understood, this wishing to be right, not the cause of something wrong.

I rode into the yard. Mama was having one of her days that began after the tragedy. So when I pulled up with the mules, I didn't have the time or energy to relate my encounter with the stranger with either her or Papa. We both kept out of her way those days knowing nothing we could do or say would make it right. Even Baby George learned to sit on his bed sucking the ends of his fingers, shaking himself smaller with each slam of a spider and iron in mama's kitchen. Our only hope was time or a visitor, someone from the outside whose presence seemed to warm Mama into her old charm that often lasted well after any visitor was gone. My stranger stopping by now would have been a blessing and I would not have found him rude in the least.

No stranger came by and so I related the encounter to no one, not even my friend Sunmiet, at least until much later.

The stranger made his way into The Dalles. Joseph said the river and the giant rapids that marked it overshadowed the little town and only later did he come to appreciate the amenities it had to offer.

The Columbia River had captured Captain Lewis and Mr. Clark and most everyone who made their way west to find it. So massive it is, so rolling and wide, the wind often whipping up whitecaps as it roars up the gorge. Especially at the rapids where the waters of a thousand miles of British territory and unsettled land pour into a canyon so treacherous that only fools or dreamers or men bent on suicide would ever attempt passage. Joseph sat at the top of the ridge looking down, in awe of a river so mighty, so broad, and so busy on its way to the Pacific.

Like tiny scraps of paper, rafts with wagons and stick-figures of men were sucked out into the current, heading downstream. Below the rapids, wharves jutted out into it, ships nudged into them leaving broken wakes trailing into the choppy water. A hotel of several stories with the name "Umatilla House" painted in huge letters on the side took up a good section of the shoreline.

Within the mist, Joseph caught glimpses of springboards, scaffoldings where men would fish. None were fishing now and so Joseph's hope of locating Fish Man lessened.

To the east, he noticed several wagons camped on the hillside, away from the river. He took his sketch book out and made notations of the angles and grades of the huge ravines. Below him, more wagons circled closer to the river and he spied rafts of pine logs. People seemed to be living out of their wagons, close to the water, waiting. He saw one small pack string heading east and thought it odd. Putting his sketchbook back into the pack, he rode down the grassy hillside, through some timbered ravines, and into the town for his initial look at the community that would redirect his life.

The level of activity amazed him. Wagons rattled through the dusty streets. Dogs barked. Men clustered on corners, smoke rising from their cigars. Wide-faced Indians walked unfettered along the boardwalks, usually in twos. He caught a glimpse of a Chinese man in his blue silks disappearing into an alley. Bonneted women whisked out of the mercantile, children in hand followed by apronned men loaded with string-wrapped packages. A man yelled at Joseph, offering a price for the kelpie claiming its hide would fetch a pretty price for shoes.

"No thanks!" Joseph said, shaking his head in wonder. He had already decided not to let the kelpie from his sight. He kept his promise to himself even while he left his horse and pack mule, his bed roll and whip at the livery and started with the dog toward the Umatilla House.

"Little dog will cost much dust at *la maison*," the livery owner said. He stood like a nail, dark and straight and hard beside the wide pine doors of the livery. Black hair scruffed out beneath a blue handkerchief forming a jagged frame around his long, narrow face. He picked at his fingernails with a Bowie knife, carefully cleaning beneath them with the knife's tip as he spoke a heavily accented English.

Joseph stopped, interpreting the man's words and demeanor. "I'll risk it," he said and began walking past the owner.

The thin man shrugged. "Would keep him here, with safety," he added, this time with more gentleness to his words, a smile and dark eyes which Joseph had missed with the man's face turned to the concentration of his fingernails.

"Louie Davenport," he said flipping the knife into a leather holster thonged to his thigh. "But my friends, they all call me French Louie," he said pronouncing it "Lou-ee" and extended his hand which Joseph shook.

"At *la maison*, um, Umatilla House. Is best place to eat and sleep." Louie said. "Or Globe Hotel on Washington and Second. Neither will welcome, um, *le petit cherie*. Very strange, your little dog, like skinny-tailed fox, *n'est pas?*"

"Not to me," Joseph said. "I'll hang on to him. Shoe leather seems a premium here and I'll not want any putting on the dog with mine."

Louie laughed, a hearty laugh ending with a gasping snort. *"Oui!* You are right." He wiped his eyes and held his foot out. "Hear this one bark?" He bent closer to Joseph and whispered: "Best leather around, *oui?*" He laughed again, more loudly. "He is your friend. Go. Take the little one. If you have trouble, um, bring him back and I will keep him in my own bed for half the price. And no shoes." Joseph left pacified, Louie having won him over.

Not far from the livery, Joseph passed a barber shop and baths, locating the lavishly furnished Umatilla House, just four years old. He planned to check in, bathe, eat, and find a barber. Instead, he located the gaming tables in the saloon even before he checked into his room.

"Pooch's gotta go, friend," the barkeep said as Joseph leaned against the polished mahogany bar surveying the players. The kelpie stood guard at his feet beside a brass spittoon. Lush ferns in pots brought elegance even into the bar of the hotel and flashed green in the mirror that covered the entire wall behind the barkeep. In a far corner of the wainscoted room were several tables set for dining. Most of the area was taken up with poker tables or men simply sharing a brew. Fragrant scents drifted from the kitchen.

Without speaking Joseph placed two ten dollar gold pieces on the shiny surface of the bar.

Surprised, the barkeep said, "Used to dust," as he turned the coins around in his fingers before dropping them into his pocket. He squinted at the kelpie. "Keep him quiet, don't want no trouble from him." Then changing the subject he said, "Not from Canyon City, then?"

"California. Is Canyon City where the gold's coming from these days?" Joseph asked.

The barkeep nodded assent, his curly dark hair a mat around his face. "First strike in '59," he said. "More coming out each day, when they can get it out. Not many folks want to make the trip or too busy thinking they'll make more money mining or moving on to Oregon City. No matter. Coming or going, they spend their money here. What can I get you? Or don't the dog let you drink?"

Joseph spent the next several hours winning at poker. He always said it was an art. He liked reading the faces of his opponents, charming them with his stories while he learned about their quirks and grimaces before they made their bets. He challenged himself by remembering what their hands held so he could relate that information to his own next bet. He liked the rush of remembering which cards had been played, who could possibly hold what remained in the deck. He always lost some at first, spending time watching and learning. And he found his opponents were more at ease with his losses and didn't seem to mind so much later when he upped his risk and energy into winning.

The kelpie slept quietly at his feet beneath the round table occasionally sniffing at the peanut shells dropped by the handfuls of the patrons. Once the kelpie stood, a square block of defiance, and snapped his jaws at some jingling spurs that walked by on a cowboy moving to the next table, but he never bit and he never left Joseph's side. He was there when Joseph scooped up his winnings as the saloon closed up for the night.

In the morning, before setting out to find Fish Man, Joseph had his bath and haircut. At both places, he heard more of the talk and energy coming out of Canyon City. He was surprised he had not seen more activity himself when he had encountered Archibald Turner near there, thin and defeated. The trail had not been crowded with either hopeful or discouraged miners. And Archibald's luck in panning for gold offered no incentive.

At the mercantile, he listened to stories about the rapidly growing city. "I look for grass train, corn train, bacon train, anything!" the mercantile owner said to several men who laughed as they stood near the egg baskets at the end of the long counter. The floor was worn smooth at that spot by the shuffling of leather as men stood and talked with Benson Hahn, proprietor. "No one wants to make the trip. All head west. Crazy! I have orders; orders!" He pulled at imaginary lengths of hair straight up from his bald head. "And cannot get them in!" He tugged at his mutton chops, grimaced. "Could at last become wealthy man and will not for want of an ox or a mule or even a pig!"

The men laughed, familiar with Hahn's lament these past months.

"I tell the truth!" he whined and they laughed again.

"What's the attraction," Joseph asked, pointing to a bin of hard pan biscuits behind the owner. He put a coin on the counter.

Hahn handed him the biscuits and leaning over the counter, scowled as Joseph bent to give one to the kelpie. "The attraction," he said straightening, "is the fastest growing city this side of the mountains: Canyon City. I have contracts for half my goods and all I can get out is one small pack. Left yesterday. They swim the Deschutes this morning and be weeks getting back. Hope to make second trip before the snow flies." He threw up his hands. "Finding good pack strings not easy here. Just when I need them most."

"Take one in yourself, Hahn," one of the men suggested to the laughter of his colleagues.

"Uch, no!" Hahn said, his speech thickly accented with German. "The mules, they are like porcupines. Must spar carefully with them every day, never rest a minute. No, want good man to work with, but don't want to take them on myself. Uch! I have enough to keep me busy. No need to borrow more trouble." He turned to tend to another customer and the men drifted away leaving Joseph alone.

Joseph spent the next several hours in the company of an east wind looking for Fish Man, speaking with merchants, bathhouse owners, shipyard workers. In the late afternoon, he returned to the livery where he and French Louie spoke again. Several Spanish-speaking people stopped at the livery along with some Chinese, Germans, and French, and Louie spoke to each in their own tongue. So when Louie gave Joseph suggestions of where he might get word to Fish Man, if he were still in the area, Joseph was quite sure of Louie's resourcefulness and asked him to see if he could find him.

Joseph finished the afternoon with a ride up into the grassy hills overlooking the town. The sunset burned vibrant against the brown hills, turned the snowcapped mountains in the distance to a blinding gloss. He noticed some young fruit trees nestled in a series of ravines and thought about the mild climate needed to nurture them. A breeze danced through his beard, dried his eyes. He liked being able to see for miles high above the river uninterrupted by timber or trees. He heard more geese calling, watched them circle, drop below the rimrocks and set their wings like open arms to the water. The snowcapped mountains looked so close he could almost pluck them like a white blossom. "Hood, St. Helens, Adams," he said, identifying the mountains for the kelpie.

Most of all, Joseph found himself drawn to the huge rimrocks that shot up from the Columbia like sentinels of stone. Their red color, rope-like twists, and lichen-licked lava attracted him. The rocks were unlike anything he had ever seen—except at the edge of the fog-shrouded crossing of Peter LaHomesh's river, just before he'd met that "sassy girl."

The thought of me and something about this grass-filled country with its dimples of ravines appealed to my Joseph, made him want to stay. This was young country, sassy itself, with the unknown visiting around every twist and turn. He inhaled the sweet smell of rabbit brush and sage and sat, the kelpie panting across his legs.

A decision made, he began moving into action when he returned to the livery and left his horse with Louie. This time, he kept his whip and the kelpie with him.

In the dining room of the Umatilla House, Joseph met A. H. Brayman who would pull it all together.

Joseph noticed that the portly man raised his bushy eyebrows in surprise either at the kelpie dog trotting behind him or the looped mule skinner's whip he wore on his hip. Joseph watched him give a look to the barkeep who touched his vest pocket ever so slightly with his fingers. He took it as a signal of his payment that permitted him this lapse in usual protocol, but he wondered who the barkeep signaled.

A. H. Brayman stood up, his shoulders wide, like a bear's, pushing out his wool suit. He had the appearance of a man who had not missed many meals and who ordered only the best when he ate.

"I hear you have an interest in an Indian I know," Brayman said pointing his soft hand out in greeting to Joseph. His grip clamped like the kelpie's jaw. "He's been working in back. Owes some money he says and is paying it off at my shipyard. Owe you money, too?" he asked, motioning Joseph to be seated at his table. Brayman hesitated a moment with a glance at the dog then dismissed it, prioritizing what mattered quickly as he usually did.

"More likely I owe him," Joseph said, sitting. "He works for me in California, then comes north to fish at the Deschutes. Thought I'd catch him there, but too late."

"Problem?" Brayman asked, talking with food in his mouth like a man in a hurry. He signaled the barkeep for another stein, holding up two fingers when Joseph nodded he'd like one too; motioned for a second platter of beefsteak and fresh greens. A pungent vinegar dressing wafted above the smoke of the saloon.

Joseph shook his head. "Just want a friend to ride back with."

"Like to talk about your riding back," Brayman said, not wasting time. "Talk is, you know mules. Packed some in California?"

Joseph nodded.

"Like you to consider that again. This is growing country. Big country. Trains'll be coming this way for years." The glow of an early gas light reflected in Brayman's round spectacles. "That land farther west will turn some off, all that rain." He chewed his beefsteak and Joseph could see parts of it wallowing around in Brayman's huge mouth, a little juice appearing at the corners. Some dribbled down his beardless chin. "Real growth is southeast. In the interior. 'Tween here and the Strawberries. Good land, less rain to bog a man down, little timber to clear, grass that won't stop 'til Doomsday. And now, gold to bring 'em in."

"I'm a businessman," Brayman said, wiping his mouth and hands on the linen napkin he pulled from beneath his starched collar. "Not sure I introduced myself. A. H. Brayman. Friends call me 'A. H.' I know who you are so here's the deal." He leaned into the table and spoke conspiratorially with Joseph, his hazel eyes clear and full of excitement. "I'll finance your string this year, wages too. No interest. You can buy me out if you want or we'll work out an interest deal. I'm not all that interested in the string." He sat up, brushed some crumbs from the linen cloth and flecked them onto the floor. "What I am interested in is the supplies. You load from my docks, not Hahn's nor anyone who's likely to find their way here in the next few years. Prices'll be fair and going rate. I take interest on the supplies at 10 percent, again, this first year. I supply all the goods. You can sell at what you can get." He threaded his pudgy fingers into each other alternately squeezing and releasing as he talked. "You take my supplies in and bring the gold out for deposit. In my bank. After two years, we renegotiate. By then, I'll have buildings in Canyon City, store more, and beat the competition.

"You, my friend," he said clamping Joseph on the back in closure, "will be a wealthy man. How's that sound?"

"Intriguing," Joseph said. He was silent for a full minute, cut several pieces of his beefsteak delivered by the barkeep and chewed fully, not in any hurry. A. H. did not interrupt, sat picking at his teeth with an ivory pick taken from his vest. Finally Joseph said, "I'd want a commission on the deposits, make it worth my while to convince the miners to bank with you. And I'd want my own string after the first year. I can get my crew," he said. He sat thoughtfully again and Brayman knew enough not to tread on a decisive man's thinking. "And I'd sure enough buy my own mules," Joseph said. "I saw five good ones just south of here a few days back."

"Herbert's," Brayman said, blasting out his first word in several minutes as if he'd held his breath while his future partner thought. "Good stock and a pistol of a girl who looks after them," A. H. continued. "George'll make us a fair price, though. We have a deal then?"

Joseph sat quietly, longer. He could feel a familiar energy stirring in his stomach, noticed his face was flushing from the excitement that such a venture would surely bring. He wasn't even thinking of cards now, but of mules and enthusiasm and organizing and making things happen. Benito was right. The mules did bring him energy; and maybe more.

"Deal," Joseph said offering his hand. Then as if to himself he added: "Herbert's mules, huh? Could be like dancing with a porcupine to negotiate this deal." He reached beneath the table to pat the kelpie and let Brayman ponder that as he marveled to himself about the paths and plans of men.

CHAPTER 13

SECOND
CHANCES

JOSEPH REMEMBERS WELL. He could feel the juices flowing in his blood again with that first call of the rooster the next morning. Such interest had not awakened him for months, years almost, he told me. It's surprising what we allow ourselves to feel as "living" and only later notice our suppression when we finally open up and tell ourselves the truth.

Joseph located Fish Man at Brayman's dock and discussed his plan. Beneath swooping and crying sea gulls, the Hupa smiled, his face filling up like a puffy cloud on a clear day. He set out for California immediately with both Brayman's and Joseph's blessing and a message for Benito.

Joseph did his explorations of the markets, talked to competitors of Hahn and Brayman, too. Then two days later, he arrived at our home, the Herberts, at Fifteen Mile Crossing.

Mama usually paid little attention to Papa's negotiations. She had her own business to tend to daily what with looking after folks, caring for them, doing her church work, and for a time, looking after a big family. So it was a bit unusual for her to take such an interest in the tall stranger who stopped by to discuss mules that early October day in 1861. It was just before my thirteenth birthday.

He rode in with his pack mule and that funny looking dog trotting beside him. Hound yelped and Mama motioned me to pen him as she walked to the gate of the fence surrounding our house to greet our guest. Mama immediately picked up on the dog, asking all nature of questions about its lineage. She commented on his unusual coloring. "Red as a hanging deer's rib cage," she noted. "Odd how his muzzle and paws and such are lighter." Even Baby George riding on Mama's hip, giggled, seemed to notice that the dog smiled, pulled its lips back, and let its pink tongue droop while it stood, panting, its skinny belly and long tail less than a foot from the hard ground.

"Unusual," Mama said. "What'd you say it was again?"

"Kelpie," the man said. "They have a temper, but usually only related to their fiercely independent and protective natures. Like some people I know." He looked at me, then smiled. I walked beside Mama, stood on the other side of the gate. I looked down, my moccasined feet digging at the dusty earth. Mama didn't seem to notice my slight flush nor the second level of our exchange.

"I've never seen the likes of it," Mama said, enchanted by the little dog, I think. Then she turned all business. "Water's at the well there," she said, pointing. "Don't forget to rinse the dipper."

"Appreciate it," Joseph said. He paused to drink and rinse before replacing the cup. "Interested in your mules," Joseph said wiping his beard with his wide hand. "A. H. Brayman says you've some for sale."

Mama snorted. "He does, does he. What big plan does A. H. have up his sleeve now?"

Joseph seemed taken aback.

"Is he not right?" he asked.

"Oh, he is definitely 'not right,'" Mama said tapping the curls on the side of her head. She shook her head in disgust. "Yes, well. No matter. We do have some mules." She also had to tell him that Papa wasn't here and wouldn't be back for a day or so as he'd gone to Oregon City on business. "Political business," she added, sending a blast of air through her nose, letting everyone within earshot know what she thought of politics.

"Can you show me the animals at least?" Joseph asked, again looking past Mama at me.

"Why, I'd be pleased to," Mama said, shifting Baby George on her hip. "Just let me find my walking slippers and shawl against this chill." A cool breeze brushed through the trees and she rubbed her arms to warm them, then turned to go into the house.

"I can do it, Mama," I said as if on cue, and stepped forward. "I've got my feet on already. And I don't need my shawl." My offer seemed to startle Mama, almost as though she'd forgotten I'd been standing there.

"Oh. Yes. Well, that would be acceptable I suppose. I'll put some tea on for when you're finished Mister...what did you say your name was?"

"Joseph Sherar," he said, taking off his hat, speaking with his deep voice the name that would change my being.

"I'll see you shortly then, Mr. Sherar," Mama said and turned away as Joseph and I walked toward the stock barns, the kelpie at our heels.

I remember being surprised to have just heard his name for the first time, spoken with a light brogue I noticed, in that deeper, seasoned voice.

"Jane Herbert," I said, introducing myself, hoping my voice didn't squeak. I felt a surprising warmth inside me as we walked, coupled with a giddy tripping of my tongue. "I'm almost thirteen," I said brightly, walking taller, turning toward him.

Joseph's eyebrows furrowed briefly and the smile in his eyes drifted back as if into his thoughts and I could tell something about my age bothered him. Too late, I remembered what Sunmiet said about telling her tongue to stop saying words that got her into trouble. I'd made myself sound younger when I was only trying to be grown-up.

"The mules are my responsibility when Papa is gone." I tried to sound all business, older.

He smiled. "A responsibility taken seriously," he said. "I have some first-hand experience, remember?"

I felt light, liked being talked to as one who was present, an adult. We walked through the stock barns, through the double doors that opened onto the pasture of velvet green. The air was still and cooling. He let me walk ahead of him, like I was a real lady. "You know Jackson and Hard Times and Puddin'

Foot." I pointed to the grazing mules. I knotted my wet hands behind my back, smoothed my calico, then re-knotted my fingers. "Actually, Puddin's not really for sale. He's mine. The others are though. Even Pepperpot. And those more." My tongue wanted to stumble. I spoke faster than normal.

We walked slowly around the pasture clipped short by the mules. Mounds of grass hay like little loaves lined the pasture, waiting for winter. "Papa's been slowly building the herd, thinking things will be happening in the gold fields. In farming too," I added, carrying on an adult conversation as best I could as Joseph eased into the space beside me.

Near the center of the grazing animals, we stopped. Joseph's eyes scanned the field lined with lodgepole fences Papa and Luther Henderson had cut and split. Maybe fifteen mules ripped at the grass near the creek that ran through the pasture. Several lifted their heads and began walking toward us.

"They're well treated," Joseph said. "Used to pampering."

"But they carry their weights good," I assured him.

He walked around Jackson as I held the animal's mane and scratched Jackson's nose. Puddin' came up behind me, pushed at my pocket for a carrot. Several other animals wandered closer and sniffed at the little kelpie who lay flat-bellied on the ground, ears alert, forward, watching them until we had a cluster of mules, people, and one dog in the center. The mules expressed their usual dislike of little things and lowered their head to the kelpie. Bandit never moved, just curled his lips to release a low growl. Once I even heard the dog's jaws snap. He bit air.

"No, Bandit," Joseph said.

"Your dog's not around mules much?" I asked.

He shook his head. "I'm thinking of packing myself. Again," Joseph said, "which should give him good practice with more than just my pack animal." He turned to me then, patting Jackson's withers and looked across the animal's back into my eyes. "I have set my bottom on the back of a mule, by the way. More than once," he said, softly.

My face turned hot and I hid it behind the mule's large head, tugging intently at twigs that demanded to be pulled from the coarse hair of Jackson's mane, concentrating on the sweaty animal smell, keeping my balance as the mules brushed close to me. "You ought to know a person better before you chastise him," he continued. He moved closer, came around to stand beside me, and I could smell the scent of leather and his tobacco, could see the rough fibers of his red vest.

There were fifteen mules in the pasture but I looked beyond Jackson and Joseph and counted them to myself, one by one, not wanting to hear the gentle mocking in the man's words.

"No need to be rude," I said finally. I straightened to my full height that did not reach his shoulder. "I did apologize for what I said, didn't I?"

"Actually," he said, lightly, "you didn't." The smirk on his face resembled a dog discovering an old bone he'd buried months before. His eyes twinkled and his smile pushed out from his mouth, making his whole face laugh at me behind his beard.

I saw red. "If you're interested in a purchase of my father's stock, we can talk," I snapped. "Otherwise, I have more important things to do than converse with some dandy who fancies himself a muleskinner." I have no idea what his face did then for with my insult I turned my back to him and kept it there.

He was speechless.

I was disappointed.

We spent the next half hour or so with him walking behind me and the kelpie behind him. I named the animals, gave him their ages, delineated their lineages, declared their temperaments, and kept my steam well under the lid, or so I thought.

It seemed to me he enjoyed baiting me. When he got his tongue back, I noticed that even his questions about the mules had teasing in them. Could he buy them for less than the going rate of $250 since he knew they were hard to handle around snakes? Would my father want me to just take them off his hands so he wouldn't have to hire someone to look after them? I did not appreciate his game and wondered if all grownups preferred to mock and criticize.

I suppose he was struggling with my youth as I was struggling with his age.

He made a few attempts to engage me in light conversation about myself and our family, which I resisted. Once, he even reached out to pull a twig caught in my braid and the interruption stopped me mid-sentence. His touch was gentle. My heart throbbed more quickly against my ribcage. I looked away and thought of Sunmiet and Standing Tall's touch, how inviting it could be, how easily it could change.

We returned wordless to the house.

Inside, Joseph treated Mama with great deference, I thought, complimented her on *her* fine stock, as though she had anything to do with it, and then offered *her* the deposit. "Please tell your husband I'll be back in three to four weeks and make my final selection. I'll want to secure them for service in the spring. Can you winter them?" he asked.

Mama looked uncertain. "We'd of course like payment when you select them. As for wintering—"

"Of course we can," I interrupted. "Didn't you see the stacks of hay?"

He nodded his agreement to Mama as though I had not even spoken. She raised an eyebrow at me, took his thanks for her hospitality, and dropped to a graceful curtsy when he bowed ever so slightly at the waist to her before he left.

He tipped his hat to me, smiled, then headed out, followed by that same strange disappointment I had sent after him before. His kelpie trotted behind his horse and pack animal to the sounds of our penned hound barking frantically. Turning to go back into the house, I remember being glad that he was going and confused by feeling sad that he had gone.

Joseph headed south, grateful that Fish Man had been wrong about the early, hard winter. This time he approached the ridge above the Deschutes in late afternoon so he could see fully Fish Man's lure.

Here stood cousins of the rocks of the Columbia. These rope lava rocks guarded the twisting turquoise water closely, more confined, as they lined the raging water that swirled and turned beneath the skimpy bridge, plunging to the lava rocks below.

He took his sketch book out and still sitting on his big gelding, made some drawings, wanting to remember, wanting to imprint the possibilities from this place.

As he rode down the ridge, in and out of the ravines, Joseph approached the falls. Water rushed faster than a wind storm and almost as noisily roared and twisted past him. He was stilled by the place, silenced by its desolate look yet intrigued by the vast starkness.

A few fishing platforms still jutted out from the rocks looking fragile and forlorn. No one stood on them to fish. Most had been put up, the long poles stashed in the rocks until spring. The hemp ropes that wrapped around boulders to hold the remaining platforms in place looked wet and frayed. Joseph wondered about the courage of the men who stood on the clapboards leaning out over the raging water to swoop their nets into the foam for fish. They'd done it for generations that way, dangerously conquering the big Chinook, competing with the rushing water.

He rode beside the river for a distance and approached the bridge he'd crossed with Peter. He eyed it carefully, glad he hadn't really seen it all that well before. It would not withstand a flood, he thought. But then, it would take a raging torrent to reach it laid there forty feet above the river's surface.

The wind came up, carrying with it a new coldness drifting from the mountains which by late afternoon had hid themselves behind angry dark clouds. Joseph urged the gelding across the bridge, rode up the ravine where he'd met Peter LaHomesh and his son, George. Joseph made his camp on the same flattened grass. A cluster of juniper trees provided shelter from the wind but Joseph said he was lonesome for the good company of the Indians.

The kelpie whined once when the wind howled through the tree branches knocking off some of the hard blue berries. "Tree is loaded," Joseph said as he pulled the little dog into his bedroll. The kelpie wiggled his way to Joseph's neck and wrapped himself around the man's head and both soon fell asleep. Only later did Joseph remember Fish Man's comment that trees laden with juniper berries were another sign of an early, hard winter.

A cold rain greeted the two bedroll partners in the morning. They broke camp quickly, Joseph ducking his head into the collar of his slicker to thwart the wind-swept rain, pulling on his hat that dripped rain off its rim. "Let's go, Bandit," he said swinging up onto the gelding and reaching for the mule's lead. Heavy rain drops pattered on the saddle, spotting the leather of the pommel before the kelpie leapt, landed, and lay panting across the saddle horn. They began the long climb out.

Joseph had thought he would use the time to think about his future more, consider how he'd make arrangements. A small, fiery girl even entered his thoughts, he claims. But at the top of the ridge, his attention turned to the steady change in the rain.

Snow. A light snow at first that seemed to melt as it touched the sage-patched earth of the ravines but stuck as it covered the tall grasses of the rolling hills. "Fish Man wins, " Joseph told the kelpie, "sure and it's good I did not bet on his prognosticating." The kelpie squirmed at the man's voice and pushed closer into the warmth seeping from Joseph's heavy slicker. Joseph wondered how deep the snow might get and how far he could make before nightfall.

By mid-morning, the trail became a white thread through dusted sage-brush and sparser grass. Joseph knew that if he kept to the breaks, he could actually follow the river south. It was new country to him as he had entered the region from the west, from the Canyon City area. Now, he headed as straight south for California as he could.

Shrouded in heavy clouds, he couldn't see the mountains most of the day. In between snow squalls, he could make out the breaks where the banks ran off to the river. The terrain promised more trees and some washes where the wind stilled. He saw no deer tracks. He looked for distant smoke, signs of other trav-elers or inhabitants, saw none. A rabbit crossed his trail. In one of the quieter ravines, snow still falling, Joseph and the kelpie made a dry camp draping an oiled skin from the low branch of the juniper. After offering a handful of grain to the horse and the mule pawing in the snow, he and the dog munched on dried venison and bread. Joseph kept for himself the warm cup of coffee brewed on the intermittent flames of the fire.

"It's only a light snowfall," Joseph said to assure himself that continuing, not turning back, was the best choice. He ruffled the dog's smooth fur. The kelpie buried his pointy nose in Joseph's pocket where he was rewarded with a biscuit before both went to sleep not knowing what surprises awaited them in the morning.

My own efforts at dealing with the first winter storm of the season took away any thoughts I might have had of the tall, sometimes rude stranger. Papa was expected back the day after the snow began to fall. Mama discussed her worries out loud, about whether he'd start out in this weather, or wait. Either way, she seemed distressed by his judgment.

"All this politics," she said. "Think a man would be happy to be home with his family." She placed the polished globe back on the lantern, setting it carefully on the wall shelf and moved on to the next. "Wants to be in the legislature or running the territory though I can't imagine what for. Yes. Well. It's time we did some work to get our minds off that man," she said.

She motioned for me to bring her clean linen from the pile. "Course tonight he's probably in some plush house at the gaming tables or drinking store tea while I make do here." She clucked her tongue in disgust. "Men mostly think about themselves," she said, taking the rag from my hand. She surprised me then by saying something that seemed directed to me. "Remember that about men. It'll make your marriage less a disappointment." She gently smoothed back Baby George's hair as she stepped past him, her wide skirts brushing against him as he sat chewing on a wooden toy on the floor. Her smile was gentle and warm for him, his eyes following her every move.

"When will I marry, Mama?" I asked, surprised that she had mentioned such a personal subject and wanting to keep our conversation going.

She turned to me, eyes narrowed, and looked me fully in the face, as though she hadn't realized until that moment that I was really with her in the room. I saw her jaw set, not unlike Pepperpot's just before he squeals in protest and I wondered if I'd stepped too far into the space she kept around her meant to keep me out.

"Well, if you're hoping for joyful cavorting or even courtship, don't," she said. "Rare's the woman these days who marries a man she knows, let alone likes, though neither's any guarantee for happiness." She sighed and turned away, dismissing me for a cleaning duty. "I'm sure your father will find some man been given the mitten by another and bring him home for you. Maybe that Henderson boy, now he's almost a man." She plucked lint from her wide skirt, brushed it, and sighed. "Your father looks after you even if he lets the rest of his family go to please himself." She reached for a second globe then and began to polish. The scent of kerosene grew stronger. "Remembers your day of birth every year, forgets mine." She sighed. "But that's the point of marriage. To provide for your children, not necessarily your mate. You'll learn that soon enough I suspect."

I wanted to disagree with her about Papa's only thinking of himself, but it was the first time we'd had a conversation about what my future held, so disloyally, I thought of me instead. "Luther doesn't interest me," I said. "He's just a boy."

"Do you think you'll have a choice?" she said, surprised. "Boy or no, if that's what's planned for you, it's what you'll do. It's the way it is for girls. Women too."

"When I get married," I said, believing it was my turn to talk, "I want to live in a big house, with lots of rooms and a parlor that gets used for happy times. One big enough for dancing." I swirled around the polished floors, dust rag in my hand, waving it at an imaginary man asking for my hand to dance. "People will come to visit and spend the night even," I said, slightly giddy from my swirling. "And we'll have parties, gatherings, the way you and Papa used to."

Mama grunted. "Sounds like a hotel," she said. "You'll have pipe smoke and tobacco juice to contend with that's for sure. And men believing they're the biggest toads in the puddle." She rubbed the globe harder, holding it up to the hazy light to check for smudges. "And tubs of laundry every week. Your knuckles will rub raw." She replaced the globe and looked over her own knuckles before she gathered up another globe. "As for partying," she sighed, "people in mourning don't. Wouldn't be proper."

"And I'd like a big family," I said wistfully, overlooking her reference to loss, "with lots of children." I was totally absorbed by the joy of my future. "Maybe four or five. Like you, Mama." I picked up Baby George's toy and rolled it to him from across the room before I even thought of what I'd just said, what unspeakable I'd spoken of following her mention of mourning.

As if in slow motion, I saw the shards of glass burst into the air and fall like crystals around Baby George who in seconds sat like an island in a sea of broken glass. He looked more startled than damaged and then seeing Mama's face—a grotesque mask of wrinkled pain—he began to cry.

I heard Mama moan and sob at the same time I heard the crash. My brother's crying moved Mama, and she threw her cleaning rags at me as she swished to pick him up, cuddle him, brush the shards of glass from his dark curls, and hold him while he howled, still more frightened than pained.

She glared at me as she faced me, as though her accident were my fault. "See what you've done to your brother, distracting me?" She pressed his face to her breast and his howling increased.

"But I didn't!" I said, feeling the burning of tears behind my nose. "I didn't do it!"

"You did!" she said. "You're the cause of it all!"

Her accusation made no sense as I did not hear the real charge. "You dropped it," I said, persisting in being right. "I didn't touch it. And he's not hurt anyway, Mama. Look."

Her outrage grew. "Don't sass me," she warned. Like a strong storm rolling across the hills she drove toward me, Baby George in arms. "Or I'll give you something to sass about." She raised her arm as though she might strike, something she had never done. Instead, she hesitated then pushed by, still holding Baby George. Mama shouted: "Do something right! Clean up the glass!" then rushed through the bedroom door and slammed it, keeping her baby safely in, me securely out.

I heard her talking softly to him in the bedroom as I knelt to pick up the shards. When a sliver pierced my finger dripping dots of red on the cleaning rag I held, I swallowed my sobs knowing I'd be my only comforter. I sat whimpering, wishing my tongue did not bring pain, sorry and angry at the same time, feeling unjustly accused; secretly believing Mama was right.

With the rag wrapped around my finger, I gathered my strength, opened the door to the cold, and tossed the shards into the snow-filled trash bucket set on the back porch. Hound lay quietly beside the wooden bucket, one eye lifted to me as I broke the silence of the snow.

Squatting, I scratched his ears and looked around. For the first time, I saw how much snow had already accumulated. The world beyond the porch was white, no difference between the sky and the land where they met at the horizon. I could barely see the barn through the wet, white curtain. If the snow stayed, we'd need to pull a rope from the house to the barn, to hang onto in the days ahead when we started feeding animals. October was early for feeding. Usually the animals could pasture on the sparse grasses until the hard freeze, often until late November. Snow in October meant we might not have enough feed for animals unless we were blessed with an early spring.

I hugged myself with my arms, surprised that after our losses I would even consider something going well, having the blessing of a late winter and enough feed. I did not think we were within the realm of anyone's blessing.

Back inside, I prepared to face Mama and do what I could to bring back the mood where we had talked and shared like sisters for just a moment. Tears idled behind my eyes. I missed my sisters terribly right then. Especially Rachel. I wished that I could hear her tattle just once more, take back all the things I ever said that sent her scurrying away, just as I had sent Mama away just moments before. Rachel, the sassy one. Now I had taken on that part of her spirit whether I liked it or not.

The cold wind whipped the door from my hands and it slammed against the wall as I opened it. With surprising speed, Hound brushed past me, scurrying beneath the table. I pulled the door from the wind's grip and latched it from the inside pulling the string, brushing the snow from my skirt.

Mama was nowhere in sight. Like the stillness of the white earth outside, everything inside was cold and quiet.

I wondered all that afternoon as I set the lights against the growing darkness, kept the fire burning, talking quietly to Hound, why I said things to Mama to make her cry. I wondered if I would ever have children running about me, have guests to laugh and dance in my parlor. I wondered who would ever want to have me in their presence for a moment let alone a lifetime as a wife.

My consolation was that Papa would be home soon. Perhaps he could tell me of his plans for my future. I thought of the tall stranger who had teased me and then rode out in the snow and wondered if he would return in three to four weeks as he promised.

For the briefest of moments, as I watched the heavy white flakes fall with no indication they would ever stop, I wished I had a second chance to talk with him. And throwing guilt aside, for just an instant, I wished it was Mama making her way through the white and Papa here to comfort me in the storm and in the morning.

U N E X P E C T E D

❦

IT WAS NOT A FREAK STORM that dropped its white that fall and quickly melted away. No, winter came prematurely in 1861 bringing with it the surprise of an expected guest arriving early and then staying late, making more demands, requiring more and more attention, giving the impression that they might never, ever leave. Everyone paid attention to that winter, Sunmiet included.

Snow piled up at the agency where the two-story brick boarding school run by the government housed Sunmiet and the other girls. All children age five and older spent their winters as required in boarding school. They learned needlework there, as though their years of doing fine beadwork were wasted. They rubbed their knuckles raw cleaning and starching their handmade uniforms, as though the skill of tanning hides and turning them into soft clothes had no merit. The boys belonged to another building where they were taught to stand in straight lines inside and outside, to work stock or grow vegetables in the spring—depending on the interests of the Indian agent that year, hoping they'd forget the roots and berries that were provided for the people to harvest each year. And they all learned about God and Christ in ways that made them think God had not noticed them before.

"Standing Tall worried for me at the school," Sunmiet told me some years later when as a mother, she spoke sad goodbyes to her own children standing at the steps of that very school. "But it was my father's desire I met that winter. He said for me to use what was not my choice and make it into something wise; to always look for the learning in a moment however much pain it carried also. At the school, I looked through my tears to learn non-Indian ways." And so she yielded her own wishes to another.

It seems to me the Warm Springs people often accommodate by sifting from non-Indians what they admire and weaving it into their own designs, making it an "Indian" way. Warm Springs horsemen kept their nomadic skills by becoming army scouts during the Snake and Bannock wars; good cattlemen have certainly risen from the reservation. And what would we Sherars have done without the Indian engineering skills I'd like to know! But that speculation's later.

In the winter of 1861, we were all bending to the demands of another: the weather.

As a boarding school student, Sunmiet found herself having to accept the thin moth-eaten blanket even though it did not take the chill from children. It offered no warmth as she lay in the narrow bed listening to the sounds of young girl's breathing and the wind rattling against the glass windows. She tossed on her cot. It was her last year at boarding school. Next year she would be married, even with child if her body listened to the traditional ways of being pregnant by the time snow covered the ground and stayed.

It was early, for no matron yet walked the aisle between the beds, clanging on the footrail with a stick to wake them before dawn, get them dressed and lined up for the meager breakfast. Auntie Lilie had been so kind to us that summer at the river, so gentle. But as a matron at the school, she became a second person, Sunmiet said: demanding, cranky. "She swallowed all the smiles she shared in the shadow of the river rocks," Sunmiet told me sadly.

One day a week they bathed. The October morning of the storm was not bathing day so even if Sunmiet had been the first to touch the steaming water— which she seldom was, now that she was almost an adult—there would be no bath that day. "It's when I missed the hot springs and the sweat lodge the most," she told me, "when I knew I could not have them."

It would have been enough, just getting through this last year, remembering not to speak Sahaptin in the daylight while refreshing herself with the language of Kása at night. It would have been enough, remembering to listen and watch, to learn what she could to bring back to her father. It would have been enough helping the little ones keep their fingers from the ruler-teacher's cracks when they made the slightest error. All of that would have been enough to keep her busy her last year. But she had her future to think of, too, how to live with Standing Tall and still not lose herself.

She tossed once on the cot then lay with her eyes open as a startling light flashed like lightening through the window, splashed against the bare walls of the dormitory.

Sunmiet slipped from the bed, wrapped the blanket around her shoulders and padded quietly to the window, her bare feet chilled by the cold floor. "Even while I scraped away the frost with my fingernails," she told me later, remembering the night she truly discovered Standing Tall's poor judgment, "Even while I breathed onto the cold glass so I could see out, I knew it was him. His actions were always forcing me to think of him, making me chose to do other than what I wished, for him."

Swirling white appeared when the light caught her eye again. Through the whiteness she finally saw it. A lantern swung methodically back and forth below her window. She could barely make out the face of the person holding the lantern so shrouded in snow was the figure. "Then it waved at me and I knew."

She worried he would get them both in trouble and felt her heart almost stop when she heard a noise behind her and turned.

Just Bubbles, sighing in her sleep.

Surely Standing Tall would not come in the night, not in a storm, unless something was wrong! But even then, her family would wait until morning before sending word, would not risk sending this wild boy out into the night to collect her. If they could wait. And that was why she risked the night and cold, because she worried about her family and what they might be needing. And because she longed for the touch of someone from home knowing it would be months before she could tussle the hair of Same-as-One or smell the herbs of her mother's freshly washed hair.

"I dressed quietly and went out into the storm. That has been my story with Standing Tall, always walking into storms."

"Why did you not come when you saw me?" Standing Tall hissed as her. "I have been waiting."

Sunmiet asked him what he was doing there besides making her feet get wet.

"You should not question me," he told her. "If I am here, there is good reason."

"I wait to hear your reason," she said. If he bore difficult news, surely he would tell her at once. Instead he lectured her on her slowness, her right to question him.

"Will I know why you're here before we are discovered and you are forced to tell the ruler-teachers in front of everyone?"

He smiled and then said lazily, "Are you not glad to see me?"

It came to her then in a burst of fury. "You come in the cold to annoy me, set me in front of the ruler-teachers to be struck, just to tell me you are *here?*"

"I annoy you?" he asked, grabbing at her arm.

"He was suddenly very angry," Sunmiet remembered, "and I was frightened."

He snapped at her. "I make a trip in the snow I did not expect to fall so soon so you would not forget me. And my presence annoys you? I see it takes little to make you forget those who care for you," he sneered. "Perhaps you have become a forever child of the non-Indians."

He finished, letting the final insult sink in.

"I could barely believe his poor judgment! Just to finish a badly started plan he had continued on through the night and the storm, called me out into risk for no reason but to announce himself! And I was foolish enough to believe he brought important news." Sunmiet shook her head.

It was the night she knew she would have to trust her own judgment or this Standing Tall, whom she did truly love and who said he cared for her, would bring her harm.

Sunmiet wrapped the blanket around herself tightly, pushed away from him, and turned to make her way back to the door. "No," Standing Tall said grabbing her arm. He saw the fire in her eyes and dropped his hand. "Stay just a minute. Give me warmth for my journey back," he whined. He reached to rub the blanket draped across her back.

"Your warmth will have to come from your lantern," she told him. "Or the embers that burned up your wisdom." She pulled away from him, leaping to find her tracks left earlier in the snow, hoping to make her way up the stairs to her cot before anyone would know.

"He did not follow me," Sunmiet said.

She padded with wet shoes into the sleeping quarters, made her way through the shadows of the dressers and beds to her own. Lying there, her heart calm, undiscovered, she found a moment to worry about Standing Tall, where he might sleep this night, survive the storm. Why did he do such foolish things? Did she wish to spend the rest of her life with such a man? Would her father understand if she didn't? "All questions I would have to answer before spring," she told me.

Her thoughts were interrupted by the sound of the matron's shoes walking crisply beside her bed, pausing.

"I thought my shoes would give me away," Sunmiet told me. "Auntie Lilie stood there while I pretended sleep. I could hear her breathing, smell the scent of cabbage left on her clothes from yesterday's stew, but she moved on."

Sunmiet planned to take what lessons she could from the early storm. Perhaps it had been sent to warn her of this man's thinking, give her time to prepare for a future with it.

In the morning, her cold fingers fumbled with the tiny dress buttons that marched like the boarding school lines up to her throat. She buried her wet socks under the covers and found a dry pair to pull up over her knees. Her wet shoes tugged over the socks told her that her feet would be cold all day. "Oh, hayah, that man!" she said beneath her breath.

She heard the chatter of the girls as they made their way to the hall, pulled their long braids over the collars of their thin coats and lined up in their dark dresses to descend the stairs. Cold air rushed at them and Sunmiet shivered, knowing they were about to enter the snowy world between the dorm and the cafeteria. It was going to be a cold day.

"But a good day," Sunmiet told me, "for I had not been discovered."

In rigid silence, the girls began the walk down the hall. In the distance, beyond her daydreaming, Sunmiet heard the scrape of the heavy door as the matron opened it into the stairwell, and the shuffle of feet as the girls began descending the stairs. "Then suddenly, the line disintegrated into a cackle of surprise and chatter and I knew without even seeing," Sunmiet said. "I pushed to the front of the line, closer to the confusion, and stared at the item of interest lying at the base of the steps. I barely heard the girls giggling. I realized in a quick moment that this would be a snowstorm to remember, one whose lessons I must quickly learn. For there at the bottom of the steps looking up at me from beneath a cozy blanket, bearing his sleepy, sheepish grin, and his lopsided look lay Standing Tall."

The storm taught Joseph lessons, too. He stayed a second day beneath his oiled skin, waiting for the snow to let up, hoping it would melt off once the accumulation stopped and the sun came out. He sketched some in his little book, read *Hiawatha* to Bandit once again. He said he'd wished he'd brought another book or two to read, perhaps the Bible his mother had given him when he'd left New York. Instead, he recalled favorite scriptures and then closed his eyes to memorize Longfellow's cadence. He shared them all out loud with the dog.

With the pile of dried branches he'd dragged close to his flames, he kept a small fire burning. Whenever he looked out, he noticed the soft pile of snow building up on the back of the mule as it stood, head drooped.

Joseph had plenty of thinking time.

It was his plan to send Fish Man on ahead while he checked out the mules, secured them for the spring, made inquiries about supply purchases, and returned himself to California. Now he wondered if he would be able to make the trip to California and return again before hard winter set in. In the spring, he hoped to arrive in the Oregon country with his own crew and assets to not only purchase the string but also buy his own supplies as well. He planned for forty mules and hoped to get them for slightly less than the going rate of $250 each. The cash would come from California. He could pull it all together as soon as he returned to the ranch. "I liked the rush of energy those thoughts of pulling it all together gave me," he told me. "Almost as good as winning at cards."

Men's plans easily find themselves diverted and Joseph did not return to Fifteen Mile Crossing in four weeks as he had planned and promised.

On his third morning out, the snow stopped and a blinding bright sun glittered and glared off the white earth. The melted snow Joseph left in his cup the night before was frozen solid. The kelpie stepped gingerly from beneath the oil skin, then, with renewed courage, skidded on the hard white surface beyond their lean-to and dropped some pellets. With two kicks from his back paws on the crusty surface, Bandit revealed his futile effort at good hygiene. He trotted back to the fire, the melting snow close to the flames clogging his pads. Joseph picked up the dog, held his hands over Bandit's paws and melted the frozen clumps. "Looks like you'll be riding again today," Joseph said, his breath forming icicles on his mustache and beard.

They spent the next three days pushing into packed snow, crashing through the crust in places, making little headway. Joseph walked often, leading the gelding and packmule on foot, the man and animals sharing the hard labor of making a path through the unknown. Two feet of the white drifted into the ravines; more on the flat surfaces on the ridgetops. Joseph kept the mountain range on his right, moved inland to find a narrow crossing of another river not yet frozen over, and continued south, into the tall timber. His thoughts were of the next ridge, the next ravine, how much stamina he and his animals had. He did not see another soul.

His fourth day out, Joseph noticed sugar pine cones larger than his own two hands peaking up from the tree wells. This was Klamath country and Joseph was grateful the wind had found another playground. "Another night and we should share Philamon's roof," he said to the kelpie.

It actually took two more nights before they spied the comforting smoke of Philamon's fire. There were no signs of the garden now. Snow already covered the irrigation canals, corn stalks, and gate posts. For just a moment Joseph watched Philamon loading hay on the sled, ready to feed cattle. He shook off his uneasy feeling. Feeding hay in early November. It did not speak well for just how hard a winter lay ahead. He hoped things were better farther south.

He clucked the gelding into pushing snow with his brisket one more time as they worked their way down the ridge to Philamon's. "At least I can exchange more reading," Joseph said to the kelpie trotting briskly beside him now along the crusty surface.

He couldn't know then that he would read all Philamon had, write words of his own, and forge a lifelong friendship with his renter. For Joseph never left the Klamath country until spring.

At our end, Papa arrived home a day after the first storm stopped. I had already strung the rope to the barn as soon as the sky held off. More than two feet of snow drifted in the winds that began shortly after the snow ceased.

Luther made his way over early on the first morning of clear sky, attempting to endear himself to me and Mama as he offered his help until Papa arrived. At least his presence brought Mama out of her silence and she began to speak with me again if only to give directions.

While I usually found Luther's presence boring and annoying, Mama's mention of him as a possible suitor piqued my interest and so I took more careful watch: of how he dealt with the cold and how slow it made all work; of how he treated Hound and the mules; of what he said to Mama, Baby George, and me.

He seemed kind enough and did not raise his voice at the animals. But I could also tell him what to do, sass him without recourse. He simply listened, didn't bait me back, and usually did what I told him. The conversations he introduced seemed of petty things: how the school teacher who stayed in their home last term chewed her meat (with tiny chop-chop bites) with her alder teeth, or how much his feet had grown ("two sizes since last year, don't you know"). Perhaps he mistook me for someone who cared about these things. I didn't, though I had wondered once about Miss Matthews, our teacher at the Walker School, and how she worked her wooden teeth.

As Luther threw hay to the horses, I watched him and imagined him dancing in my parlor, or myself looking at his pimply face every day of my life as Mama looked at Papa's. I could not see my future reflected in his eyes.

Several times that winter, lying deep in my goose-down comforter, I dreamed of someone tall, someone special. I walked just behind him, sometimes beside him and reached out to touch him, to have him turn so I could see his face. In the dream, his face would have no features, just whiteness, like the snow, and so I never saw who lived there, in my dream.

After Papa arrived home, we found that the winter simply consumed us. The temperature never rose to permit thawing. Clear days meant no snow but air so cold Papa said his words froze and we could chop them from the air and save them, break them open to listen to whenever he wasn't there. I didn't believe him.

Overcast days threatened new snow piling on old snow, its only redeeming grace being the clean look the whiteness brought, if only temporarily. Everything we did could not be done without first contending with the snow, the frozen creeks, the cold. Getting hay and water to our stock, keeping the fires going in the house to keep ourselves from freezing, rationing supplies so we would not be forced to make a trip to The Dalles, all took our energy and time.

Christmas came and left with even the joy of cutting the tree taken from us as we were forced to tromp through deep drifts and arrive home cold and wet, almost like any other day that winter.

We greeted 1862 with the enthusiasm of mourners.

Only once did Lodenma and Senior May venture over with their little ones so much work it was, so risky to show their faces to the cold. The Mays talked with Papa about opening this eastern part of Oregon, of more travelers that would surely come in spring, and how Papa could make a profit possibly with his own string or teaming up with someone else. Mama reminded him the mules were already spoken for. Papa simply nodded. Later, I heard their voices raised in argument, something about mules and cash and cards. "The money's not been squandered," Papa said. "Trust me on this, 'Lizbeth. You're thinking in areas a woman ought to let be."

Lodenma and Beatrice and even Senior May spent that night on their one visit and Senior May took the occasion to show me how to hold his antler-handled knife so I could carve a piece of rough wood as he did, whittling animals and toys carrying the scent of alder and pine. Mama snorted that such was man's doings. Papa smiled, encouraged me, said perhaps I'd be good enough to sell them someday to support myself "in case no suitor meets my requirements," he said and laughed.

I liked sharing conversation with the adults. When visitors came, Mama often spoke directly to me and she smiled. And though she never sent me off to care for Baby George, I didn't mind as much. Other's might never know of our dissension if they only saw our little family tightly sitting in the parlor with our guests.

The creation of small things from wood filled those dreary days, brushing blond chips from my skirts, pulling little slivers from my fingers, inhaling fresh-cut wood as we sat before the fireplace in the evenings. I thought of Pauline often and her little carved gift. I wondered who of Sunmiet's people had made it as I chipped at my own.

Papa made only occasional trips on the sled through January and February, not wanting to tire the mules living on sparse rations. Once he made a trip south, to Tygh Valley to Muller's store. The shelves held little. "Neither grass nor corn trains coming through," Art Muller told him, sadly shaking his head as he moved Arbuckle coffee cans around on his sparse shelves.

In The Dalles, Papa heard news of low hay supplies and only scattered shipments as little arrived in the region, the snow said to spread from the Cascades clear east to the Rockies. The mighty Columbia River froze completely over.

Papa said the only good news came from the China boy, Tom, a cook at the Umatilla House, who said the tea leaves predicted a harsh but sudden spring sometime around April.

We did not go to church in The Dalles at all that winter, instead finding ourselves on Sundays reading from the scriptures. Once or twice, word spread and we gathered at the school for music and prayer with neighbors becoming preachers for the day. We missed the weekly fellowship though most of us were too tired and too compassionate to spread the animals strength out over our wishes instead of just onto our needs.

And I confess, I thought often of the tall Californian, the way he had spoken to me as a young woman, an adult. Once I even wondered if it was his face who would someday fill the whiteness of the stranger in my dream.

In April, the floods began seemingly overnight. One day the snow still drifted with dirty veils of dust beside the barn. The next day, the drifts began to sink, seeping dirty water beneath them that became fast moving flows over frozen roads, thawing fields, rock-washed ravines. Passive pasture streams roared torrents that kept some families split: half holed up in the barn where they were when the little stream became a raging river and the other half in the house. Roads and bridges washed out and at the mouth, the Deschutes spread like a dark stain into the Columbia.

I wondered, idly, if the flooding would keep the Californian away.

CHAPTER 15

THE PLANS
OF MEN

❧

"SO WHO'S THE DANDY with the dog, J. W.?" my father said, nodding to his card partner. He spoke loud enough for Joseph to hear despite the clatter of dishes and men's voices in the bar.

J. W. Case, my father's card partner, uncrossed his size tens from beneath the gaming table knocking dried mud from his boots onto the polished floor at the Umatilla House. Smoke swirled around the players and diners like flies on a day-old carcass. Joseph watched them in the back bar mirror. J. W. rubbed his eyes with his fists like an overgrown child, glanced up briefly from his cards to see Joseph staring back at him.

J. W. couldn't have recognized the tall stranger wearing a well-cut jacket and turquoise bola who had just entered carrying a pointy-eared dog beneath one arm. For like the long-awaited spring, Joseph had just arrived.

A mule skinner's whip coiled at his hip above Mexican leather boots that captured his pants inside.

"Don't know him," Joseph heard the lean man answer. "Looks like he's been on the trail, judging by the mud. Maybe he come 'cross the river."

"Benson's friendly enough with him," Joseph heard my papa say though he didn't know then who Papa was. He watched Papa adjust his hat with a nervous gesture typical of him. "Look at that. That barkeep just slipped some silver into his pocket," Papa said.

"You could use some of that, hey, George," J. W. told him, smiling. Take the sting out of losing."

"I win enough," Papa said, still loud enough for Joseph to be unintentionally eavesdropping.

"Loud when you do," J. W. razzed, "and you're pretty quiet tonight." He laughed his high-pitched laugh and slapped another card on the table. "Call!"

"I don't think a man should bring his dog into an eating establishment," Papa said, laying his cards down flat on the green felt to make his point. He adjusted his hat once again pulling it farther forward, shadowing his good eye.

"Leave it be," J. W. said. "Stick to your hand." He scratched at some hairs growing out from his nose. "Hey! Your cards are getting wet. See there." Moisture from Papa's whiskey glass seeped into the table felt turning a spot beside the cards a darker green.

Papa said: "Forget it!" He picked up his soggy cards, took one last look, probably calculating his losses, and folded his hand. "You've already got most of what I have," he said and pushed his chair back from the table.

"You can't just quit!" J. W. said. "I'm on a roll here! You owe me!"

"I've paid. In full," Papa said and stood up.

In the mirror, Joseph watched the transaction, watched my papa dismiss J. W. with the palm of his hand as if grateful for a diversion; approach him.

"New policy?" he said to Benson, the barkeep. Papa's voice held sarcasm; his eye contempt as he eased in beside Joseph, keeping him to his left where his good eye could watch him. He rested his foot on the brass rail and pushed his hat farther back onto his head. He was only a few inches shorter than Joseph. His bad eye watered and he dabbed at the marble in it.

"Nothing new," Benson said, wiping off the lip of a whiskey bottle. "Man just likes to drink with his friends. Happens this man's friend is a dog." Benson set the bottle down, moved his cloth in a circular motion over the bar polishing what was already shiny and smooth.

"Doesn't say much about a man, can't find anyone to eat or drink with besides a dog," Papa said.

"Both're well behaved," Benson said quietly. "Don't make anything more of this than it is, George. Just go back and finish your game with J. W."

Papa's words were even, contained. "I got a wife to tell me what to do," he said. "Don't need advice from you."

Familiar with Papa's sour, sometimes uncompromising attitude, Benson backed off. "Look, let me introduce you. This is someone you should know."

"Don't know anything I'd have in common with a man who drinks with dogs," Papa said. His good eye floated over Joseph smooth and slippery as a catfish in a murky hole.

"There's a seat there at the window table," Benson said hurriedly to Joseph, motioning him out of the tension.

Joseph paused, deciding about this intrusive person then tipped his hat at the barkeep. He turned to walk toward the window when the kelpie twisted its head around to look at the surly man, rolled its lips back, and breathed a low, menacing growl.

"Look at that!" Papa said. "Dog's mean!" He turned his back to the bar, his voice even, loud. Men stopped their card playing and looked. "Hear that? Growled at me!" He reached for Joseph's arm, to grab the dog, but Benson grabbed Papa's arm instead.

"Leave it!" he said. "The dog's fine." Then softer, so few could hear it though Joseph did, he said: "Starting a scene won't do anything 'cept spread bad talk. Which I know you don't want. Not with the election and all."

Someone near the back laughed out words about "some beast." The tension lowered and Papa calmed. "Got a hound of my own I'll bring in since you've decided to serve dogs," he told Benson, brushing his arm off and turning abruptly back to J. W.'s biscuit-sized eyes.

Joseph kept silent. He didn't know who the man was or why he'd decided to be so cantankerous toward him, and he was too tired to really care. If the man wanted a fight, he could give it. If the barkeep could avoid it, more power to him. He had enough on his mind.

Joseph ate quietly, thinking of days past, the kelpie at his feet. Much had happened since he'd last been in this bar negotiating a deal with Brayman. When winter finally broke, he left the Klamath ranch and headed to California to determine his losses. He discovered that Fish Man had gotten through, given the message to Benito; but efforts to sell off the sheep had failed before the snow fell. Without cash from the sheep sales, Benito had been unable to buy up mules before winter. They'd had severe losses with the sheep.

The cattle, fortunately, had survived well despite the weather which had not been as cruel in the Hupa Valley as here, along the Columbia.

Once he headed to Oregon, though, Joseph could see the destruction of the cold and raging floods. It had taken them nearly two weeks to bring fifty head of cattle and his small band of fifteen mules on up from California.

He reached for another biscuit. He planned to sell the cattle here, as he knew the losses from the winter would be great. He had not planned on there being so little cash available for purchases. Worse, more and more men were leaving for the gold fields perhaps with nothing to keep them in The Dalles and the promise of riches luring them east, so he wasn't sure who was left to buy cattle. He planned to use the cash from their sale for the mules. He only briefly considered that the winter might have stolen his secured mules as well as stable men's plans.

Brayman told him two pieces of news that could be taken as good or otherwise: Joseph now owned a ranch at Fifteen Mile Creek, not far from the Herberts, as he'd requested Brayman negotiate in his absence; and he had competition from three other stringers. J. W. Case, J. J. Cozart, and D. N. Luce, all men so busy they had no time for names, just initials, had pack strings ready to head into gold country.

Joseph realized that with their outfitting complete, mules would be at a premium.

"Should have let me set the string for you," A. H. told him when they met earlier in the day. "But, so be it. Just let's get going as soon as we can."

Now Joseph wished he'd brought more mules north rather than counting on finalizing his agreement made late last fall. As hard as the winter had been, Herbert's mules may not have even made it. And he wasn't at all sure that the Herberts would consider a trade. Cash he'd set for the ranch would have come in handy now. Herberts might be wanting cash too, something he'd find out the next day.

Benson brought a refill on his brew and said softly so only Joseph could hear, "J. W. is one of the stringers." He nodded his head in the direction of the surly man's card partner. "Set to leave in the morning. May want to talk with him about the route and all. He's a good egg. Hard-worker. But best save your discussions for when he's alone," Benson added cautiously.

Joseph thanked him but he knew he wouldn't be talking with anyone right then. He had all the information he needed about the trail, first hand. The rerouting because of the swollen rivers and the washed out roads had put him and his men and cattle and mules into a maze of ravines and ridges.

He had been within a day's ride of The Dalles when he and Benito and his men moved the cattle down Buck Hollow. He looked forward to crossing on the narrow bridge, sure that so high above the water, it would have survived. He was close enough to allow himself to think of a featherbed following a seven-course meal.

Instead, he'd faced surprise and disappointment. The little creek in Buck Hollow was swollen three times its normal size. It swirled with juniper branches, grasses and roots, waterlogged snakes and foam. Crossing it took an extra day, with ropes and horses and cattle getting in each others' way and growing more agitated by the minute.

And when in the morning they moved the cattle toward the bridge that he and Peter Lahomesh had stepped carefully across, Joseph found himself fighting away tears of frustration. For ahead he could see that the bridge he needed to cross the Deschutes was gone.

He was angry with himself that he had not listened to Philamon about taking the roads through the reservation, up the western side of the Deschutes. He had remembered the bridge and believed he could save time by taking it. He'd also looked forward to seeing the falls again, the terrain that led to it.

But not that day. There'd been no choice: he faced the falls and blood-red rocks that lined the gorge without the presence of the bridge.

The men blew their noses on their patterned kerchiefs, rubbed their hands with goose grease to soften the calluses, cinched their saddles extra tight as though it were the horses' fault, and turned the cattle back to cross, again, swollen Buck Hollow creek. A light rain fell.

Animals died this time. And when they headed north and reached the Columbia, they were again thwarted by the unruliness of rivers and streams. For where the Deschutes disgorged itself into the Columbia, a massive river twice the normal width churned angrily with dark red mud. Islands like thin green paint strokes sliced the rolling brown and blue. Tree roots, limbs, remains of bloated cattle, and sagebrush bobbed like wood chips in water, swirling, going under. No Indian offered canoes for passage, a sure sign that whoever was on this side was meant to stay. "We cannot cross, yes?" Benito asked him.

"We will cross, yes," Joseph said. "In a few hours or days maybe." He lifted his hat and ran his hands through his sweat-stained hair. "We'll see how much it drops."

They had waited nearly a week before risking the crossing. All the time, they suspected others were ahead of them, loading and preparing for transport into the gold fields. What made it worse for Joseph's men was knowing that this would be the same route the pack string would now have to take to Canyon City since the bridge at the falls—Joseph's idea for a shortcut—had been taken by the flood.

Joseph shook his head to brush away the agonizing thoughts. He wiped his beard on the linen napkin hanging from his stiff collar. Tonight, his first evening back in The Dalles, he simply wanted a warm bed and no more effort.

The kelpie perked up, swatted his skinny tail against the floor in friendly greeting, giving Joseph advance warning of Benito coming into the saloon behind him. "All is finish," Benito said as he sat down. "French Louie, he make arrangements. For cattle for night. And mules. You sleep soon?"

Before Joseph could answer, the kelpie skittered forward from under the table and growled. Joseph looked up to see the man with the bad eye approach his table, his sour disposition still in tow.

Papa stopped, looked at Benito sitting at the table and he said something he would not have thought to say I'm sure without rye whiskey in his blood. "Greaser," he said. He spoke it softly, Joseph remembered, almost like a hiss. He spit his next insult directly at Benito. "The Umatilla House really does serve dogs."

His nose red, he moved quickly past their table.

Bandit barked. Joseph's chair tipped in the speed of his rising, his temper tested by the insult and flared by days of drain. The room froze into silence. Benito grabbed at Joseph from across the table. "No," he said. "The man, he is not worth it."

Torn, Joseph stood a moment, watching the back of the lean man ease toward the door. When he saw Joseph would not pursue, he turned and adjusted his hat in triumph just before he left. Such contempt should not go unscathed, Joseph thought though he could see Benito's point. The man wasn't worth it, even if Benito was.

Voices in the saloon resumed talking, forks scraped on plates at the nearby table. J. W. wore an embarrassed face as he stood and moved his bowed legs to another card game, looking at Joseph over the head of another player.

Joseph sat back down, leaning to retrieve his white linen napkin from the floor. Benson, the barkeep, brought another brew over and said something about the man loosing an eye to a whip coming across the trail and grateful that Joseph had not pursued the bait.

"Good," Benito said, as Benson left them. "Good you do not pursue. Men of little minds do not deserve the energy of greatness."

"Greatness?" Joseph scoffed, tossing the napkin in a clump on his plate. "You, my friend, are even more tired than I if that's what you think!"

Pleased the tension passed so quickly Benito said: "Yes. And tired makes me say things out loud I sometimes only think. But I will not be so tired in the morning." He smiled. "My bones will ache from keeping up with you on our *paseo*. They wonder why I take them from soft beds for all of this." He stood and rubbed his backside as if to massage away the aches. "No, *crazy* will be the word I think to call you then."

"And few would disagree," Joseph said. "Only a few."

When Joseph rode into our ranch at Fifteen Mile Creek the next morning, Mama and I were at the dying tubs, tending to yarn left long in the sheds. We stood with walnut husks and dried goldenrod in gourds at our feet ready to color the yarn, aware of the glorious day. Meadowlarks warbled away their cares, little songbirds and nuthatches bopped about bravely pecking at the nuts. In the pasture, tiny yellow butterflies rallied at the slowly drying mudholes. Fifteen thin mules grazed hungrily on the new shoots pushing through patches of old, melting snow. Though the cattle had not been so fortunate, the mules had all survived.

I almost didn't recognize the Californian as I'd taken to thinking of him. His shoulders seemed wider, leaner. His face wore the bronze of a man who easily tanned or who by May had already spent hours in the sun. He sat taller astride a big bay gelding. A small, dark man with a mat of unruly hair rode beside him, a large hat held by a string at his throat bounced upon his back. They led no pack animals.

The kelpie barked back as Hound roused from his lounge on the porch. I stopped my stirring and smoothed my dark skirt, tried to hike up my stockings with my shoeless feet and walked forward toward the gate.

Mama recognized him immediately.

"George!" She called out to Papa who was mending fence and nursing a headache near the barn. "We've company." To me she said, "Hurry inside and put the bread and jam on the sideboard. We'll take tea in the parlor."

I must have looked surprised because she added, "Parlor sets a propensity for good business. Now go." She watched the men tend to their horses and added more cautiously, "I'm not sure about his man…" She eyed Joseph's darker companion and nodded her head with approval when he took the reins from Joseph and led both horses to the hitching post. "Yes. Well." She said then, always carrying with her remnants of her Virginian past, "It's his man-servant. He'll most likely wait outside." She walked forward to greet the Californian, wiping her hands on her always immaculate apron.

"Please forgive my appearance," she said, touching the snood nervously at the back of her neck. "You've caught us unaware." She seemed giddy, girlish, I thought, with some annoyance.

"It's we who ask forgiveness," Joseph said, bending at the waist to greet her. "For arriving unannounced. And not returning last fall. It was the winter. I wasn't sure we'd even be welcome——"

"*You* certainly are…" Mama said. She eyed the darker man as he left the horses to stand beside Joseph.

"My friend and partner, Benito Donario," Joseph said.

"Well. I'm pleased I'm sure," Mama said, flustered by Benito's offer to shake her hand. As her fingers adjusted her snood again, Benito awkwardly returned his work-stained fingers to the rim of his large hat now held in front of him. "My husband will join us shortly," she said looking at Joseph. "Shall we go inside?"

She didn't wait for their answer. Instead, she lifted her crinolined skirts discreetly above her work shoes and walked toward the porch steps. "Jane," she said as she walked by me. "Let's serve our guests." She walked quickly inside.

My feet seemed sucked into mud; my hands stuck to each other like pitch to fingers behind my back. My smile worked and I gave it to Joseph as he removed his hat and stopped in front of me. His friend stood beside him, saying nothing. Joseph threaded his wide fingers through his thick brown hair, looking me over with the kind surprise a distant uncle shows for a niece not seen in years.

"You're a tad taller," he said, "and a whole lot prettier."

His words embarrassed me, and so I did what I do best when someone does something out of my control: "Do mule skinners always travel without mules?" I said, with only a little lightness to my barb.

"Glad to see the winter didn't freeze your sass," he said. He smiled wide, revealing a softness that filled his full face, his kind eyes. "I figured what this mule skinner needs spent the winter here."

"I did," I said. Then, my face ablush: "I mean they did. Spend the winter here. The mules. Did." His friend had a funny look on his face.

"Jane!" I heard Mama call out and for once I was grateful for her interruption.

"You'd best go on," I said. "Papa'll be along any minute." Then I led Joseph, Benito, and the kelpie inside, waiting for Mama to shoo the latter two out, but she didn't.

Later, I would try to reconstruct what happened, to see if a path through the tangle could have been hacked out some other way. Wisdom, of course, carries with her both the future and the past while we humans have mere memory.

My father entered next, stomping mud from his boots. Mama touched his arm as she began to introduce Joseph who had just turned to face him, eyes adjusting to my father's form standing in the backlight of the door. The kelpie growled. Mama stepped back in surprise when Papa stiffened, recognizing Joseph first.

Papa held his hand to his side as Joseph offered his, not even looking at him, Papa's eyes beyond. "We've a foreign guest," he said as he spied Benito standing next to the fabric chair, hat in hand. He had risen with Papa's entrance.

Mama was soothing. "He is Mr. Sherar's partner," she said. Then moving quickly said, "Mr. Sherar has come for his mules. Remember, I told you. He left the deposit?" To Joseph she said, "We are so fortunate. My husband put up extra stocks of hay and our mules, while thin, will fatten nicely with this snow-stained grass." She took my Papa's arm more forcefully. "Let's sit, George," she said firmly.

At the sound of my father's name, Joseph dropped the offer of his hand. I noticed caution now in his eyes. And then some kind of recognition.

Papa recognized him at that moment, too, though neither Mama nor I knew how until much later.

"The man who drinks with dogs," Papa sneered.

I thought he was looking at the kelpie standing at Joseph's feet, lips pulled back, teeth showing, no tail wagging.

Mama gasped at Papa's poor manners. "George!" she said. "Yes. Well. I never—"

"Shall we have tea, then?" I said, interrupting with my tray of things, trying to move past this awkward moment, feeling more like my mother than I ever had till then.

"Yes. Tea, then. Here it is," my mother said, her wide dress swirling about her legs as she turned to the sideboard, quickly, to help me.

Joseph's words were deep, even, spoken with an Irish tinge to our backs. "I'll not be drinking tea, then," he said. "Not with a man who cannot bide his tongue."

I turned to look at him and saw his neck was red and his eyes a stony blue directed at Papa.

"In a man's home, he can say what he wants," Papa said, and I was inclined to agree. "Have who he wants to tea," Papa told him, spitting at the "tea." "And even sober, I don't want the greaser."

Benito shifted uncomfortably from foot to foot and said softly. "I will wait outside—"

"Sit!" Joseph said. "I'll not walk away a second time."

"Now, George," Mama said, her voiced higher pitched. "We have a business arrangement to complete. Surely we can do that without rancor."

"I wait outside," Benito said as he moved to pass Papa.

"We will both go outside," Joseph said. His temper still ran his thinking as he pushed past my father, followed by Benito out onto the porch.

"Please! George!" Mama pleaded. She twisted her fingers on Papa's striped shirt sleeve. "For heaven's sake! Control yourself!" Mama seemed frantic. "Complete the deal and then express your politics!"

Papa pulled away from her and out to the porch. I stood in the doorway, my stomach a knot of hornets.

Joseph and Benito digested the events near their horses, their faces close to each other with strong feeling but not in anger it didn't seem to me. They were working something out between them.

Papa seethed at the gate. Having won his argument, he seemed uncertain about how to proceed. Mama pushed by him to stand before Joseph. I heard her express apologies and they exchanged some words and then Mama led him back toward Papa and the gate.

I'd never seen her quite so muddled. "None the worse for wear, shall we say, Mr. Sherar?" Mama smoothed and straightened her snood. "Mr. Sherar would like to complete his exchange," Mama said, "and be on his way."

"Mister Sheer," Papa said, glad to have some steps to his uncertainty. He put a "sneer" into Joseph's name and added, "has no reason to stay. There is no deal to 'exchange' as you put it, Elizabeth."

"But he left the deposit—"

"Which shall not be returned as he did not keep his end of the bargain." He looked at Mama now, daring her to challenge him. "He was to have brought the principal in three to four weeks. He did not."

Mama gasped. I heard it from the porch. "Excuse us," she said to Joseph. "For the moment." She tugged on Papa's sleeve again. He brushed her off.

"There's no need for privacy, Elizabeth. The deal's done. When we didn't hear, I sold them. J. W. bought the animals in March. Will be heading out momentarily, I expect."

Mama looked genuinely pained. I didn't know then of the debts adults incur or how relying on one thing to happen serves as hope and drops one deeply to despair when the thing is changed without recourse. She was so stunned she didn't see Joseph walk closer to my father. "I had your word—"

"My wife's word. You did not keep yours, sir. I'm not obligated to keep hers."

They stood close, like two bulls who eye each other for one moment in honor before striking.

What possessed me to speak into that tense vibration still remains a mystery to this day. Perhaps I felt my mother's humiliation, my father's need for control. For whatever reason, I did and so entered into the fray adult's call life.

"Puddin is mine," I said, my voice cracking. And looking straight at Joseph added, "So at least one Herbert mule is still for sale."

CHAPTER 16

JOINING

I HAD NEVER SEEN Sunmiet so still, standing in the shadows like a blue heron, steadfast in the water. It was summer and the tribe had gathered at He-He in the mountains for the celebration. In the distance, beyond the lodge at the cool mountain campsite, I could hear children laughing, men talking, drummers warming up.

Sunmiet reigned serene despite the chaos that drifted around her like the heady fragrance of honeysuckle.

"Hurry, Bubbles!" Sunmiet's mother said. "We are almost ready, just waiting for your lazy body to find that bundle!" Morning Dove, Sunmiet's mother, appeared the most unsettled I had ever seen her. "The one painted green and white with fresh buckskin laces," she continued, chastising her niece in the midst of the excitement.

"Did I not tell you to guard it as though it was the summer's roasted camas?" Sunmiet's Auntie Magpie spoke to her daughter, Bubbles, without gentleness.

"You would not be careless if it was fit to eat!" Auntie Lilie said.

"My mother brings her beaded bags," Bubbles said with some authority in her voice. "And the cornhusk ones you made last huckleberry time. The blankets are here. All the *shaptákai* are here. Everything is here...." Her voice always seemed to whine at the end, as though tired of having to defend herself each time she spoke.

"Not everything," Magpie snapped. "It is the bundle I sent you to bring that worries me. It holds the beads of Sunmiet's *kása* from the Spokane people of her father. Oh, what did you do with it?"

Morning Dove rustled around again in the blankets and bundles lining the floor of the anteroom of the longhouse, stirring up the pungent scents of alder-smoked buckskin mixed with wind-dried salmon. Her daughter stood quietly off to the side, seemingly patient. The drummers began a slow, heart-beat cadence and with the first high-pitched song of the wedding singers, Morning Dove's frenzy increased. "Look! Look!" She said to Bubbles and me and her sister, Magpie. "Find it!"

I looked, even though I wasn't sure of the bundle's appearance. At least I felt useful, something I hadn't felt since arriving three days earlier. I'd never been to an Indian wedding before and knew myself both privileged and nervous at the same time, wanting not to make mistakes and yet to take in every beaded detail of the day.

"I can be persuaded," Bubbles said, tapping her fore-finger beside her cheek, "to remember...." She closed her eyes, earning time to think and I noted idly as I watched her that Bubble's eyes were the shape of her hide scraper, arched at the top, round at the bottoms.

"Oh, hayah!" Morning Dove said. "You will just fall asleep," Irritated, she advised, "If you brought everything I told you, then go look outside. See if it has been set in with the baskets of food out there by mistake."

She watched Bubbles ease her way through the narrow opening into the sunlight, the hide door catching briefly on Bubble's beaded roses that kept the ends of her braids in place. Dust glittered in the ray of sunshine that pierced the lodge when Bubbles left.

"Who could have known this day would come so quickly!" Morning Dove said to me—or no one in particular—anticipation and loss joined in her voice. She clutched at the necklace she wore, rubbing the tiny seed beads beneath her fingers as she thought. Then with her hands she directed my searching again, motioned me to look here then there, beneath the stacks of buckskins, fur hides, trade beads, dried fruit and meats, talking as we turned up and inside out, looking for the small *shaptákai* that held the precious veil.

Morning Dove buried her head in a basket, searching. "When Sunmiet was born," she told us, remembering, "we accepted the gift of Standing Tall's parents and their request to join our daughter to their son. We used the time until the full moon to consider, invite them back to share a meal and give our answer." She shook her head in amazement. "The day of our promise disappeared like the moon behind the clouds. We knew it was certain to be there, but hidden from our vision just the same. Until now."

"I am glad you waited," Sunmiet said, speaking for the first time since the search for the bundle began. She stood in the shadow of the lodge, dressed in white buckskins from head to toe, the deer's tail still attached to the hide at the hem as was the wedding custom. She was as beautiful as any bride I had ever seen. 'Course, I'd not seen many by that age and never an Indian bride. Sunmiet had told me that each detail of her regalia had been carefully thought out and planned over the years, just for this day. From the tiny red and blue seed beads sewn into her moccasins to the matching design on her leggings to her beaded belt and bag worn at the back of her waist. Even her wrist bracelets and the ermine woven into her braids that eased over her breasts, just whispering to the dirt floor, each detail spoke of care and respect, family and tradition. The entire bodice of her dress had been beaded by her mother with beads she'd traded bags and buckskins for over the years.

Sunmiet cooled herself with her eagle feather fan. Her cheeks were as flushed and soft as a baby's bottom as she said quietly, eyelashes fluttering, "I'm glad you permitted me one more summer, even though my flow began last fall." Her voice was tremulous, shaky with gratitude and a bit of fear.

"We could be laughing, remembering all this commotion for a whole year already instead of searching, searching, readying ourselves for this wedding yet to come," her Auntie Magpie said.

But Morning Dove heard the fear in her daughter's voice, stopped her frantic search and came to her. As she spoke, she touched Sunmiet's cheek flushed with emotion. "We thought you were too young," Morning Dove said, her fingers tracing her daughter's fine cheekbone to her chin. "And you are our only daughter." She brushed some wispy tendrils of hair that stuck, damp, to Sunmiet's temples, weaving them with her fingertips back into Sunmiet's braids. "And your father reins in his views with the skill of the good horseman he is. So it was not so difficult to persuade the family of your husband-to-be to wait one more year."

She turned her daughter around, checked the necklace of porcupine quills she wore at her throat, adjusted the braids parted at her daughter's neck. Her fingers, callused from the years of joining beads to buckskin gently touched Sunmiet's skin. "Your father did not wish the boarding school pain on you. But you will understand the non-Indian ways better, for the good of your children's children."

"Standing Tall did not wish it," Sunmiet said, facing her mother again, searching her eyes.

"No. He took issue."

Magpie interrupted, believing they wished to know her thoughts. "He thinks you pay him back, for his foolish visit in the snow that cost you big time at the school," she said, remembering.

"Sunmiet does not have venom," Morning Dove told her sister. "And Standing Tall is a good son. We made a wise decision those years ago choosing him for you." Morning Dove stood back, surveying as she spoke. "He is a good hunter. Good fisherman. He listens to his mother and his *kása.*" I wondered if Sunmiet had told them of her fears about him or if she would let them only see his good side. "He will provide for you and his family," Morning Dove finished, straightening something on Sunmiet's dress. "So he had to wait." She shrugged her shoulders. "It is not the first time."

"Nor the last," Auntie Lilie said and giggled.

The long fringe on Sunmiet's buckskin dress flowed like water as she moved her arms to straighten her beaded belt, ignoring her auntie. Her mother stepped closer, held both her daughter's hands out before her, admiring the gentle drape of the hide over her daughter's slender frame, the tiny stitches and network of beads, the elk's teeth and shells that decorated the bodice. Many calluses had been grown for this moment.

"You are a good berry picker," Morning Dove told her daughter. "And a good root digger. Only a good root digger receives a *kápn* from both her mother and her *kása,* is that not right?" Sunmiet lowered her eyes in embarrassment at her mother's high praise. "Perhaps someday you will be one of the seven to dig first roots. You *will* be a good mother," she said, lifting her daughter's chin. "You *will* bring joy to your husband's bed and his family's fire and pride to our hearts for what you will do for your family. You will bring us roots in our old age and we will not go hungry." She reached her hand behind her daughter's head and touched her gently. "You are beautiful on your day. Your husband will forget he was asked to wait, he will be so pleased to see you. It will be as it should be," she said, with finality.

"If only we can find that bundle," Auntie Magpie sang out, spoiling the moment, beginning to rustle about once again.

The music seemed louder now and Kása, entering, had to speak more loudly over it. "What holds it up, then?" Kása said, puffing. She trundled into the dressing area bearing a huge basket before her like a last-minute pregnancy. With a grunt, she delivered the basket to the dirt floor revealing her skinny body dressed in a freshly tanned hide, covered with beads. Deep lines like rivers flowed down either side of the island of her mouth. She looked upset. But I had begun to understand that Kása always looked upset.

"We're looking for the bundle with Sunmiet's veil," Bubbles said lazily, coming in behind her, as though there was no hurry. "Do you have it?"

Kása looked briefly at the chubby girl she claimed as granddaughter, scowled. "Who would trust you with something so precious?" she said, looking into her woven basket filled to overflowing with stacks of homemade gifts of bags, smaller baskets, food utensils, and supplies. She shook her head. Three younger girls poured through the opening carrying baskets as well, filling the already cluttered space with women and woven things. Kása scanned the bounty of their baskets. They too were filled only with the gifts for the wedding dinner.

"You should have taken care of it yourself," Kása told her daughter.

The drumming music increased its pace.

"It is not here, then," Morning Dove said, her voice holding a mixture of regret and alarm. Then deciding said, "We must find another way. Let me think on it."

Kása, Morning Dove's auntie, clucked at her the way Morning Dove sometimes did her own daughter. "What way is there? The drums beat faster. There's no time now. She will have to marry without it." She shook her head. "It will be a stain."

Morning Dove ignored her. "It should look like purifying water cascading over her head, covering the part in her hair, her eyes and face, down to her throat, until she is joined...." She was thoughtful, stepping over Kása's negative view that nothing could be done. She scanned the baskets, seeking a solution. Something of what Morning Dove said triggered my memory and my eyes roamed the room looking for a particular basket I'd noticed during the search.

The drumming grew more forceful, the wedding singers' voices more piercing in the August air.

Finding it, I reached into a bundle of buckskin laces, inhaling the smoky fragrance and pulled out a mass of fine sinew threads and thin, feathery light, white buckskin lengths. "Can we use these?" I said, holding them cascading over my fingers. "Tie knots along each length, to look like beads of water, string some wild grapes—"

"And antler beads. And dentilium. Yes! I saw them somewhere," Morning Dove said, excited now. "Quickly. Bubbles, Auntie," she said, directing, "you and Huckleberry Eyes take these and tie the knots. Leave space for beads and berries we will tie with sinew. You," she spoke to the younger girls, "go bring two handfuls of plump grapes. But almost dried so they will not stain," she called out to them as they scurried out the door. "Quickly! Quickly."

"It will not work," Kása said, dropping her bird-like bones onto a pile of blankets off to the side. She adjusted her colorful kerchief, wiggled her bottom into the blankets before resting her scowl on me.

Morning Dove pulled the beaded necklace she wore off over her head. "We will use this too," she added tenderly fingering the intricate design of the white bird beaded onto a brilliant blue circle of sparkling cut beads. "With a branch of red willow around this." She set the perfect circle on her daughter's head. "From which we'll hang the laces and the beads." Her lips pursed in approval. "I will ask your father to get the willow, now," she told Sunmiet. "We will make your own veil, from the things of this place and your life, made with your family and your friends." She looked at me before she slipped out the doorway, "It will be a new tradition, from both Indian and non."

Sunmiet's veil was exquisite, even if it was conceived in part by a non-Indian. Having never seen what one should look like, I truly enjoyed the finished product put together by the women those last minutes before the ceremony. Our fingers worked in eel speed and just as smoothly until Morning Dove placed the beaded work on her daughter's head and led her out to her husband-to-be.

The two were married, then, at He-He, "laughing," there beside the Warm Springs River that bubbles out of the mountain called Jefferson. Standing Tall looked as a grown man with his breastplate covering his dark chest and his beaded arm bands accenting his strength. He wore new buckskin leggings and soft moccasins. I noticed he raised his eyebrows in question as he looked at Sunmiet's veil. We heard some chattering behind fingertips from the wedding guests.

Then Standing Tall smiled at his bride, held her hands gently as she smiled back. They stood that way, as though none of us were even in their presence while the elders sang the prayers and spoke the words over them that would join them forever. It seemed to me Sunmiet had come to some peace about him for she had never looked happier.

Just as the words ended, Sunmiet's parents and Standing Tall's parents came forward carrying a Hudson Bay blanket. Standing behind the couple, they wrapped the blanket around their shoulders, swaddling them together as though babies ready for their cradleboards. There was much laughing and giggling and more words were spoken in their language, and only later did I learn that their families had truly joined them together with the blanket embrace.

The wedding exchange had already taken place, a few weeks before. One beaded bag made by Sunmiet's family equal to three Hudson Bay blankets brought by the family of Standing Tall. Sunmiet's family offered many gifts made by their own hands. Tanned hides, baskets, beaded bags, dried fruit and salmon to better furnish the cooking place of Standing Tall's mother. His family offered store-bought goods, from Muller's store or the agency, as was the custom. Blankets and calico and tools and things purchased with the tradegoods of Standing Tall's family and dried venison, to show that he could provide.

After the exchange, dozens of guests had sat as they did now, on willow mats, to eat salmon, venison, *piaxi, lukus,* wild celery, and finally huckleberries, in that order, the way Sunmiet's people believe the Creator gave them the food. We began and ended with *chuush*, "water," always with the life-giving water.

Morning Dove had cooked for days with her family to prepare the meals, grateful to be higher in the mountains where the nights were cool when wearing buckskins brought unwanted perspiration. Sunmiet's younger cousins, both boys and girls, served the food and everyone ate until they were full.

Many people, more than those I'd spent time with at the river, sat around the circle on the mats, eating. "Sahaptin-speaking Warm Springs people and more Wascos, tribes put together by the treaty whether they wished it or not," Koosh told me handing me a bowl of steaming *piaxi* that reminded me of potatoes. "They thought we would kill each other off. We have fooled them and we get along, in our way."

On the other side of me sat George "Washington" Peters, explaining, pronouncing. A quiet boy, he and Sunmiet had ridden three days before to fetch me. George had said almost nothing during the long ride from Fifteen Mile Crossing to the reservation letting Sunmiet talk about family history inspired by a view of Mutton Mountains or the river. But during the ceremony and after, at the dinner and the pow wow, it was George who seemed to know before I even asked what I might be wondering about. Like the change in music, the meaning of the songs, how the dancers competed with the drummers, anticipating the final beat that to my untrained ears seemed abrupt, unplanned. He talked about "old ways."

"Some do not believe non-Indians should even witness our ceremonies," he told me leaning back on his elbows, chewing a long strand of grass. "'They will steal them as they have stolen our land', they say." He was thoughtful as we lounged on the striped wool blanket. His face was a sharp profile against the dusk, like it had been cut with Mama's sharpest scissors. "You will dance?" he asked as people formed two circles. "An honor dance, to shake the hands of the family of Sunmiet and Standing Tall who are joined this day."

He pulled me forward into the circle and led me, toe-heel, toe-heel. I hugged Sunmiet when I reached her in the inner circle, lingered in her embrace. She would go away now, to the lodge of Standing Tall's family and I did not know how much more of her I'd see.

"Who can blame them?" George continued after the dance as though we had not interrupted our conversation. I fidgeted, wondering who might wish me gone from the circle. Standing Tall perhaps? He did not like how non-Indians were changing his world. "Sunmiet wished your presence," George said as though reading my thoughts. "So you will always be welcome. It is why her father asked the agent to speak with your father, to have you join her on this day of her beginning."

It must have been quite a conversation. Mama told me later, when I came in from the potato field, that Sunmiet's father and the Indian agent had been there, spoken with Papa. As she and I pulled weeds from the herb garden, she said: "The agent was headed to The Dalles, to the Fort I'd say, and stopped by as a favor to Eagle Speaker." She brushed the hair from her eyes and left a smudge of garden dirt on her forehead. "So. You'll attend Sunmiet's wedding." Her voice held a strange quality.

Anyway, you could have knocked me over with a whiff of basil so stunned I was to hear they would agree to such a thing since I had wounded Papa greatly with my sassy talk that day with Mr. Sherar. Mama said something about "teaching the heathens" and must have justified my going by assuming they would learn from me. Instead, I learned from them.

Now, in the midst of all the joy and learning as part of Sunmiet's wedding, I decided I must have been forgiven for what had transpired those months before, when I first defied my father.

Joseph did not buy Puddin' that day, of course, or any other. Papa would never have permitted that. Joseph would never have negotiated such a transaction "with a child." But my offer, coming when it did, did the damage by itself, forcing my father to see me as something more than just his child.

"They all belong to me!" Papa bellowed that day. "I'll not have a child of mine seize the moment to make herself above her elders!"

"He's mine," I said, and did not whine. "You gave him to me. I choose to sell him. Now." A huge silence seemed to fill the air around our home, settling onto us like a scratchy, suffocating blanket.

Papa started toward me, enraged by the turn of events that day and by my defiance. I hunched my shoulders in anticipation of a blow almost deserved by my betrayal. I stood my ground, glaring at him. Baby George looked up, his eyes big in question. He turned, as I did, and Mama and Papa too, when Joseph spoke.

"I'll not buy from the child," he said, speaking with his deep voice like a man who could bite rocks for breakfast. "You've no need to spend your anger on her." He called the kelpie and the little dog left Baby George's side, scurried to Joseph, and sat straight-backed in the dust before him. Joseph squatted as though idly patting the dog while keeping a wary eye on Papa.

Papa had halted mid-stride. I think he would have challenged Joseph, believing he would take my bait, but Joseph's lowering himself and patting the dog took the edge off a moment stretched out with tension. Papa's outrage exhaled to mere irritation.

Joseph stood to take the reins Benito offered him. "We'll make other arrangements," he said to Papa. Then of me he said, "Your daughter has a kind heart. I thank her for her wish to sweeten a deal gone sour." He held the reins and swung his lanky body up onto the saddle with grace and agility rarely seen in so big a man. "Perhaps," he added, patting his thigh for the kelpie to leap to, "when she is older, we will meet again. Under gentler terms. And I shall return the favor."

He touched his hat to Papa, Mama, with barely a glance. Then he looked at me, took his hat off, held it to his chest for just a heartbeat, smiled and nodded once in my direction and then rode out.

I heard what he said, watched what he did, and believed, young and inexperienced as I was, that he had spoken to my soul.

Mama and Papa had their own words after Joseph and Benito left. A kind of seething expectation descended on our home, like the rattle on a wet snake. I learned in bits and pieces that the mules had been committed in a card game or somehow mortgaged; Papa had never found a way to tell my Mama. He hoped Joseph would simply not return and thus avoid the confrontation.

J. W., old enough to be my Papa, arrived one fine morning that same week to "smile at a grasshopper" he teased, and take the mules off. Mama, furious, kept a cool distance from my father for some days thereafter. She had counted on the sale more than the integrity of her commitment to Joseph; and with

Papa's choices, had lost both on one spring morning. I learned something about the strain of business deals bogged down in the muck of poor decisions and the accompanying boil that could split a union if allowed to fester.

Joseph was fairly well occupied after he left us, changing his life.

"The Army, um. It has need for cattle," French Louie told Joseph and Benito when they arrived back in The Dalles. They stood together in front of the livery, desperately watching another pack string make its way to the Deschutes.

"They've a wait," Joseph said of the string. "At least we have the high water going for us. We're all stuck for a while yet." He cursed himself for not bringing more mules from California, wondered how quickly he could get the word to those left south, perhaps to Philamon, to buy up more and head north. This whole adventure was curdling like sour milk before his eyes as he tried to recall the strong feeling that had initially led him to commit to all these changes.

"You do not listen, my friend," French Louie persisted. "The Army. Needs cattle. Will buy. My sources, they say the Indian agent, he makes the trip for fresh beef in few weeks. The tribes, um, do not eat well this winter. Many cattle die. Deer, elk, too, are thin. High water hurts the spring run of the Chinook. So they look for beef soon." He picked at his fingernails with the knife as he talked, popping little pieces of nail onto the boards in front of the livery office.

"It will bring some cash?" Benito asked.

"Oh, yes," Louie said. "Or maybe some Army script. For trade." He pushed the knife back into his leg sheath.

"Only trade I'd be looking for is beef for mules," Joseph said listening to the hammering of a building going up down the street. "Do they have mules, Louie? That would make your sources worth their weight in dust."

The Frenchman grinned. "I see some fine animals in the paddocks, my friend. You want I should explore?"

"I want," Joseph said.

And thus was the pack string of Joseph Sherar put together that spring of 1862. It began a year of lucrative activity for Joseph. His crew of men already knew and trusted each other which gave his venture a head start even with skinny, unknown animals and the other packers leaving first. Half the success of any venture is finding people to share it with you, willing to ride the roads of peaks and valleys that come with great ideas. Joseph had that in Benito and his family and he was adding men like French Louie as he moved.

The Army mules rounded out the string of forty mules, two lead men, and one cook, Benito's Anna, who rode a gray bell mare. They set off to Canyon City in early May. At the mouth of the Deschutes, they loaded their supplies of pick-axes, beans, flour, shoes and shirts, and even wheelbarrows onto rafts manned sometimes by the Celillo band of Indians who fished on the Columbia. They swam the mules across. Joseph kept an eye out for the bell mare not just for Anna's protection. The tinkling bell on that gray horse would lure the herd bound mules. And keep the cook happy.

Reloaded, they headed south, following The Dalles' military road, or trail, such as it was, making their way to the Strawberry Mountains, Canyon City, the gulches, gold fields, mines, and men.

It took little for people to see the quality Joseph packed with him. He sold his goods for top prices and carried gold dust out promising security by his demeanor and air of integrity. He learned of other stringers' problems: skirmishes with Indians, incompetent handlers, lost animals and packs, and highway men without conscience. He even encountered J. W. once and thought he recognized Jackson, one of our old mules, our last encounter drifting gently to his mind.

Mostly, he heaved sighs of satisfaction each night he and Benito and the kelpie shared the lush aroma of Anna's tortillas on the trail.

He helped make Brayman a wealthier man.

He helped himself to that condition making several trips that summer and fall: into the gold fields as far as Idaho, back out to The Dalles. I kept hoping to see him the few times I rode with Papa to The Dalles. I never did.

Joseph said he spent the seasons hoping for a shorter, better route between The Dalles and Canyon City, one with less difficulty in crossing at the mouth, one that would take less time. He thought that finding one would finally grant him the restless peace that escaped him. He thought, too, of the falls, he told me. Too late, he learned that John Todd, owner of the land beside the Deschutes had sold it to Lodenma's brother-in-law, Robert Mays. Mays hoped to build again across the river, his efforts leaving Joseph wistful.

On each packing trip, he'd vary his route a bit, take scouting forays he said, looking for that perfect route though I suspect it was variety, avoiding boredom, that truly moved him. He'd ride through painted sand country south of an area known as Black Rock where the hills wore rainbows of color. Often, he loaded his packs with rocks with imprints of leaves, ran his wide fingers over the image of tiny animals somehow left there. "Fossils," he called them. Led to many a lively discussion in the saloons and later, with Pastor Condon in The Dalles who shared Joseph's special interest in the rocks.

Frankly, it seemed to me he inhaled the scent of wild roses and sage in places that did not promise a shorter, safer road. Instead, they promised intrigue and interest and substance for his sketch book. And new paths.

Joseph might have stayed at packing, still searching, I suspect if it had not been for that one scouting trip near Canyon City and the events that ultimately changed his lifecourse, as surely as Sunmiet had just changed hers.

CHAPTER 17

CELEBRATION

"BANDIT!" JOSEPH CALLED. "Here, Bandit!" He kicked the big gelding closer to the fracas but the horse was edgy, didn't want to approach. "What snakes is that dog wakin' anyway?" he said to his horse as much as to himself, a wary relief at hearing anything from the dog at all. He could hear the ruckus beyond the thick undergrowth, the single bark in spurts and the snapping jaws of the kelpie coming up against some other guttural, feral sound.

He stepped off his horse, pulled his rifle from the scabbard and waited, isolating the noises. He pushed back the branches of the buckbrush, searching. A light breeze billowed out the striped sleeves of his shirt, ruffed the wool of his brocade vest.

A few hours before, Joseph had planned to head back into Canyon City, the afternoon wearing hot under the October sky, the evening promising to come on cool as it did in the high country. He had ridden along the top of a rocky ridge of white stones that seemed to typify the Strawberry Mountains. Tiny clusters of red lichen chiseled their way through the stony ground like the fine cracks in Philamon's old ironstone plates. Joseph wondered if the ground was as brittle.

As he rode, he picked up signs of little used trails and understood why they were abandoned when they ended in deep ravines and ledges dropping away to boulders and brush below.

The afternoon brought no new insights to a shorter route. He'd not even stopped to sketch. Something about the area seemed vaguely familiar. He hadn't ridden that way before, he was sure. And would not be likely to again.

Instead, he'd planned to head back.

Then the kelpie disappeared.

He and Bandit had ridden inland, away from the edge of the ridge, away from the rocky ledges. And then Bandit simply vanished, leaving no sounds of his panting, no rustle in the brush. Joseph had called and called, listened for the stir of the kelpie wrestling through the snags and tangles of branches, hoped to hear his sharp bark, surprised at how attached he'd come to the little dog, how dislodged the dog's disappearance made him feel.

He'd called until his voice was hoarse, then listened to the hot stillness. Nothing. He'd called until the late afternoon wind came up, then listened to the breeze in the pines and the junipers. Nothing. He called until the night breeze ceased and his eyes looked into a silent dusk before he admitted that the kelpie was lost.

He considered leaving his vest somewhere in a clearing, hoping the dog might come to it. He decided better to simply make a camp, a small fire, and spend the night himself, continue looking in the morning.

That's when he heard the ruckus.

Night always asked to stay up late in the summer of the mountains, and now, just enough pale light gave Joseph hope that he could see something, see well enough to shoot if necessary, depending on what he found beyond the tangles.

Easing himself through the thicket, barely aware of his horse's agitation, he let his eyes adjust to the growing dark, focused on the growling, a kind of hissing whine, hoping his scent would scare off whatever Bandit had attracted.

"Bandit," he said, speaking quietly when he spied the dog, neck hair bristling. "Easy, Bandit," he said, stepping back, his arms clear of the buckbrush, his eyes moving upward to the low branches of a Hackberry tree growing crookedly from the side of a rocky ledge. "Easy, Bandit," he repeated when he spied Bandit's challenge hunched on the branch, taut muscles, claws and jaws poised for disaster. "Easy, Bandit," he whispered bringing the Sharps to his shoulder taking aim at the cat.

The blast echoed through the still night and Joseph swore he saw the cougar drop before the red lichen gave way at his feet crumbling the side of the ridge with an avalanche of rock.

Joseph fell as in slow motion, a kind of stillness filling up his soul despite the roar of rock that seemed to flow like an ocean wave around him, drowning him, taking his breath. A hundred thoughts rushed through his head at once, not jumbled, not sequential, wondering if he hit it, if he'd die, what's the purpose in it all.

Then the thud, the crack of bones, the air pushed out from lungs, the rush of dust so thick he could not catch his breath, the sense of being driven into earth and rock like a spear spiked into soil; the knowledge that he lived followed by the pain, searing, piercing pain. Then silence.

It has always been my feeling that people truly bonded felt a special sense together: that parents knew when their children hurt though they were out of sight; that good friends often posted letters to each other on the same day though they lived a thousand miles apart. But when I learned of the day of Joseph's fall, I could recall no sense of him at all. And so I have concluded that while I may have intuition about which wrangler plans to want his pay cut earlier than most or which friend is now with child, I am not clairvoyant. Joseph's falling taught me that.

I celebrated my fourteenth birthday on the eleventh of October, Joseph's fateful day, and had a fine day of it at that. Mama let me have a party after church and Luther came, and others whom I would go to school with when it began later that month. Lodenma brought along her Beatrice and her youngest, William. Her husband "jawed" with Papa, and Mama engaged her with talk of recipes and wish book items from the catalog. Luther's mother was there, still repeating the ends of phrases of whatever Mama said, her head bobbing in agreement. We were joined later by Papa's partner, J. W. Case. Mama was civil to him, I noticed, but then, she always was at her entertaining best.

Lodenma and I talked a while of growing up. Maybe it was knowing Sunmiet was married and already with child that set me thinking in those terms. Maybe it was seeing Mr. Case and knowing he was packing into Canyon City which put the Californian into my growing-up thoughts.

Lodenma wanted no talk of her marriage; she wanted to be a child again and perhaps later, talk of mine.

So we played stick ball, over Mama's protest. Our dresses flounced, scaring up our pantaloons as we ran the bases having hit the leather ball stuffed tight with coarse horse hair. The boys shouted as much for our running, I think, as in surprise that we could hit the ball!

Luther looked on in open admiration when I struck the leather and hiked my skirts up, not afraid to run, slide into base, and dirty up the satin bow that bounced behind me. I was amazed I could run and breathe at the same time!

"I think he fancies you," Lodenma said, breathless as our team moved out to catch the hits of Luther's team.

"Luther?" I asked.

"Do you like him or not?"

"I have to think on it," I said, hoisting my bow around to the back.

Luther was still a kind boy, gentle. I'd even grown fond of him though that was not a word I would have used just then. He was comfortable, like a brother. Even the kiss he'd stolen earlier in the summer had seemed a simple thing, friendly, without intention. I had been talking about Mama's new modified poke bonnet, fashion being something that, oddly, seemed to interest Luther. I used my hands to describe it in the air. He'd stepped closer—I thought to better see—bent his face to mine and kissed me. I simply kept on talking, never missed a word. We both just acted as though two other people had entered our bodies for the moment and done something neither he nor I knew anything about.

"You'd best think hard and fast," Lodenma said, interrupting my thoughts. "I hear your papa's been talking with Luther's papa and an agreement's being hatched sure as the crickets'll sing tonight."

I felt my chest tighten and the bee sting in my stomach. "I'll tell them I'm too young," I said. "Not ready."

"You'll tell your papa plenty from what I hear," she answered as we separated in the outfield. Then over her shoulder added, "It won't make no difference once he decides you're old enough. And you are fourteen. Isn't that what this day's all about?"

I watched Luther as he came up to bat. Lanky, his feet still looking like the anchors of an un-sturdy ship, he settled himself into the ground, stepping his feet up and down, two or three times. He pulled on his hat, taking it off, putting it on. He lifted the bat, pointed it to the sky then down to the ground, once, twice, three times, his routine so excruciatingly predictable even Smithson, his friend finally yelled, "Hurry it, Luther, we've not got 'til spring!"

And in that moment, of watching this boy-man do each thing the same, perform each routine predictably with no hope of surprise, repeating his life the way his mother repeated her phrases, I gave up "comfortable" in my mind. I didn't know what I preferred instead, but "comfortable Luther" wasn't it.

I thought of the studious George, Sunmiet's friend, his curious, searching mind and liked the memory. Koosh, the brother of Standing Tall, came to mind, too. He had danced an owl dance with me at Sunmiet's wedding and I remember looking up at him, felt the firmness of his hand around my waist, the confidence of a young man asking a non-Indian to share his steps in front of elders who might not approve of his decision. Both were much more interesting than Luther, it seemed to me, though much less likely to share my life.

I even thought of Standing Tall, his wild impulsiveness and daring and his protective ways and wondered if that's what Sunmiet found appealing enough, after all, to marry him. Or did she do so mostly because her parents had it all planned out?

And, of course, I considered the tall Californian, who seemed to blend all those qualities of the young men I had encountered who had the added advantage of making me feel older, wiser, and sassier, all at the same time.

The game over, Lodenma walked with me, arm through mine, to the house where Mama served a light cake. Called "angel food" she'd drizzled maple syrup frosting over it, receiving "oohs and ahs" just as she planned, taking some attention from my day as she often did.

Still it would have been the perfect day—a girl does not turn fourteen but once—if not for Papa's announcement.

Joseph's view came through eyes caked with dust and shrouded with pain. Heeled into the avalanche of rock like shoots waiting to be planted, he was upright, at an angle, all except his head entombed in chunks of granite and branches and black dirt and chalky dust.

He breathed even, uncluttered except for pressure of the tightness of his new-sprung tomb. He could move his head left and right without much pain. The fingers of both his hands wiggled though buried beside him. His legs were the worry. He could move his toes on the right leg. But even the thought of moving his left leg sent pain racing up his thigh and back to an explosion inside his head. So, the left leg was damaged and then for just a fleeting moment he wondered why it mattered since he'd probably not be freed of his surprise sepulcher before dying anyway.

From high above him, thirty feet or more, on what was left of the ledge, he heard Bandit bark. He could not see the dog and efforts to move his head around that far produced a numbing he did not want to repeat. He tried his voice. "Bandit!" Coughing up dust, he tried again. "Bandit! Here boy!" It was a whisper.

He could hear the little dog whimpering and didn't know if it was pain or being so far away from his master that brought the sounds. He called again and heard skittering sounds, then silence. Looking out from his forced grave, Joseph tried to orient himself. Too dark. He felt shivery though the night had not yet cooled. The injuries, he concluded, his body already shutting down. Through the limited dusk light, he made out the forms of trees, shrubs. He saw no evidence of his horse and hoped the ledge break had been far enough out that the horse was safe and perhaps even now on its way back into the livery at Canyon City. Someone might come looking for him, trail him back, if his route was noticed and a good tracker available. He didn't see the carcass of the cat but it, like Joseph, could well be buried beneath the avalanche of rock. Taking a last look around before darkness settled, he remembered Peter's Indian word for "help me": *páwapaatam*. He couldn't believe he remembered it! Little good it did him. No one to hear it, his voice too parched to speak it. It was amazing he should even recall it. He wondered if he'd be alive in the morning.

He told me later that he prayed. I don't know what it is about a man that makes him hesitate to say he prays, like not wanting to admit he needs instruction when he does. Anyway, he remembered a psalm: "The steps of a good man are ordered by the Lord... Though he fall, he shall not be utterly cast down for the Lord upholds him with His hand." And a verse from Chronicles pierced his thoughts and became his prayer. "It's your battle. You know I'm here. You know why. And if I'm to be still here in the morning, then make there be a way to get me out," he bargained. "Otherwise, I'd appreciate a speedy trip to heaven's gate."

His eyelids were heavy. His whole body shook with cold chills, keeping blessed sleep from him. He heard rustling to his left, scraping sounds, and then light pressure as he smelled the breath of the kelpie, close.

The dog licked his face, laid down, became a muffler of fur curled around Joseph's head and neck. "Keep me warm, huh, Bandit," Joseph coughed. "We'll see who wakes up first on the wrong side of the bed." The kelpie whined and panted then fell asleep. Warmed, Joseph stole his own fitful sleep from the silence.

"We've some special presents for you, Janie," Papa said, all expansive on my birthday, happy with the growing evening and his limited imbibing. He stood beside Luther in the comfort of the main room as we circled the leftover cake. Luther's face was reddening and I stole a look at Lodenma, whose wink at me caught my breath up short. Not *now!* I thought. *Not him!* I prayed all the while noting that even the announcement of my destiny with Luther seemed destined to be predictable.

"Janie," Papa said. "This here's an important day for you. Turning fourteen, having your friends around you." He patted Luther on the back, looked around at Lodenma and others gathered there; J. W., too. "And I have the privilege of making it even more special." He smiled at me, pulled me closer to him, hugging me.

"J. W.?" Papa said inviting his partner forward. "Would you like to propose a toast on this occasion?"

J. W. grinned. He had legs so bowed a pig could run through them without touching either side. Those legs took him now to the front. "Don't mind if I do," he said. "Everyone got their ginger ale? Good."

Papa smiled and looked out over the gathering, prolonging my worst fears. "Go ahead," he encouraged.

J. W. cleared his throat once or twice and, considering the looks on people's faces, committed some social impropriety when he began his toast with: "Here's to swimmin' with bowlegged women and divin'—"

"No no no!" Papa sputtered. The men chuckled, Mama looked aghast, Lodenma blushed, and J. W. just seemed perplexed.

"Never mind, J. W.," Papa continued, more formal. "My girl here, is just as sweet as any future bride to be," he said to me, patting my shoulder. My friends and the others gathered, chuckled, seemed to know what was coming.

"Today," he continued, "someone has asked for my daughter's hand in marriage. He noted that she is a fine young woman, which she is." People murmured politely. "Her skills with mules are without equal. She sets a fine table and she has weathered well these hot Oregon days to be the fine looking young woman she is." Everyone applauded politely to my growing embarrassment. "And I've consented to this offer of marriage." I looked across Papa at Mama standing on the other side of him, just beyond Luther. She brushed at the folds in her skirt ignoring my stare. Luther wore a dazed look, like he didn't know why he was standing there so close to J. W. and Papa who continued.

"He has offered to look after our only girl." He choked a bit on *only*. "He's promised to keep her not too far from her mother's house. He brings his considerable resources to this marriage bed, and I believe my daughter will be well tended."

Considerable resources? Luther didn't have that much nor did his parents, I didn't think. But before I had the opportunity to sort that out, Papa sorted first.

"With great pleasure I announce the betrothal of my daughter, Jane, to my good friend and partner, J. W. Case. J. W.?" he finished, turning the stunned silence over to him.

Mr. Case held a glass of ginger ale in his hand and I noticed, idly as he lifted his glass to me, that he had dirt beneath his nails. I wondered what the "J. W." stood for, what on earth this could mean?

Mama had looked annoyed by J. W.'s attempt at a toast. Now, genuine surprise formed the "Oh" on her lips as J. W. moved to stand between me and Papa, his arm slipped awkwardly around my shoulders.

She could have looked no more surprised, however, than I.

Just being alive surprised Joseph. As light eased into the day like a reluctant relationship, he could see how his condition had permitted him to live. The angle he'd been driven into the debris forced the heavier rocks from his chest and legs. Smaller rocks, heavy, pebbled earth, and split branches shrouded him, kept him pinned but without the pressure of boulders to crush his breathing. "I'll probably die of starvation," he said out loud, surprised at the still raspy whisper of his voice.

He noticed some of the red lichen clinging desperately to a fragment of white stone and replayed what had happened in his mind: the ruckus, the kelpie and the cat, the rifle blast which he decided came after he had begun to feel the earth give way beneath his feet. Nothing he could have done differently.

Still, he was alive and he wondered why. Was there some purpose he had yet to accomplish? Had he been stubborn as a mule about something and this was God's way of getting his attention? Was there a point to catastrophe besides just bad timing? "Did I just draw the low card in this cut?" he said.

His words woke the kelpie who eased himself from around Joseph. He gently slipped down the angled tomb, stretched, tail wagging to the air, panting through a happy, tongue-washed smile. Closer to where Joseph's feet must be buried, the kelpie stood looking up, his tongue dripping, waiting for his sleepy master to get up. He barked once.

"Not this morning," Joseph said. The kelpie cocked his head sideways, back and forth, confused by the hoarse voice emitting from the rocks, the lack of movement.

Joseph assayed his condition in the daylight. He noticed that his right hand might be worked free. This he did, with effort, the kelpie even getting into the act, digging with his paws, dirt skittering out between his short legs until he'd made an impression deep enough to lay in, and did. "No, Bandit!" Joseph said. "Off!"

The dog moved reluctantly as Joseph's free hand finally grabbed one of the branches that blocked most of his view, pushing it out of sight. Almost immediately he was sorry. First, because pain from the effort raced up his leg and back as he moved and secondly, because too late, he realized he could have used the branch to dig with. "Not thinking clearly," he said.

The effort fatigued him. He closed his eyes to rest, listening. Crows called in the distance. A breeze rustled the branches of nearby trees. He heard the kelpie panting, closely. Efforts to stay alive seemed futile. He felt tears burn behind his nose and he swallowed. Perhaps these were the last details he would ever experience. It seemed a bitter irony to him that he who had a great vision to come west, do something extraordinary, make a difference in the world, should die alone, in the midst of rocks, having accomplished little in his life, having shared nothing of real import, not having caught his dream.

He had played his cards, won several hands. He'd finally lost the game and would be going home early. He'd likely not live to celebrate his thirtieth birthday. He slept.

When he awoke, he had no idea of how long he'd been asleep. The scent of pungent earth came to him along with the smell of something rotten. The air was still and he noticed a deer moving on porcelain legs down the ravine. She passed below him without noticing either him or the kelpie who slept at his feet. Joseph's mouth tasted like wool.

As the deer moved on out through the junipers and thickets of manzanita and buckbrush, Joseph recalled something familiar. Was it the deer? The terrain? Perhaps just the peacefulness of the deer's presence. He couldn't place it.

He thought about his family, his friends. He wondered if they'd recognize his body when found, perhaps months or even years from now. His turquoise bola might give him away. And his leather-bound sketch book, should they dig it out. He wished he'd sketched more, wished he'd written more to his mother, wished he'd read more, acted on things he considered rather than simply compiling them into a list in his mind. He wondered if people close to dying made bargains with God, offered commitments should they survive. His would be to act more on what he felt. Like pursuing the feelings associated with the Herbert girl and coming to some settling about what he wanted for the rest of his life.

The breeze picked up, warmer, like it might be mid-afternoon. He smelled the rotten scent again, thinking he'd killed the cat after all. The carcass could bring vultures to peck on his head. Or coyotes. He hoped the rotten smell was not his own.

He grunted at that thought, winced, remembered other events connected with strong scents like the day he encountered the reptile pile. "She'd not be too pleased to know I associate bad scents with her," he said to the kelpie. "Wonder what sassy thing she'll say when I tell her that?" Talking hurt his voice, even in the whisper he'd just mustered.

The thought of me and of having what was happening be part of his past, encouraged him, he remembered. That, and the faint smell of smoke.

Smoke! Someone might be close. Or was it the smell of flaming forest, a disaster burning his way? "Hello!" he attempted to shout. Only a hoarse whisper came out. He heard nothing but began digging frantically with his free hand, the pain causing him to stop and start. He lifted his nose to the breeze.

Campfire, he thought, excited. Perhaps not too far off. He did not smell the smoke again. He tried to call, his voice barely projecting loud enough to wake the dog.

Bandit had been roused by his activity and now began to bark. Short barks, with a listening pause between. Joseph heard nothing in the pauses and he did not smell the smoke consistently, but the dog never wavered once he began his staccato bark. He kept it up, as though sending a signal: a yip, pause; yip, pause; yip, pause; yip.

Suddenly, Bandit rushed down the rock tomb and disappeared into the brush. Joseph felt a moment of panic. The dog continued its steady barking cadence in the distance for what seemed like hours until it scrambled back through the shrubs to Joseph's sight.

"Good boy," Joseph said, realizing how much the dog's presence comforted him. He tried to pat the dog, but Bandit slipped beyond his grasp, kept up his yipping cadence, this time facing the underbrush instead of Joseph until both heard the sounds of movement: some large animal stomped just beyond.

Bandit increased his barking, scuttled out through the underbrush again, returned and stood a wary guard, back to Joseph's tomb, hair raised, until the brush parted.

Legs and the chest of a horse came first. Then Joseph saw the man.

Joseph had a moment to study him as the man tried to locate why the dog barked at the base of a pile of rocky debris. Tall, blond, he looked vaguely famil-iar. Like his mother's milk toast, Joseph thought, the realization bringing back the man and the event. "Turner!" he said in his whisper.

The man looked, isolated the sound. He seemed healthier than the day more than a year ago when Joseph had given dried venison to a hungry man and his family.

"Lordy, Lordy!" Turner said, finally locating Joseph's head in the rocks. "Couldn't figure out that barkin' sound. Knew no coyote yipped like that." He had dismounted quickly, grabbed his hide canteen and bent now, holding Joseph's head gently to the moisture. Sweet water dribbled from the corners of Joseph's mouth making paths in the dust. "Thought I recognized that funny looking dog when he come out through the brush," he said. "Couldn't figure why he'd be here."

Joseph closed his eyes, relishing the sweetness of the water. "Thank you," he said.

"Don't thank me," Turner said, still kneeling beside him.

"Then the dog," Joseph said, resting his head back onto the dirt.

Turner looked at him. "I was thinking Someone higher," he said. "He's what led me this way. Hadn't planned to be up this ravine looking for scrubs, least not 'til next week or so. Figured this was too close to home to worry about."

"I thank him," Joseph said, "More than you can know."

Turner nodded his approval. "Let's see if we can get you out of here," he said next, surveying Joseph's condition. "Francis'll look after you while I get the Chinese doc. Let my little ones romp around you while you wait, keep you up half the night. But you've prob'ly had enough rest," he said, smiling, "laying around like you have."

Joseph eased back while Turner began the slow process of removing the debris. He was aware now of the throbbing in his leg. He knew the trip to wherever would be painful, wasn't sure how badly his leg was damaged or if it would ever hold him to walk again. But he was alive, thanks to God. That was all that mattered at the moment. "I'll be thirty years old next month," he said. Turner's odd expression told him he was rambling as the man eased Joseph's mangled leg from the debris. Joseph didn't care. He had more than a birthday to celebrate.

CHAPTER 18

A FUTURE
AND A HOPE

FRANCIS TURNER WAS A SAINT long before she died. I never did meet her, but she became my rival just the same, one all the more difficult to compete with after her death. I covet the time she had with Joseph. Though he says I would not have liked him much those months—his recovery taxing his patience—I would have risked the encounter not to have later shared his memory with a saint.

The Turners' home sat on a ridge not far from Joseph's forced entombment. Archibald Turner whistled softly when he uncovered Joseph's left leg. Impaled on a sharp branch, Joseph's calf resembled a bloated cow before the knife was pulled to release the captured air. His knee looked oddly crooked too.

"Don't think I should try to take out the splinters," Turner told Joseph, looking up at him with wary eyes. "Just cut what I can and leave the wound plugged."

"Agreed," Joseph said wondering already about the infection, his own beginning fever, the chills that were turning to a clammy sweat now that his body was exposed to the air.

Turner made a sturdy travois of old hackberry branches and alders and eased Joseph onto it though as big a man as he was, Joseph had to sit up—more or less—to keep his leg from dragging in the dirt and shrubs. With no sign of

Joseph's gelding (or his Sharps), Turner led his own horse back to a trail wide enough to drag the travois through. Bandit trotted faithfully by his side.

Joseph could not recommend the trip. His leg, twisted at the knee with its open wound, throbbed until he felt nauseous. He passed out.

When he came to, the angel bent over him. Wisps of gold surrounded her narrow face, pug nose, and heart-shaped mouth, and blue eyes stared into his with worry and concern. Her hands were cool to the touch as she wiped his forehead leaving a lavender scent. As she leaned over him, Joseph realized she was with child.

He heard noises, little voices, and then "Shush, now!" as she turned to quiet four small children. "Mr. Sherar needs his rest," she told them. She coughed, as if to clear her throat. "And the dog does too, I suspect." He heard scrapes of little feet and then eight doe-like eyes in stair-steps gawked down at him in faces that were perfect replicas of their mother's. Bandit's head and front paws soon appeared on the edge of the bed. The cornhusks shifted within the comforter with the dog's weight.

"Our children," she said, with both apology and pride mixed in the introduction. She coughed, pressing her fingertips against her full lips. Then, "Cris, John, Martha, Susan Ella," she said touching each small head as she spoke. "We shorten the little one to 'Ella', but they're the same little imp." She coughed again. "The dog you know." Bandit panted happily, nuzzled Joseph's neck.

"You awake, Mister?" Susan Ella, the youngest asked, her face close to Joseph's, examining. She looked to be about five years old. She had two dimples in plump cheeks and the same blond curls, same blue eyes of her mother. "Can we play with your dog?"

"Little late for asking that. Dog's played out these past days," her mother told her. To Joseph she said in explanation. "He wouldn't stay outside. Just barked and barked when we put him on the porch, so we let him in." She coughed. "Didn't know his name. Children called him Weasel cause he wiggles so, and he comes."

Joseph smiled, tried to speak. His mouth felt like wool again, and Francis noticed, apologized, and offered him cool water. It tasted strange but the liquid was clear. "What's in it?" he asked, laying his head down with the help of Francis's hand.

"Herbs. From the Chinese doctor. You children, shoo now, go play with Weasel."

"Bandit," Joseph said. "His name is Bandit."

The children swarmed around Bandit, calling him correctly, running with him around the table in the center of the single large room.

"Some folks don't take with him," Francis continued, turning back to Joseph. "The Chinese doc," she said in explanation. "But he's made me feel better." She coughed again, harder, catching her breath. "I am better, really," she said to Joseph's wary eyes. She smiled at him. "I couldn't even sleep I coughed so hard." She set the empty cup down on the bedside table and added: "He's mixed a concoction to cut your fever and a poultice for your leg. See," she said, pulling the covers back, "he got the branch out and most of the splinters. I change the bandage twice a day. It's still weeping some, but now your fever's broke, I think you'll be all right." She coughed again, "In time."

Joseph watched the children playing with Bandit. The dog seemed to like the attention, didn't snap his jaws or run away. He behaved as though at home and Joseph wondered how long he'd been here in this simple house. Joseph felt weak, thought his legs looked bony, lacking muscle. He wondered when he'd eaten last; how he'd even stayed alive.

"How much time?" Joseph asked warily. "Or did he say?"

Francis shrugged her shoulders. "Several months if we can keep infection out. He set your leg, too. Good thing you were out. Just watching was enough to make me faint." She shivered.

"Several months?"

"It's a very bad injury," Francis defended. "He said you were fortunate just to be alive." She wiped his forehead with her cool fingers, looking into his blue eyes. "We'll take good care of you. Small return for your help for us. A few months will mean nothing. You'll see."

It was the exact same argument I attempted with my father and my intended. "A few months will mean nothing," I said, though I knew I'd be using the time to plan a way out for us all. I wasn't sure what was in this arrangement for Papa or for Mr. Case. Discovering it would be the key to my reprieve.

"Yes. Well. You should do as your father wishes," Mama said. We sat in the parlor a week after the celebration. Mama kept her eyes on her needlework, talking into her skirts.

"I want to do as Papa wishes," I said, my heart pounding, my own unfinished needlework resting on my linsey-woolsey. "I just want more time to do it." I pulled my shawl around my shoulders to ward off the morning chill.

J. W. sat next to me on the divan. "No need to fear, girl," J. W. said, patting my knee with a familiarity I did not prefer. "I'm an experienced man. Can take care of a little thing like you." He grinned revealing his tobacco-stained teeth. He stretched his long legs out in front of him like a comfortable cat, put his hands behind his head, making himself right at home. Mama lifted her eyes from her work, gave him one of her looks. He stared back. She out-looked him and he straightened, pulling his knees up and keeping his boots flat on the floor, his big hands now folded awkwardly in his lap. He rubbed his eye with one fist, waiting.

"Janie can hold her own," Papa said, rising to stand by the window, behind Mama sitting on the caned chair. "You're getting a real lady who will also be a helpmate for your business," he said to J. W.

Papa's observation gave me my opening.

"Right now, you're on the trails into Canyon City, aren't you Mister Case?" I asked, honey dripping from my tongue. It was the first time I'd spoken directly to him since our "betrothal" and I wished I hadn't noticed the dark hairs peering out from his nose, the large pockmarks on his cheeks. His face formed a distraction to my thinking.

"Just call me J. W., girl," he said, smiling at me. He started to pat my leg again but I tried one of Mama's looks and he returned his hand to his territory. Still, he seemed pleased I had at last spoken to him. "I leave again in the morning. With my fine set of animals, I might add, thanks to—"

"What's his packing got to do with waiting, Janie?" Papa asked quickly. I could tell by Papa's voice that he wanted to make this easier for me, give me some choice. I wondered what had happened to Lodenma's rumor about Papa promising me to Luther or what had transpired to bring in Mr. Case.

I improvised. "A wife wants time to know her husband, know his likes and dislikes, how to make him happy," I said. J. W. watched me like a dog watching a muskrat dive, with interest, wondering if he could catch me if he just plunged in.

"So the sooner the better?" he offered. "So's you can know me?"

"We could consider things in the spring," I said. "Give me the opportunity to sort the seeds, store them, have a cache for planting. Give me time to paddle flax and spin thread." I tried to think of things I needed to do to borrow time. "And court," I offered, looking as demure as I could.

"Child's right about that," Mama said, looking up. "No reason not to court. You owe us that much," she added, not letting reference to the mule deal slip by.

"Courting?" J. W. said as though just considering it. "What would that be, exactly?"

"Well. Time here," Mama said, smoothing her skirts, then clasping her hands over her needlework. "Perhaps some walks when you've a few days between trips. An exchange of pleasantries and some baubles. Every young girl likes baubles." She adjusted the snood at the back of her neck, primping.

"Not to mention baubles for the girl's mother," Papa said. He laughed. Mama did not join him.

J. W. was quiet and I could see he was a man who liked to do things right even if it meant depriving himself of some pleasures.

"It could be in spring," J. W. said thoughtfully. "And then you could join me on the trail. I'd be the envy of all them packers," he said, "wouldn't have to leave you at home. Them Mexicans take their women along and they eat real good!"

Mama frowned. "Doesn't seem a proper place for a lady," she said.

J. W. thought again. "Well, just once or twice," he said agreeing. "So she'll know what it's like for a man, know what comforts he'll be missing, and what to do to please—"

"It's settled then," Papa interrupted. He seemed annoyed with all the talk of sparking. "In the spring. March? April?"

"May," I said putting it off for as long as I could, batting my eyelashes again at J. W. He blushed. Then I hedged again. "We could *consider* it again. Come May."

"May, then," J. W. said. "And we begin the courtin' now."

"'For I know the plans I have for you, declares the LORD, plans for your welfare and not for calamity, to give you a future and a hope. Then you will call upon me and come and pray to me, and I will listen to you.' Jeremiah 29:11-13." Pastor Condon read the scripture at the New Year's Eve service taking us from 1862 to '63.

All the people did not take the chill from the old church, but the words lifted up my sinking spirits, warmed me, as nothing had for months. Sometimes I thought God's plan was to punish me for my judgment with the babies; sometimes I didn't think he cared about my life at all, so small a person was I.

The impending commitment Papa had made in my name hovered over me. I kept waiting for Divine Intervention or some worldly act to come between me and becoming Mrs. J. W. Case. I liked making things happen, not just waiting to see; but for this, the biggest change of my life, inaction crippled me. I was at a loss to make something happen.

On New Year's Eve I did pray. On the return from church in the back of the buckboard, with my feet resting on the hot stones, bundled up beneath the robe, I asked that what plans God had for my good and not my calamity would be revealed before May.

J. W.—who had been christened with only initials, one from both his father's and his mother's father's name—did not join us on New Year's Day. He had business to attend to "elsewheres."

When he visited The Dalles, he did not always come courting. When he did, he spent more time with Papa than with me discussing their business connections, inventions such as a new barbed fence, or the gold fields. Often asked into their presence, I was then ignored, becoming part of the furniture or scenery depending on the terrain. I imagined it might be so come May and then thereafter. My mind could wander in their presence, though, as it did within the potato patch and now the corn fields that I helped tend.

J. W. was not an unkind man, I noticed. He often brought me gifts, awkwardly handing one to me and another to Mama. She seemed more taken with her bolt of cloth or a pewter spoon than I with my hair ribbon or bright colored marbles. I decided that if I were married to this older man my life might be much the same as now. I might even remain in this house while J. W. packed every few months into the mountains. Or perhaps I'd move to another parlor where friends of my husband would gather and like now, I would simply serve. My marriage might change little of my life except who shared my bed. I'd be exchanging Baby George for grown-up snores.

My day dreams were still filled with many children, a house large enough to have dancing in the parlor surrounded by family and friends. J. W. did not seem the fathering type and I couldn't imagine dancing with him anywhere let alone in the parlor.

My night-time dreams still held a stranger with no face.

"A hope" as scripture promised, appeared in March. The sun warmed a wet earth. Yellow bells bloomed early, the winter having been so light of snow. I should have seen then the promise that always comes with spring. I saw it sure when J. W. said in passing to my Papa that he had heard the Californian had been located after all and "would recover." I had not known he was even lost and the thought of it punched a hole in my stomach.

"Staying with who?" Papa asked. We three were standing at the corrals, the men conversing, me listening, standing straight like the corner post I'd become.

"Some mudlark family with a passel of kids," J. W. said. He spit a stream of tobacco into the dirt. "Woman is a good-looker even if she is sickly. She and the Chinaman doc tended him all winter." He leaned on the corral fence, chewing a long arc of old grass the winter wind had not destroyed. It hung over his thin lip, bouncing beneath his mustache as he spoke. "Month before anyone knew for sure where he was. Almost lost his leg. That dog hate's you helped somehow. Lucky, that's what he is."

"Not so lucky," Papa said. "You got my mules." I noticed he didn't gloat over the observation as he might have the year before. I believe that being elected to public office buoyed Papa, made him less likely to stand on another in order to be taller himself. Perhaps his new perch as the county's commissioner permitted him to appreciate Joseph some. Afterall, he had not pursued the failed mule deal which might have brought to Papa both embarrassment and loss. Papa seemed only to have continued irritation with his actions to contend with still.

J. W. nodded. "His Mexicans—I know you don't think much of 'em,

George—but they kept his string going, like always, even before they knew Sherar lived. Just trusting, I guess."

My ears perked up at his name.

"You've talked with him?" Papa asked.

J. W. nodded. "Rode out to Turner's last month, looking at scrubs he'd corralled. Pitiful place." J. W. shook his head in amazement. "Kids running around chasing that funny-looking dog Sherar eats with. Dog worried their shoats some, lying in wait for them pigs then snapping at 'em. Woman looks puny but still carries a glow. Looks to me like she's the glue holding what little they have together. Turner don't give her much to glue that's for sure."

J. W. was thoughtful, remembering his visit. He took the grass he'd been chewing from his mouth, rolled it between his fingers. "Walks with a stick cane yet, but moving around. Funny thing is, he asked about my intended when I told him who it was," J. W. looked at me for the first time in the hour. "I told him she don't say much, but she's spoken for, come May." J. W. had a quizzical look on his face as he added, "Said a curious thing then."

"Yes?" Papa asked, looking at me.

"Said, 'Wonder what she'd think of April?' What'd you suppose that means?"

He wasn't asking me, but I blushed, knowing my answer was "grand."

Joseph's words to J. W. rolled around, repeated in my thoughts along with the few other times we'd shared a word, a look or two. Sometimes I wondered if I was dreamin' into make-believe, like I did when I was little; sometimes I knew exactly that his words meant he'd be coming for me, would find a way to save my May.

"It seems too early," Francis said between coughs. "More time will make the leg stronger. You'll have less limp."

"Don't care about the looks of it. Just need it to work well enough to hold me up and let me ride. It's good enough for that," Joseph told her. The Turner children circled his horse; Archibald Turner held the bridle and the gelding steady. Francis let Joseph steady himself with her frail shoulder before he eased himself from the tree stump onto the saddle. "Be awhile before I can mount without a step," he said, as he landed with a hard thump onto the gelding's back. He grimaced. "I'm here. Just have to plan ahead where I'll be getting on and off for awhile."

Francis wore a worried look. "Just seems too early. We could send word through Benito. There's no need to rush."

Their discussion was familiar, tenderized by need and time. Over the antler-chip checkers, Joseph had told Francis much about himself and about me those months while he recovered. At the stump burned black in square patches, he'd won and lost the checker games. He'd shared his fears and joys. He even talked of the empty space that would be filled up when he reached the falls and whatever it was that called to him there.

It was of that kind of sharing that I both loved to hear about, years later, and at the same time envied Francis for having had instead of me.

Joseph had even told Francis of J. W.'s passing comment about a planned May marriage.

"I heard him say it," Francis said, "and thought the dog must have jumped on your leg, you look so pained."

"Felt as though I was back in that rock tomb Archibald pulled me out of," he told her. "My chest was so heavy." Francis handed him some straw for the skips, continuing to cover the wild bee hives as they spoke into the unusually warm February morning. "Guess it was the thought of that girl marrying someone else come May that choked me up."

"Pay attention to that," Francis said, coughing as she moved on to the next hive. "Some folks don't hold much with Archibald, but I knew first time I saw him that he'd be for me. And so he has been, through thick milk and thin."

They'd talked together, eaten together, and as he healed, walked and worked together. The Turners had taken no pay for their care though Joseph offered. They did accept the food stores Benito brought out when he conferred with Joseph. That was all they'd accept. Archibald was adamant that what they gave to Joseph Sherar was only a small return for his generosity to them the year before. "Besides," Archibald told him one evening, "Scripture says 'give and it will be returned to you, a good measure, pressed down and shaken together.' You gave and now you're receiving."

"Helps explain the 'pressed down' experience of the rock tomb then," Joseph said, smiling.

Archibald gave him an irritated look, one allowed between men of shared respect but where one finds little humor in Scripture.

It was Francis who gave him real encouragement, helped heal his physical wounds and permitted him to look farther inward, to wounds he'd hung onto, some about his oldest brother and his father. "Keeps you from trusting, from knowing your own feelings and wishes when you give such power to others," Francis told him. Their bond was unique, bred freedom in their thoughts and discussions.

"Will she have you?" Francis asked one day as she rippled the flax seed in the late afternoon cabin light. She lifted her eyes to supervise Susan Ella paddling the dry threads with the brake. The child was young to be so skilled, to take on so much work that her mother couldn't.

Joseph picked up the silky thread, rolled it between his fingers, knew Francis spoke of me. He said the threads made him think of my dark hair with a hint of chestnut and the fact that he'd never touched it, might have died before he could. "Believe she will," he said. "If I can get her past her sass."

"She's young?" Francis asked.

Joseph nodded. "But wise, I think. I'll know, of course, if she takes me."

J. W.'s unsettling news had the advantage of hurrying Joseph's healing so by March, he not only walked, but rode.

On that first crisp day Archibald handed the reins up to Joseph where he steadied himself on the horse Benito brought out for him. Archibald said to his wife, "You've done all you could. He lives, he walks, and now he rides, all from your care."

"And God's," Francis answered looking up at Joseph. "God did the healing," she said, and she coughed.

Archibald nodded agreement, slipped his arms around his wife's thin shoulders, pulled her head to him, stroked her thick, gold hair. "Come on around now," he said to the children. "Ella, step out of Mr. Sherar's way. He wants to take a ride 'round the yard here, get a feel for it 'fore he leaves us in a day or two."

"Take me?" Susan Ella asked, refusing to move from her stand beside the gelding's withers.

"Susan Ella!" Francis scolded, pulling away from her husband, reaching for the child.

"In a bit," Joseph said to her, not even thinking it a promise. "Move aside, now. Don't want you getting hurt the last days of my stay." Sweat from the exertion beaded on his forehead. He felt shaky in the saddle, concentrated on Ella to keep his mind from the discomfort.

He adored the child, her dimples sewn like tiny tucks taken in her plump cheeks. "Let's try the kelpie first," he told her and with that he slapped his thigh and the little dog squeezed through the legs of the Turners and leaped. "Hey!" Joseph said as the dog licked his master's face, safe and secure once again from his perch on the horse. "You remembered what to do even though it's been, what, five months?"

Then to the Turners' he spoke of me and of our future and a hope: "My only prayer right now is that she remembers too."

CHAPTER 19

THE GIFT-
HIDE OF MY
HEART

❧

KOOSH SAT AT THE DRUMS, beating with the hide-covered stick while beside him his father, uncles, and three cousins pounded the stretched hide and sang their high-pitched songs. The spring Root Feast had been celebrated for two days and the dancers and drummers and singers switched off to give themselves rest.

Sunmiet and I lounged together on the fur hide set in the shade of the old juniper near the Simnasho Longhouse. Our fingers were stained black from peeling the skin from roots. It was afternoon, April, the shadows growing longer. We were several miles from the falls, in the oldest encampment on the reservation. Kása lived here, away from the agency and its boarding school, Indian agent and his meticulous wife. Morning Dove had grown up in the little cluster of buildings nestled in the dimples of sagebrush and juniper-dotted hills. Sunmiet spent her winters here and the Root Feast was always held here, where the elders announced that the earth said the roots were ready for digging.

Once again, Papa had consented to my time with Sunmiet. It would be the last for awhile. Mama said it was "unseemly for a wife to spend time with

Indians. Better for her to be with her own kind," she'd said, "teaching her own children and not gathering wild ideas from Indians."

Papa surprised me by saying: "Warm Springs Injuns are all right. Peter's a smart man, peaceable. George is good. Their folks volunteered as guides for the army to bring those Snake Paiutes down. Puts them in good stead. Not like those Yakimas, always arguing about this and that, squabbling over the treaty terms. Been almost ten years! They forget they're lucky just to be left alone in their defeat. No. Warm Springs are all right."

I had arrived in the company of Peter and George just as the ceremonial roots had been gathered by the seven selected to dig first. The blessings complete, we'd feasted and then the rest of the tribe could gather roots for their own family and for storage for winter. Kása had consented to taking me out with her after Sunmiet had pleaded with her to show me what to do.

"She has no grandmother to teach her these things," Sunmiet told her sweetly.

"Oh, hayah!" Kása said, shaking her head in disgust, but she had taken me.

"Why did I agree to this? You stupid girl. Hold the *kápn* this way. As I tell you!" The old woman held the root digger made of antler and pushed the sharp point of it into the soft earth. "See. It is not so difficult even for an old woman. What is wrong with your hands?" she asked. "They don't look puny."

I had learned that she gave her tongue-strapping to everyone and did not sass her back. It was good practice for getting along with cantankerous people. That day, I simply picked up the antler and pushed again against the earth beneath the slender leaves.

"Deeper! Deeper!" Kása cackled. "Yes! Yes! That's it, *piaxi,*" she said reverently, naming it as she reached down into the upturned earth to pluck the deep brown tuberous roots. "That is what we look for! Good!" She ripped the green from the roots I handed her and stuck the tubers into the woven corn husk *wapas* bag hanging from her skinny waist. "Maybe you are not so useless," she cackled again.

Hearing a compliment from her was almost more frightening than bearing her irritation. I must have stood before her, dumfounded. "Oh, hayah!" she said, irritated. "Here." She handed me the dark roots that stained my fingers the color of walnut. "We take some skin off in the bubbling water," Kása said, teaching, "and dry in hot sun for four days. Did you taste ones we had for feast? You liked those?"

I liked their taste with the pinch of precious salt added and herbs. I liked the smell of spring earth and the companionship it took to gather them up. I had eaten my fill of the roots at the feast and now, on this second day after feasting and digging, I was ready to rest with my friend.

Sunmiet had not danced at all during the feast days. Her time for delivery was only a few months away though she was as large as some due soon. Instead, she watched the little ones, laughing when either "Same-As-One" ran by, their chubby legs carrying them through spears of blue lupine. Furballs of dogs chased after them into tall grass. When they were older, the twins would have their own names so the "wind will recognize them," Sunmiet told me. "It will be a special ceremony to name them with Indian names, maybe even with names of the ancestors, if the family agrees. I have some names to recommend, when they pester me like ants," she added, laughing.

Same-As-One always brought Loyal to mind. He would have been their age now, had he lived.

The feast days bristled with activity and I noticed riders coming and going from the paddock and now several walked to the small clapboard house of Peter Lahomesh and disappeared inside.

"I wish a boy for my husband's pleasure," Sunmiet said over the noise and activity that always amazed me at these feasts. The sounds of my life were quiet ones, of crows and meadowlarks, of geese calling or the Seth Thomas clock ticking in the parlor. Most often, my still days were broken only by my mother's requests or directions, she and papa's terse words. Rarely was I pleasured by the chatter of family, gossiping and laughing.

"But a girl for my own," Sunmiet continued. "There is much work to do in my husband's lodge," she said, sighing, her voice breathy, like the whisper of wind in the tall firs. "A girl would help, someday. My husband's mother makes a good ruler-teacher," she said, looking at me with a wry smile. "She cracks my knuckles with her hide scraper if I do not work fast enough or hard enough to suit her. She gifts me with memories of the boarding school," she said.

"Doesn't Standing Tall complain?"

"Only about my laziness," she said. "He would never complain about his mother."

"J. W. has no mother, living," I said, speaking louder, to be heard over the drums. "At least he's never said anything of her. Or much else about himself, for that matter." J. W.—with my Papa near by—spent little time conversing with me on his visits. And I noticed that he lingered in the kitchen over Mama's fresh cobbler topped with cow's cream, often choosing that room over time in the parlor with me.

"His mother would be older than Kása!" Sunmiet said, laughing.

"So I won't have a mother-in-law to contend with at least," I said, thinking it small compensation for what I would have to face marrying a man who seemed more taken with my mother than with me.

Something about one of the riders going into Peter's house looked vaguely familiar. Was that Fish Man, the Hupa, already heading for the falls? No, not fluffy enough, I decided.

"You'll have other things," Sunmiet said. "The worst is sharing a lodge with a man you have no feeling for except as *pimx,* 'uncle.'"

"Mama says it could be worse." I stood, put my hands on my hips, as Mama. "'Yes. Well. You could be stuck with a drinker or a beater or one who never comes home except smelling of another's perfume.'" I could imitate Mama pretty well and enjoyed seeing Sunmiet smile. "Course I can't say any of those won't be true once we're wed." It was an unnerving thought. I held my stomach, anticipating the pain.

"My life is not so difficult," Sunmiet sighed, shifting awkwardly. "I see my mother and father each day, have time with my brothers. Sometimes I believe I have only moved into a new lodge, traded the kind words of my mother for the sharp tongue of Standing Tall's." She adjusted her bulky body, winced, leaned against the tree and rested her hands on the shelf of her belly. She took a large gulp of water from an old army canteen set beside her then added, "This one will make it different." She patted her stomach. "I will have more respect from my husband's mother. I will be allowed to have time with my baby and not always be under the feet of his grandmother. And Standing Tall anticipates the baby. It will be better. It will be so for you also," she said to encourage me. "You will see."

I sat back down. Babies would make it different, I hoped. Perhaps they'd make me forget the dark hairs in J. W.'s nose, the pocks in his cheeks, the faceless stranger in my dreams. Taking off my bonnet, I leaned back onto my elbows, thinking. With a baby, I would have someone who loved me no matter what I did, what mistakes I might make. A baby would never, ever leave me. With a baby, I would be treated differently by Mama, have things to share with her, to talk about on equal terms.

It was the fanciful thinking of a fourteen-year-old girl.

Still, with a baby, I believed my life would begin again, with newness. This time, I'd let no harm befall them. That was my dream, my promise to myself and to God, though I doubted he was interested.

"But it would be better if the baby came into the arms of one who loved its father," Sunmiet said breaking into my thoughts.

"'Yes. Well. Love is a luxury,' Mama says. And I'm not to have luxuries," I told her wistfully. "Only baubles."

The drums stopped abruptly as to me they always did. I could hear the stomp of horses in the corrals, some whinnying to another. Dogs barked and in small packs with their long tails wagging, roamed the grounds seeking leftovers. There were shouts in languages I did not understand and some in words I did. Giggling bubbled up from a cluster of girls and young men near the Longhouse. I thought I saw Standing Tall there with his friends and some others, laughing loudly, passing something between them. Dancers quietly moved off from the grassy arena, drifting toward the gourds of cool water, snatching up mouthfuls of jerky and dried fish. It was a place of simple pleasures though I knew sadness and sorrow lived in these hearts as well as my own.

Sunmiet cleared her throat.

"Would you like more water, Sunmiet?" I asked, thinking I had heard her speak. When she did not answer, I turned to look at her.

She held her stomach, and I watched the color drain from her face. Her eyes were wide and I could not tell if it was in pain or surprise. "Is it the baby?" I asked, kneeling over her, the thump of my heart beating loud in my ears. A grimace of fear rippled across Sunmiet's face.

She held her belly, her slender fingers spread like a fan over the mound of her body. Panting quickly, like a dog, her eyes seemed to bulge and then sunk down deep in her head showing more white than the brown. Her eyelashes fluttered; her body shook. A rattly sound back in her throat threw me into action! I thought I'd heard those sounds before!

"I'll get help!" I told her and scrambled to my feet, frightened, smelling death at the door. With a twist I turned, ran, shouting, "Morning Dove! Standing Tall! Kása! Come quickly!"

I headed straight to Eagle Speaker's house, racing across the circle and disrupting the dancers still mingling about. I stumbled into the opening, my eyes adjusting to dark, words jumbling out. "Follow. To come. Sunmiet, the baby. Something—"

"What's wrong?" Morning Dove interrupted me.

"Where is she?" Eagle Speaker demanded.

Morning Dove pushed me out of the opening. "Take us!" she said.

We raced, seemingly so slow, yet wind was forced into my mouth. I barely noticed the faces flashing by me as I gasped. "There! By the juniper!"

Morning Dove pushed past me, her husband close behind. They hovered over their child making throaty sounds, her body shaking less now in the dust.

I stood there feeling helpless, panting, watching with frightened eyes. Kása came running. Eagle Speaker bent across his wife who was holding his daughter. Someone told Standing Tall and I saw him rush across the dance grass. Everything happened so quickly and yet as if part of a slow-moving dream.

So later I did not blame myself that I overlooked J. W. Case standing in the cluster of men I'd raced by or that I failed to notice the pointy-eared dog until he laid at my feet. And who could fault a fourteen-year-old girl so frightened for her friend that she did not recognize her future and her hope when he stepped out of Peter's home and into her life, forever.

Red earth, red rocks, and a lake of red water marked the area. That's what Logan, the agent, had told Joseph when he stopped at The Dalles his first trip out from the Turner's care. It was luck he'd found the agent there instead of having to ride to the reservation to discuss his ideas. It was a miracle, Joseph thought, that the agent volunteered information about the "Herbert girl" and where she was.

"They'll be feasting," the agent told Joseph. "Don't know how receptive they'll be to your coming, talking about business. Sure you can't wait?"

"Some of the business can wait; others not," Joseph said, not wanting to reveal all that he had on his mind. "It's already April and I took a time-eating detour, to those falls."

The falls. At the falls on the Deschutes he'd finally put together the puzzle pieces that had piled up in the corners of his mind. At the falls, the builder in him saw the pattern, finally. And what had been only a wispy dream began at last to form into a plan.

He kept to himself his other reasons for seeking out the Root Feast, kept to himself the visit he would need to make at the Herbert ranch to face a father before he headed south.

The agent shrugged his shoulders. "You know anyone you can talk with or talk for you if you need?"

Joseph was thoughtful. "Peter Lahomesh and his son, George. If they're there."

"You mean Washington?" Logan asked, surprised. "Thought that was Peter's son's name. Washington."

"Way he introduced himself to me at the falls," Joseph said, thoughtfully.

"Everyone here calls him George Washington." The agent laughed. "Thought they named him that." The agent grunted, his freckled forehead wrinkled in thought, his bushy red eyebrows like lazy caterpillars over his eyes. "No matter," Logan said, dismissing the thought. "Names mean nothin' to 'em or they'd stop changing them all the time. But if you can find Peter and his son—whatever's his name—they'll help you. Feast should be over before long. Everyone will spread out, digging."

But Joseph could hear the drums as he rode down over the ridge into Simnasho and exhaled his relief. The feast was not over. "She should still be there," he told the kelpie and the man who rode at his side. He kicked his gelding, Nugget, and they picked up their pace, the kelpie perched on the saddle in front of Joseph like the sentinel he was.

Joseph discovered me in the midst of great anxiety over Sunmiet.

Kása had pushed by me, thrown a blanket over Sunmiet, and held her head in her lap as the convulsions ceased. Morning Dove wailed in distress, hovering. Kása silenced her. "Quiet!" she told her daughter. "She lives. I have seen this, when the baby is big, big for its time and the mother craves water. The baby will breathe air later than planned; not this night. She needs rest now." Sunmiet focused her eyes on me, a confused, frightened look flooding her face.

"It's a-right," I said softly, moving in closer, stroking her arm. "It's a-right," I repeated, remembering what once comforted Pauline. "Kása says not to worry."

Kása closed her eyes, sang her prayer song over Sunmiet and the girl calmed, seemed to return from some far away place. "Leave us," Kása said. Her words were gentle but gave no room for discussion.

Defeated, I put on my bonnet and turned to face the surprise of my life—Joseph Sherar standing behind me.

His dark hat shaded his eyes but his smile lit up the remainder of his face. Thinner now than when I'd last seen him almost a year before, he wore a well-trimmed beard that outlined his full, bronzed face. His hair had been cut with a barber's scissors. The bulk of him still cast a long shadow standing beside J. W. whom I confess I truly did not see until he spoke.

J. W. said, missing the conversation going on between my eyes and Joseph's, "Told ya she didn't say much. Sure you know what you're doing?"

Peter and the others who had been standing with the men moved quietly away, leaving the three of us non-Indians to step out of Sunmiet's circle of activity, stand off by ourselves.

I don't know how long we stood there, just staring until finally Joseph swallowed, removed his hat, and ran his wide fingers through his newly barbered hair. Hesitation may have visited his thoughts earlier, but not his words now. He spoke directly, soft eyes looking into mine, his deep voice vibrating to my very core.

"J. W. agrees to let you choose," Joseph said. He did not let me wonder about what. "And while it has been some months since we have spoken, it is my hope you will consider me in marriage as I have the license and the justice of the peace arranged." An Irish brogue drifted through his words like a soft afternoon breeze blowing over the Warm Springs river. He bit at his lower lip. "We only wait the arrival of my friend Philamon Lathrope from the Klamath country," he said with finality.

He must have seen the quick flicker of annoyance cross my face for he thought better and added, "And your answer, Jane. I await your answer, as it is your choice."

If he had said my name before I must not have heard it for his speaking it with deep and melodious tones seemed to tear me open, lay my soul before him on the gift hide of my heart.

I chose not to tell him that there would be much more to do than simply wait upon his friend before we married. I did not make corrections. For once, I chose not to risk the loss of happiness at the expense of being right.

"Yes," I said, the word catching in my throat without sass. "Yes. It will be my pleasure to become your wife."

Joseph reached out to take my hand then, and lightning passed between us. Later, I thought it happenstantial and a sign that our first touch should bring with it the features of a storm.

J. W. accepted the situation with dignity, standing there in the presence of a mind-changing. He and Joseph had conferred about "deals gone sour" before they rode together to the feast, French Louie having teamed them up in town. "Whoever she'll have," J. W.'d said to Joseph, confirming my belief about him wanting to do right, once he learned of Joseph's intention. "I'll withdraw my offer if she consents to you. Hasn't really said yes to me. Waiting on May, as I recall." He had no strong feeling of me except for fondness and a wish to please my papa and mama. "Don't want no woman what'll be dreaming of another," he said, both fists rubbing his eyes like a sleepy child.

I wondered about the conversation Joseph must have had with my father, but I did not want to doubt the outcome so I kept my caution silent. Having lost the choice, J. W. meandered off seeking stick games, looking to make some bets, not knowing they were not allowed at Root Feast.

"There is nothing we can do to help Sunmiet," I ventured, "so maybe we could walk?"

Joseph nodded, bent his elbow to my hand, and we walked with Peter Lahomesh (keeping his word to Papa) a respectful pace behind. We drifted around the circle of the dancers in full view. Fires lit the dancers' faces and I suppose ours too, if anyone watched. Few words popped out of my usually fresh mouth. The strings of my poke seemed especially tight across my throat, and I wanted to take the bonnet off so I could see him better and at the same time, wished to hide behind it. Mostly, I found myself gazing more at my moccasins as they slipped out beneath my skirts than at the man I had just consented to marry.

It is a powerful event to be faced with the appearance of a miracle, an answer to a prayer made one New Year's Day. Fearful, too. I sneaked a glance at the man who walked with a slight limp beside me. What young girl wouldn't bear some fear that her prayer to be out of a poor marriage by May was answered by a tall Californian a whole month before? Had I jumped from the long-handled spider into the flames?

"I'd not rush you," Joseph said as we walked back to Eagle Speaker's lodge, Peter close behind. The moon was out, not quite full, but cast some pale light over the teepees of visitors and the small homes of the residents. Some still danced to the drums beating like a pulse. "I'd give you more time to think of having me or not. But I want your father not to reconsider."

"You think he will?" I said, looking up at him with alarm. I noticed the artery in his throat throbbing steadily against the skin of his neck.

"He has reneged before, over something not as consequential as his daughter." He spoke with me as someone who had known me always, without hesitation as he added, "And your mother was not present during our discussion. The wheel's reversed. So there is that to yet contend with."

A kind of quiet silence surrounded us as we stood before the doorway of Eagle Speaker's lodge. Wild irises released their sweetness into the air competing with early lilacs in bloom. A night owl hooted high above us in the firs. Joseph took my hand in his, held it gently, running his fingers over my nails. "I am pleased beyond words," he said softly.

My pounding heart greeted my racing thoughts as long-absent friends no longer certain of their relationship.

Releasing my hand, he untied the strings of my bonnet, pushed it back off of my head, the long sashes pulling like silk against the velvet of my throat, falling noiselessly to the earth. In the darkness, I could barely make out his features and knew he could see little of mine. He leaned toward me then, my heart pounding. With both hands, he lifted my face, his touch both tender and firm. His fingers wore the scent of leather.

I thought he would kiss me.

Instead he said so close I could smell the sweetness of his breath: "You've pulled me from some suffocating place, and I am grateful." He seemed to study my face, memorize its features in the darkness, as though he might not see them again. "My life," he added, dropping his hands, "has just begun."

He nodded his head to me next, touched the brim of his hat he replaced on his head, then disappeared into the darkness.

In the morning we checked on Sunmiet before leaving. "She sleeps well," Kása said from the doorway of Sunmiet's house. Her toes lifted a plump puppy out of the way before it slipped inside. "Go now. When next you see her, she will be a proud mother." I nodded once and resisted my wish to hug her, to tell her of my happiness, afraid of her rebuff.

We mounted, me on Puddin' Foot, Joseph on Nugget. Peter stayed as he'd promised my father he would do, escorting me, until we saw the corn fields of our home at Fifteen Mile Crossing. J. W. would eventually ride on to the Columbia, but for now, he and Peter rode behind us with our privacy in mind.

Something about the freshness of the April morning and the burst of purple phlox and early lupine added to the joy and awe I felt in riding here beside this man. I told Joseph of that feeling when we'd been wed some years. "Did you not feel awed upon that day?" I asked him.

"Not by someone whose huckleberry eyes looked at me as an equal," he told me. "Saw you that way that day. Always will."

Perhaps it was that sense of equal I felt that fragrant morning that gave me courage to ask of his encounter with my father, how this life I hoped for had even come about.

"He considered throwing me off his land at first. I know he did," Joseph said. "But I had made my mind be humble beforehand. I went there with one purpose and I thought, 'What would make a man as willful as your papa think to look at me anew?' And when I figured I'd come across it, I set out. Believed

I'd see you there too, but it was better that you weren't. And knowing he consented to you spending time with Sunmiet told me he did have some open places in his mind."

I laughed but saw that Joseph did not see the humor in his words so serious were his reflections. "So I arrived at your father's place just two days past, hat in hand, with not the dog nor Benito neither. Left Bandit with J. W. well beyond your place. So it was just me and him that met, man to man.

"Your papa stood on the porch, above me, still chewing some dinner I suspect, a napkin fisted in his hand. 'I came to make a truce,' I told him before he could swallow and speak, 'and to express my apologies.'"

"You apologized to my father?" I asked, turning to stare at this man I really didn't know. "What for? He's the one who should have said he was sorry, for being rude, for not keeping his word about the mules." I was a bit indignant wondering if Joseph's judgment kept him from seeing what was right.

"No room for shoulds when a man has a greater purpose," he said. "Nor too much pride, either. Can't let being right stand in the way of winning. What mattered was that your papa see me differently, allow me to press my case about you. The road that way was rocky but not impassable." He smiled at me, lifted the brim of his hat from his wide forehead revealing those sky blue eyes. "No road is ever impassable if you set your sights clear. And you don't have to push someone off just for you to be on it. Just make a good survey, be willing to reroute, and never lose sight of where you're going." His words fascinated me.

"'Apologies!' your papa grunted. 'Plenty room for them from your mouth I'd say.' I just agreed with him, gave him no new fuel to add to embers he'd been burning with my name on 'em all this time. Told him I understood that some folks did not approve of dogs inside saloons or parlors and that he must have thought me pretty inconsiderate, tired though I was. Told him a man has the right to decide who comes inside or out his home, too. He just kept on chewing. Told him he was right, too, about the deposit. That a man's word was his only calling card and when I left mine and then did not return, there was no reason for him to think other than he did, that I'd changed my mind and would not be back for mules."

I could picture my father standing there, jaws set, getting ready to dab at his bad eye with that ball of a napkin.

"And then I risked the big one," Joseph said, taking a deep breath. "I said I felt differently than him, too, about the Indios, the Mexicans. His eyebrows shot up but I added quick that I could see he was not a man to discount all who were different or he'd not let his daughter share time with Warm Springs folks nor set himself up to run for office like he had. An elected official had to see a passel of points of view, pour water on different kinds of flames, and I could see he knew how to do that, knew how to settle disputes in ways to keep a man's face."

"Papa heard you say that?" I asked.

"Seemed to. He let me keep talking. I just held my hat and looked up at him, hoping he'd hear. He seemed to be thinking. Said I expected voters could respect a man big enough to change, that only that kind of man could really lead a changing country. He grunted then and said, 'Getting hot here on the porch. Why don't you come inside where we can talk in comfort.' And then I knew I'd opened the door to this day."

"But about me," I said. "How did you ask him about me?"

"That was delicate. Took some time getting around to. Had to talk about the packing and gold fields and how I'd managed my business while being laid up. But eventually I told him that J. W. and I had spoken about you, and that J. W. knew too that your father was a man who felt kindly about his daughter, wouldn't want her to be unhappy if there was a way around it. He didn't protest that comment, so I ventured that it was the trend back East, where women weren't so scarce, to let them choose their own. That in these times only a strong man, solid and wise could afford to let his daughter make her own marriage bed and learn to sleep in it. 'If a girl's prepared well with a good head, she ought to be able to,' he said. Pretty progressive for here, I told him. He sat awhile and then he said, 'Will she have you?' And I had to tell him that I did not know, but that like him, I was willing to risk her choice. And so I did," he said and reached across the space between our mounts to brush some wispy hair from my cheeks.

So only my mother's absence to the deed let apprehension share the saddle with me as we passed through the gate at Fifteen Mile Crossing.

When Mama joined us—Papa, Joseph, and me—and learned of the plans already made without her having taken part, she protested. Joseph had plowed the courting field quickly, he and Papa made it ready for planting. Mama had been caught unawares, wasn't ready with her seeds.

"It seems there's no need for me to partake of this discussion," she said, her voice like nails scraping on the school slate. To Papa she said, "What chip has Mr. Sherar called in that makes you so easily alter your agreement with J. W.?" She sat erect on the cane chair, hands and jaw clasped tightly while she waited for Papa to speak.

"Now, 'Lizbeth," he said, his voice a patting hand on her head. He chuckled, awkwardly making light. "Wasn't anything like that. The man truly cares for our Janie. Came all this way. No," he said, "no deal. J. W. seemed fine to let the girl choose. Would have myself if I had known of another suitor. Takes a good man to let a daughter make her own way. Shows she's been well-raised—"

"There was a promised transaction," she said. "And you have simply let that by?" She spoke to Papa but glared at me, as though once again I had distressed her well-planned life.

Her question raised the wonder, though: had there been some bet lost and now I was the pay?

"Just a change, Lizzie," Papa smoothed.

I wondered what kind of change.

Papa stood behind her, put his hands on her shoulders, to calm her. We could all see her agitation rising like day-old sour dough starter.

"So there is to be no exchange, then?" She searched for something.

"No chips, Mrs. Herbert," Joseph told her. "I'd not bargain for your daughter as I did the mules. Nor let a bad winter keep me from either if I had known then I'd left my heart here, too."

She paused, staring at him. "Fancy words will not win me over as they did my husband," she told him. "Honeyed-tongues have left their stickiness with me before." She smoothed the folds in her skirt draped over her plump knees, pulled abruptly at the seam threads as though they were the most important detail in her life. She frowned watching Baby George who played with the kelpie near the window, on the floor next to the Sheraton.

"Then hear the truth," Joseph told her. He stood above her, all of us, in fact and walked closer to her, leaning casually, his elbow against the desk. His shadow caused her to leave her seam and Baby George and look up at him. His words were clear, precise, nonnegotiable, and it struck me as I watched him that he stood before me with both strength and flexibility, both tenderness and steel.

Mama gave him one of her looks, but I noticed Joseph did not back down as J. W. had those months before.

"J. W. has withdrawn his offer," he said quietly. "Your husband and your daughter have consented to mine which is to make a good life with her. There's no win in it for you to intervene."

I could tell that she considered that. Like all of us, she liked to win.

"It's complete except to set the date," Joseph said, "and await some friends' arrivals."

"I suppose you'll take her far away," Mama said, changing her tactic. I heard a whining in her voice, noticed the scent of her perfume grow stronger. *Why should it matter?*

"A mother needs help—"

"We didn't discuss that, Lizzie," Papa said. "But I'm sure Mr. Sherar means to remain in the region." To Joseph, "You still have your place along Fifteen Mile, don't you? Wouldn't take our only daughter far from us?"

My future husband nodded. "No wish to cut into your family," Joseph said. "Just add to it, in time."

They talked around me as though I wasn't even present, my life being tossed about like cottonwood fluff. I knew he kept his mules at a nearby ranch. I hadn't known he owned it! Nor had I thought to ask that question yet about where we'd live, so much had happened in less than a day.

"So where do you plan to make our home, Mr. Sherar?" I asked.

"Someplace you'll be happy in," he said, turning to face me fully as I stood behind the divan, my hands gripping the mahogany frame. "Not decided yet, of course." He had a twinkle in his eyes as he added, "Wouldn't confirm anything so important until you and I talked."

He was quick. I gave him that. And he could read me like one of his books, knew when I was close to spitting fire, had cool water ready to pour on it.

Mama was silent and into that space Papa finished expansively. "It's agreed, then!" He walked to the wooden box that held his best cigars, pulled two out, lit one, inhaled deeply, and handed one to Joseph.

Mama stopped him for a moment. "Yes. Well. For now," Mama said, "It's agreed for now." And I knew then we would marry, but that her argument against my happiness, for whatever reason, wasn't over.

Despite Mama's protest, our marriage did take place in the parlor five days later on the 26th of April 1863. I carried a fresh bouquet of white lilacs mixed with wild yellow roses, both blooming early, just for me. We'd had little time to plan and so I wore a dress Lodenma loaned me, taken in at the waist with a long satin bow added to the white lace. Lodenma May stood as my witness; Philamon for Joseph. The justice of the peace spoke the words, the minister of the Methodist church being on the circuit. Later, the few guests and several of Joseph's packers, including Benito and his wife and A. H. Brayman, charivaried us. Fish Man and some Warm Springs friends joined them too. French Louie led the procession with their noisy calls, banged pans, whistles, and gun fire, arousing us from our quarters at the Umatilla House, not leaving until we invited them in for drinks and entertainment.

Pulling the frightened kelpie from beneath the bed, we partied late into our wedding night, singing and laughing, listening to bawdy comments I only half understood made by the men. It was like being allowed to stay up late with grownups, not being sent early to bed.

Joseph eventually rid the room of them.

I have often chuckled through the years about what follows, wedding night stories being shared only among close friends. But this one was different. For when the bridegroom returned from escorting the well-wishers off to the saloon and returned to greet his bride, he found her—and the kelpie—on the freshly laundered sheets of our four poster, already quite soundly asleep.

That night, I dreamed again of the stranger who would share his life with me. This time he wore the face of Joseph Sherar.

PART II

DREAM CATCHING

BEGINNINGS

"I'VE LOOKED it over. It's a fine site."

"I'm not disagreeing," I said.

"Hard to tell."

"Just want to make up my own mind," I added, always wanting the last word.

We had ridden out from The Dalles to the donation land claim Joseph had acquired, a 640-acre detail he had not shared with Mama. At various stops along the way—Three Mile Creek, Five Mile Creek, Eight Mile Creek, and others—he had consulted his sketch book, gotten off his horse, walked here and there, his hands moving as though he were talking. He spoke mostly to himself.

Elmer Wilson's house at Five Mile was already a stage stop for people traveling south to Tygh Valley, Wapinitia, and Nix's bridge not far from the mouth of the Deschutes. At Wilson's, at least, he spoke out loud to me: "It all fits in," he said.

Riding on down Tygh's Ridge, we skirted a steep trail that twisted like a snake to the Deschutes and instead followed a hollow that dipped and rose until we reached a small, year-round stream. He noted where he believed our claim began. The surrounding land had a gentle slope to recommend it.

"No need to build right at this spot, but there's water and an openness I like. Can see the mountains on a cloudless day. No trees to break the view. And there'll be less wind down here." We rode farther around the sidehill of the gentle ravine following the gurgle of the fast-flowing stream. "Over there, see those stones?" He pointed to a marker pile in the distance. "Meeker graves. Still don't see how they could've gotten so lost," he said, recalling the fateful wagon train where so many died on their way to The Dalles. "Twenty years too soon, I guess."

I looked around at the sparse sage popping up through spears of grass. The hills and hollows looked the same in spring, all soft shadows and green. I could well imagine how hungry, exhausted people from the Meeker's train could have become confused and taken the turn away from both the White River and the Deschutes, ending up here, on the crest of a ravine, discouraged, starving, barely able to bury their dead.

"There's water on the other side of the hollow, too." Joseph moved his arms expansively, directing my attention. "Comes into this one and where they join is the perfect rise for the house I think. Not far from that trail. With a little upgrading, we'll bring more packers through here. And it'll be just the beginning, Janie," he said. "There'll be roads and people and settlers all coming our way 'cause of what we lay out, get ready for them." He was enthusiastic about his puzzle pieces, letting me in on bits and pieces of his dream that still seemed foggy and wispy to me.

As we sat on the horses looking across the horizon to the stream before us, I realized the site was familiar. Sunmiet and I had sat on this ground having followed the little stream up from the Deschutes the summer Joseph entered my life. At this "Y" in the stream, Sunmiet and I had talked of Standing Tall; here we'd picked choke cherries and carried them back into the chaos of Koosh swinging by a rope from the scaffolding. "Don't the Sahaptins and the Wascos own this?" I asked. "Isn't it theirs?"

Joseph shook his head. "It's part of their ceded lands. They can dig roots and hunt, just not own, according to the treaty. Our claim doesn't go to the river anyway. Stops short. That'll be the next step. May owns what's next to the river and the bridge that crosses it, such as it is. Built that pretty fast after the floods last year. Too fast to stand the traffic there's bound to be." The latter he spoke more to himself than to me.

"And you'd build this trail into some kind of road?" I asked, wanting to be sure I understood his intentions.

"Eventually. For now, I just want us to have a home, place to run cattle and settle down on soon as I sell the string and the other place at Fifteen Mile. And we get something built. Here first." He added, "Eventually, the falls." I didn't pursue his addition though it was the more significant for our future.

Instead I tried to imagine what this site would look like with a house on it. Where the smokehouse, barn, and buckaroo bunkhouse would sit. What view over my doughboy or out the privy door would I see? How long would it take for the lilacs to bloom? How hot would it get in the summer? At least these questions would be answered someday. I wasn't so sure about some others that had emerged from my marriage bed.

We rode on down to the place of joined streams, tied the horses to one of the wild rose bushes, and walked. The kelpie scoured the grass and sage for rabbits, his skinny tail beating birds from the bushes as he moved. Joseph reached for my hand and I let him lead me, feeling the warmth of his fingers coiled around mine.

We'd been married but three weeks. It was the strangest of times for me sharing intimate space with a stranger, trying to live up to the adult he seemed to see in me. Must have been strange for him too, now, looking back all these years. What does a grown man do with a mere child he has taken into his life? How does he wait until she grows into a woman? What can he do to nudge her along without first strapping her for her sass, without destroying her spirit?

Joseph neither strapped nor destroyed, a rarity among married men I believe. Joseph already knew of my strong will. He did not know it rose partly from my confusion, not being certain of the rules. It came forth, too, from my wish for approval, my wanting to do things correctly and right, my fear of being put aside if I didn't. That discovery took time and experience, for both of us. What he learned early the morning after our marriage was that he could not simply tell me what to do and expect it to happen as he requested.

First, he announced we would be leaving immediately on a bridal trip to New York.

"Not New York," I said. "Not now." I picked at the side of ham floating in maple syrup at the dining room of the Umatilla House. It was our bridal breakfast and I found I wasn't all that hungry. "First I want to know where we'll return to," I told my husband of twelve hours. "That should be settled. Then I want to see where you take the pack string into Canyon City, meet the people who have known you before me. After that, we could consider New York."

His amused smile did not escape me though he tried to hide it behind his linen napkin as he wiped his mouth and beard. I felt myself bristle but I simply waited, took a bite of johnnycake and chewed, staring calmly into his eyes. Little spider webs spread out from his blues and I noticed a sprinkling of gray in his hair. He bit on his lower lip, a habit I noticed accompanied deep concentration.

Clearing his throat, he gave me reasons we should travel back east now: before I became with child and couldn't travel; to select furniture we might wish shipped out; to meet his family. Once he began speaking, I think he actually liked talking out loud to someone besides Bandit, exploring options this way and that. Unlike the dog, I talked back, and I could see by the look on his face that my opinions startled, often amused and always intrigued him. It was an auspicious beginning. I won the first round.

He learned I needed time: for explanation, answering questions, analyzing, so I could decide on my own. I learned I could sometimes get my way though I didn't know then it was less my skill at argument and more my husband's fondness for me that set me on the upper step. However it came, I liked the feeling.

The land claim was one example of the shifting going on in our relationship. Our visit that May morning was the third trip to the site and I approached readiness for a decision.

"We have five years to build," Joseph said. "But we do have to begin sometime before then."

I scowled at his sarcasm.

"Five years," he noted. "And then it's ours. We can add what you might want. Don't need a cat and clay chimney. We can use stone or even some bricks. Be safer."

"I'm not worried over the construction," I said. "You'll handle that well."

"What do you need to know then, to decide?" I sensed some exasperation in his voice.

The answer wasn't easily brought forth. I had only that day understood that I dawdled because the site was barely five miles from Mama and Papa's. I wasn't sure if it was too close or too far away. Part of me kept thinking I would find the right and perfect answer to every big decision if I just waited, asked better questions; another part said "decide," make corrections later.

Which is what I did, finally.

"Let's build it here, then," I said, and marked the dirt with the new boots Joseph had bought me at French & Gilman's store in town. "So I'll have a view of the streams and the wild roses."

A blast of air exhaled from him. "My idea exactly," Joseph said and smiled. "And I've something to honor the occasion," he added, delight in his voice. "Wait here."

With his slight limp, he hustled back to the horses switching their tails against flies. From the pack behind his saddle he pulled out a roll of white cloth the size of a linen napkin bound up with a burgundy bow. From behind my saddle, he untied a blanket roll and carried both back to me, a smile on his face.

"Hold this," he said, giving me the linen package. "But don't look." He unfurled the blanket in the shade of the roses, away from the dust of the horses. Then he sat and reached for my hand, pulling me down beside him.

"Didn't have time to get this before we were wed," he told me, reaching for the package. He untied the dark ribbon that bound it. "Even 'on the frontier' as Benito calls it, a man can find a fitting present for his wife."

The burgundy box he handed me fit in the palm of my hand, the name, "Cosner & Sons, Jewelers," imprinted in gold letters across the top. My fingers lingered over the letters, wanting to savor the elegance of the box, anticipating the gift inside.

"Open it," he said, his excitement more evident than my own.

A tiny hook and latch kept the box closed and I opened it, a gasp escaping my mouth as I peered inside.

"Do you like it?" Joseph said, eagerly. "When we go to New York, I'll get another for you. A gold one, but I hope this one's good for now." He leaned closer to me, seeing my view. A certain anxiety came through his voice and I realized he wasn't certain of what his young bride might like. "Go ahead. Take it out. Here, I'll put it on you." He reached for the silver chain.

"Wait," I said holding his hand back. "I just want to look at it first, hold it."

After a few seconds of pleasure, I reached inside and lifted from the box the most exquisite silver oval I had ever seen. Not much larger than Joseph's thumb, the oval hung from a silver chain that draped like silky liquid between my fingers.

"Open it," he urged.

I lifted the oval cover with my thumbnail and peered at a clock face surrounded by a dozen tiny diamonds. "It's beautiful," I whispered, feelings caught in my throat. "I've never had anything like it. So delicate and perfect."

His voice was thick with emotion. "I wanted perfection for you. And a watch. So you'll know I think of you with each minute of the day. And will, all the minutes of my life."

A great stillness filled the space between us. Even the kelpie sensed the moment and walked back quietly, not bothering us, lying with a soft "plump" at my feet.

"It's more…" I said, wiping my eyes with my fingers, not making much sense. "Thank you. I've never…" I fingered the pendant. Something was coming to me from a far away place. "It wasn't just a 'deal' then, like Mama said?" I asked him.

Joseph looked startled, having forgotten our discussion in the parlor. Then, "No deal," he said firmly. "You must never think that." He was thoughtful. "I loved you for longer than I knew. Perhaps from the moment I first saw you take on the snakes." He smiled, folded my fingers over the watch, and held both of my hands, looking at me. "I didn't recognize it, Jane. Not until I almost lost the chance to recognize anything, and then I had no way of knowing you might want me, too. There's been no deal, no arrangement. I wanted you for my wife. It is my greatest luxury in life that you might want me, too."

I didn't tell him that I was a girl meant only for baubles, if my mama was right. For this moment, I would bask in the lavishness of his love. And perhaps as a woman, be worthy later of the luxury he offered.

"You can put a photograph in the frame," he said, moving his eyes from mine. He pointed out the tiny silver frame across from the watch face. "Maybe of me. Or my dog," he joked, "who seems to have transferred his loyalty quite readily." Bandit wagged his tail, knew we spoke of him. "Now may I put it on you?" he asked, eager. I nodded and lifted my knotted hair at the bow from my neck while he moved behind me to catch the clasp. The watch hung perfectly over the tiny tucks of the burgundy store-bought dress I wore. It rose and fell with my breathing, resting at the crest of my emerging breasts.

Joseph pulled me back into his chest, his arms sweeping around me, holding me close. I felt his chin resting gently on my head as he rocked me, smelled the perfume of the laundry's soap from his shirt. His breath was a sigh. "I love you," he said, his voice a deep whisper. "And only hope someday you'll feel the same."

Looking down, I found the watch and rested it on his forearm. I lifted open the face cover again, to look at the dark hands, read the tiny diamonds that marked the hours. He had loved me for a long time, he'd said. And would with each passing minute. He'd placed no conditions as yet, nothing I needed to do to earn it except just be me. The feeling was foreign.

As if my heart had room for more, Joseph coughed nervously, moved me slightly to retrieve his sketch book from his red vest pocket. "Something I wrote while I was recuperating," he told me. He took a deep breath and I knew he was sharing himself, heart and soul. "It's about you," he added hoarsely. Then he read the words that still tick away in my heart.

"To be so loved,
that time stands still
when I'm with you,
and does not start again
until you've gone away,
and I am left alone
to wonder
why the hours move so quickly
when you're with me,
and so slowly
when you've gone."

He turned the watch over to show me the engraving in tiny script on the back. "To Time Standing Still: All my love, JHS to JAS 1863." The words marked the moment I truly fell in love.

I couldn't have been more excited about the trip if it had been to someplace exotic like New York. Canyon City was the second largest town east of the Cascade mountains in the new Oregon State. Bigger and better gold strikes marked the news that came from there with each returning pack string and now people moved there, having discovered land ripe for sheep raising and for cattle and families too. Joseph said along with the gold, the Homestead Act would bring thousands into the area and if he planned things well, their hunger for land and riches could feed our dream at the falls.

"Our dream" he called it though it still seemed more his than mine. While I could be sassy about some things, I found myself holding back, not challenging him yet about things I didn't understand.

It was the trip that interested me that June. We would be gone for several weeks, spending nights on the trail under one of Joseph's San Francisco tents, seeing country I had never seen before. I imagined the hustle and bustle of the packers, listening to Benito and his wide wife, Anna, exchanging opinions in Spanish, watching Joseph work with his men, master the mules and the elements as we traveled the two hundred miles.

It would be my first trip away from the familiar setting of my childhood. Along the way, I would meet people who would only know me as I was beginning to see myself and as I was now introduced: Mrs. Joseph Sherar. At the end we'd meet the Turners, and I would come face to face with Francis—"the saint," as I had taken to thinking of her since Joseph never spoke of her in less than heavenly terms.

While in Canyon City, Joseph planned to finalize the sale of his string and his "good luck" route to Robert Heppner. My Joseph had never had a loss in all his trips, had kept every agreement for the miners. While other men told of Indian raids, lost animals, and troubled hands, Joseph's stories spoke truthfully of good fortune. "People think everything I touch turns to gold," he said as we rode past the Meeker grave markers. "They don't know how much gold I've already buried."

"Not to mention your own burying for a time," I reminded him.

"That didn't involve the string, fortunately. So Heppner is buying my good reputation along with my mules."

With the string of forty mules, we had ridden out from The Dalles on the west side of the Deschutes, past Fifteen Mile Creek to the Tygh Ridge and down the ravine where men worked on our house. If we had not wanted to monitor the building progress, we might have taken the steep route that crossed the Deschutes at Nix's new bridge a few miles south of The Dalles. "Bridge won't last there," Joseph said. "Another winter like '61 and it'll be gone. And the roads are no good to and from. That's the key to a route that will last." He didn't tell me which route he thought would.

At our homesite, we spent scant moments, just enough to answer simple questions about the barn going up first; confirm where the house would rise. I could tell Joseph wanted to be there, building; but he kept his promise for our wedding trip.

With impatient animals and energetic men, we moved on down the ravine on the old trail to the Deschutes with the plan to take the skimpy bridge that Todd had built.

"First day out, Mrs., is always worst," Benito told me. "Get kinks out of ropes and how you say, 'routines.'" Everyone seemed relieved when we reached the river and I felt my own excitement growing as I heard the roar of the falls and wondered if I'd see Sunmiet.

We made camp that night with the Indians nestled in the shadow of the rocks. The spring Salmon run was on. Fish charged up the falls, leapt unknowingly into the nets dipped from the scaffoldings. Taking only a moment for a fond reunion with Joseph, Fish Man, in his element, returned to spear salmon from the slippery rocks. Joseph traded for wind-dried Chinook to take with us into the mines, talked with Peter and others about the trail, the weather, the bridge. Benito directed the men to hobble the mules, unload and make camp, making plans for an early start in the morning.

Seeing Standing Tall, I assumed I'd find Sunmiet.

"She is still wearing her big stomach," Bubbles told me from her squat in the shade of a juniper. She waved grasses to cool her chubby face though it seemed to me she had lost weight. "Kása says soon, very soon. The baby waits until he is ready to walk before he joins us." She laughed. "He is not persuaded it is better here than there, that one."

"Where is she?" I asked.

Bubbles shook her head. "She and Morning Dove stay at Simnasho. They will join us when the baby appears." My face must have shown my disappointment, my wonder too at whether Mama would be with me at my first; whether Joseph would be like Standing Tall, not near his wife.

Bubbles shrugged her shoulders, scratched at her thick thigh. "I will say you asked of her," she said. She noticed Joseph walking up behind me. "Ha!" she said, looking provocatively at him and then my flat stomach, slender hips. "And how goes your baby-making? Do I have something to tell Sunmiet when I see her?" Her grin was wicked.

"If it was your business to know I'd tell you," I said, haughtily, hiding my own disappointment at having nothing to share even if it had been only two months. I turned my back on her to meet Joseph. He looked at Bubbles over the top of my head and at me with a question on his face.

"It's nothing," I lied.

In the morning, the June sun rose early on a hot, clear day. We took a trail along the east side of the river, south and then east, away from the water into the high, dry country. A slender line of green marked a stream in an area hot enough to bake bread on the rocks.

I wiped sweat from the band of the hat I had taken to wearing instead of my bonnet as we made our way up the single-lane road. It twisted and turned like a lazy snake and below us, we could watch mules loaded with packed panniers led by men on horseback as we inched our way toward the top.

"Someday," Joseph told me. "This road will be wide enough for wagons and stages. And they'll stop at our rest stop, when we own the falls."

I looked at him, askance. "Surely you jest," I said, sounding as wise and old as I could to hide my disbelief.

"Nope. That's the way it will be," he said in a voice with no arguing.

When we reached Cross Hollows, a place where two dry ravines fed into each other, it was late and we camped immediately. "Named this myself," Joseph told me. "First trip out. Be a good place for a stage stop, don't you think?"

I had difficulty imagining a stage arriving on the road we'd just mastered.

The sunset on this high plateau was extravagant. Spears of light radiated from the fluffy clouds that hovered like dumplings over the mountain peaks on the horizon. Joseph took time from the string to walk with me in the dusk. White mountains dotted the horizon, as bright and brilliant as a necklace of pearls against a dark blue sea. Joseph pointed out the mountain's names, gave words to the vast expanse that led from California to the lands north, toward the Columbia. A chill wind rose over our camp. By nine o'clock, dusk still hanging on to daylight, the two of us curled under blankets, savoring this bridal trip as my first real taste of being grown.

In the morning we headed toward a place Joseph called Antelope for the beige and white striped animals that roamed the area. That road was not for indecisive people as it permitted few changes in plans. With few turnouts, it offered limited places to pull aside to let another pass. We'd gotten an early start, hoping to reach the bottom before anyone else started up. Then at a particularly narrow section, just as the thought entered my head that we were fortunate to be the only pack string on the road, I noticed dust below us, coming our way. We had listened for the bells and heard nothing before we started out. I shouted to Joseph who had already seen the cloud of dust and signaled a halt to the string down the line, voices in English and Spanish rippling down the ridge like echoes. We waited, checking packs and cinches, our animals twisting their necks, biting at flies, stomping their impatience.

Finally, the dust below us coughed up one man and team in one unloaded wagon who pulled up facing the string.

The driver, wiry and worn, wiped his face with his bright-colored neck scarf. "This is a pickle," he said.

Joseph nodded his agreement.

No one could turn around. Fortunately, the freighter was a single wagon with only one team instead of the usual six or eight horses. Still, the wagon could not be backed up far enough to reach a turn out. There was no going around him or him bypassing the string. Benito made his way on foot toward the front of the line, weaving in and out beneath the necks of the mules to reach the front. No one seemed distressed though I couldn't see a solution.

Finally, Benito signaled in Spanish and several hands made their way with effort through the ropes of mules and men to the front, listened carefully, and then spread out around the wagon where they promptly took it apart!

Perhaps the packers were pleased by the diversion though I wondered what might have happened if the mules had chosen that moment to protest. But they didn't. Even the team of big horses with their bearded hoofs allowed themselves to be unhitched and led away from the wagon. The wagon dismantled, its parts stacked close to the inside bank, our string moved on down the road, inching past the wagon's team where we stopped again, sending men back up the line to put the wagon back together.

"All in the day's work," Joseph mused as we continued and the hours wore on. "It's exactly why the road is so critical, why what we build will bring them in. We'll have wide turnouts and a solid base and people will choose to cross on our bridge, you wait and see."

For me, it was watching the impossible become probable. The only ingredients needed were ingenuity, shared energy, and time.

A Brent's Pony Express rider passed us not far from Canyon City. The rider waved, the only attention he paid us, so serious did he take his work. "Perhaps he carries some news written line by line then turned upside down," I said.

"And more written between the lines and then diagonally, making three pages on a single side. Probably so important it will change a life," Joseph said, just joking, not knowing. "Everyone now has news that can't wait a week or two. Used to be we waited months. Even years! Now, got to be a day or two. World is moving faster, Janie," he said, "we'll have to get on board."

Only later did we learn how Joseph spoke the truth without his knowing. For the rider carried with him a letter from my Mama, responding to J. W.'s inquiry about her willingness to help a family who had lost their mother in childbirth.

Mama was always willing to help another. That's what J. W. told the grieving widower seeking good homes for his children. Just two more days, and Joseph and I would have been there, would have known of the letter he'd sent asking our help. Just two more days and the widower Archibald Turner would have turned to us in his sorrow instead of who he did.

CHAPTER 21

REPUTATIONS

FIRECRACKERS EXPLODED in bursts of sound and color. We celebrated the Fourth of July in Canyon City, the event and the day being hotter than a highjacker's pistol. "Oom-pa" bands accompanied the festivities interrupted by political speeches to respectable people who now populated the remote area. Bits and pieces of conversations spoke of General Lee's invasion of the North, President Lincoln's plans for emancipation though the war seemed far from us. Food stands dotted the perimeter of the celebration grounds sending up a mix of fragrances to honor the varying tastes of visitors and locals. A pinkish man rolled pasties in a hut off to the side and Joseph whistled low under his breath as we strolled by. "I'll be. O'Connors!" he said. "They've a reputation for always being where the boom is next." His eyes searched quickly past the man. "Wonder where Eleanor is?" he said out loud, promising to answer the question in my eyes, later.

I could wait. People-watching, not eating near the pinkish man, consumed my time in Canyon City, such a mix of personalities displayed themselves that day. My ears picked up a dozen different languages spoken here and there: German, Irish, something that sounded Greek which Joseph said probably was.

Only those voices and the wind of the paper fans we carried broke the still July air.

Few Indians or dark-skinned people exposed themselves beneath the red, white, and blue bunting banners that hung like a necklace across the street. I noticed a fair speckling of Chinese. Joseph said the Chinese not only worked the mines, but performed much of the menial tasks the locals chose not to. As if to confirm his words, I watched several clean-shaven men appear in starched shirts from behind the Chinese store-fronts smelling of sweet scents, serving as ready advertising for the "baths and laundry, 10¢" signs that appeared at intervals along the boardwalks. Wearing silk pants and tops like soft pajamas, the Chinese seemed to hover on the sidelines like the flutter of hummingbirds near the bloom of wild roses; gentle, yet vibrant in their presence.

"Their doc, Dr. Hey, I think his name was, gave Francis herbs that kept my fever and infection down," Joseph told me, noting my fascination with the foreigners. "Lots of tricks up those wide sleeves," he said. "Good cooks, too, they say. Francis'll tell you more when we see her tomorrow. Kind of thought we'd run into them today." His eyes scanned the crowds fanning themselves like dozens of yellow jackets in the heat. "They don't get out much," he added idly.

We walked, my arm through his as a good wife, the kelpie trotting close at my feet. Joseph stopped often to introduce me as his "new bride." I felt myself blush to the bare heads of men as they removed their hats; felt awkward to the looks of women. A few matrons smiled out in kindness from beneath their bonnets. Many more wore a haughty look. They glared at me—or perhaps the silver oval I wore at my neck—able to see another woman only as competition. Joseph talked of business to their husbands while they gave me the business with their eyes. It didn't matter. I was as good as them, now. And it was my honeymoon trip and I adored it.

"We'll meet with Mr. Heppner to finalize the sale tomorrow. Six thousand two dollars, cash," Joseph said as we continued our promenade around the city's commons. "It's a good price, Janie. Heppner says he likes the aura that goes with it, my reputation for luck." Joseph hung his thumb in his watch pocket in exaggerated punctuation.

"You are a fortunate man, Joseph," I said. "You captured me."

"I believe Heppner referred to my business relations," he said, laughing.

"Hopefully, he's not privy to my personal ones." He patted my half-gloved hand resting over his arm.

Joseph and Robert Heppner had just finished arranging their meeting time when the first explosions of fireworks from the rimrocks above the creek lit the dusk sky. Applause, "oohs" and "aahs," whooping and hollering, followed the rockets of light that burst in the air falling like waterfalls over the river canyon giving the city its name. Whiffs of sulfur drifted through the night heat as one arc of color followed another. Shouts from the ground greeted each burst of flame as men rushed with water buckets to put out the glowing embers, their faces a mixture of grimness and delight reflected in the firelight.

"Another gift of the Chinese," Joseph said, speaking of the fireworks. "Hope they've got enough water in Canyon Creek to put all the fires out," he joked, his arm around my shoulders. The band broke into "My Country" and then an Irish tune Joseph said was from County Derry. It was a sad song, a man singing to his son, Danny, who had died in battle. I blinked back the tears that rose unbidden on the sad strains of the phrase, "It's you, it's you must go and I must stay," grateful that my husband did not tease me for my sentiment.

Following the song, we headed with the throng of people to the Elkhorn Hotel for a night meal and eventually to bed.

I thought later it was good we had that evening of celebration together. Even the O'Connors' presence seemed to buoy Joseph, remind him of a good decision made years before, and at the same time confirm his belief that Canyon City and the interior of Oregon would grow, his plan for our part in it getting clearer, the trail to our future being better defined. Only later in my marriage did I equate times of joy and sureness as forewarning of disasters to follow.

As we rode up to the picket fence that surrounded Turners', I held a mix of emotion. Soon, I'd be meeting my rival, the model of a wife and mother Joseph held in high esteem. He had written to Francis the morning after our wedding and I was not asked to review his message. I had felt a tinge of something I would later call envy. At that moment, envy was too large a word to fit into the first day of my marriage.

At the same time, riding to the home of the woman who had nursed my husband back to health, I felt full of pride in my status: I arrived at Francis Turner's home as the wife of Joseph Sherar.

Whatever Joseph felt, he was not sharing. I noticed he chewed his lower lip as he scanned the yard. The place seemed unduly quiet. "Not even chickens scratching around." The skips sat idly in the shade on plank shelves, no bees nearby.

We "howdyed" them, Joseph calling out to Archibald and Francis and each of the children. Even the kelpie barked into the silence, his "yip" pause, "yip" pattern going unanswered. We tied our horses to the rail and I stepped through the picket gate Joseph held open for me, aware of a strange apprehension brought on by more than the afternoon heat.

Archibald appeared on the porch so quietly, a gasp marked my startle as I had already started up the steps when I saw him. Thin as a hickory switch, he stood before us, eyes all hollowed out like coal lumps in snow, his beard knotted, clothes hanging on him like they were meant for someone fuller, bigger in body and spirit. He looked right through me, then came from some far away place to bring Joseph to recognition. When he did he moaned and reached his hand out as though seeking his balance.

"You got my letter, then," he said, his voice weak. "So good you sent J. W. on ahead." He held Joseph's hand, clinging. "Ella said we should wait. If I'd known you would almost pass, we could have." He talked like we understood his reference.

"Where's Francis?" Joseph asked.

Archibald's eyes narrowed in pain at the sound of her name. He took a long time answering, swallowing. "She's lost to us, Joseph, like I wrote. God took her home two weeks ago. Baby too," he said, his voice ending in a half-spoken word. "Buried 'em together."

"We've received no letter," Joseph said, his voice even, full of patience. "Ella, and the other children? Where are they?" he probed gently.

Archibald sighed. "Boys are with friends in town. They can stay. Martha's in The Dalles with the Gilliams. And Ella's with J. W., on her way to Mrs. Herbert."

"Mama?" I said, taken aback. "That Mrs. Herbert?"

Archibald looked at me for the first time. "J. W. said she'd look after Ella good. Used to looking after folks." His voice defended, like he was being asked to respond to too much, losing his wife and infant and now being challenged on the choices he made for the living. "J. W. said she was looking for a young girl to keep, all her children but one being gone. Said you'd be having your own in time and you not having a place and all, wouldn't be good to add an almost seven-year-old to the mix." He rubbed his temples with the tips of his fingers as if wiping the pain away. "Wasn't what Francis and I agreed to. Figured she'd understand." He dropped heavily onto the plank wash bench and leaned his head back against the house, closed his eyes. "Already dead a week by the time I wrote to tell you what her wishes were."

"You want us to take Ella?" Joseph asked, still putting the pieces together in the present tense.

"Wanted," Archibald corrected, making it past. "Your mama made good sense in her letter. And J. W. happening out when he did seemed God's message to us, too. Thought you'd sent him. Don't want to burden you, with a new marriage and all."

"It would be no burden," I said to Archibald, speaking up.

"You'd want Ella? Even with you being newly wed?"

"Surely Mama was only acting to be helpful, temporarily," I said.

Archibald moved his hand dismissively. "You work it out," he said. "Ella's fond of Joseph. Francis wanted it," he sighed. "But I've no energy now."

"When she understands our willingness and Francis's wishes, Mama surely won't stand in our way," I said.

"Won't she now," Joseph said, his voice far away and strained yet a step ahead of me in his understanding.

I could see he was dealing with a range of disappointments. I didn't know what he would do with the loss, how large Francis would come in his mind over time, how badly he wanted to battle for her child. My side began to hurt. I didn't want to lose the friend I hoped my husband would become. I didn't want to compete once again with the dead.

I took Archibald's bony elbow and moved him gently back into the house, aware that of the three of us, I was least attached to Francis, dealing with less grief, more focused on what we could do in the present, how we could impact the future.

"Perhaps we could overtake J. W., to avoid confusion before it starts," I suggested.

Joseph shook his head. "Too far ahead," he said. "But if he doesn't cross at the falls, we might make it to your mama's before too much is nailed together. Need to settle things here first, though."

My eyes scanned the cluttered room reflecting the emotional cave Archibald had crawled into. "Start a cook fire," I directed Joseph, who surprisingly did as I asked. I located a pot and walked outside, pumped water from the hand pump and returned. "Some tea will clear our thinking," I said, "Then we'll eat something, help us know what to do next."

The men accepted my directing. The cooking directed my thoughts, distracted me from hearing Archibald tell Joseph of Francis's last hours, from having to decide what we'd do next.

The "next" turned out to be riding with Archibald back to Canyon City that afternoon, settling him in with the boys and their keepers. Joseph held a hasty meeting with Heppner and Benito and we saddled up. We rode out hard, pausing only for a moment at the fresh graves.

As sometimes happens, we took different routes to the future.

Joseph and I slipped quickly through Cross Hollows, down the dugout road, and headed back across the falls with only a brief stop to learn from Auntie Magpie that Sunmiet's baby had arrived "big and long and wiggly as a eel" and that all was well.

J. W. and Ella, however, took the northern route, crossed at the mouth on Nix's bridge and rode on to Fifteen Mile Creek arriving at Mama and Papa's two days ahead of Joseph and me.

"It makes no sense, Mama," I said, frustrated. "Her father wants Ella with us. So did her mother. And Ella too. She knows Joseph, feels safe with him."

"Yes. Well. The child's wishes are of no consequence. She's too young to know her wants. And her father agreed she should come with me for a time."

Mama sat in the kitchen at the small spinning wheel feeding flax fibers into the groove, making thread.

Ella stood at her side, wide blue eyes following Joseph's movements as he paced around the room. She listened, her stiff child's body rigid with tension, her dimples hidden in uncertainty. She wore two black ribbons on either side of the center part in her gold-spun hair.

"He didn't know we'd be willing," Joseph said firmly. "Now he does. He wants us to look after the girl."

"The man's deranged with grief," Mama said, her foot moving rhythmically below the wheel. "Doesn't know what he wants for sure. Times like these," she motioned Ella to hand her more fibers, "cooler heads need prevail. I've seen it before. People in sadness making decisions they later regret. This is the best place for Ella. She'll go to St. Mary's Academy in the fall, get a good education. It'll be easier from here. Might just move into The Dalles for the school year. Once your house is finished, you not living in a hotel, we might discuss it again," she said, adding a drop of sweet to the sour.

As always, there was truth in what Mama proposed. I did believe it would be difficult to add a seven-year-old to our quarters at the Umatilla House. And St. Mary's was a good school and a good idea.

A part of me, selfishly, wanted more time alone with my husband before adding a half-grown family not of my making. But those beliefs were not enough to make me want to thwart my husband's wishes. And there was Ella herself, all sweet-smelling and soft.

Joseph stopped pacing. "There's no need to disrupt the girl more. She comes now, so neither of you feels the pain later. You'll have ample time to see her. We'll arrange it."

Mama acted as though she hadn't heard him. She just paddled away on the spinning wheel, the thump and hum of it filling the room.

"Come, Ella," Joseph said, reaching out for her, testing the tension.

The girl hesitated, looked at Mama as she began moving away. Without looking up, Mama reached her hand around Ella's waist, pulled her, announcing her control, into her side.

"Well," she said then, stopped her spinning and stared at Joseph. "You cannot always have what you want, Mr. Sherar. It's a new experience for you, I'm sure, but the girl stays. Salve your grief some other way. Go make the marriage you wanted. Finish your house and we'll talk again. Ella," she said, patting the girl's arm, "fetch me a dipper of water. My old bones are tired." We watched Ella leave, looking back over her shoulder at us. Mama sighed and looked first at Joseph, then me before she said, "Reminds a soul of Rachel, don't you think? Just her age when she died."

"But I've never had trouble," Joseph said. He was agitated as I had never seen him before. "What happened?"

Benito carried the information from one of his trips into town for a wagon load of shakes to roof the house with. The shakes would be extra protection against the leakage of the sparse rain though greater snow accumulations expected later in the year. "Nothing to be planned for," Benito told him, unloading the piles of cedar. Puffs of dust burped out from piles as the shakes slapped the earth. Benito wiped his brow of the August heat, stopped to describe. "Cayuse attack on dugout trail. No place to go. Wounded many. Cut ropes and slash bags and kick everything over sides. Many animals destroyed. Flour and sugar snow on sagebrush until first rains." He shook his head sadly, "All is lost."

"It wasn't your fault, Joseph," I said, trying to calm my husband. He seemed decidedly upset. "Didn't you tell me it was a risky business? Mr. Heppner must have known that too, decided he could live with the risk when he bought the string."

Joseph snapped his response to me, startled me. "I didn't just sell him the string. I sold him the idea. Told him settlement would be increasing, things were safe. Everything he had he put into that string." He wiped his face with the linen handkerchief he pulled from his shirt pocket.

Benito shook his head sadly, spit a stream of tobacco. "Mr. Heppner, he wiped out on first trip on his own."

"No one holds you accountable for the loss," I said, touching Joseph's arm gently, still attempting to slow his irritation.

"Doesn't matter." He brushed my arm away. "Hold myself accountable." He jabbed his finger into his chest as he spoke. "My integrity's at risk."

"Mr. Heppner," Benito told him, picking up on my cue, "he does not blame you. He is just glad he lives and no lives were lost. He is just not sure what he will do next."

Joseph grunted, ending the conversation but not his thoughts I was sure.

The men finished unloading the shakes, enough to roof two houses, ours and Anna and Benito's being built down the slope. We had lived two weeks in our home, a two-story frame structure built with extra bedrooms on either side of the stairwell at the top of the second floor. I missed some of the hustle and bustle of living in the Umatilla House; but I liked the privacy, the freedom that being in my own home afforded me, the opportunity to know my husband as a friend.

I brought up cool water from the well, offered it to the men in the sultry morning, pondering Joseph's word *integrity*. Joseph wiped the cold liquid from his upper lip and mustache with the back of his hand. He emptied the dipper with a flick of his wrist, sprayed water beading up on the dust. He rinsed the cup, refilled it from the bucket, and handed it to Benito as he spoke, decision clear in his voice.

"I'll replace the string."

Benito's eyes grew large above the rim of the dipper he drank from. He looked first at Joseph. Then at me.

"Replace it?" I said. "You don't owe him that!"

"It's not what I owe him, but what I owe myself—what I can live with."

"Can we afford such generosity?" I said, though my voice held an opinion more than a question.

"Can't afford not to," he said. "Sold my reputation for success along with that string. My reputation for giving people good advice. Heppner took my words on as his dream. He trusted my judgment as much as anything. Don't want my name bandied about in any way other than respectable."

"But six thousand dollars!" I said. "We can't manage that, what with the cattle, the ranch, and all."

"You didn't make the money," he said, "or my reputation."

"Maybe if you'd let me participate in both I'd see it differently," I snapped back. I swallowed to keep the tears from stinging my eyes. Bandit appeared from nowhere, sat primly at my feet.

My outburst startled my husband, I think, told him he had more to contend with than just his reputation. He took it one step at a time.

"We'll stop for the day," he said to Benito. "Time for you to head back into town, ask Heppner to come by his earliest convenience. Tell him I'd like to talk."

To me he said, "Change—if you'd like. We'll ride to Tygh Valley, discuss this money thing. Maybe stop by your father's."

He knew both offers would please me. I wanted to know more about his financial affairs, wished to be a full partner in this life we were carving.

And it had been several weeks since we'd seen Ella. We'd stopped frequently at first. But our visits were frosted by the cool presence of my mother. It was time to bring up the subject of Ella's move with us again, now that a bed and dresser awaited her; time to face my confusion about truly wanting her or not.

He began putting his tools, the adz, a saw or two, into his tool box. I noticed an odd looking saw, one with a handle and very thin blade. He liked teaching me, and I thought it would tenderize our feud if he told me what it was.

"Coping saw," he said.

"What's it used for?" I asked.

"Fitting things into tight places, like a cabinet into a corner." He turned the small saw over in his paw-like hands.

"What's so different about it?" I asked. "Why do they say it 'copes'?"

He looked at me, saw I was serious. "It has both strength and flexibility," he said. "Blade is very strong, good, hard steel. But it bends. If it was too strong, things you're trying to fit would splinter. But if it was too flexible, bent too much, then you'd leave big gaps in what you're trying to bring together."

"Kind of like trying to cope with Mama and this thing with Ella," I noted.

He nodded. "And with Heppner. And even with building this place, buying land at the falls, trying to make our way here. Even with the two of us, making this marriage a fit." He lifted my chin with his hand, held my gaze. "Coping takes the whole saw, both its toughness and its suppleness. That's how we're building, coping, before things start to splinter or split. Let's both try to remember that," he said, and pulled me close and kissed my forehead.

CHAPTER 22

AFTER THE STORM

⁓

"SCHOOL WILL BEGIN soon," Mama said. "Why not wait until spring. You'll be more settled in your house." She pulled at the weeds in the garden plot, Ella kneeling at her side.

"You said once we were in the house, Mama," I told her, sitting, hugging my knees.

"Yes. Well. Ella's become such a good help to me, especially when your Papa's gone. And she'll be gone herself from me soon enough. To St. Mary's. You wouldn't want to deprive her of that, would you?"

"She's young for boarding school," Joseph said. "Needs to know where home is before she leaves it again."

"The Sisters understand young ladies. They're prepared for some sickness for home. Teach in spite of it," she added. "And children learn."

I watched Ella quietly working in the morning cool beside my mother. Even in a few short weeks, her plumpness was easing into her height. She was growing up before our eyes. Ella watched me out of slate blue. I thought I recognized longing. I was twice her age as Joseph was twice mine. Once she was in school, we'd see so little of her, her childishness would disappear before we even knew it.

Joseph wanted her. That much I knew from the way he talked of the child. He'd even begun the adoption proceedings, gathered the required papers. Mama knew, even encouraged it which I suppose added to our false hope.

I wondered if perhaps Joseph's attachment to Ella was a connection to Francis. And yes, I recognized the ebb and flow of my feelings about taking on this child. But for Joseph's sake, I pleaded for her, made myself supple for the fit.

I tried to imagine what argument would appeal to my mother. For the child's sake? For Francis? Surely not for mine. None held water with her.

"You said when the house was finished Ella could live with us," I reminded her, petulant.

"I said we'd discuss it, to be more accurate," she said. "And so we are." She wiped her hands on her long apron, stretching out her power. "Where is that Baby George?" she asked idly. Ella pointed toward the paddock where the youngster made mudpies from the horse-trough leaks. "Yes. Such a help you are, Ella," Mama said. Then to Joseph and me: "She goes to St. Mary's in the fall." She left no argument. Then she smiled a sticky sweetness. "We can discuss again her living with you in the spring, when school is out. Yes. It will be better to think of a move then."

She stood. "Shall we take some tea the sun has readied? Inside. It's cooler there." She breezed her face with the imaginary fan of her hand, flushed with victory. "Come, George," she called to my brother. "Ella? Fetch him, dear." She turned to walk inside as Ella slipped past us to the paddock without a second glance.

We had lost. But in the conversation, I knew I wanted Ella for more than to just please Joseph or to thwart my mother. I wanted her for her, to be there for her as I once had been for Rachel, Loyal, and Pauline. To share her child-hood before it slipped away.

Over sun tea, my mother did consent to Ella's joining us on the day ride. "As far as Tygh Valley and back," she said sipping tea at the table. "But be care-ful. Watch her." She pinched my guilt.

Papa came out of the barn to talk with Joseph and me, help Ella onto her horse. His face looked thinner and he walked with tired steps, not saying much, less the politician and more a sad but busy statesman. "Mama has tea," I told him. He smiled and turned back to the barn instead of walking to the house or watching us ride away. I was conscious that this was no longer my home.

On her own horse, Ella rode like an egg with legs, gingerly, her stubby limbs sticking straight out over the wide back of the nag. The three of us talked quietly in the morning heat, cantering occasionally, our voices mixed with the creak of leather and the jangle of the horse's bits. Ella seemed a somber child. "Not the way I remember her," Joseph whispered to me as we rode.

The day of no demands must have offered safety, for as we crested the last rise before Tygh Valley town, Ella began asking questions about where we lived, what things there were to do there. She squealed in delight when her tentative call to Bandit resulted in a lap full of wiggly dog. It was the first time I'd seen excitement lift Ella's blond curls from her cheeks.

"I bet there are more things to do at your house than you could do in one day with one dog," she said.

"Good bet," I said, winking over her head at Joseph.

"Mrs. Herbert doesn't like me to ride much," she volunteered. She urged her horse to keep abreast as she rode between our mounts. "Says sitting with my legs split isn't lady-like. My legs aren't split," she said, chastising foolish adults. "They're all tied together with skin, see?" She pulled her pantaloons up toward her knee to show me. I thought her old for little girl's pantaloons.

"You're right," I said, smiling. "Smooth as an alder branch."

"And I told her, 'I bet Mrs. Sherar rides that way.'" She looked at me and said, "And you're a lady." She kicked the horse again to keep her moving.

"Bet she loved hearing that," Joseph said.

"One of your better bets," I quipped.

"She *did* like me saying you were a lady," Ella insisted. "She told me all kinds of things you do as a lady. 'Shoot a Kentucky, steal your papa's heart, change your mind.' When I asked to do those, she got upset. Sent me out to pull weeds. Do ladies do those too?" Ella asked, her dimples resting in question.

"Ladies do what they have to," I told her, "even when they'd rather not."

We reached Tygh Valley. While Joseph completed his business with Mr. Staley, Ella and I located a shady place in the shadow of the rimrocks that arched part way around the grassy flat forming the town site. The smaller end of the Tygh Creek bubbled out beside the rocks. "Watch for snakes," I warned Ella as we found a place to sit. "They like the cool this time of year too."

"I never step on snakes," she said. "I talk to them."

"Me too!" I said, amazed.

Ella threw small rocks into the river, stepping closer to the grassy bank.

"Careful," I called out. I felt the familiar anxiety associated with small children beside water. "Careful, Ella," I said again, sitting up straighter, better to see. "Don't get too close." I'd said those words before, too, and for a fleeting moment I imagined what I'd say if something happened to her, how I'd explain. I shook my head of the thought.

Tygh Creek ran full here, but it wasn't flooding, wasn't pushing past its banks. Still, memories prickled unbidden to my mind.

Joseph walked up behind me and gently touched my shoulder, startling me. "Don't do that!" I snapped.

"Didn't mean to scare you." He sat beside me, removed his hat. "Thought you heard me coming. What's the matter?" he asked, looking at my jaw set, eyes staring toward the river. "Looks like you've seen a ghost." He turned to watch Ella remove her shoes. "Something with Ella? What's wrong?"

I had never told him of what had happened with my brother and sisters, never shared with him how quickly guilt arrived disguised as fear or grief. It never seemed the time to tell him. I never really wanted him to know of my poor judgment, how things I loved just left.

But that day, as we sat beside the water watching a child we hoped might come into our lives, I shared my soul. Perhaps I wished to rescue my own reputation as someone who could be counted on to care for another. "Integrity," I told him. "Maybe that's why I want to care for Ella and a dozen other children. Maybe to prove to myself—and my mother—that I am able to keep a child safe, love her into being grown."

Joseph sat quietly as I talked, swallowing tears. His fingers parted and sorted a soft patch of grass. When I finished, he reached for me, wiped my puffy, crying eyes, held me. I began truly loving my husband that day for he heard my story and did not judge me harshly. With Joseph, I watched, again, a child at play beside rushing water.

"Perhaps God will keep children from me," I voiced my deepest fear, "to punish me."

"You did not cause it, Janie," he said as my body sank into his safety.

"I must have! I let them get wet. I didn't want to spoil their fun, have them be upset with me. Then I let them get beyond me, out of my control!"

He shook his head. "It was not your fault. They could have fallen into that creek, been drenched and cold to the bone, and their deaths would not have been your fault."

"I was careless," I said, sobbing. "Mama said so."

"Your mama is wrong in this." He rocked me, safe in his arms. "Diphtheria...it isn't caused by water or colds, but by something that goes between people, quickly. No one knows what or why some people suffer and others don't. But it isn't from them slipping into the water, that much I'm sure."

I so wanted to believe him.

We held each other, still watching Ella.

"Best you come back," I finally called to her, wiping my eyes, aware that the day slipped away.

She looked at me, pretended not to hear and kept on walking. I felt some irritation.

"I don't believe the Lord works that way," Joseph said. "By withholding children. There's time yet for babies of our own." He squeezed me. "Yours is a young life to be faced with losing so much," he said. "But like the song from Derry, some must go, and some must stay. Those of us who live bear the greatest pain."

The refrain from that mournful song settled in my head as I sank into the comfort of his confidence. I did not know then that he, too, spoke from experience. I was simply grateful that he did not faint from touching a person who may have caused the death of someone else.

Ella chose the afternoon to demonstrate the disobedience of an almost seven-year-old and we ended up staying longer than anticipated beside the river, chiding her to put her shoes on, settle down, get back on the horse. She didn't accept my fumbled explanation for my red eyes, kept prodding, curious. I wondered fleetingly if I had the energy to deal with a defiant child, then decided if Mama could do it, so could I.

We arrived back at Fifteen Mile Crossing as the sun set and after the wind rose but well before darkness and the impending storm. This fact escaped my mother who stood on the porch agitated enough to chew up farrier nails.

Her anger seemed well beyond the infraction we'd apparently committed by coming back later than we'd thought. Mama said: "I see once again you cannot be trusted."

"It's early yet," Joseph answered, surprised at her vehemence. He did not sound apologetic. "Just supper time. Not even dark." He stood off his horse, helping Ella to the ground.

"I decide what's early or not," Mama countered. "Been lightning over the ridge for the past hour. Not safe at all for a child to be out in it." Soft lights from the kerosene lamps glowed through the house windows, looked inviting. I saw movement inside, Papa and Baby George coming out to stand on the porch.

"Come Ella," Papa said, "there's some supper waiting on you."

"I'm not hungry," Ella told him in a petulant voice.

"Did you have a nice time, child?" he asked.

"It was all right," she said, stomping up on the porch.

"That's good," Papa told her softly, his voice betraying his wish to get her away from the storm he too felt brewing. "Take Baby George inside. There's cold milk on the table for you in the kitchen, some sliced venison and cheese. Then off to bed."

Ella started her stomp into the house, punishing us I guessed for making her leave the river, ride back, do what needed to be done. But then with a child's ability to forgive and forget, she turned, ran back to hug me as I stood beside my horse. I squatted down to her height, felt the warmth of unfettered caring that only a child's arms can give. I held her, buried my face in her curls, my fingers remembering the touch of lean little backs through thin calicos.

"G'night," she whispered.

I held her a bit longer, until I felt Joseph's hand on my shoulder. Ella reached for him as he bent down to pick her up, brushed her face with his beard.

"Sleep well," he said. "We'll see you again soon."

A flash of lightning lit the night sky somewhere in the distance. "Stay," she pleaded. "The storm."

"They need to hurry home," Mama answered for us. "Got lots to do there, I'm sure."

"We'll be fine," I assured Ella. "The storm is far away, see, on that ridge? We'll ride the other way, where the moon is full. It will light our way home."

Ella seemed skeptical as Papa walked out to take her from Joseph's arms. "You're welcome to stay," he said for our ears only. Joseph shook his head, helped me mount up.

Papa and Ella headed back into the soft lights of the house. Mama started to follow them in, carrying her skirt up the stairs with her fingertips. Then she hesitated, turned back. She said: "Your presence disrupts the girl's life. I've had time to think, waiting." Her tightly clasped hands now formed a fist together in front of her as she faced us full. "She goes to St. Mary's in the fall. Until then, I'll thank you not to be stopping by, filling her head with thoughts of what her life might be like living with you. If you care for her—as you say you do—then leave her be. She's had enough loss and change and needs no more from you." My heart pounded in my ears and seemed to understand her words before my head did. I stalled for time, to change her meaning. I said: "But we didn't do anything wrong! Only spent some time with her. Why take that away from either of us?"

"Why not?" my mother said. She shrugged her shoulders as though I'd asked her to explain why she served carrot cake instead of angel. Her lightness infuriated me, as though we spoke of meaningless things instead of someone's love and life. Her power over the outcome made it all the more intolerable.

"The adoption papers are ready," Joseph said. I heard both alarm and anger in his voice. "Let's just finish what Archibald wanted, stop this dallying. We'll pick her up in the morning."

Mama glared at him from behind a thin smile. "I'll not say my daughter is the cause," she told him, not looking at me. "But I have only one child under my roof that is of my own birthing. The rest are gone. Dead." Her eyes matched the word.

"It wasn't my fault, Mama!" I cried.

"Whose then?" She turned on me. "Three babies. Dead within three days."

Then she hissed the words I'd imagined her saying, dreaded ever hearing: "And you live."

"That's not fair!" Hot tears poured down my cheeks. My breath stuck in my chest, choked out my words.

"You dare to speak to me of *fair?* There is no fair in life," she seethed, "or I would have my family." I could see tears forming in her eyes, too, heard the catch in her voice as her chest heaved back growing sobs.

"Your loss is great, Mrs. Herbert," Joseph said. His voice soothed as he stepped toward her. "Don't compound it. Jane did not cause their deaths, nor your pain."

"What do you know of it!" Mama said then, openly, irrationally enraged, moving out of his reach. Her eyes bulged. Her chest heaved. She clasped and unclasped her hands at the sides of her skirt, her knuckles bony white. "This child, Ella," she shouted, then calmed herself, through evenly enunciated words. "This child, Susan Ella Turner, is mine to care for." She glared at Joseph. "She is here by God's good grace, and neither you nor your young wife shall ever take her from me."

She bore no further argument, simply turned and went inside, pulling the latch string behind her when she closed the door.

I looked at Joseph, expecting he could see the hole my mother's words had exploded in my heart. And so he must have, for he came to me, touched my shoulder, and then held me in my grief.

We rode on home, lightning over the ridge sending flashes that lit Joseph's set jaw, pierced my tear-swollen eyes. Thunder cracked within a few seconds, rattling the horses who skittishly moved sideways, picking the trail home in the darkness. They needed more concentration from their riders for control.

Then, as though our grief was insufficient, we both smelled the smoke.

"Lightning strike somewhere," Joseph said, looking into the night sky. The strike could have been miles away, could have happened hours before. Smoke could drift great distances in the ridges and ravines, settling over a homestead miles from its source. Or there could be a wall of flames just over the ridge. "We'll have to stand night watch," he said.

"No matter," I answered. "I doubt I'll ever sleep again."

The next hours were lit by flashes of lightning ripping across the ridges like a sharp blade flashing against the sun. The thunder rolled and cracked, startling the horses who ran in circles in the field until we caught them up and tied them close to the house. It worried the cattle, even bothered the mules who looked up into the flashing night sky.

I moved as in a nightmare, my mind thick, body tired from crying. It seemed fitting that a range fire should light the empty darkness.

We were as prepared as we could be. Anna and Benito and the hands all had buckets of water dipped from the well and the creeks. In the dark, we slopped the water around the house, splashed up on the walls. The smaller animals we let run loose assuming their instincts would best protect them. The kelpie kept close to us as we ran here and there with more buckets, more water. Finally, the thunder moved on, and we waited to see what the lightning had left us.

The low, fast-moving flames reached us in the early-morning light, their red and gold crackling of the dry bunch grass preceded by a wall of dark smoke.

"All the buckets to the barns!" Joseph croaked in a smoke-husky voice, and he and Benito and the buckaroos moved from splashing water around the houses to the largest barn. We had already decided that the houses were best protected by their position in the Y of the two creeks. If the flames did not jump the water, they'd be safe; if they did, nothing would protect them.

The barns, however, sat on the far side of the split creeks where their wide doors opened onto the corrals and green grass in the spring. But this was August. Hot, dry August. If the flames moved to the upper end, they could easily move toward the barns. Anna and I and several other hands wore calluses into our hands digging a fire line around the upper end of the barns. Joseph and Benito and other men formed a bucket line from the creek, hoisting bucket after bucket of water to splash on the barn walls and up onto the roofs. When it seemed we had dug what we could, we joined the bucket line, pulling buckets of water from the horse troughs, slopping them up on the walls and on the dirt fire line we'd dug beside the men. Dark smoke billowed around us. We watched the grasses burn fast and pick up speed in their own wind, moving down the ridge toward the creeks.

I supposed the intensity the fire demanded was good, in a way. It kept my mind from considering the emptiness and loss.

Joseph attempted to yell something, his voice lost in the thick smoke. My eyes burned and my nose filled with the scent of singed sagebrush. I looked around for Bandit and then saw what Joseph yelled for: Bandit, swirled in smoke, lying beside the creek closest to the barns. "Bandit!" I yelled, "Oh, please God, not Bandit, too," I prayed and knew that if I lost the dog, I would not wish to wake up in the morning.

"Bandit!" I called again, searching through the smoke, and God answered my prayer. The little dog lifted his ears, coughed, then splashed through the wetness of the creek to my side.

We were all taken care of that night, despite the fire searing and roaring on down the ravine to the Deschutes, burning up the nettles and the choke cherry trees and exposing the rocks and ridges of the pack trail as it moved back and forth across the now naked stream. At the upper end, the fire burned above the barns and disappeared over the ridge to be consumed by the White River. Our dug lines around the barns held the flames at bay.

The morning revealed a black, exposed world. Around us, the land smoldered with drifting smoke. Nothing brown or green; just black beyond our fire lines, as far as our eyes could see. It fit how I felt. Joseph took my hand and we turned back from the barns, smoke still clinging to us like a nightmare that lingers into morning.

"Looks bad, but not much real damage done," Joseph said. I marveled at my husband's optimism. "We've still got this island of green." He gazed at the tiny space of sparse grass growing between the houses and the barns. "And a whole lot more since the buildings were spared." He pulled a dipper of water from the well, handed it to me, surveyed the bleak, pastureless horizon. "My mother used to say 'a fire is as good as a move' for cleaning out the old, forcing you to appreciate what you have and look to whatever is new." He took a long drink of the cold water I handed him, wiped soot from his forehead with the back of his hand. "So that's where we are, Janie. We're cleaned out of the old; got to get on with the new."

CHAPTER 23

TRANSITIONS

"THE SWEAT MIGHT HEAL YOU," Sunmiet told me. "Relieve you of the hurt that sits on your heart." She rested her needle, thread, and red bead on top of the buckskin lying on her lap. Her fingertips idly rubbed the colored beads she'd traded dried salmon for, examining the hummingbird design as she paused. Aswan, "little boy," and Anne chased each other in the center of their Simnasho home. She had named her second Anne, a non-Indian name. Standing Tall initially protested, agreed only when Sunmiet's *kása* promised to have a naming early, before Anne was full grown. The children flopped in laughter onto the bedrolls, tickling each other, rolling then racing again. "Oh, hayah! Go outside now," Sunmiet said, scooting them out the door. We watched their chubby legs disappear through the opening, heard them laugh as the newest puppies attacked them on the outside.

"You have beautiful children," I told Sunmiet. She smiled and nodded, better about receiving compliments.

We sat, our backs against the wood frame, leaning into the leather hides hung on the walls. The leather kept the cool October air from moving too quickly through the cracks in the wood. The soothing scent of smoked leather filled the small space packed with baskets and furs and herbs hanging from the ceiling like black moss dripping from the firs.

"Many of my people take the sweat, to feel stronger, to move the bad spirits out of their pores," she told me. "To be cleansed, refreshed, and free," she added. "I will ask Standing Tall to heat the rocks if you wish it." She returned to the beadwork, completing a design that had been her grandmother's and handed down to her. "If I ask him, he will do it, even for a non-Indian."

Did I wish it? I wasn't sure anything would heal what ailed me. "Our spirits grieve," the pastor had told me, "and in time, as the Lord heals, we are given newness. It's that way with loss. It is all right to feel sadness, even anger. In time, both will go away and leave only a small emptiness in a corner of your being. You'll receive greater fullness, then, as you will have stretched your heart, made room for the Lord's blessings."

His words had comforted me at Papa's funeral, helped ease the pain of Papa's loss.

But now, as I approached my twentieth birthday never having given my father a grandchild, with no change in Mama's distance or Ella's closeness, I wondered if too much loss might simply shut me down.

"Shall I ask him, then?" Sunmiet said, breaking into my thoughts. "You will sweat with me and the children? It will heal your body even if you do not let it heal your insides," she told me. She straightened herself with a sharp intake of breath as Bubbles came through the door, unannounced.

"I need to think on it," I told Sunmiet.

Bubbles noted Sunmiet's brief flash of pain. I thought it because of her intrusion. Bubbles took it differently. "You need the sweat to heal the blood spots on *your* body," she said to Sunmiet, having listened at the door, knowing some secret. "You married the wrong brother," Bubbles crowed. "You should have waited for Koosh."

"I did not wish Koosh," Sunmiet said, irritated. "My husband is a good provider. He gives me a house of my own, even if the door does not keep everyone out."

Bubbles snorted. "Your own house. Yes, so no one will hear your cries when he treats you like a slow horse."

"Is that true, Sunmiet?" I asked, alarmed. "He beats you?"

Sunmiet looked away, her eyelashes fluttering in embarrassment or shame, I couldn't be sure. "Only when he drinks the whiskey. He is always sad it happened when the night is over." She looked up, defending. "It is so hard for him. The arguments over the fishing. The Wascos at the big river are of one family. They have fished there since time began, and now, they are told to stay away, come here, where other families care for fishing sites and he does not belong. It is too hard on him."

"Does your father know?" I asked, missing again my own father.

Bubbles answered. "Everyone knows."

She plopped onto a corn husk mattress spread across from Sunmiet and changed the subject as though we had been discussing choke cherries. "When did Kása give the hummingbird design to you?" she asked Sunmiet, too sweetly.

"Long ago," Sunmiet said.

"She promised it to me before that," Bubbles said, pouting. "Mother says you tricked her out of it. You are always there, being her hands. You never let the rest of us come around."

Sunmiet set her jaw, as irritated as I'd seen her. Her eyelashes fluttered. "No tricks. She gave it to me. You might have had it. But you can never be found when Kása needs huckleberries picked or salmon dried or roots dug. She gave it to whom she wished. And so will I."

"Can I persuade you to give it to me?" Bubbles asked, looking with envy on Sunmiet's fine beadwork.

"I will think on it," Sunmiet said. "As Huckleberry Eyes thinks on the sweat."

Bubbles raised her eyebrows, surprised I'd been asked. "I need to give it more time," I said, uncertain. I wanted to confer with Joseph about it, and about Standing Tall's behavior.

Sunmiet nodded, understanding that I needed to hang onto my wounds, for whatever reason, would let them go only when I was ready and in my own way. We shared in that, I think. She offered her healing with the sweat, and her willingness to wait.

Joseph stuck his head through the opening, Bandit pushed past him onto my lap. "Ready?" Joseph asked. I nodded, touched Sunmiet's fingers lightly, told a lounging Bubbles goodbye, and with Bandit bouncing at my feet, we left the reservation, heading back home.

Joseph's mood always lightened after time with Peter, chiding him about his eagle-feather, teasing, trying to trade him out of it even after all these years. They always spoke of cattle and sheep and change. Joseph found a fellow visionary in Peter and sharing his company proved ample reason to ride with me to the reservation even if he had little to say to my friend's husband.

"Standing Tall…" I began as we rode, broaching the difficult subject with Joseph. I tried again, "Sunmiet says Standing Tall hurts her. Well, Bubbles said he did and Sunmiet didn't deny it. Everyone supposedly knows. Why don't they stop it?"

We rode side by side, mounted, watching the weaving grasses like waves of water through the ears of our horses.

"It's their business," Joseph said, uncomfortable with the subject. "They have their ways."

"I don't think we can dismiss it as *their* way. I mean, it's a human way, the way we treat each other. It makes a difference, it seems to me, regardless of your race or family or tradition."

"Don't get involved in this, Janie," he said. "It is something you don't understand. We wouldn't want someone telling us how to be with each other, would we?"

I thought for a moment. "If you were hurting me, I think I'd be very pleased to have someone stand beside me, help me fight back for what is right."

"There's the difference," he said. "You'd fight back. Sunmiet won't. It's their way I'm telling you. Stay out of it."

It made no sense to me: not Standing Tall's behavior, not Sunmiet's, and not my husband's ability to dismiss the pain of someone else so easily. He always reached out to others. This time, he held back as though to honor Sunmiet's people. I struggled with the quality of such honor.

"Sunmiet thinks the sweats might help me," I said. "Even Kása said perhaps the Indian doctor could assist me. It's a great honor, I think, that she would ask me."

"Honor. Yes, it's that, I suppose," my husband said. His hands tightened on the reins. I could tell there was a hesitation for him.

"You're reluctant? About the sweat?"

"Let's see first about the Chinese doctor, Dr. Hey. We've not considered him."

"What's the difference?"

He was thoughtful. "One's religion," he said. "The other's herbs. We could go to Canyon City in a week or two. Looks like an open winter."

"It isn't *my* religion," I said. "I wouldn't be doing something that was sinful. Just seeing if the sweats could get me restful. Cleanse me."

"You're clean enough," he said, irritated. I could tell the subject bothered him, something about the sweat. Or perhaps just the subject of my fertility itself distressed him. Or maybe his distress arose from the constant wondering of what part he might play in our inability to advance our family. "Suit yourself," he said, dismissing it. Then he added more kindly, "As I'm sure you will."

Since my marriage, the only children I'd spent time with belonged to someone else.

Lodenma had another. "Easy as a hog skinning," she said, "long as you can stand the stench. Not to worry," she added, her wide hands patting mine kindly. "You'll have one soon enough." I felt her embarrassment at her fertility in the presence of my lack.

She was less hopeful, mentioned it less often as I turned twenty, still childless, with neither an Ella or my own. Sunmiet shared her children with me, helped fill my days. A natural mother, Sunmiet's children each arrived larger than the one before. But she had no throwing fits. After Anne, she'd been healed enough within a day to move about. Of course, having her mother and auntie and Standing Tall's family close by made nurturing as available as mother's milk. I envied the family Sunmiet's children were born into.

Even Bubbles delivered a healthy boy the summer of '68. Still stocky though sporting a waist now, she had mended some of her ways which had persuaded a handsome Koosh to claim her. Their union seemed fitting since she'd once claimed him from the river.

For Joseph and me, there was no baby-planning, no vanilla-smelling toddler splashing in the copper boiler; no little voices crying in the night. I played catch with Benito and Anna's children since they lived so close; took them on rides to spots where deer slept, even introduced them to my pistol, with their parents' permission.

Joseph never spoke of our disappointment though he must have felt it. I'd see him watching Peter and his son riding together, their heads bent in planning, their voices raised in laughter and I knew he must have missed it terribly, that rawhide tightness that comes from well-matched strands.

We caught glimpses of Ella sometimes when the St. Mary's girls went on outings near The Dalles and we happened to be near. From a distance, we watched Ella go from being a little girl to quite a proper young lady. Joseph and I did not discuss her, keeping what we felt for her inside, to not hurt the other.

I had not spoken with my mother since the day she shut Ella from us.

For Joseph and me, those were years of coping a marriage and a friendship rather than a family. And though we each took time when we could to be with Sunmiet's children or made ourselves favorite auntie and uncle for Benito and Anna's two, Joseph and I mostly spent our time together, learning each other's ways, not the ways of children.

I discovered how Joseph liked his venison fried (thin-sliced, lightly floured, and seared once on each side) and that he loved to give—gifts of silver, gifts of time, gifts made from wood. He discovered I liked the feel of things: rough wool woven into warmth, alder cut and carved into a child's toy, and the grit of earth beneath my fingers and the vegetables and blooms that grew. On our rides together, Joseph often took the time to mark a flowering plant, promising to return later to transplant it in the fall. And this he did, expanding the variety of flowers that pushed up through the worked soil each spring creating splashes of color around the weathered wood of our home.

It turned out Joseph's temper was for things that didn't always work the way he wanted; he rarely used it against people. He demanded much but treated others with more tenderness than he did himself. He assigned work well, built on the strengths of his buckaroos.

Joseph also spent hours in quiet walking, sketching, allowing me to sometimes simply stroll beside him in the silence. I watched satisfaction appear readily on his face when he saw his sketches rise to real—to barns and smokehouses and especially to the pack trails he reinforced across meandering streams, up steep switchbacks. Trails that looked like some giant had dragged his finger across steep hillsides, cleared rock and ridges with his fingernail into narrow, twisting roads. Joseph loved seeing accomplishments where some said none could be. He was always a giant in my mind.

And like an attentive husband, he noticed and remembered things to make a difference. That I liked early morning rides regardless of the weather. That it would please me to have him ask permission to join me in them, honoring my privacy and my right to choose. And no gift he ever gave me had more meaning than one received each morning while I slowly met the day. Half asleep, his arms around me, my head resting on his chest, I'd feel his lips upon my forehead, hear him whisper through my rest.

"What is it?" I asked the first time it happened.

He was quiet. I felt him swallow, then he said, "I'm prayin' on ye, darlin.' It's how I start me day."

Nothing ever lifted me on my sometimes weary way as remembering his lips against my skin asking for blessings on my day.

And we nurtured each other's dreams: mine, to have a family still; Joseph's, to own the falls, build a home there and a bridge, open up the interior of Oregon.

In all those years, I counted myself privileged to be married to my best friend.

"I don't understand how you hope to bring a stagecoach down the ridge," I told him one morning as we curled under the down comforter together. Dawn eased up the hollow like a lazy dog, slow but sure to arrive through the starched white curtains over the bedroom windows. Over the years, Joseph had shown me portions of his ideas in his sketch books. Still I struggled with understanding what he planned to really do.

"Let's get up," he said, impulsive. He pushed the down comforter away from our faces presenting us with a blast of November air. "Ride down to the falls so I can really show you." Thinking further he added: "Pack a lunch and we'll picnic. Make a day of it, ride up the other side where you can really see it."

"It's November!" I said. "Picnic?"

"Where's your sense of adventure? Have you lost it with your youth?" He poked my midriff, still slender, showing no signs of aging. Or of birthing.

"Oh, pooh!" I told him. "I'll always be younger than you, old man." I poked him back, his small paunch showing the signs of regular food cooked with loving hands.

He laughed, pushing me out of bed, the rag rug delaying the squeal I always made when my feet hit the cold floor beyond it.

"Bundle up," he said, getting dressed. "I'll bring up the mules."

"O-o-o-h," I said, "we really are going to ride up steep slopes if you're bringing on the big guns."

"Don't want to take any chances on slick surfaces riding with an old woman on a skittish horse," he assured me as he stomped into his boots. "Wear your fur boots. It'll be warmer. And the split skirt."

"I know, I know," I told him. "I'm old enough to dress myself."

I grabbed my clothes, bounced past him on tip toes into the main room to stand in front of the glowing embers of the fire. A shiver passed through me and I reached for the bellows to fan the flames. I still held them when Joseph came up behind me. He wrapped his arms around me, brushed his beard on my face. "I love you," he said as he released me then shot out through the door, chanting, "old and aging as you are."

I threw the bellows at him. They hit the closed door.

It was a wonderful trip! And for the first time I did truly see what he saw.

"And we'll build a huge house here," he said, "a hotel, two, three stories of the finest wood, with huge rooms and glass windows so people can look out onto the falls. We were standing on the narrow strip of land that bordered the river, just beyond the crossing.

"They'll practically step out onto the bridge," I pointed out, "if you build so close."

"There'll be room," he said, "for the road to run past the front and turn east, to cross the bridge. I've checked it. A big bridge, wide enough to accommodate wagons and stages and herds of cattle and sheep. That rope lava, over there will be the backdrop for the hotel." He turned my shoulders around so I faced the row of rock posts Pastor Condon said were of the Clarno Period, unique in their thickness as they rose up from the river canyon forming a steep, flat ridge at the top. He spoke more loudly, to overcome the roar of the falls.

"What about my garden?" I said. "Where will that be? There isn't even any soil here, just rock." I was thinking of what I would leave behind, the rich black soil that gave up fresh vegetables and good seeds for the drying gourds each year.

"Beside the ledge," he said. "We'll bring in earth, loads of it, enough for a garden and an orchard. And over there," he pointed to the base of the Tygh Ridge, moving his finger and my eyes up to the top of the steep and dipping ravines dotted with sagebrush and junipers. "We'll build up the pack trail. Bring it all the way down to the bridge. Improve the crossing then build a real road up the other side. Cut through that lava and open up the way to Bake Oven and Canyon City. Rocks and sagebrush roots as a base so the road'll withstand the rain and snow. People will know it's safe to go this way and take less time." His enthusiasm grew with each shared detail.

"Who will build it all? It'll take dozens of men, just for the buildings. And the roads... How do you propose to pay for these grand ideas," I said, popping holes in his dreams. I'd become more familiar with our finances over the years and found that Joseph was never restricted by ordinary resources such as cash.

"There'll be a way," he said. He walked closer to the roaring falls, stepped off distances from the base of the ridge to the river. "Room for a barn here, this side. For stock changes. One over there, too, for cattle, blacksmith." He was off on his own. "May sold it to Hemingway. Hemingway to O'Brien. Every time I think we're close to buying, someone else slips in.

I heard the frustration in his words but more, his absolute commitment that someday this land would be ours.

I persisted. "It will take thousands of dollars. And years. Look how long it's taken just to build up the pack trail," I reminded him. "Now you want to widen that to bring down stages and freighters, too?"

"More people use it," he told me. "Just like I said."

"And how will we build? Get everything down here. Who? Let alone the road—"

"There'll be a way," he said, reassuring. "I've seen it happen time and again:

set your course and amazing things happen. To quote my old friend, Frederic: 'Plan, then mit faith, do.'"

I wanted to share in Joseph's enthusiasm. Still, the unpredictability of it alarmed me. For a brief moment I remembered Luther up to bat and wondered if marrying him—and predictability—would have really been so bad.

"And where will we live in the meantime, while you're building and building?"

"At our Inn," he said to my surprised face. "Small one to begin with, but room enough to serve stageriders and sleep them overnight." Joseph stared at the choke cherry trail we'd just ridden down. "Put it there for now, close to where the stream comes into the Deschutes." He talked as if we already owned it. "Have seven or eight rooms. Enough to board and bed until we build the hotel."

A hotel! I thought. "You'd better plan to build some privies and keep people for quite awhile," I said only half in jest. "After coming down that road you propose, people'll be stopping off at the outhouse for sure; then do some building of their own."

"They will?" Joseph asked.

"Building courage to go up the other side."

He laughed. "Look," he said, pulling me to him, wrapping me against his bulky coat. "Trust me in this. It'll be a good place for us. With the bridge and the roads, we'll give to the future, not just take from it. And the change, maybe it'll be good for us." He held me still. "Here, there'll be room enough for all our children," he said softly. "And for that garden. Even for the fancy parlor you always wanted. Big enough to dance in. Right here," he said, marking the space with his heel. "In fact..." He moved away from me.

I knew he was up to something. He wore a delighted look on his face pink with the cold. He took my mittened fingers, bowed low, and said: "Is your dance card all filled?"

"I believe it has your name on it," I said and curtsied in my boots. He lifted my hand, bowed ever so slightly, and we danced while he sang.

Have you ever heard tell
of sweet Betsy from Pike,
who crossed the wide prairie
with her lover Ike.
With two yoke of oxen and
one spotted hog,
a tall Shanghai rooster
and an old yellow dog.

There beside the river, to the tune of "Sweet Betsy from Pike," we danced. While the mules stomped impatiently at their tethers, my fur boots catching on the rough rocks, we danced. Cold air settled down around us like the wispiness of a dream, and we danced. Bandit watched us warily. Joseph limped just a little. I stretched on tiptoes to place my hands on his wide shoulders and he lifted me, swung me gently about, setting me down facing the falls.

"Here's where we'll come to then," he said, his arms tight around my shoulders, pulling me into his chest and his dream. "And God willing, we'll build it all, Janie. We'll build it all, together."

CHAPTER 24

CLEANSING

STEAM ROSE OFF Sunmiet's bare back like the mist over a high Cascade Lake in early morning. Wet, and black as obsidian, her hair cascaded over her shoulders like a waterfall at night. My nose tickled from the heat, became more sensitive to the piercing cedar smell. I watched as she bent over the rocks, her face lit by the firelight, her hair a veil on either side of her face. The other women and children had sweated earlier and left. It was just the two of us still in her family's sweat lodge.

When Standing Tall started the fire, the rocks were almost perfectly round and nearly white. They burned red now, with dark centers that seemed to flicker with life. Sunmiet lifted another rock from the flames with the long-handled rake, slipped the hot rock onto the deer shoulder-bone strapped to the end of the stick, and gingerly carried it to the lodge. "Step into the river," she said. "Cool your body. Drink some water. Then return."

Snowmelt from the mountain made the Deschutes River even colder than ice but I did as instructed. It was the fourth time that night I had looked at the moon, felt the cool air tingle my hot skin, braced myself for the cold after bearing the heat. The excitement of the new experience did not decrease my reluctance to face the water. I overcame it, plunged in, and sucked my breath as the water shocked close my pores, covered my head with the tingling of a thousand fingers, filled every part of my body. Submerged, I lasted only a second or two before I shot from the water, gasping for air.

With goose bumps for companions, I walked rapidly the short distance from the river to the small rounded lodge covered with mud and hides and blankets, lifted the hide door and on hands and knees, crawled into the welcoming heat inside.

"So sweet it smells," I said, squeezing water from my hair, dribbling it on the hot rocks. The immediate, steamy warmth of the lodge felt wonderful. I could not see Sunmiet in the darkness, just felt her there. As my eyes adjusted, the glow from the rock pit near the door gave enough light to see her face, a ripple of shadow over serenity.

"Rose water," she said. Onto the rocks she splashed water from a tin cup. "It has special meaning for us and smells good too." The water sizzled against the hot stones like water in the spider at the hearth but with a sweet fragrance. "The cedar branches symbolize strength and purity and healing."

The hot, black quiet drained all cares from my body, made me restful as I had never been. Time traveled over us without leaving tracks.

When my breathing seemed labored, Sunmiet's voice came from a great distance to remind me to go outside, inhale the fresh air, slip again into the water, drink to cool my parched throat, and then return. "We have already added ten rocks," she said. "You are doing well for the first time, enduring much heat, taking in much cleansing. Do not harm yourself by trying to remain too long."

"I'm all right. What about you?"

"A little more time." She sat quietly, her silence urged me to remain.

"Standing Tall worries me," she said into the dark. "He is angry at the changes in his life. He blames others but hurts himself. I am afraid for him. And for my children and myself."

I didn't know what to say so, like a listening friend, said nothing.

"Sometimes, I hear the elders who have gone before," Sunmiet told me. "I see them, too, in the faces in the rocks. They speak to me of what to do." She was silent. "They are friends. And old *kásas*. Go out now or you will bring yourself damage. This is a healing place, but we can let it harm."

I crawled out through the opening, my knees taking on the impression of the cedar twigs and branches on the ground. I gasped in the cool air, aware that my lungs seemed fuller, more expanded. The fir tree offered balance. I waited, caught my breath, felt the rough bark against my skin, the dizziness in my head.

The sweat was cleansing even if it did nothing to increase my chance to have a child. None of the specialists' suggestions had worked though we'd visit any new one we heard of. It was almost the new decade and we still waited for a child of our own. We had not yet made the trip to the herb doctor and Joseph had finally, reluctantly, only to honor my judgment, agreed to the sweat.

Once more, I plunged into the creek, noting the thin ice lining the water's edge like lace. Shivering, I rejoined Sunmiet in the lodge.

"It is a time to pray," Sunmiet said. Hunched over, I could feel the willow sidewalls, the low, arched ceiling, sense the branches that kept the heat from escaping. My nose burned with the dry heat; my hair felt heavy on my shoulders, smooth and wet beneath me as I sat on my own long strands.

Sunmiet sang a song in a language I did not recognize. She spoke a prayer out loud in words I did. Her prayer spoke of thanksgiving, then asked for strength for me, to heal my heart of sadness, to help me forgive so I could make room for new life to be planted in me, "if such is to be." It was a prayer not unlike what I prayed for myself each day except for the forgiveness part.

"What's forgiving my mother got to do with it," I said when she ended, tossed rose water on the rocks. The lodge was as dark as the inside of a cow's stomach.

"*You* were forgiven," Sunmiet said. "Though it is your not forgiving her that will matter."

"She still blames me! What do I have to forgive? And what difference does it make anyway?" I felt disoriented in the dark. A rock suddenly glowed brighter in the corner so I could see shadows on Sunmiet's face.

"The ruler-teachers say we are all forgiven, for wrongs we never even tell ourselves, by Someone who cared and died for us. He is as the liquid of the water, they said. And the Creator as ice, and his spirit as the steam. They are all children of one family, each with its place in forgiveness. If you do not give up your suitcase of anger toward yourself and your mother, you will not have room for the good things the Creator has planned for your life. Your vision will be clouded by steam and you will miss the Creator's other forms."

"Do you think we pray to the same God?" I asked her, diverting her.

"The Creator made the world," she said. "Gave us all we have. Roots and berries, land animals and fish, each other. We have done nothing to deserve them, we must care for them, only. It is what keeps them in our lives. Is that not like your God?"

"God created everything, yes," I said. "And gave us people, each other. And more."

"The power to heal," she said, and I could almost sense her single headnod of finality. "The ruler-teachers say healing is from the Son. Do you believe that?" she asked.

My skin felt tight as though stretched in one large thin piece across the bones of my body. My thoughts were light. I wondered if I would hear music as Sunmiet said some did. A rock shifted in the pit, glowed brighter, settled next to another, taking strength from the flame beside it, like friends, bonding. I felt a strength I hadn't before; clarity.

"I wish that believing would answer my prayer," I said. "I wish the memory of my brothers and sisters, *yáiyas* and *nanas,* would not cut so deep. I wish my mother would give up Ella. I wish I could bargain so God will give me a child." I took a deep breath. The scent of cedar pinched my nose.

Sunmiet did not fill the space with her words, allowing the hot darkness to open up more than the pores of my skin.

"But do I believe he can heal?" I asked, repeating her question into the darkness. More time to consider, more water sprinkled on the rock pit, more time to remember, to attend to my breathing, to pray. "Yes," I told her. "I believe in him. And I believe he can heal me if I let him."

"Then it will be so," Sunmiet said with sureness. "You will be healed whether you are chosen to bear a child or not when you forgive and accept his gift for yourself."

How ironic, I thought, Sunmiet bringing light to my beliefs, the religion of my parents. Joseph would be surprised to see my faith grow stronger with the sweat, not more distant, giving me a future and a hope.

I had envisioned living an interesting life with Joseph Sherar, and so it was. We had our differences but shared more preferences. Like the cattle and sheep we raised and his willingness to let me become a greater part of the work considered "men's" by most standards of the day. I think that was a difficult shift for him, his always treating me with such deference. He wanted to take care of me, I knew that. But he also loved me enough to let me be myself.

As a result, my interests on the ranch kept with the general operations more than the usual household activities. Oh, I performed many duties typical for a woman: provided medical aid to young buckaroos, even soothed a lost love wound or two. Only a few years older than me, most buckaroos still found any married woman reminding them of their mother and they let me advise them not knowing I had so little experience of my own. I mended and canned, helped Anna with the wash, organized the cleaning and the meals.

But my greatest love, I discovered, was working with Joseph. Together, he and I planned the day's events, the jobs that needed tending. After, I drew up the work lots, decided who would go with whom to do what tasks. I had a good sense of how long things would take, whose skills best suited the effort, and after very little experience, Joseph trusted that judgment.

There were occasional encounters with buckaroos who disliked taking orders from a small woman. They either got over it or left. In general, both my husband and his men treated me with respect for my thinking and my mind. I found I liked the feeling. Joseph seemed to enjoy my ability to outline work for the men and handle conflict with their ways. "Better'n me," he said. "Keep wanting to find excuses for them, give them one more chance. But you," he told me with a certain pride, "you just clear the bunkhouse."

That, of course, wasn't always desirable. We often needed extra help to rope and brand, take up the hay, make fences and repair them, assist with the fall round-up, spring shearing. Even finding available men who knew their way around a cow or lambing shed and were willing to remain sober long enough to demonstrate their skills proved no easy task despite the steady influx of men from the east, escaping memories of a bad war. We needed to treat the buckaroos well enough so they wouldn't move on. My sharp tongue sometimes sent them on their way a tad too soon.

The constantness of uncertainty filled our days: uncertainty about the weather, about the calving, about which bull to invest in, about which rams to let go. Little predictability entered our work lives, gave me small reason to know boredom. The constantness of the seasons and the ever-presence of our love were predictability enough.

For diversions, Joseph and I sometimes took in races at the Indian race track on the east end of The Dalles. Next to the beach along the Columbia, men took out their brag on bets against their mounts. Joseph never shared with me how much he wagered, as he ignored my clucking tongue about wasting money. Instead, he'd cheer with me at the finish line when the Indian spectators would wave their blankets startling the mounts so unprepared. Those blankets brought many wins to Indian horses trained for such surprises.

We traveled to Portland once or twice a year where we stayed in grand hotels, swirled in custom clothes beneath giant kerosene chandeliers and talked of investments with bankers who seemed awkward in my presence. Joseph introduced me to the financial world. I found I could step through it with dexterity and verve despite (or perhaps because of) the discomfort of most men. With the War Between the States over, the markets for wool had dropped dramatically. But people still needed to eat, and so cattle remained as steady as gold and took up much of our discussion with the men of finance.

After our meetings, we would walk along the wharves to watch the line of drays waiting to load onto the river boats heading up the Columbia. "Settlement," Joseph would say. "Look! There's the *Jason P. Flint*, ready to steam up to The Dalles. Now there's the evidence that the interior will burst open. Just need to complete the land routes that will work."

Over tea, Joseph and I would discuss what we had seen in the bankers' meetings and at the wharves. Once we were even included in one of Ben Holladay's parties at his lavish Astoria home near the ocean. But when Joseph saw the effort was to win us to his views on railroads and elicit our investments, we declined future invitations. We had our own plans for investments. We made a good match, we two, able to capture with four eyes and ears nuances that would have been lost with only two of each.

While money was not a problem, we were still thwarted from accomplishing the work at the falls. We'd been unable to purchase the land beside the river despite several attempts, several changes in hands. Now O'Brien had his own ideas about expanding the bridge site, we learned. And he had instituted a toll as a way of paying for the upkeep, such as it was.

"Toll idea is a good one," Joseph told me a few weeks after our visit with Sunmiet. We walked up from the corrals to the house. "Unless he makes the roads accessible, not enough will use it to make it pay." He poured water into the wash basin as I unstrapped the pistol bound to my hip, hung it and the holster on the branch.

He watched me wash my face at the wash bowl shaded by the lilac bush that arched several feet over our heads. Then he washed his own. Grabbing the towel, he spoke through the linen so I almost didn't hear. "The Dalles Military Road was approved in the legislature last week," he said. "Going to be a land grab, that's for sure. Money to create a road already been a trail for years. Crazy! I saw a team dragging a fir log and the rider told me he was 'road constructing.' If that's what it's to be, it'll be money in someone's pocket. Looked like the road meandered into fields it didn't need to, into good soil." He grunted his disgust. "That'll become part of the Act we'll all pay for. Be months before the inspection team decides it's passable."

"Won't the road at least be maintained?" I asked him.

"Parts of it." He wiped his face, stood behind me wiping his hands. "Enough so maybe O'Brien will get cold toes, want to sell rather than face the competition. But getting people—stages and wagons—getting them down the grade and across the river, that's the key." He wiped the back of his neck with the towel, hung it on the back rod, poured fresh water to rinse the bowl. "Look at Gordon's site. Nix would never have sold to him if he'd realized what that place could be. Tom's planted over seven hundred orchard trees at that bridge crossing!"

"They have soil there," I chided. "Not like all those rocks at the falls."

He ignored me. "It's still too low, I think. The bridge'll be washed out, you wait and see. And it only goes to that uninviting Military Road." He ran a comb through his thick hair, pulled on his beard as he talked. "No, O'Brien's site is the best." He was thoughtful for a moment more. "He isn't focused on the roads and he's making enemies there, if his way with Indians doesn't change."

Peter Lohomesh had reported a growing tension between residents at the falls and the Warm Springs people who camped beside the river each year. Sunmiet had spoken of altercations, too, between packers and the Indians. "We stay away," she said, "from the people. They seek us out, walk up Buck Creek to pick at us as though we were some scab they will not let heal. They tell us to go back to the reservation, leave the fishing we do all our days. Sometimes they laugh at the eels we dry or maybe bring their faith words to us because they think we have no inner life." It would not be long before such insensitivities resulted in more than emotional pain. Joseph thought that too.

"Maybe that isn't where we're to build," I told Joseph. I used my hands to smooth the hair back behind my ears and into the bun at the back of my neck. Freckles dotted my nose despite the hat I always wore and the grease I spread across my face. I could see Joseph's reflection behind me in the mirror I looked into.

"Obstacles don't mean we're on the wrong track," he told me. In a quieter voice, "Think we're not supposed to have children?" He kissed the top of my head, held my shoulders. "Didn't mean that to be painful. Just a reminder that if it's what we're supposed to do, things'll happen." He released me, started walking toward the house. "No, the falls are where we're to be," he said with sureness. "Just not sure how or when."

I grabbed the pistol I'd taken to wearing and we headed toward the house, hand in hand. "No need to carry that," he said. "You just imagine snakes out this time of year." Joseph bent deep to kiss my cheek.

"I've shot my imagination, then, on more than one occasion," I said and giggled as we entered the house.

"Like children," Anna said with mock disgust as she placed platters before us. "Always playing."

Anna prepared the meals. In our years together, we had worked out the arrangement where she would cook most meals so I could work beside my husband. "Until babies come," she'd told me, flour drifting over her ever-widening midriff. "Then the Señora will want *en la casa,* with them, not pushing boots in dust beside Señor Sherar. He will want that, too," she'd added.

I was beginning to think my boots would always be beside my husband's, never have reason to slip beneath the cradle of a child.

To be twenty, married nearly six years and childless was not what I had envisioned by becoming Mrs. Sherar.

Any plans to bring Ella into our lives had disappeared with Papa's death. He had been our fishing line Joseph set into troubled waters every now and then, seeing if Mama might nibble at our bait. She never did, wouldn't now, with only Ella and Baby George to be with her. When Papa died, he took our life-line with him.

I did my best not to think of my childless state, and so, of course, that was all that filled my mind when I was not engaged in work. Every late day of my flow held me captive with anticipation. Every time I rode too far or over did in the garden I would ask myself, did I do damage? I even gave up my whale bone corset believing that if I found it hard to breathe then perhaps an infant would have insufficient air to find breath too.

Mama told me once before I married that to conceive I must behave like a lady. "Do the work God gave you to do. No riding and working like a man."

But my mind went crazy in the quiet house. Anna had her place in our home and liked that I knew mine. Even quiet efforts to whittle made little inroad on my constant thoughts of children, especially knowing that Joseph, the garden, cattle, the rolling grasslands, and deep ravines called just outside.

Oddly, I also found myself sometimes moving physically away from my husband, a strange behavior I always thought. "I don't understand why I'd want a child so much and then make myself so tired," I told Sunmiet once. We gathered roots together, placing the tubers in her *wapas*.

"Maybe is easier to be tired than face disappointment," she said. "You work hard, enjoy your husband's sweetness in the day and then fall asleep. He asks no questions of your sleeping, you work so hard beside him."

I knew that if Joseph thought my efforts on the ranch with him meant risking an infant, he would give up the time we shared, want me to, too.

I was relieved when the newest specialist Joseph and I conferred with in Portland told me activity was best. He knew of no reasons why I had not conceived, told me to just go home, that I was young and healthy and would likely soon begin my family, that I was just doing it in a different way and with unique timing.

That winter, when we learned of five children in need of a home, I thought perhaps the specialists were at last correct, that children would come to me in time, in another way than what I'd always thought.

J. W. brought the news, riding with his string down the road past our claim. He'd become a puzzle for me. Not just because I could not look at him without wondering what my life would have been like if I had married him; but also because he appeared in my world at strange and opportune times.

An open winter meant the packers and freighters could continue carrying supplies back and forth to Canyon City and beyond with little fear of snow or bad weather to prevent their movements. Even Indian raids along the trails had settled down so that J. W. was one of many—Heppner included—who worked their strings regularly along the road.

J. W. complained about O'Brien's toll as he stopped to talk with us. "Specially when that dugout road's so poorly kept," he said. He rubbed his fists in his eyes like a tired boy. "You folks looking good. Missus." He tapped his hat at me, called me the title he'd helped me claim. Then, "If I can speak of something delicate," he said, his voice lowering. "Know you have no young'uns yet. And I know Sheriff's looking for someone to take in five children. They got parents, but not taking care of 'em, living in some tent. Heard about it?"

I shook my head.

"Five, they got." He counted on his fingers. "Yep, Five. Youngest one just born last week. Folks irritated kids are left to rain and cold."

"Where are they?" I asked.

"Well, that's a case," he said. "In a crumbled down arrangement near that Wamic place they call it, other side of Tygh Valley. Been there quite a time. Now, some are on their case saying the babies'll die to exposure without better care."

"What 'some'?"

He fidgeted. "Oh, charitable folks. Don't like the conditions they live in when they deliver goods. Think the young'uns should at least be in decent homes."

In the expansion and the settlement, more and more families experienced difficulties in locating housing sufficient against the Oregon winters, finding work to sustain themselves. Some were forced to accept food and shelter from people taking on airs with their good intentions.

Tolerance of different ways was not one of the area's strong points I noticed. Not ten years earlier Oregon citizens had voted to prevent entry to Negro people, an unenforced law. Once or twice in The Dalles, I'd even overheard snide words made about Benito and Anna. It was as though people who looked a little different could be blamed for the misfortune of many more who might have trouble making their way. People hired the Mexican families to pick apples and work the pack strings—perhaps because they moved on. Those that remained to make a living in the region that had once shared a border with Mexico itself, often found themselves sharing bad comments along with Indians and Chinese and even Negroes newly arrived from back east.

"Is the family from here?" I asked J. W.

"From South," he said, "but white. Hit on hard times and now, just trying to make it. With winter coming on, and five little ones, parents might be willing to let their kids have shelter under someone else's roof. Thought you might be willing to take one or two in. Can get ahold of the sheriff in The Dalles if you're a mind to."

"We can't take on five!" Joseph said when I brought the subject up. December waited in the wings and while it had been a mild winter so far, there were always promises of unexpected snows and a drop in temperature cold enough to freeze the water in the bedroom pitcher by morning. "Maybe one or two."

"I was just thinking of Ella and her brothers and sister," I said. "She almost never sees them, being separated so. It seems criminal to break a family up."

"Maybe we could give the father work instead," Joseph said.

"Possible." We sat by the fire, the spine of a book lying upright in my lap. "I hear he is a man of fragile temperament."

"Not so fragile he'd let others raise his children," Joseph said, surprising me with his sarcasm.

"It wouldn't be something anyone planned," I said. "And things happen. You know that. Look at Archibald's state those years before and how they still found help for you."

Joseph was silent for a time, remembering. "You're right," he said. "I'm in no position to judge. I should be passing that kind of goodness on."

"I think the Lord is tapping me on my shoulder," I told him, standing up, decided. "And I don't want to disappoint him."

"I just don't like to interfere," Joseph said, cautious. I wondered if he was also thinking of Sunmiet.

"We're just offering help," I said. "Temporary. Even St. Luke said we should give in order to receive."

My husband pondered that a moment more, stirred his Arbuckle's, added sweet milk to the black. "Francis and Archibald used to quote that verse," he said. He thought a while longer before he said, "Let's ride over and see what we can offer up."

We took the buggy and loaded a second wagon full of food stuffs that Benito brought behind us with the team. The road to Tygh Valley had good use and the frozen ground made the buggy glide across the usual ruts and ridges. At Staley's store, we added cloth and thread and children's gifts and five fresh oranges Art said were just delivered. Then we headed southwest, toward the mountains and the reservation and the settlement of Wamic on the way.

Such a mixture of emotion filled me as we rode, my feet warmed on the foot box newly refurbished with embers from Staley's fire, my hands holding themselves, coiled inside a fur muff. The air was crisp, nipping at our cheeks. A hawk stared down at us from its perch on a cottonwood tree startled free of its leaves. The wind lifted my bonnet, Joseph's beard, almost to the rhythm of the "clop-clop" of the horse. Bandit lay panting at my feet, his breathing a comfort to my ears.

Refreshing. That was the word to describe this bracing ride to give and perhaps, receive. Refreshing and clean, the very words Sunmiet used to describe part of the mystery of the sweat! The opening of oneself that resulted in cleansing, free from the inside to the out, free to give, and to receive.

I leaned into Joseph, grateful for his generosity and God's provision of it. "Will they want us when we get there?" I asked him.

He shrugged his shoulders, his hands steady on the reins. "No sense wondering. Be there soon enough."

But I did wonder. Would someone else have already separated them, sent two children here, two more there? Would the children wish to live with us, total strangers? Were they girls or boys?

With J. W.'s directions, we followed the Barlow Trail, twisting up the switchbacks out of Tygh and then across an open, wide expanse dwarfed by the white brilliance of Mt. Hood. There, on the edge of the flat, my wondering was interrupted.

We approached a small wood and canvas structure one could hardly call a shelter. It sat back from the road without benefit of trees to break the wind that raced across the top of the ridge. It had no rock foundation. None at all, in fact, and three sides of the structure seemed to slide into themselves while on the fourth side, a canvas flap hung loosely. A small wisp of smoke made its way out of the top. I could see movement through the splintered walls and holes in the canvas.

Benito pulled the wagon up behind us, stepped off, and walked abreast. "I knock?" he asked.

"We'll all go," I announced, straightening my bonnet strings. "Bring Bandit with us. Let them know it's a friendly visit, from one family to another."

"You heard the little woman," Joseph said squeezing my hand as he pulled the blanket from my lap and helped me step out. Bandit bounded past me, stretched on the frozen ground, tail wagging in readiness. Joseph took my hand and we three—plus a kelpie—walked up on the silent porch, walked up to face our future.

CHAPTER 25

FAMILY
MATTERS

SOME YEARS TUMBLE into themselves and cannot be distinguished from another. Newspapers and archival experts well record what transpired of import. But such accounts do not stimulate the pangs of memory like the scent of fresh lumber taking on moisture in a January drizzle or the clatter of a train making its way across the country. If I had not made notes in ink to preserve the highlights of 1869, it would be lost, pushed down by the pressure of weightier years. This way, as they say, "cream rises" and so does 1869.

What better example of cream rising than to discover the depth of Joseph's generosity or the breadth of my own capacity to care?

Chief Paulina of the Paiutes had been hunted down and killed; after months of controversy, President Johnson had barely missed impeachment in the Senate and at election time, he was replaced. Finally, we had a new president, a fighting man, Joseph said, meaner than even Paulina: an Ohioan named Ulysses S. Grant.

And it was "a fighting man" I thought of when the wild-eyed man gripped the tent flap that day. He snapped it open and we felt the blast of fury in his eyes.

"What do you want?"

His eyes were dark, set into a cow-like face dominated by his wide, flat nose. He wore homespun pants and shirt, a weary jacket made smaller by the exposure of slender forearms sticking from the sleeves.

"We've brought some food for you. An early Christmas gift," Joseph said, responding to the fear more than the fight in the man's eyes.

"Appreciate your interest," the man said, less hostile, "believe we'll be all right." He stepped back a bit, so we could see the children huddled around a small sheepherder's stove, chimney stack poked out through a hole in the tent. His wife, suckling a child, sat toward the back, a thin blanket draped over the shoulders of her dark linsey-woolsey. From the shadow of the lean-to, she smiled at me. Her eyes flashed the pride and sparkle of a new mother tempered by the wisdom of the status of her brood.

Putting her finger to her lips she signaled "sleeping" and lay the child in a bundle of blankets kept warm by the fire. The baby, eyes closed, sucked at an imaginary nipple, rooting at the blanket that nestled close to its face and then slept soundly.

"Is it a girl?" I asked softly, slipping gently inside, concerned about the cold draft our presence brought. The man hesitated, then let me pass. "Such lovely eyelashes," I said. Her mother nodded, smiled again, tucked the blanket from her infant's face. "What's her name?"

"Eleanor," the man answered. He looked on kindly at his wife who blushed as she examined her hands, clasped and unclasped them, fidgeted with the baby's thin blanket. To one of her other children, she signaled and a boy smudged with soot on his nose snuggled into the crook of her arm. A gathering of tenderness circled parents and child, held them safe, together, despite the desperation of their circumstances.

"We've little to offer," the man said, still standing not far from the opening. His voice had softened some with his introduction of his daughter. "You're welcome to warm yourself a bit at our fire before you leave." He opened the flap farther and Joseph followed me inside, ducking considerably. Benito hesitated a moment but the man urged him on into the smoky dim, having reconciled himself to our intrusion. He dropped the tent flap behind him so that we now all huddled inside, including Bandit who dropped at my feet.

Tidy and compact, the family nonetheless looked as poor as Job's turkey.

The shelter held little else, save the children, their parents, smoke and a steamer or two stacked in the back and being used as a table and child's bed. One, I noticed, was covered with a thread-bare Hudson's Bay blanket, the black and red stripe faded into the grey. On it lay a toddler staring at us, scratching his leg against the wool with one hand; sucking his thumb with the other. They were barefoot. Old quilts covered the dirt floor.

Five children, counting the baby. Five, well-loved children, to look at their faces: they all lacked the doe-eyed stares of children nurtured only with food.

Joseph spread his wide hands before the fire, rubbing them to warm, accepting the man's hospitality. He nodded toward the wagons outside and said: "Appreciate it if you'd take those stores off our hands."

The man shook his head, said quickly: "Not necessary." I noticed the woman watched Joseph when he spoke, a quizzical look on her face. Her husband continued. "Gustauf, my oldest, already nine," he ruffled the boy's hair and spoke with obvious pride, "has shot us a good-size buck which we've skinned and cut. It should hold us through the week. The game remains ample thanks to God's generosity. Not much after the month," he said, shooing two children out of the way so Joseph and Benito could sit. "It will be spring. We'll plant corn first thing and vegetables next and be fine." He motioned me to be seated on the steamer beside the toddler. "And we've seedlings. Apples and pears and sweet grape starts we've brought with us. Shall I fix some tea, Eleanor?"

The woman nodded and I realized she and the baby shared a name. I marveled that this father of five had found the place in his heart to assist his very quiet wife with her household obligations. Eleanor nodded and started to rise to help him, but he pressed his hand on her shoulder as he stepped past her and she sat back down. He pushed aside a sack of eye-pocked potatoes as he reached for the tea tin. His pants hung from him; worn thin at the back. A respectful grace flowed between husband and wife and their children, all of whom were beautiful despite their pale and paper-thin faces. Two middle children pushed next to me on the steamer trunk, patted Bandit still at my feet. I felt their warmth, smelled their clean bodies, which was no mean feat considering I could see no hand pump and the nearest water would be some distance to be hauled for bathing.

The man dipped water from a crude bucket and heated it in the pan on the stove. The children remained attentive, subdued. Still, only a blind man would have missed the easy way this family stayed at peace with each other and their circumstances. I watched my hopes for the presence of any of these children living in my home, disappear.

"Surely you'd accept some fresh oranges for the children," I said. "And Eleanor needs variety and fat to make the baby's milk."

"And shelter," Joseph said. "Not to add insult to your agony, but a place like this is good for old miners, not families. Why, these walls are so thin any fat doe just sneezing as she walked by would give your whole family a shower. And doesn't look like you'd have linens to spare to wipe yourselves up."

The man did not take offense as I thought he might. Instead he nodded agreement with my husband. "We have little but enough to share and so we lack nothing. Truly. We're fine just as we are. Though some take issue with it," he added, frustration sifting through his words.

"That should be a worry to you," Joseph said.

Again, Eleanor stared at my husband.

"It is," the man said. "We've learned there is a move to take the children from us." Then for a moment his face formed a loathsome look. "It's not you been sent?"

"No," Joseph assured him, "though we would invite you to have the children stay with us until the winter or this crisis has passed."

Despite the stove's fervent heat, I felt a cold chill on my face as a blast of air hit the tent side. Into the awkward silence that followed I said, "You've chosen good land. What made you decide to build your shelter here, Eleanor? It seems so far from water. And into the wind."

Her husband answered for her. "It's a distance from the stream over the side but we like the openness, the mountain to watch over us. And there's little timber in this clearing so it did not seem to matter where we set the tent and built the lean-to. We have five years for a permanent structure; plant and harvest and then it will be ours. You probably know that Missus... Why, I've forgotten to ask your names," he said.

"And we to offer them or find out yours," Joseph said. "Joseph Sherar. My wife, Jane, and our friend, Benito."

Eleanor's head jerked, she stared openly at Joseph. I thought I saw a flicker of recognition on her face as her husband gave us their name, "Blivens," he said, offering his hand. Eleanor signaled something to her husband using her fingers and he answered back, surprised. "Really?" He turned to Joseph. "She says she knows you. Both of you," referring to Benito.

Eleanor looked delighted, excited, nodded and again spoke with her fingers. "You were in San Francisco some years ago? Ate pasties near the wharf?"

Joseph narrowed his eyes to look at Blivens and then to Eleanor. He turned his head left, then right, the way Bandit does when he is considering. Joseph studied Eleanor's lines and angles and then he burst out a gasp of held air. "Well, I'll be," he said. "Eleanor O'Connor. You look warmed and happy so I hardly recognized ye! And you were about to walk!"

"It's Blivens now," her husband said, "But you're right about the O'Connor part. She does look happy, doesn't she, now?" He looked at her feet. "Made her wooden shoes and she walks just fine. First thing I ever made of wood," he said proudly.

"Eleanor-with-her-writing-pad O'Connor. No wonder this tent looks familiar! Did Strauss make it for you?" Joseph asked, delight on his face. He looked at the seams and the lighter patch at the top. The woman nodded, her face aglow. I vaguely remembered Joseph and Benito mentioning the woman who could not speak or walk and the little German who sewed up one of Joseph's ideas.

Eleanor signaled again and her husband laughed. "She says the tent aided her escape or she might still be sitting at some wharf slicing potatoes and carrots surrounded by difficult brothers. Instead"—he improvised for her, looking at her with kindness—"she is living happily among her children, loved dearly by all of them and their father."

"No doubt she could be happier," I said, "without wolves at her door or the fear of some well-meaning person swooping in to take her children." I didn't mean to sound harsh nor to describe myself in the process, but there it was.

"You're right on that," Blivens said, contrite. He glanced at his wife who wore open trust on her face, looked adoringly at her husband. "And I would give what I could to make it different. But it isn't." He poured the tea for us in a single tin cup which we shared and passed between us. "So we will do what we can and hope the authorities will see our good intentions rather than our current circumstance."

"They're not likely to," Joseph told him. "Word is, you're risking your children to the elements. Especially with the babe. There'll be a move to change that, with you or without. This weather shifts for worse and the sheriff'll be here faster than a flash flood to separate your family."

Benito spoke now, suggesting he bring in some of the foodstuffs in the wagon.

"Good idea," Joseph said. "You're welcome to spend time with us, till spring." He looked across the small room at me, checking where my thoughts were.

"We don't live that far away," I added, "and it would only be for a short time." My husband nodded his agreement to me. "We have plenty of room and love having children—and their parents—don't we Joseph?"

"That we do," he said softly, and I watched his face take on its idea look.

"We daren't leave here," Blivens said. "We risk loosing the land."

"Let the children come, then," I said. "And Eleanor, with the baby."

Into the silence that followed Joseph said: "We'll bring some things in while you think on it."

We three visitors bent through the tent flap and stepped out into the greater cold. "What they need," Benito said as he pulled on his gloves, spit through his teeth, "is not all this food, but a safe roof."

"Yes," Joseph said, "and if he'll let us, I know a way to give it. If you'll agree, Janie," he said, pulling me into his side as we walked.

And when I knew of it, I couldn't help but agree.

So it came about that Eleanor Blivens and her husband, Ray, a former singing teacher from Illinois, and their five surprised children spent the next few weeks not in our home but in watching, and as they could, participating, in the raising of their own.

It took some convincing on Joseph's part to get Blivens to accept our offer, pride holding him back, his disbelief that no conditions were attached to such generosity. But once accepted, Blivens was agush with appreciation, speaking, he said, for both him and his Eleanor. "We have never had such a gift," he said. "And will never be able to repay you."

"Not expected," Joseph told him more than once. "We've the pleasure of giving and the hope that it will be returned, pressed down, shaken together, as Scripture says."

It was a great event, the very best way to begin a new year.

Joseph had milled lumber delivered from Tygh Valley, carried by a string of double freighters that included J .W. as a driver, up the grade to Wamic.

Getting the lumber took the longest. We built the bunkhouse shelter first to house the men. Then with Joseph as their architect and guide, Ray and Benito and several of our buckaroos along with the Pratts and others from Tygh Valley who learned of the plan, formed the frame and stood the walls of the Blivenses' two story, four bedroom home.

It was too far for us to travel back and forth, so Joseph dug out one of Strauss's tents and he and I stayed not far from Three Mile Creek while Eleanor and I cooked in it on a sheepherder's stove to feed the men who built the house.

We had a day or two of cold drizzle that sogged the lumber and slowed us; but then the sun came out and you would have thought it April instead of January so warm did it beat on the workmen and us.

I had not expected to experience such pride in watching the house go up. I had thought I'd feel sadness that my hope for the children to live with us had been so quickly dashed. To my credit, I was wrong about myself. Watching their faces as each square nail made its mark; laughing with them as we baked pasties in the small oven of their lean-to; holding baby Eleanor after her feeding, sinking into the liquid of her eyes, all gave me such richness of feeling I failed to notice what I thought I'd lost.

Joseph became thoroughly engaged in his own creation. And when he thought the building moved too slowly, he sent Benito to the reservation. His right-hand man returned with Peter and George and several other young men, eager to put their shoulders to the effort. Joseph paid them a fair wage as he did his own men who initially shied away from the Indians. Finding them hard workers and good followers of directions—with Peter and George to interpret from the common Chinookan language spoken by so many—the buckaroos formed a bond with the Warm Springs people and the Wascos who entered into change.

Such a mixed crew made swift work of the Blivenses' home.

Sunmiet rode over with her children, her latest bounced swaddled in the cradleboard carried at the withers of her horse. She did not speak of Standing Tall and I did not mention him. She and Eleanor communicated with their hands while I shook my head in wonder. We laughed together, watching the Blivens children and her own make games and play together.

Sunmiet honored me with her observation: "You live always with children," she said, "even if not of your own. Maybe you have more family than most."

The day the Blivens moved into their home, they prepared to spread blankets on the floor as beds for the children but Joseph and I had another surprise for them. We unloaded from the freighters rope beds with down mattresses for each child and a double one for the Blivens. Eleanor kept shaking her head in wonder, squeezing my hands in appreciation, almost floating as she spun around the wood floor of her home. "We did not get the cradle yet," I told her, gently patting the infant snoozing on my shoulder as we stood in their home. "It was promised, not delivered." She moved her hands in the air to mean, "Fine, fine, this is too much."

"I have cradle," Peter said, overhearing us as he carried items from their tent to home. "From my people. One like my mother make for me."

He created for her a hammock, with two hemp ropes strung parallel across a corner of the kitchen. He wrapped a blanket around the lines in the center forming a child's cradle. He kept the lines separated with a frame of willow in the shape of an oval, covered with the blankets. With some caution, Eleanor laid her baby in the center of the oval and its soft form sunk into the womb of the cloth. "Push," Peter said, directing, and Eleanor gently pushed the ropes as the baby rocked at her mother's shoulder height. She floated there, like a feather in the wind, hung above the clatter of children and activity but with a bird's eye view of the world.

"Here," Sunmiet said, putting the finishing touches on a memorable event. She reached for her own child's cradleboard. "Hang this from the hammock," she said and removed the dreamcatcher with its oval frame. "For her bad dreams to be caught in the web and her good dreams to call to her in the morning."

"And a prayer," I said. "That God will honor her dreams and give her a sweetness to the soul."

And so it was that Baby Eleanor spent her first night in the Blivenses' new home asleep in the gift of the Warm Springs people with God's blessings to keep her warm.

We did not give up on seeking a family of our own, but the pressure lessened. Joseph noticed my increased comfort. As if to honor it, in February he gifted me with my first Esther Howland hand-crafted valentine, all covered with cut lace and flowers straight from Massachusetts. I'd had valentines from my school chums and little paper ones from my Joseph. But this one was elaborately designed, had been ordered up special, for me. I was delighted, a joy that continued when Joseph surprised me again later, with the rail tickets and my first visit to his New York.

"Is it a good time to leave?" I asked him, being practical when he would have me just accept. We sat in the dusk of the long July evening. I looked at my watch. Still light at 8:00 P.M. We both rocked gently in the wicker chairs set on the porch to look onto the creek that disappeared toward the Deschutes in a tangle of willows and weeds.

"Benito can manage it. We'll be gone but six weeks."

"Maybe we should ask to take Anna's children, or even Ella."

Joseph shook his head. "You'd best put that girl from your mind. She belongs to your mother now and that's how it's to be." He took my small hand in his, rubbed my palm gently. "This is our trip. The one I promised you the day we wed and you refused to take. Wanted Canyon City instead, remember?"

"I remember. It would be fun though, to see your world through a child's eyes." We sat serenaded by crickets. "Guess I'm a little wary of meeting your brother after all these years, wondering what he'll think of a mere girl but twenty-one. And all your other brothers and sisters."

"Old enough to keep me in line," Joseph said "so I imagine they'll adore you as I do. Only way to find out is to go."

And so we did, making our way with our leather satchels, riding all nature of vehicles from stagecoach to train including a nervous sleep in one of Mr. Pullman's new cars. Joseph promised me tours of the Metropolitan Museum of Art and an afternoon watching the newly formed Cincinnati Red Stockings play baseball against a New York team. He kept his promises.

A million sights and sounds made their imprint on me, an impressionable young wife in the presence of her handsome, older husband. I even spent the money Joseph gave me to indulge myself finding first a dress salon that fitted my small body with the latest striped silk fashion adding an ostrich feather hat and parasol to match. Next, I kept an appointment with a photographer who made my likeness. Later in the week, with the new photograph in hand, I headed for Tiffany's where the gentlest of men in a fine black suit with subdued ascot smiled profusely, spoke with the softest lisp, and patted my hand gently before he found me a silver watch to fit the picture. A chain and fob and the engraving completed my afternoon's adventure.

"You look like the pupil who's outsmarted her teacher," Joseph said as he escorted me across a profusion of color and design into the dining room at the Grand Hotel.

His eyes admired me and he held my half-gloved hand just a moment before he kissed my fingers then helped me ease the fullness of my dress over the chair. "New York agrees with you," he said, smiling. "I almost hate to take you north, afraid the distance will tarnish some of the glow."

"Oh, pooh!" I said. "I'd glow wherever I'm with you. What are we having?" I asked, referring to the menu.

"Cracked crab, dipped in drawn butter. The perfect meal to test a new whalebone corset. Though I can't imagine why you didn't wait until Nicholville. To have one made at the shop."

I raised my eyebrows at him. "I'd never ask your brother for such an item." Then whispered, "How did you know?"

He returned my whisper, leaning toward me at the table. "Your waist is even smaller than when you left this morning. And you're having trouble breathing."

"The shallow breathing is because you would choose to bring up so delicate a subject in a public place," I chided him. "And you should recognize the waist whether surrounded by whale bones or not." I sat straight, away from his intimate posture. "You've held it often enough."

"Ah, the sassy one is back," he said, throwing his head back in laughter. "Let's eat!"

Our trip was filled with the delights of a honeymooning couple, and several people commented to us about our "recent" marriage. At one cafe we took coffee, sat close together, our faces shadowed by the brim of my ostrich-plumed hat. A waiter brought us each a dish of ice cream, the vanilla bean so fragrant it must have just arrived from Mexico. "For the newly married," he said in a loud voice. "Compliments of the gentleman at the far table." He gestured and we both smiled appreciatively at the elderly man who sat behind a red checkered table-cloth and nodded our way. The small crowd had heard the waiter's declaration and applauded lightly, their gloved hands the sounds of rain drops on the roof over our Oregon home.

Joseph said he felt like a young boy instead of a man approaching thirty-six. His eyes watered when I handed him the Tiffany box and with one thumb he opened it to see my likeness. He read the engraving, the opposite of the words he'd placed on mine. "Your wedding gift," I said. "After all these years."

"You're the gift," he told me. "I've never wanted for more."

I savored his words and didn't immediately notice that he looked hesitant.

"What is it?" I asked, fearing something.

"I had planned to wait," he said. "To give this to you in Nicholville. But I think now's the time." From his pocket, he lifted a thin box wider than the palm of his large hand. It too, was embossed with "Tiffany's."

"What have you done?" I asked, pleased. He motioned me to open it and when I looked inside, my heart nearly stopped. There, wider than my thumb nail and half my height in length was a solid gold chain. A large purple amethyst intertwined it and moved up and down it like a bola. The chain held something else: a watch of heavy, shining gold that opened for two portraits.

"It can be pinned," he said, excited about the engineering of it. "And then the watch hangs from it." A smaller chain connected the watch to a dress pin over my pocket while my breast would be laced with links of gold.

"It's stunning," I said, breathless. "I...I don't know what to say. It's so lavish, so unique, so delicate, strong, all at once."

"As are you," he said.

I turned the watch over, sure there would be an inscription. "All my love, always, JHS to JAS."

"I could find no stronger sentiments," he said, "than love and truth."

And so we spent our holiday lost in love and laughter. At least most of it.

We did venture into the wood-paneled offices of specialists in female disorders. Most prodded through my new silk clothes and asked questions. "You're young," they all said. "No reason for you not to conceive. Give it time. Take warm baths." Others said the same about my youth, but told me to soak in cool water three times a day, take naps, and most definitely indulge less in physical labor. I did not ask them their opinions of regular riding in the rugged ravines of Tygh Ridge.

In all, the visits were depressing, offering no new information, reminding me only of my inadequacies. Joseph couldn't have been more encouraging. Still, the pall over our visit remained even when we left the city and by boat, took the canal and then by coach arrived at now his brother's store in Nicholville, New York. Perhaps the pall was merely a premonition of what would follow.

James greeted us politely. He was not as I had pictured him. I had made him bigger in my mind, more the size of Joseph though he was shorter, slender, and held himself like the stiff collar he wore at his throat.

"Eliza expects you for supper," he said formally. "And you are welcome to remain with us while you visit. Caroline would be happy to have time with her western uncle and aunt. And you should meet Henry, too, our youngest."

James's stiff demeanor did not change during our visit. He and Joseph shared only words of business talk, the markets, stock raising in the West. He filled Joseph in on other nieces and nephews, some we would see in a week. James looked pale, I thought, not well. I know my husband looked for some sort of connecting with his oldest brother but it was not to be, at least not that trip.

James behaved so formally that I expected Eliza to be as reserved and was pleasantly surprised when she wasn't. She greeted us with open arms scented with lilacs, her wide hoops circling out behind her as she hugged first Joseph and then me. "Welcome! Welcome!" she said. "And do not let James intimidate you," she told me smiling, slipping her arm through mine, though I suspect she spoke to Joseph too. "He is a somber man but a good husband and father." She moved us gracefully into the parlor, commenting as she did on my lovely watch and Joseph's eye for beauty. "Carrie!" she called. "Put away that mirror and comb and come meet your Aunt Jane all the way from Oregon. Henry! The cat belongs on the floor. Please wash your hands!" She turned back to us. "Children can be so trying, just when you want to show them off. Ach! No matter. You'll know soon enough when you have children of your own."

I became wistful during our stay. Perhaps it was seeing another happy family however different Eliza and James were from the Blivens or the Mays or even Sunmiet and Standing Tall. Perhaps it was the steamy August air, the gathering of relatives, Joseph's nieces and nephews, my new sisters-in-law and their children, seeing them laughing, chiding their charges into adulthood. Perhaps it was being in a space that belongs to someone else. Whatever the reason, we shortened our visit and soon headed home.

On the return, lying on the Pullman bed, rocking less than gently through the night, I lay awake, thinking. First, about the gift of my marriage and the joy we'd shared in being "newlyweds" these past few weeks. I wished to keep that feeling, that closeness that made others notice us while we noticed only each other. Joseph turned over in his sleep and I heard him start to snore, then stop. A good man. God had given me a good man despite my less than worthy state.

While the train chugged vigorously across the plains, I thought too, about my child. No one knew her but me. Not yet conceived, she had become a being in my mind, soft, with brown eyes and skin as smooth as corn tassel and hair as yellow. I did not name her. That would have been too much to risk. Bringing her to real was wrapped inside my one last hope: Joseph's Chinese doctor. Perhaps there was the answer to my prayer to have a family of my own. It posed no threat, I thought, by trying.

CHAPTER 26

TO TRUST
IN THE
PLAN

❧

THE WINTER OF '69 and '70 left little time for travel. A hard season plagued the region, a time of struggle with the wind and snow and cold unlike any we'd known since ten years before. This winter, at least, I did not wonder where Joseph was and he did not spend his spare time reading books with Philamon in the Klamath country. Philamon had returned to working with his father when we sold the ranch. Joseph and I weathered that winter together though spending so much time with snow piled against the windows often made for short tempers and stale air.

Benito and Anna and their children plowed their way through deep drifts on snowshoes to spend days with us playing checkers with antler slices on the soot-blackened checkerboard stump or dealing cards with no money risked. We sang old songs and the men told stories of their days along the Isthmus and in San Francisco. Anna told of meeting Benito in Northern California and their whirlwind courtship and marriage. I entertained the children with a story or two I remembered from Sunmiet's family, about how Bear lost his tail, how Dog got his name, the tricks of Coyote. "These can only be told when snow is on the ground," I reminded them. "That is the way of the Sahaptin and Wasco and Paiute people."

"So much snow means lots of stories, Auntie," four-year-old Corlamae said, her nose pressed against the frosty window. A look at the depth of the drifts made a body wonder if we'd be telling stories still at Easter.

Unlike some, though, we had enough to eat. After a harrowing trip by sleigh across crusted snow, we shared lean beef with Sunmiet's family and some others, horrified that the Indian agent could gather so little for the tribe, saddened that like stockmen everywhere, the Indian herders too were forced to watch their cattle die.

When the weather broke once in January with a false promise of a thaw, we learned that all went well with the Blivens's five. Joseph and Benito sledded supplies to Mama and Ella though even that did not thaw her freeze.

What hay we had we took to the high country where the cattle raked for grass, pushed their big heads to clear a way to the frozen shoots of grass oppressed by winter. Many cows gave birth to calves that could barely stand to suck before they succumbed to the cold. At night, their mothers bawled. In the morning, we would see them, tails switching, standing guard over the bodies of their dead babies, watching warily any who approached.

Then, as before, in one day, the sun came out, warmed up to sweater weather and the creeks began to rise.

It is a phenomenon not easily appreciated, the spring thaw. The hard ground so quickly turns to mud and muck that streams flow through every uneven ridge making even flat surfaces slick and splashed with dirty water. Piles of dirty snow sink before your eyes pouring out liquid like an orange half squeezed over a glass juicer. The earth smells of wet leaves, pungent decaying grass as the high water cleans ravines of rotting carcasses left over from the toll of winter. Meadowlarks sing of drier days and yet gratefully, of the spring and summer yet to come. Greater Canadas high above us in their V-formations move on North, announcing what we already know: spring is here.

Such volatile gyrations of nature also forewarn disaster.

From the window in the kitchen, I watched the two creeks on either side of us swirl by with debris and flotsam, foaming at the edges in their surge. Where they met at the base of the Y near the rise the house sat on, they formed a dirty plait rushing on down to the Deschutes. The pack trail grew closer to the creek as the water rose and I wondered how Joseph's rock and root supporting system would hold up.

Joseph wondered about O'Brien's bridge though he wisely did not suggest we ride there. "I bet it goes," he said. "And Nix's too." His voice held a certain anticipation to it.

"You're not hoping it's so, are you?" I asked, wiping the Tea Leaf ironstone plates, standing them, tiny copper designs all facing upright, in the cupboard.

Joseph ignored me. "The Military Road will be awash as well. I'm going out. See how the trail fares. Coming?"

"Give me a minute to put my old boots on. This mud," I said shaking my head, "makes a mockery of housecleaning."

"Need spring standards," Joseph said. "A little lower than the rest of the year."

"Need to have everyone wear slippers," I said, "including the man of the house."

"Coming?" he asked, sweetly, holding out his hand.

We squished into soft, saturated ground, our feet leaving little levies around our prints before ponds formed each place we stepped. Puddles appeared in Bandit's footsteps behind us. Joseph held my hand and we leaped across rivulets of water to stand closer to the creeks. Both still rose, leaving the knoll with the house and smokehouse and bunkhouse still well above danger. But lower, nearer where the two creeks met, where Benito and Anna and their children resided, the water seemed more ominous.

We walked toward their home, and I noticed that the cattle we'd herded into the corrals for calving and easier feeding stood now in a foot of water. They bawled to their babies who seemed oblivious to any danger.

Benito and Anna and their children stepped carefully up the rise to stand beside us. "We do what we can to prepare," Benito told us. "Can help with cattle. Then we wait." The watchword for spring flooding: wait.

"Wait at our house if you like," I said. "We'll move them."

"I help," Benito said, though Joseph protested.

"Do we have time to saddle up?" I asked.

Joseph assessed the creeks, nodded, and we saddled Sage and Buttercup. "Bandit and I'll cross, move what we can. Stay here, unless we need you."

His instruction annoyed me and I showed it, but his argument held water. "I don't want to rattle them any more than they are. One horse and a dog may be enough. I'll signal if I need you."

He started across the creek, water swirling around the white legs of his horse. "Don't come," he yelled back at me. "Swifter than it looks."

I could feel anxiety burning in my stomach, watching the dirty liquid push against my husband. I'd been in swift, spring run-off water, seen how quickly it could rise. He'd picked a place to cross that looked safe enough. The memory of a flooded creek came. I pushed it from my mind.

Bandit leaped in after Joseph and swam, passing him up, the water carrying him downstream a bit, swirling him around before he pulled out and shook himself on the other side. Joseph reached the sloppy ground near the corrals and turned to wave.

The kelpie nipped at the cattle, biting at their heads to push them back or snapping at their heels to move them forward toward the now open gate. Cows can always find a hole through a fence yet rarely see an open gate.

Bandit worked. More than once he came away with his mouth full of hair, some blood, spitting and shaking his head as he moved on to the next cow-calf pair. Being kicked didn't seem to stop him as he'd roll into a ball like a caterpillar and land with a thump, shake himself off and return, his tongue hanging, panting, almost in a smile, his eyes sparkling with the intensity of effort.

They moved most of the pairs together, man and dog, and were nearly finished. Joseph had gotten off his horse to lift a halter left hanging near the gate. He didn't notice that one last cow and calf returned, disoriented by the water, not wanting to leave what seemed familiar. As if in a bad dream, I watched as the cow circled back, somehow putting Joseph closer to the fence and her calf. The mother turned on Joseph. Bawling, she moved her one thousand pounds with more agility than would be imagined.

"Joseph!" I screamed. "Watch her!"

Joseph turned in time to see the cow charging toward him. He stepped back. His leg weakened, he could not quickly climb the fir pole fence. He turned and flailed his hands before her eyes. She startled, stopped, bawled again, backed up, then lunged once more, this time closer. Again, Joseph threw her off, struck the side of her head with his palm and threw himself to the side, still grasping for the corral, the water slowing him more than the protective mother who stopped only for a second. I watched her big red and white Hereford head lower, the gleam of her horns. She attacked again.

I stood so helpless! I could do nothing from where I stood but pray and that I did, hands pressed to my mouth.

Then from the corner of my vision I saw a familiar reddish streak strike out for the big cow's heel, pushing the cow toward Joseph!

Bandit barked and bit, drawing blood at the cow's heel.

I held my breath, heard my heart thud, expecting the cow to throw her half-ton of weight directly at my husband, smashing him against the rails as she escaped the kelpie's bite.

Instead, the cow swirled to attack the dog.

Water sprayed in all directions. The cow's lumbering body took a sideways turn as she lowered her head, bellowing, at Bandit. She butted the dog, and sent him flying higher than her head. Joseph slipped beyond the mother, up and over the fence rail and out of striking distance, deciding wisely to let her move her young one when and where she wished.

Bandit hit the ground with a splashing thud. He lay still. The Hereford bellowed and with her calf beside her she stood by the still form; nudged it. Bandit did not move. The old cow bellowed again, butted at her calf and sloshed away from the corral, away from the rising creek.

Joseph circled around, bent to Bandit, and I knew he would be shedding tears for that small dog.

"I'll come across," I shouted, tears already brimming.

Then as Joseph knelt beside him, the strangest thing happened: Bandit sneezed. Dazed, he stood. His legs wobbled, but he lived! "He's all right!" Joseph yelled at me, his voice cracking. "Fall must have been broken by the water!" With Joseph's help, the dog leaped into his open arms. "Good boy!" Joseph told him, over and over, letting the dog lick his face. "Good boy! He's earned his keep!" he yelled to me, waving. Remounting, he rode upstream. "Cross where it's narrower," he signaled.

With the horses, I rode a mile or more up the bloating creek, paralleling my husband and Bandit before finding a place safe enough to cross. Once there, I leaned from my horse to pat the dog, let him nuzzle me. Then I touched the face of the man I'd married, grateful he rode safe and sound beside me.

Thousands lost property that spring of 1870. Barns and animals and homes joined trees and carcasses and snakes on their way to the Columbia and the far Pacific. Benito and Anna's home wore water damage but still stood. Joseph's pack road needed repairs where the water eddied back behind the sagebrush roots, washed out dirt to expose rocks, bore a hole or two in the surface. The trail held firm, though, would still be safe to use even if it had been wide enough for wagons, which it wasn't. Yet.

The Nix bridge was lost to high water as Joseph predicted. O'Brien's bridge had damage too, in a section where a tree root had caught then pulled splintered lumber with it. While it did not wash away, neither did it invite safe passage, this place where my husband hoped to build a wagon bridge and our future.

Out of disaster can come triumph if one does not faint or fall away. Joseph was nothing if not persistent and so he approached O'Brien, riding down to the site where the log bridge gaped open in places like an old man's bad molar. It didn't seem possible that a man could want to build another bridge knowing two had been lost within ten years. But O'Brien was made of tough stuff.

Oddly, the day Joseph rode to talk with him about the land, O'Brien stood again with Robert May, Lodenma's brother-in-law. It was the spring of 1870, the start of a new decade, and Joseph hoped to capitalize on that new beginning for us, convince O'Brien it was an ending at the falls for him.

"Quite a sight," Joseph said, walking abreast of the two men as they stood peering over the side. He nodded to O'Brien and to May.

O'Brien grunted. He stood head to head with my husband, older, carried less than the 220 pounds my husband bore. His brow wore worry furrows. Bushy brown eyebrows speared out from his face giving him a wilder look than what his deliberate behaviors promised. Robert May removed his bowler hat, wiped his face and shiny head of the June heat. He said nothing.

"S'pose you're here to barter," O'Brien said, turning to him.

"Only make a fair offer," Joseph answered, "if you've a mind to sell."

"He does," May said.

"You speaking for him?" Joseph asked.

O'Brien turned away, stared out at the water. May spoke again. "Ezra and I think he should sell. No sense to rebuild." So here was another name. Ezra was Ezra Hemingway: banker, businessman extraordinaire, another person involved in this venture? Joseph had checked the records at the courthouse and only O'Brien's name appeared on the deed.

"It'll go," O'Brien said. "Make the bridge wider, sturdier. We know more now. You can't quit in the middle. You'll never get to the other side."

May ignored him, said to Joseph: "What kind of offer do you have in mind?"

Joseph noticed O'Brien's shoulders stiffen. May's eyes prodded for an answer. Joseph could see O'Brien was dealing with dreams while his apparent backers dealt defeat. My husband wanted to purchase the land fair and square, not to wheedle while a man was down, to buy so both buyer and seller were pleased with the exchange.

"What makes you want to hang on, Ben?" Joseph asked to O'Brien's back. "Ye've lost two to high water."

"Same thing as makes you want it." O'Brien paused. "Put in bigger timbers. That's the key." He turned to Joseph, a man with a vision staring into the eyes of a kindred soul. "You know it," he said, "where they don't."

"The Military Road will kill any competition," May said. "People would rather ferry at the mouth than go up and down these canyons." His eyes gazed upward at the ridge that loomed nearly two thousand feet above them. He shook his head, removed his hat again, wiped his bare head with a blue silk handkerchief, stuffed it back into the small vest pocket. "Not to mention the savages. Unpredictable regardless of how peaceful they act."

He looked at the distant scaffoldings holding men handling nets. "Forced even them to use canoes way upstream, swim across in places. But they got their eels and fish to motivate 'em. Most don't have anything to make 'em risk these ravines or a new bridge for." He walked a little along the rocky ledge, bent down, squatted, returned to a silent Joseph and O'Brien. "Good investment a few years back," he said. "Now, too costly for us to consider rebuilding." He checked his watch, slid the gold piece back into its pocket. "We can talk, Mr. Sherar. Bring your offer in," he said handing Joseph his card. "We'll be making a decision within a month or two, won't we Ben?"

O'Brien did not respond.

In the spring of 1871, Ben O'Brien agreed to sell his property to us, Joseph H. and Jane A. Sherar, the land the river ran through. We named our venture Til Kinney Road and Bridge Company. Joseph arrived home from a trip to The Dalles elated, overjoyed, surprised, and dealing with the newness of achievement, the effort of the long, hard journey not yet in his mind.

"Be careful what you wish for. You might get it," Joseph said, waving his offer before my face. "My father said that more than once. Guess we'll find out what it means!" He picked me up, swirled me around the kitchen. Bandit yapped outside the window, excited over the activity going on inside. "Let's tell Benito and Anna!" he said, taking my hand and pushing open the door.

I held back. "Details," I said. "Give me the details." I crossed my arms over the watch hanging at the tucks of my dress. "How much does he want? What do we have to sell to give it?"

"Later," he told me. "Let's celebrate now. Come on! Get your shoes on." He pulled at my hand again like a boy urging his dog to play.

"I want to know. Now." I liked living where we did. I liked the familiarity of our home, knowing what part I played in our life, having some say in decisions. This new venture did not promise me as much, especially when my husband chose not to share with me his usual details that gave me comfort and control.

He stopped, annoyed that I poured water on his hot fire of anticipation. "Seven thousand and forty dollars," he said. "And a pack string of mules. It's a fair price," he added, responding to the look of disbelief on my face. "Includes what he's started on the bridge, small barn, that little house, and the lumber sits there for adding on."

"It may be fair, but it's more than we have, cash on hand," I said. "You've not looked lately at the books."

"Didn't need to." He grinned. "Wasn't going to tell you this, but I've a stash."

"What stash?"

"From California times, when I risked some Merino rams sent across the country and came out good. I've never spent it. Just kept it, in case."

"Where! What bank?"

"In a safe place. No bank."

"Why would you not tell me? I thought of us as partners." I sat down. The kelpie came in through the open door, panted at my feet.

"And we are! Don't make a thing of this, Janie. Not now, not when we're so close. I only told you so you wouldn't worry over money as you do sometimes."

"I worry because you don't. Now I see why. You've kept some back for when *you* decide we need it."

"It was mine earned. Didn't think I needed to clear everything with you." He chewed on his lower lip.

"Not permission. Just sharing," I said. "Seems little enough."

He came to me then, kneeled, pushed at Bandit's bottom to set him aside. He lifted my chin with his calloused fingers. "I'm sorry, Janie. Look. This is what we've said we always wanted. When the door opens, you put your foot in to keep it from closing. Go looking for something to pry it open with and you'll as likely lose your gain."

"You could let your partner know how big your foot is before you knock on the door," I snapped.

"They're tens," he said, trying to tease me from my mad. "Always have been. And they've just walked us through the door we said we always wanted."

"You wanted. More," I reminded him, cooling some, still not looking at his eyes.

"It's for both of us, isn't it? Didn't you tell me once it was your place of belonging, being at the falls?" I nodded, sighed. "We'll build a big house there," he said, "fill it with the voices of people. And children. Not at first, maybe, but eventually. I'm sorry about not telling you of my stash. I can see now how you'd read it. It was meant to surprise you, to keep you from worrying." He pulled me up. "Come on, let's let Benito and Anna know. They'll be pleased to be coming with us, I'm sure of that."

I still hesitated. "We'll need to sell it seems to me. To build. And do the roads. That's the key you said, the roads?"

"There'll be a way."

"Something more you've kept from me?"

He sighed. "Nothing more," he said.

"Where did you keep it, your stash?"

Joseph was quiet a long time. "Just around. Can we not discuss it later?" He took my hand. "For now, it's time to celebrate."

"Not sure what we're celebrating," I said, knowing I did.

He took both my hands in his, pulled me to standing. "A new path," he said. He looked into my eyes. Liquid formed at the corners. He blinked it back, wetting the crows feet that reached out toward his temples. "I feel it. Sense it," he said.

"And if you're wrong and this new path turns into more trouble than we've had? If we go to the falls and we don't have children, can't build a better bridge, the road doesn't work, and your vision isn't real, will it be worth it then?" I wanted assurance that if this move did not bring children, add to our happiness, that he would not hold it over me, hold me as accountable as I held myself.

"Man's got to be somewhere, doing something," Joseph said. He spoke quietly next. "Children? I want those for you more than for us. Because you want it so. It will make our lives no less a gift if we live it out together without some of our own. For me," he said, his eyes sparkling now, "working at the falls—with you—is what I believe I was meant to do. It's why O'Brien has decided to sell now, I'm sure of it. It's time to bend, Janie." He lifted my chin, looked into my eyes. "This course has been mine since the day I first saw the falls out of the mist, the day I felt something special between me and you. It was like God let me see the falls and then meet you, see you both for what ye could be. I don't mind that some folks think it's too hot, too far from people, too rugged to live on. Remember Frederic? He said you can't let fear and disappointment or what others think set you back. Trust me in this," he said, folding his big arms around me, burying my face in the wool of his vest. He rested his chin on my head. "Just trust me," he said softly. "And in God's plan for our lives."

His arms promised strength; he merely asked me for some bend. And so we adopted those coping-saw qualities of life and nurtured them into our future.

CHAPTER 27

THE FALLS

"TO THE LEFT! Hold it! Get the blanket, Jane!"

I followed Joseph's instructions, wrapping the headboard of the fourposter with the old wedding-ring quilt. Joseph and Benito set the bird's eye maple bedroom set into the back of the wagon with a "thump!" The mules grunted at the weight, danced a bit in their harness. "Hold 'em!" Joseph shouted at young Dick Barter, the driver.

"Imagine it'll still get marred," I said, stepping back, "if the other loads are any judge." Joseph threw the rope to Benito to criss-cross the bed set, and I placed old shoe leather under the stretch points hoping to protect it however little we could. "Can't be helped," Joseph said, "We'll take as good a care as we can but there'll be some rub marks, sure—until the roads are improved."

"Well, there's little left to load, at least."

The men tightened more, wrapped as they could around the trunks and wooden boxes stored under the bed, on top, wherever we could fit things until the wagon sat jammed as tight as my corset, leaving no room, we hoped, for shifting.

Finally, Joseph gave the order. "Take it down, Dick. Let Janie by you with the pigs first. I'll finish loading here and bring up the rear."

"Right so!" the young man said. Big and tall, he wore a leather belt from his waist to his armpits, to hold his back as stiff as a timber to handle big teams on rugged roads. Dick released the foot brake, slapped the backs of the mules, and with a jingle of harness and crunching wooden wheels, set out with the last of our worldly goods. He headed down the ravine, pulled to the side to wait for me to pass him before we both moved down to the Deschutes.

I'd made the trip four times myself that past week, surprised that even with Joseph's work on it, the trail was still treacherous, almost as much as when I first rode on it with Sunmiet and her family. That had been ten, maybe eleven years before. I'd never taken the trail in October to the river. Never had a need to go there after the rains had washed out deep ruts and new rocks. Until we moved.

It was the week before my twenty-third birthday, 1871, and the move had not gone as we had planned.

The pigs resisted leaving their roaming grounds, being herded like cattle to new spots. Bandit, confused by our efforts to treat the spotted hogs like cattle instead of the pets they had become, simply lay on his belly and watched, tongue dripping, eyes following our efforts, but not lifting a leg to help. We had a dozen shoats who both kept the snakes down around the house and tidied up the place. Attached to their wallows near the lilacs, they resisted the move. After some effort to push them with the horses down the trail, I suggested we catch them and toss them squealing into the back of a wagon that I now stepped up onto.

"Don't think this is the best idea," Joseph said. "They'd eventually come with us. Riding in this wagon...."

"Let's give it a try," I said picking up the reins.

"You've got to move fast enough to keep them in there—but not too fast," he warned me.

We started out well enough.

With great care, I began down the twisting, winding descent of narrow road, feeling the wheels drop over rocks that seemed to appear overnight in the trail. My legs were tense, beginning to ache. My feet jammed the front board, my hand gripped then released the brake, setting, releasing, my arms aching in the effort to help the horses hold back the wagon with its load. A doe and her fawn startled, distracting. The pair lunged up the steep side hill, the fawn a muted shadow behind its mother.

This road was some of my husband's best work up to that point. Difficult to believe that the governor of this state would someday call him the "Greatest Roadbuilder of the West." That fine governor should have been riding with me in that pig wagon!

I wondered how Dick was handling his much heavier load when I heard him coming up behind me. He shouted, though I didn't know what and my team became agitated, maybe because they thought he got too close with his. At any rate, mine picked up speed.

I tried to slow them, saw their ears flick back and forth in agitation. Half standing, I pushed my weight against the front board, whoaing them. They pulled and jerked the harness, the tongue of the wagon bobbing up and down like a chattering child. My leg cramped, my forearm strained from holding back and I shouted, "Back off, Dick!" but by then it was too late.

Our action broke a rock loose, startling the horses more as it fell, bouncing and careening like a cannonball off the boulders below.

"Whoa, now, whoa!" I said, trying to keep alarm from my voice. "Easy, now." The horses had another plan and then theirs was thwarted, too, as the wagon picked up greater speed and jerked over rocks and ruts like it was a rock itself, bouncing off the narrow canyon, the wheels riding up on the side. I could feel my heart throbbing against my ribs, my breathing shallow, and I'm praying now, out loud, "Please, God, please, God, please," hoping he will know exactly what I need. I hear another squeal and think I see a spotted form fly out of the back and tumble down the ravine.

The wagon wheels crunch, horses lunge, as though escaping the very thing they drag behind them. The rear of the wagon careens around the switchback shifting the weight of the pigs from side to side, sending the wagon up on two wheels then dropping, hard, as we twist to make the next turn. I hear Dick shouting and realize by the closeness of his voice that he's moving faster than he should be, too. I can't take time to look, my wagon is rushing, pushing, way too fast, and I'm bouncing on my seat, standing, sitting, pulling on the reins, wondering why I cannot get the wagon stopped despite my desperate slamming of the brake.

It has taken on a life of its own, my wagon, with the shoats protesting, bouncing in the back, and I am sure we will not make the next tight twist in this excuse for a road when we round the bend and the ground levels out, blessedly, to run more gently beside the rushing Deschutes River where the horses at last, slow.

I breathe prayers of thanks while catching my breath, and finally pull the horses up and stop. Dick hauls up beside me.

"Whooee!" he shouted, his dimples deep, his boyish face washed in grin as he towers over me. "What a ride, hey, Mrs. Sherar? You can drive for me anytime. Whooee!" He lifted his hat and wiped his forehead then made a sweeping, gallant bow. He was full of compliments while I was feeling fury. He jumped off, helped me down, and balanced me a moment on my shaky legs before he checked my wagon and what was left of the squealing pigs.

"You were way too close," I snapped at him. "Scared the horses and me half to death. Could have gotten us all killed."

He looked surprised. "Just trying to warn you. The leather split, dropped off back on the trail," he pointed behind him. "You didn't have no brakes to speak of. Pulled back soon as I saw you were having a hard time with 'em. But hey, Mrs. Sherar, you done good! Lucky no bells rang. We had the road all to ourselves. Really put the steam on. Just the way I like it."

Later, when passengers stepped off the stage at our hotel, I always had a special sympathy for those who rode with Dick. Many reported walking down that grade rather than ride with the Wheeler Stage Company's handsome young driver. I knew how he liked to take his big Concord down the steep twisty road at breakneck speed. He grew bigger with the thrill of that steep grade while I shrank smaller than my five feet.

We finished the drive in the shadow of the rimrocks, noticing the tangled remains of a raven's nest and the resident's white droppings dribbled down the red rocks. I heard the falls, could see the turquoise twist of water surging through the lava cuts roaring beneath the splintered bridge. Then we stopped, presenting fourposter and pigs to the base of the canyon and our new home.

We had survived the day. Even the tossed-out pig found his way to his mates having taken a short cut. Once we actually lived at the river, I worried we'd lose pigs, that they'd wander too close and fall in. Only Joseph's assurance of their intelligence—"they can probably swim"—and the thousand other demands coughed up by our decision to move kept me from dwelling long on the shoats' fate.

The stove, too, proved troublesome to move. And we had to take with us a winter's supply of pinewood and fir so we'd have other than brush to burn through our first winter at the river, there being no trees where we had chosen to live, just rock.

But the most difficult and unexpected part of the move was Benito and Anna's response to it.

"Is not personal," Benito said, stirring the spoon in his coffee a little too vigorously the day Joseph carried his enthusiasm to Benito and Anna, announcing his purchase of the falls. "We stay here."

"Ye don't wish to be part of it?" Joseph asked.

"We do our part. Here," Benito insisted. "Buy this claim if you let us, run cattle, this place. Or other." His finger tapped into the tabletop with each phrase, tentatively emphasizing his point.

"I need you," my husband said, still surprised. Corlamae climbed onto Joseph's tall knees, sat in her "uncle" Joseph's lap. Aware of the tension, she sucked on her fingers and leaned her head into Joseph's shirt. "It won't be the same if you don't come," he said.

Joseph had not considered that Benito and Anna and their children might have different plans. I suppose he figured he had discussed his wish so often with Benito that he expected his friend would share in it as he had with all the rest. Or perhaps he never asked.

"This is what we came north for," Joseph persisted. "You're the one who urged me to come all those years ago. Now you want out?" Anger in his voice hid the pain.

Benito nodded his head in disagreement. "Not out. Different." He smiled and I realized for the first time that it was not a smile of pleasure I often saw, but a habit, a way of expressing his discomfort, of buying time. I could tell he did not relish this discussion, disagreeing with his life-long friend over something so important as the future. He diverted his eyes from Joseph's face, studied the crack in his cup. "This is our home now," he continued. He reached around the waist of Anna who had moved to stand beside him. Her arms crossed over her chest, she willed her strength onto her husband in this. "We stay here, yes? Or we take other claim," he said.

"You'd move somewhere. Just not with us." Joseph said. He chewed on his lower lip, patted Corlamae's arm as she tensed on his lap.

"Is not personal," Benito said, "against you or Missus. But is for us. Personal." He sighed, struggling with the words. "We...to have own place. Not always ride drag behind big friend. Do not want to start again, far from things. Want to do things...different...even make mistakes."

"Haven't I treated you fairly? Haven't I—"

"You have a right to your own dreams," I said. "I doubt being fair has anything to do with it."

"What if I don't want to sell?" Joseph said.

I squeezed my husband's shoulder gently as I stood behind him. "Each has a different path. Isn't that what you've always said, Joseph? It isn't about you and Benito. It's about Benito and Anna, what they want for their family."

His gaze went to his hands hugging the small child. He was quiet.

I looked across the table at Anna. We each stood behind our husbands, our eyes sharing a message. *The friendship matters,* her eyes said. *But more, my husband's pride, of who he is and yet will be away from the shadow of Mr. Sherar.*

"You'll visit?" I said, lighter than I felt, aware at once of how much I would miss them, their ready laughter, good sense, the smell of Anna's cooking, the chatter of Spanish mixed with English. "Bring the children?" My words caught in my throat. Oh, how I would miss the children!

"Yes, *si,*" Benito said. "And will help with roundup. Share, still. Just set own pace," he said, his eyes pleading with me, with Joseph, to understand.

Anna left her husband's side and came to mine, her eyes searching, each knowing what we would miss, each supporting the loves of our lives. "I save seeds," she said softly, "so you can plant at the river. We will share some of the same view. Come. I show you," she said, and we walked arm in arm outside.

I'm not sure Joseph understood until much later. Sorting out the change in their relationship and how it would affect our move to the falls took energy. It was as though he had to ruminate on other old connections, with his brother, his father, have them work to the surface whenever some current encounter attached to the past. Slowly, though, my Joseph washed his feelings in the soothing water of time and we moved to Sherar's Bridge without his life-long friends.

It was called Sherar's Bridge almost immediately. I never understood that. Todd and May and Hemingway and O'Brien—not to mention the Tyghs and Teninos and Warm Springs people—all had their marks on that piece of the river. Somehow "Sherar's" stuck.

O'Brien had begun work on a wooden flume to bring spring water from a grassy ravine above the rock ledge to a storage tank near the cabin. It was our water supply. Finishing that task took Joseph's first energies, begun even before we began the move. Then he started on the house.

The place came with a single-story frame structure, made up of a large kitchen with a room to eat in and gather, a small parlor; and on the other side, three bedrooms, two for weary travelers. Almost at once, Joseph determined to add on, to enlarge the small parlor into a saloon. He wanted to expand the kitchen area, create a long, rectangular dining room with eight small bedrooms sticking out from the saloon. Each little room would house a narrow bed, a washstand for a chamber set, a Chatham-square mirror, and two clothes pegs pounded into one wall. I wondered how weary travelers could sleep with their tiny bedrooms attached like nipples to the belly of the bar, but they did.

Thirteen rooms in all. Finished, it would be larger than the home we left behind, very different, as we prepared for the increase in passengers Joseph was sure would follow with his improvements in the road.

I always appreciated that he tended to the house first even though it must have galled him some. He knew the roads so badly needed work. Perhaps he concentrated on the house because it was October, and he knew it was futile to begin the real road work before spring. I prefer to think his efforts reflected his remembering: my wish for a house with room enough for a large family to slip their feet beneath the table; room enough to strike up the fiddle and hear the shuffle of smooth soles across the polished floor; room enough to house all my memories and hopes.

At the same time, the bridge itself did require his attention. He wished to secure it, make it sturdier, and widen it to accommodate the larger loads and traffic he imagined would come down the ridge and cross. I often wonder if he ever imagined that just ten years later Jess and Stephen Yancy would bring five loads of thirty thousand pounds each to that bridge, having eased their way down the grade, the owners trusting in his construction enough to creak their heavy, ponderous fifteen-ton load of a light plant to the water's edge. They hoped what they carried in their wagons would illuminate the entire town of Prineville, south of Cross Hollows—if they could only reach the other side. I marvel that my visionary husband could have engineered something that inspired such confidence, especially that first fall.

And there were other pressures on us as we moved to our new home. Developing a crew was one. We needed men to handle the livery animals, harness and tend to traveling teams. If we were successful in building roads, we'd have stagecoaches making that treacherous grade. They'd require feed to refresh their mounts to make it up the other side. There'd be passengers to serve, tolls to collect, food to prepare for travelers and our own crew, assuming we had one.

"So who will we hire for the road work?" I asked my planning husband. "There'll be enough work to keep what buckaroos we have busy without releasing them each day for the road."

"Been thinking on that for a while, now," Joseph said. "Going to make a ride to the reservation. Want to come along?"

He knew he didn't have to ask twice.

Sunmiet greeted me with a warm embrace and invited us inside. Seeing us, Standing Tall bristled, grunted a greeting as he pushed his way past us to the outside without further comment. He left unmended dipnets on the floor. "He is busy with the horses today," Sunmiet said awkwardly, "and forgets his manners. Please, sit." She made room for us on the furs and blankets and it dawned on me as we sat that there were no chairs in the room. Nothing, actually, of the white man's world. Rock pestles, spear shafts, snowboards, all hand made. Even

Sunmiet wore the buckskins of her own tanning. "You like dried salmon?" she offered.

Joseph declined, saying he had really come to see Peter and would do that now. I accepted her offer though I wasn't hungry. I knew that giving meant much to her. "You stay," Joseph urged me. "Visit, while I look for Peter."

"You look young, happy as a child," Sunmiet said. "And still so slender, as an eel. Tiny waist," she laughed, "not like mine." She patted her stomach, sharing her secret.

"*Iyái?* Again?" I said, surprised and happy for her as she smiled. It pleased me that I felt no jealousy for my friend's happiness.

She blushed, blinked her eyelashes. "We cannot seem to find the cause," she said, laughing. "And so it keeps happening."

"When?"

"In the spring. During salmon feast. He will be a big baby, like my others, Kása tells me. Aswan!" She raised her voice to bring the youngster from his digging in a basket. "No more candy for you! You'll be sick! Maybe I will call the Whip Man, to help you remember to stay out of what is not yours!" Aswan quickly pulled his fingers from the basket as though bitten by a snake. He said something in Sahaptin which his mother answered in kind. Then to me she said, "He has seen the Whip Man at his friend Tepo's. Bubbles called him in and the Whip Man disciplined Tepo with a willow swat to his legs. The other children too, but Tepo got the worst. It works." She smiled as her oldest son picked up a spearpoint and scurried out the door. "We will see you at the falls?" she asked. She already knew then, of our move.

"We'll be there always, now," I said, and something made me ask, "Does Standing Tall resent our being there?"

Sunmiet looked away from my face. "He does not think any white man should live where the fish come up the river. He says their presence will scare the fish away. He is not alone in his thinking." She fidgeted with the fringe on her dress. "Others disagree. There is much discussion in the council." She looked back at me, her eyes tired. "Some argue about white man and fish. Others say the Modocs are the trouble." She sighed. "Maybe it is because the men have little else to do now, so they talk often and long."

I didn't know how to respond. I felt sad for her, for Standing Tall. Yet we were not the first to have lived at the bridge. And I knew Joseph would take care there, though I wasn't sure about the Modocs' intentions. Surely we wouldn't hurt the fish or her family's livelihood.

"Now I can see you every summer," I said. "And Aswan and Anne and this new one when it comes. You can put me to work, cleaning fish again, or watching the babies." Sunmiet reached for her beadwork, began work as we talked. "You'll like how we improve the bridge. And the roads, for easier traveling."

"Standing Tall says there are too many people passing there now. A better bridge and roads will bring more. He says new men come with books and drawings to cut up our world like a hunted deer. We will be left like dogs with only the bones."

"And your father? What does he say?"

She looked back at me, her brown eyes showing a depth of pain I had not noticed before. "He and Standing Tall disagree. My father stands with Peter and others who say the white man is here forever, like the fish jumping up at the falls, pushing themselves over the impossible because they have a place calling them, a place to go to. And living with them, taking their ways and making them fit into ours, molding them to our ways, stretching them on our drum rings, will be better for our people than trying to stop them from being here at all." She worked again with her beads, talked into the design. "It is my experience that non-Indians never turn deaf ears to their calling over impossible places."

Eagle Speaker's and Peter's views prevailed that day. For when Joseph returned to pick me up, he was elated. "Peter will bring men," he said, "in the spring. Some who helped at Blivens's like that kind of work and the steady pay. There'll be twenty or thirty—of families who camp there every year and fish. Some new people. Peter seems to think they can do both: fish and build roads. I like his attitude. So we'll see. Following round-up next two weeks, he'll come by." He put his hands out for me to step into, push up onto my horse. "We'll ride where I want to build and he'll see what I mean, translate to those not speaking English." Joseph's joy was complete.

As we rode back I heard him speaking beneath his breath, his hands moving this way and that as he does when he's in deep thought. "What?" I asked.

"Just remembering," he said. "Never imagined when I rode down Buck

Hollow the first time and shook hands with Peter and his son, that one day we'd be working side-by-side. Funny, isn't it, how when you're on the right road, life has a way of meeting you over and over at the switchbacks?"

Our fall had one last big event before we settled in to our first winter at Sherar's Bridge: round-up. Work on the bridge and the house and the general moving in all halted for that process of gathering animals from the ridges and ravines, driving them through grasses torn short to the corrals near the Y homesite now occupied by Anna and Benito. As before, buckaroos roped, flopped calves, held the bawling animals' legs with one boot holding their necks and the other driven into the dirt. With strained arms and legs, they kept the animal still while another buckaroo wielded the hot branding iron, burned a J in the red hair on the left hip side. The area reeked of singed hair. As before, we doctored leg injuries, pulled cheatgrass from eyes, and drove curious calves sporting noses filled with porcupine quills into the wooden chutes to pull the barbs, leaving behind bloody noses and calves wondering if we'd really helped. I suspect the bull calves we converted into steers wished to ask the same question of our efforts with a sharp knife. And as before, we culled out animals who had not made the weight gain we would have liked, made plans to sell the calfless mothers with no yearlings by their side. The steers we'd cut at spring round-up stood fat and sleek, now ready for market.

The final step meant driving cows to join herds bought up by eastern buyers in their silk vests gathered at the Umatilla House or the Globe Hotel in The Dalles.

Joseph always thought making the eight-hundred-mile drive of cattle from The Dalles to the Union Pacific railroad at Kelton, Utah, would have made an interesting time. But we sold "on foot, as is" and let the buyers find their own buckaroos to drive the cattle south. "Enough trouble getting the hard-headed horn-growing bovines twenty miles to town let alone another eight hundred miles across the territory to Utah," Joseph decided anew each year.

It was the last time Benito and Joseph worked side by side and I was conscious of the bittersweet event even if Joseph remained silent about it. We all behaved as though nothing had changed, Joseph and Benito laughing through the dust, speaking of the feistiness of calves, never mentioning their friendship. Anna and I readied baskets of food for the dozen buckaroos; she served and cleaned, freed me to ride and rope. My mind would not let go the thought of how I'd miss not having them close to my side.

But the Lord never closes a door but that he doesn't open another.

By spring, I knew something else of Anna's I truly missed: her food handling! It wasn't that I couldn't cook. I did, and liked to. I could stir flour, salmon, and milk into Sunmiet's lumpy gravy known as luckameen as well as anyone. Joseph called it "spring run off with rocks." The two or three buckaroos we held over the winter did not complain. Joseph did. In truth, I think he wanted more time with me beside him, less of my efforts in the kitchen. He didn't express it that kindly.

"We need ourselves a cook," he said, sawing through the beef steak I'd gotten a little too done on the cookstove. "The crews won't take to your way of making steaks, Janie." He chewed. No juice dribbled from the slab. "Not that your meals don't show care," he added quickly, seeing the defense in my eyes. "And I suppose well-done kills off the critters." He grinned.

"Sunmiet says its bad medicine to touch food when you're upset or angry," I said. "So if you want me to cook again, best you not complain too much."

"No offense intended," he said, lifting his hands in protest. "Travelers want a hot, fast, *tasty* meal. Personally, I like a foreign touch." He leaned back in his chair, pretending satisfaction.

"Suggesting I'm 'foreign' to a kitchen?" I said, taking up the dishes. Water heated on the wood stove for cleaning them.

"Not my meaning," he said, smiling.

"I miss Anna, too," I said. "I actually like cooking, just not having to choose between doing it or spending time on the books or being with you."

He sat quiet. "Thought I'd check with Chinaboy Tom at the Umatilla House." He stood, walked to the window, looked out at the river, swirling. Sea gulls screeched at the base of the falls, dipping and swooping for early, weakened fish making their way upriver against the rapids. It was March, early in the salmon run.

"Why do they call a grown man, older than you even, a *boy?*" I said. "Seems demeaning to me."

Joseph brushed a spiderweb from the window, held a cold glass of spring water in his other hand. "Never considered it," he said. "Doesn't say much for me, does it."

I shrugged my shoulders, dipped the plates into the steaming water. "Wasn't being critical. Just wondering."

"Suppose some folks still see Tom as a boy, from when he first came there working in the kitchen and taking care of the chandeliers, cleaning and all. Thinking on it, though, no boy would have stuck it out so long. Or been so quiet doing his work. Not complaining, just sending his money back to China for his family." He took a drink, swallowed. "Something to think about. Anyway, we could ask Chinaboy—Tom—if he knows any of his countrymen who would cook for us, passengers, and crew."

"He'll most likely send us to Canyon City or John Day town," I said. "Gold mines petering out there might free up some cooks. But we haven't time for a trip now, pushing on roads like we should be. And didn't you say you wanted to build a bridge across Buck Creek too this year?"

My clanking of dishes filled the silence. "That might not be such a bad plan, if we do it soon enough. Before Peter gets here with his men. Put two chickens in one pot."

"What?" I asked, still steaming the plates, not following where his mind had gone.

"If we head out to John Day town now, we could seek ourselves a good, authentic Chinese cook to add to the Sherar's Bridge family."

"That's one chicken in the pot. What's the other?"

His voice gentled, letting me know he spoke of something of import, something that truly mattered, and something he had not forgotten. He turned from the window to face me. "We could collect some advice from Dr. Hey while we're there. About expanding a family of our own."

CHAPTER 28

UNPREDICTABLE

SUNG-LI'S ALMOND-SHAPED EYES slid like a slow snake down Joseph's body, halting at my husband's feet.

"No need for that," French Louie said, clearing his throat. He added something that sounded like Cantonese, repeated it in English as though talking to a child. "Don't challenge this man."

Any who needed translating in the gold fields of Canyon City called on Louie at one time or another. Today, Louie came to the cooking hut of the Lodi mines to help his old friend, Joseph Sherar, find a cook with a reputation.

He found us a temperamental cook, though any other kind was rare.

Sung-li moved his eyes slowly from the blue morocco on Joseph's boots, gauging his wool pants, appraising the value of the turquoise stones at the end of his belt, the soft weave of his vest. He ignored Louie's command and boldly looked into Joseph's eyes instead.

"I speak Engli," he said in a voice as loud and brash as the dinner gong that called the men to eat. The blue silk of Sung-li's pajama-like shirt pulled tightly across his back as he braced his legs and crossed his arms in front of himself. He hid his small hands in the folds of the wide sleeves. His mouth was a straight line beneath a small nose and he wore his coal black hair straight away from his face, pulled tight and hanging in a queue down his back.

"Good," Joseph answered. "It'll save time. The question is, can you cook?"

"I cook good for many here," Sung-li said as he turned his back on the older men and walked like a satisfied king behind the throne of his butcher block. "No mind to leave," he added, picking up the cleaver, turning it over in his immaculate fingers. He handled the blade like a new weapon. He never took his eyes from Joseph's. Defying his look of confidence, his feet stepped back and forth in one spot, as though stepping on hot coals. He seemed to realize his strange habit and stopped, abruptly.

Joseph pulled on his beard. The man was bold, but I suspect Joseph liked that, liked someone with confidence. Yet something about him struck a tender note too, I think. Perhaps the smallness of the slippered feet that shuffled nervously again on the floor. Joseph ran his tongue back and forth like a metronome over his upper lip. His tongue stopped abruptly with his mind made up. "You will work with my wife? Take directions from her?"

Sung-li paid attention to me for the first time. With that same boldness, he looked me over, checked out my wide-brimmed hat, tiny earrings, paused briefly at my eyes, my throat; easing his eyes imperceptibly down to the parasol I held in my hands. Looking back at Joseph, he nodded his head slowly in concurrence. His demeanor nudged a caution in my mind, but I set it aside.

"But no wish to change," Sung-li said, his voice still loud but closer to a whine.

"You come with good recommendations," Joseph said. "Louie here heard you were looking to leave. But we've no need to disrupt a happy man. Nor to beg," Joseph said, fingering the turquoise bola at the end of his belt. "Guess we came for nothing." He tipped his hat to the man and I took it as a signal that we would leave the closeness of the hut and the heavy scent of herbs. The four of us filled the small space to overflowing; I liked the idea of leaving.

"You no go," Sung-li said, a desperate note in his voice. "What you offer? Wages?"

"Five dollars for a seven-day week, your own room, and a saddle horse as needed. And we don't hold to spitting on the bread."

The smaller man nodded his head. "No spit," he said, "but one day week.

For my time." He slammed the cleaver onto the block a little too hard I thought. He must have thought so too as he shot his hands back into his sleeves. Sung-li's feet swished on the hard dirt floor, that nervous hot-rock step.

"A day a week!" Joseph said, his deep voice filling the small cook hut in Canyon City. "That's robbery! I've an inn to run seven days a week. No," he shook his head. "That won't do. Tell him that won't do, Louie."

Before Louie could even open his mouth, Joseph took my elbow and we turned to leave, the fullness of my dress filling the hut door as I started to push through into the sun-filled April air. Joseph bent to pass through the low door behind me then stopped. When I turned, I saw that the smaller man must have touched the sleeve of Joseph's short coat, then stepped back, submissively. I couldn't believe how quickly Sung-li had flown around the butcher block to reach us!

"Half-day, mine," Sung-li said, stepping back beyond a fist's reach, "to send letters home." His eyes dropped like a rock, staring at the embroidery on his slippers.

"Home." Joseph said, chewing on his lower lip. "What's your thought, Mrs. Sherar?"

I hesitated and Sung-li's eyes got smaller, softer as he lifted them to peer into mine. "He does come highly recommended. We can manage, I suspect. We've need to hire a girl or two anyway and one could be trained for kitchen help, to cover Sung-li's half-day off."

"Well, Sung-li," Joseph said to him, smiling. "I suspect you're hoodwinking me, but except during round-up, half day a week is yours. Every man needs at least some time to call his own even if I haven't found any myself. It's a deal then?" He extended his hand to Sung-li who lifted his head, smiled a vacant smile that only later reminded me of a sneer, then bowed. He did not proffer his hand to his newest employer.

"Must just be their way," Joseph said as we departed with plans to pick up Sung-li later in the day.

"The mine foreman says he has some weird ways," Louie said as he helped me into the buggy we'd rented from the livery. "But, um, he is harmless enough."

"Why's he want to leave do you suppose?" I asked.

"Something about relatives in The Dalles. Wants to be closer."

"Can't begrudge a man for that. Sure drives a bargain," Joseph said with admiration in his voice. "Don't remember many Chinese being bold enough for that."

Dr. Hey, the "herb doctor" as Joseph called him, had a temperament the exact opposite of Sung-li's. Warm and inviting, he remembered Joseph, asked about his leg. Then with tenderness and skill and the gentlest hands of any who had poked and prodded my body, he examined me. Looking into my eyes, as Sunmiet had that very first day, Dr. Hey smiled but I could tell he saw something different there than "huckleberries."

I knew that my eyes looked unusual. They seemed to push out from my face at times, showed white all around the dark blue when I looked in the mirror each morning to tie up my hair, powder my face.

"You take Oregon Kidney Tea? From Stark Medicine Company?" he asked, referring to the Portland druggist's latest cure. It surprised me he was so well-versed on current medicine. We sat in the Chinese doctor's tidy office surrounded by small ceramic and blown glass vials that lined the dust-free shelves. Herb bunches hung neatly from the ceiling giving the room a sweet yet pungent scent. A small pewter frame with a fading picture of a woman and child sat behind him on a shelf, staring out at us.

"Sometimes I take it," I said. "When my stomach hurts. Is that wrong?" I was suddenly worried, hoped I'd done nothing to counter my chances for a child.

He shook his head and touched my gloved hand softly, to reassure me. "Just wish to know what you do. To care for self. And Pfunder's Headache Wafer?"

"No, I don't have headaches. Just sometimes feel tired though usually I can go the day without stopping. My friend Sunmiet says I move like a sandpiper at the sea always running close to the water but never getting wet."

He smiled, made a tent with his fingers, touching them lightly as he thought. He moved around the room as though floating. I studied the embroidery that marched in tiny stitches hemming the sleeves of his silk jacket and the hat that fit like a small box on his head. I envied the smoothness of his olive-colored skin, his gentle eyes. Beyond him, through the washed window, I could see a slender woman walking hand in hand with a small boy across the muddy yard, the child's single braid bouncing as the boy looked up, talked and smiled to the woman who must have been his mother. I turned back to the doctor.

"I never will have children, will I?" I said, finally putting words to my fears.

He walked behind a small desk table and motioned for Joseph and me to sit in the high-back armchairs across from him. He sat, his hands reformed into their thinking tents. "No way to know, for certain," he said kindly. Joseph reached for my fingers, held them gently as the doctor spoke. "Sometimes birds born in nests we do not think could bear them, resist the storms. Others come to perfect branches with best material. Eggs are laid. But do not hatch. Something happens." He lifted his fingers like birds in flight. "It is the way of all life." He rested his hands flat on the desk now, kept looking into my eyes. "Your body shows me no reason why you do not bear children. Eyes like yours, sometimes, mean pressure, many headaches, but you do not have these." He shrugged his shoulders as if to say it could go either way. I stared at the half moons of his well-shaped nails arched high. "Is best if you live full life. Baby arrives more quickly to restful nest. And if no baby comes, then you have not waited, hung on so long to hope for one thing, you fail to find joy carried on other wings."

"Do what I've been doing, worry less, and get on with my life." I said with resignation. "That's what you're telling me, isn't it?" I swallowed back tears. "We came all this way for you to tell me that." Anger and disappointment mingled. I sounded like my mother and my voice cracked as I spoke. Joseph squeezed my hand, to steady me.

"You have much to give," Doctor Hey said, his voice still soft and calming. "Do not wait to offer it only to the child of your dreams or you miss great joy, perhaps pass by dream caught for you by another. Each labor is different for each child. Labor is not only of your body but of mind also."

He rose, approached the shelf of vials and selected one, removed the cork and poured the tiny flakes into a piece of parchment paper rolled into a cone. "For the bee stings, in your stomach," he told me. "Brew in hot water." He handed me the cone, folded the top over. Joseph took it, holding it like a white candle in his big hands; the other arm around my shoulders. We stood, readying to leave.

"Each child arrives to different family," the doctor said. "Though may come of same mother and father. First child comes to parents; second to parents plus one." He held his index finger to the air. "Next child, plus two. Different family, distinct. Perhaps your child come in separate way, too, looking for own family, own place of belonging."

It struck me that his words described my sense of belonging that day at the falls, the first time I felt a part of a family, after the babies died. Perhaps the falls would provide my family after all, if I let it. If I let "family" be different than I'd thought.

Sung-li proved a good traveler: quiet, undemanding. Unfamiliar with a horse to ride, he bounced a bit, but hung onto the little mare we bought for him. He made no complaints as he followed behind us, all his worldly goods bobbing in the canvas bag that hung from the side of the saddle. Even down the steep grade we called Hollenbeck's Point, following skid marks from the wagons using the Barlow cutoff, Sung-li did not protest.

Only his demeanor with Bandit when we arrived concerned us. The dog growled at him before doing anything else. Sung-li kicked at him. Joseph said "Hey, hey! That's Bandit! He's old! Won't bother you if you let him be!" The dog dropped flat on his stomach as though guarding, circled Sung-li close to the ground with quick-quick steps before dropping to his stomach again, stalking, wary. Sung-li scoffed, turned his back on the dog, and stepped inside.

"Where room?" he said in his gong voice.

Our life with a temperamental Chinese cook began.

He proved a worthy man, one well needed for the crew Peter brought the following week. Sung-li knew what thickness of salt pork the men liked, had a good sense of how much flour and oil to order for the weekly trips I made to town. His feet moved steadily in their hot-rock step as he cooked. Surprisingly, he and I worked well together, I thought. He occasionally resisted my suggestions for a meal, but nothing drastic. Except for his annoying habit of humming, we got on fine.

The sing-song nasal quality drowned out my words if he did not want to hear me. The humming provided a curtain for ignoring me. Later, he feigned innocence when I had to touch him, cause the humming to abruptly stop, to bring his concentration onto what I wished to tell him. The humming proved a caution to me, and I thought well before I caused its interruption.

Sung-li did not work well with Alice M., however, a child we were forced to name, as what she called herself sounded like a foreign language. It just came out to us as "Alice M."

We guessed her to be about eleven on the day she arrived, on foot, wandering down the first of the roads that Joseph and his crew began working on that year of 1872. But the depth of pain in her eyes said she was probably some years older.

Appearing from nowhere, she fairly dragged her frail body down the grade from Bakeoven, her buckskin and sagebrush clothes hanging in shreds from her, exposing calloused knees and scratched arms and thighs tanned to a bronze leather. Her brown eyes stared out at us as though from far away. They were the most prominent feature of a face that looked to be chiseled out of jasper. Oddly, she initially spoke a language only Peter seemed to understand.

"Sounds some like Paiute," he said. "She speaks as someone who did not grow up with the words, but learned them late. She is not Indian," he added to our surprise.

But she needed shelter, food, and she was, after all, just a child. We ran an ad in *The Times-Mountaineer* under the advice of the editor, William Hand. It ran next to notices about missing wives. We heard nothing from anyone who might claim her and as the weeks wore on, I pulled the ad and hoped no one would.

I liked the name Alice, and she did not seem to resent it, nor me as I eased my way around her, deciding whether to become attached. She accepted what was given, made few demands.

Alice's communication moved from indecipherable Paiute to signs and English words she heard us say. Quick with her movements and her eyes, she soaked up the world around her. She stayed off to the side when travelers arrived from the stage but kept a close accounting of which baggage went with whom, rushing to deliver luggage correctly to the sleeping rooms. She had a way with the animals, too, I noticed, and Bandit adored her.

"She copies you," Joseph commented one day as we watched her near the rock wall in front of the inn, tossing a line into the river.

"Oh, I think she knew how to fish before she ever arrived," I told him. "She does it quite naturally."

"Yes, but see how she stands, one hand on her hip as she tosses the line. Looks just like I've seen you do."

"O pooh!" I said turning back to the butter I churned. But his observation pleased me. I felt a smile touch me from the inside. I thought of the herb doctor, my nesting while looking for peace. Perhaps Alice was that bird looking for a place of belonging, and this was the way our family would grow.

"Alice M. agitates Sung-li," I told Joseph as we sat one day months after both had arrived. It was our evening to complete bookwork in one of the bedrooms we had converted into an office. I sanded the ink, gently shaking the paper. "Though I can't determine why. She follows his directions to perfection, at least when she understands what he wants. Brings him coffee from the bin, scurries out for sour milk from the summer kitchen. But he barks at her and she shrivels up before him like a winter's leaf."

"Probably doesn't understand," Joseph said. "She doesn't know much English, or at least it sounds strange when she says the words. Peter's asking for help with reading English. Maybe I should hold school," he said, laughing.

"That's not a bad thought."

"What? Oh, no. I've no time for that. Too much on my plate already without adding your sauce."

"But perhaps that's what annoys Sung-li," I said, "her not understanding."

"Life annoys Sung-li," Joseph said, stretching his big arms over his head.

"Be serious."

"I am! The man cooks well, but he's a brooder. I almost look forward to his half-day away. Maybe we should just give him the full day, for our sake. Alice's hovering is probably just too much. I'd say find someone else to be the cook's helper and let Alice learn English day by day. From you. Let her help serve meals. She seems to want to. Travelers are so tired they won't recognize good English anyway. Be different when the bridge is rebuilt and Wheeler's stages start coming down.

"Then they'll be so glad to set their feet on solid ground, they won't question what country it is no matter what language the help speaks. Especially if Dick's driving the stage." I remembered Dick's wild ride the day we moved, and laughed.

"But think on it," I persisted, hanging onto my idea. "About teaching Peter writing. Maybe in the winter. And Alice can learn too. You could include George and that chore boy you just hired, John Suhr. Lord knows the boarding school doesn't teach the Indians any real skills. Only how to sew and seed. Who knows what might come of Alice and Peter's boy spending time together."

"No scheming," he said. "But I'll think on it. Where would I be without ye?" He didn't wait for a response, just leaned over me, closed the drawers in his desk, placed the jade tea-kettle ink well over my papers signaling an end to the discussion. Then, for that evening at least, he kissed me out of my scheming.

Alice's presence added brightness to each day. As she began to trust that we would not put her out, she behaved more like a child, resisting some, acting like she did not hear or didn't understand when we wanted her to help with laundry or gather eggs. Still, she sometimes surprised me with her tanned hand slipping into mine as I stood at the dinner bell to call the men. She was someone I sponged time with.

Sunmiet's people and their seasons formed a frame around our picture of life at the falls. In the spring, I watched the Indians fish, traded beef for salmon, new cloth for plump huckleberries. Sunmiet shared her children with me and giggled when she announced still another on the way.

And on Sundays, Joseph and Alice and I sometimes made the long trip to the Congregational church in The Dalles where Thomas Condon preached (avoiding the Methodist church of my mother). There, I let in the peacefulness of God's promises as I sat between two that I loved, nestled among my family.

Work on the Bakeoven grade begun in the spring after our move proved the most demanding of the road work. The Indian crews gathered daily to create the picture Joseph carried in his head. Day after day, the men walked and rode up the steep ridges, tethered their horses, and began chopping and pounding and hand-carrying rocks. With pick axes, they cut trails into the steep ridges, widened them, reinforced the lower banks of the rugged road with sagebrush and rocks. From a distance, the road appeared like a fingerswipe in chocolate frosting following the dips and curves of the steep ravines arching ever higher out of sight.

The biggest challenge had been slicing through a lava outcropping thirty feet thick and twenty-four feet high that ran from the top of the ridge to the river's edge and stood between my husband and his plan. Sweating men chipped and hammered for months to carve a slice through the Clarno lava rocks wide enough for wagons and stages to run through. A remarkable feat, everyone said when it was finished and the men moved to another challenge.

But Joseph knew the real push forward would come with the redoing of the bridge.

The May day in 1873 when we began widening and reinforcing Sherar's Bridge, making it safe enough to transport stagecoaches and large freighters, herds of cattle and sheep, and any other thing the inventors and investors of the West could think to move, proved doubly memorable. In the midst of the chaos and scattered intentions of twenty men and horses attempting something dangerous and new, Sung-li chose the day to display his true colors.

Joseph and I had planned this day for months.

Milled lumber from Tygh Valley stood in stacks near the water's edge, having arrived with great difficulty and care down the twisting road past our old homestead, across the creek to the falls. Up Buck Hollow, Peter's crews had marked four huge pine trees with trunks so thick it took three men to reach around them. Weeks earlier, they chopped them down, stripped them of their bark and with teams of horses, dragged them down the creek, across the mouth, and then along the pitted lava shelves that marked the steep and treacherous gorge along the river.

The morning of Sung-li's indiscretion found Peter's crew already sweating in the May canyon heat as they worked to bring the four logs into two giant "A" shapes. When the A-frames were nailed in place and reinforced with rawhide straps and ties, the horse teams stomped nervously as they backed up to the edge of the river. While some steadied the teams, other men eased the frame across the roaring rapids, lowering it like a chair standing on one leg then slowly dropped to straddle spilled water.

The air fairly prickled with shouting, yelling, signaling with hands, the smell of men and animals mixed with spring breezes under a perfect blue sky. Joseph moved here and there as delighted as a boy with some new toy. He was always happiest when building, converting his ideas into real. Peter spoke rapidly in Sahaptin, switching in a flash to English as was needed, keeping everyone in stride until a leg of the brace dropped over with a solid "thud!" and the first "A" supporting Sherar's Bridge rose up from either side along with the cheers of men.

Teams of men steadied the big logs while others dug into what little earth there was, strapped coils of rawhide and hemp around nubby rocks and then the braces to secure the frames. James, one of Peter's crew, volunteered to be lowered out over the roaring rapids. "Like fishing!" James said, smiling. With a rope around his middle, his friends lowered him down the side of the steep gorge, and held the ropes while he secured the bottom of the braces to the rock outcroppings.

Sunmiet's people had arrived from their place up Buck Hollow and despite the salmon run, they too became involved in the bridge excitement, standing, watching, being enlisted with brawn or brains as the situation demanded.

With a shout of success, the men hauled James up and applauded, another step finished. We were another day closer to a bridge wide enough for stages, sturdy enough to secure our dreams.

Sung-li had the meal prepared as planned. Pans of fresh bread heaped on the plank tables we'd set out in front of the inn, accompanied by chicken fried to crisp, bowls of mashed potatoes draped in melted butter, leafy lettuce picked by Alice from the early garden and slabs of salt pork, fresh roasted salmon, and dried apricots we'd revived with spring water. A spice cake with fresh sweetened cream globbed on top became dessert. Jugs of tea cooled in a river pool washed the full meal down. Alice and I swirled around, pouring tea, serving, refilling platters, rushing back and forth from the outdoor table to the kitchen, catching in snatches the chatter of the men. The kelpie lay tangled in feet beneath the table, snoring until Joseph gently pushed him with his foot and the men laughed about the sounds and smells of growing old.

Inspired by their morning success, the crew took little time to digest their food, wanting to see both "A" frames set before the sun did. They returned quickly to the bridge.

"Sung-li not hot water plates," Alice said quietly to me as we cleared the dishes. She spoke to the side of my face, rarely giving me the pleasure of seeing her eyes.

"Hot water plates?" I asked, confused by the concern in Alice's voice. "What's your meaning, dear?"

"No hot water. On plates. Like Missus say." She motioned washing dishes and left out the hot steaming I required after every meal. With so many different people eating, I insisted that each plate be squeaky clean, so no one would complain of illness taken from our inn. Sung-li knew it was how I wanted the dishes handled. Why had he picked this day to challenge it? Well, there was nothing to be done for it.

"Finish clearing things here," I said and walked inside.

It's funny how events crystallize in your mind. The house was cool, a little dark, and smelled of spice. I could hear Sung-li humming in the kitchen as I walked toward the closed door. I picture him standing at the cutting board, head bent to his chopping block. Spiders and other frying pans rested in their places. Knives, cleavers, herbs, and garlic all hung from the ceiling. It was my kitchen, I reminded myself.

Sung-li did not look up when I entered. He continued to chop onions with his favorite cleaver, a large steel blade one that he'd brought with him from the mines. He did not stop humming. "Sung-li," I said in my firmest voice. "Please look at me."

He did not stop humming.

I decided to press my point to the top of his braid bent before me. "It has come to my attention that you did not steam the plates. Is that so?" I clasped my hands in front of me, for courage, resisted wiping their moistness on my white apron.

He did not stop humming.

"This is a significant matter, Sung-li," I said, getting rational, ignoring the pounding in my heart. "It is required. I know you understand that. If you are too busy, I can have Alice help you, but the plates cannot be simply rinsed and put away. People will become ill. Do you understand? I need you to look at me, now, Sung-li. And steam the plates."

He ignored me.

"This instant."

With that, he stopped his humming. Slowly, his eyes lifted to mine like a snake raising its head over the edge of a rock, seeking, searching its prey. "It is woman's work," he said, his voice a seething whisper, "so do it."

"We'll not have that kind of manner in this house," I said, my breathing becoming shallow. "You know the requirements. Please proceed." When he simply stood, boldly staring, I thought I'd up the ante, much as I preferred to keep it just between us. "Shall I request Mr. Sherar's presence?"

Sung-li smiled at that, seemingly pleased about where he'd taken this disagreement. He said nothing; started to hum. "Well!" I said, exasperated, and turned on my heels. I strode through the door, angered that I had to seek help from my husband, that I couldn't deal with this cook without him. I didn't notice where I stepped and so ran straight into Joseph.

"Alice says you need me," he said. "What's it about?" He looked over my head at Sung-li standing, cleaver in hand, sections of onions lying in piles on the block.

I felt like Rachel tattling to Papa and it angered me more. I took a breath. "Sung-li refuses to steam the plates," I said, facing our cook.

Joseph walked closer to Sung-li, towering over the small man. "No need for this," he said, his voice gentle.

Something in Sung-li's eyes forewarned me. Or perhaps it was the glint of the sunlight on the steel cleaver. Maybe that he stopped humming. I shouted "Joseph!" and shoved his shoulder just as the cleaver sailed through the air, slammed into the door, between and behind us.

Joseph lunged across the butcher block for the man, grabbing at his arm. Sung-li had already slipped around the block holding now a long butcher knife in his hand. "I do nothing," Sung-li hissed. He held the knife at his waist, his elbow set to thrust. He slithered his way around the block toward my husband, his eyes glinting, his mouth a sneer. Joseph kept a step or two beyond him, moving, saying quietly, "This is no way, Sung-li."

Too busy, Sung-li did not see me slip my hand beneath my skirts to reach the pistol I still kept with me. I set my feet, held the gun with both hands pointed directly at Sung-li's face. "Put it down," I said in my firmest, loudest voice. Both men startled, stared.

"Good, Janie!" my husband said, recovering quickly. To Sung-li he said, "Jig's up. She's not afraid to use it. Put the knife down."

Sung-li hesitated just an instant, shifted his weight toward me and that was enough. I took aim, shot. Even then I wondered about the blast in so closed a space, the mess I'd make.

The smell of gun powder filled the room accompanied by a momentary loss of sound, my ears reacting to the explosion in the kitchen, the clatter of shattered plates. Through the smoke, I watched Sung-li stare in wide-eyed surprise while Joseph sprang forward to disarm him.

The room was suddenly filled with men; Alice hovered near my side. Joseph pushed Sung-li out the door, handing him, unhurt, subdued to Peter, shouting orders, "Take him into The Dalles to his relatives. Send two or three along with him! Don't go alone! Get his things—but make sure all the knives stay here."

Then he turned to me, took the anniversary pistol from my fingers, wrapped his big arm around me, pulled me to his shoulder. "It's the first time I've actually shot at a person," I said. "I wasn't really aiming at him, just beyond his head, to scare him."

"That ye did!" Joseph said, as he gently patted my arm, "Among others." We stared at the splintered ironstone plates that lay like shards of old pottery scattered across the floor. Through the hole in the cupboard, we could see outside light. The dust of gunpowder settled around us. Looking at the broken dishes Joseph said, "It does seem a drastic way to steam the plates."

"Yes. Well. My oldest daughter was never known for doing things as everyone else," a cool voice behind us said. We turned. There the last person I ever expected to see in my kitchen filled the doorway. And behind her stood the lovely Ella.

CHAPTER 29

BRIDGES

~&~

"ALICE. PLEASE SHOW Miss Turner and her companion to the parlor," I said, my voice sounding to my ears as though coming from far away. "Let them know we'll be right along." I couldn't actually see their faces, the back light from the room keeping them dark, but I imagined them perusing my home and did not want them wondering about the state of my kitchen. "And then, if you would, dear, please tend to the kitchen. Do you have any questions?" I asked, buying time, nervously filling space with my words. Alice shook her head and her slender form slipped past me showing my mother and Ella to the horsehair sofa in the parlor. Then she rushed back past Joseph and me, disappeared into the kitchen.

"I'll stay with ye," Joseph said, and he took my elbow.

"What are they doing here?" I whispered to him as we followed them to the parlor. He shrugged his shoulders. I slipped my arm through his, reassured by his presence, wondering if he could hear my heart beating.

My mother's back, straight and unbending as a wagon tongue, presented itself to us as we entered. With her monocle, she peered into the glass china cupboard set next to the window. "Lovely," she said, hearing us enter. "Your husband has provided you with lovely things." She had stopped to examine the silver and gold crumb chaser and pan. "Such luxuries," she said, turning, dropping the glasses into her silk wrist purse.

"Not a bauble in sight," I said. They were my first words to her in nearly ten years. "I especially like the silver napkin rings. Joseph had them engraved for us at Tiffany's, in New York, when we were there last time." I liked seeing the look of envy that passed briefly over my mother's eyes. At least I thought it was envy.

"Please. Sit," Joseph said. "You too, Ella. Ye've grown into a lovely young woman. And you, Mrs. Herbert, are handsome as always."

Ella blushed; my mother flashed a forced smile.

As they settled wide skirts over narrow chairs, I had time to study my mother a bit. She looked older. More crow's-feet escaped her intense eyes. Lines formed an arch around her mouth fading into her strong chin. Her skin still stretched tightly across solid bones, though. Her lips were full, slightly red. She wore a deep blue dress under her pelisse and I had to admit that Joseph was correct: she was still a handsome woman.

Ella, on the other hand, was something more than handsome. She was beautiful. Her wine red dress set off the pink of her cheeks, the depth of her dimples, the pale blond of her hair that peered from beneath her matching bonnet. Her dress molded itself tightly over a fully developed sixteen-year-old form. Perhaps a little too tightly, as though her body had just recently surprised her with its changes. Tiny hands removed dark gloves, one finger at a time. She rested them quietly in her lap, her breathing even, unlabored. When I looked directly at her, she smiled ever so slightly, showing one broken tooth and revealing a touch of sadness in an otherwise flawless face. She dropped her eyes to her lap.

"I thought it time we should visit," my mother said, fluffing herself on the chair like a hen, nesting. "And having not received an invitation or being sure of the day you receive, I hope you'll not think less of us for having just dropped in."

What was she thinking? How could I think less of her than I already did? She'd told us to stay away, to have nothing to do with her or Ella! How could she have expected an invitation? And now, just when I was beginning to enjoy my life, she arrives, carrying with her both old memories and the promise of new pain.

"You're welcome any time," my gracious husband said, ignoring the look I shot him. He waited then, like me, wondering about their reasons. The Seth Thomas calendar clock ticked quietly. We heard the shouts of men at the river, moving toward success. Bandit yipped his aging bark in the distance. I noticed the large fern behind my mother had dead fronds that needed removing. More silence.

"Yes. Well," my mother said, clearing her throat though not the raspiness of her voice. "I will get to the heart of it. I'm to be married next week. To Mr. John Cates. A fine man, Mr. Cates." She said the latter defensively, I thought, though no one chose to argue. Neither Joseph nor I knew the man, nor did I think I wanted to.

"Our congratulations," Joseph said. Again we waited. I twirled her astonishing news around in my mind.

"Mr. Cates would take a honeymoon trip back east though I prefer the southern coast of France." She played nervously with the ribbons of her bonnet. "It's said to be a lovely place." Imaginary lint disappeared from her pelisse.

Only the Seth Thomas ticking filled the quiet.

"Let me get some tea," I offered, starting to stand, looking for a reason to escape. Ella glanced up at me as I rose.

"It is not a place for young ladies," my mother continued as though I hadn't mentioned tea. With her gloves, she motioned me to sit and I obeyed. "The sun at the South of France can be so beastly to the faces of young women." She blinked her eyelashes, waved an imaginary fan before her face. "Isn't that so, Ella, dear?"

The girl had not yet spoken. Her hands were calm in her lap. I noticed her nails were chewed to the quick. "It's what I've heard," Ella said in a voice as soft as a baby's breath.

"And since she has not seen you," my mother proposed, "for so long a time, I thought perhaps you might wish to spend some time with Ella. Perhaps you have need of some help here, what with the inn doing well. Maybe at the post office?"

Neither Joseph nor I said anything, dumbfounded. Ella's working for us had never entered our minds. "And, of course," my mother continued, "there would be no objections should you wish to complete adoption proceedings. It has been her father's wish for some time. Her older sister has a place with the Gilliams, in the Mitchell country. Her brothers remain with their father in Vale. Only Ella is without. That is, if you've still such a mind to. A child needs a family, after all."

Adoption? Now? It was an incredible suggestion. I took in the wonder of it and felt it explode into fury inside my chest.

"When you no longer have need of her," I said, "you send her to us. Is that it? Or is it that your Mr. Cates does not like the burden of a family? What about Baby George? Do you want us to adopt him, too?"

"Well." Mother fidgeted on her chair. "I thought you would be pleased." She picked up her gloves, strained them through her hands, put them back in her lap, strained them again. "George is going with us, of course. But Ella, well, I thought it better if she remained. And she agreed."

Joseph asked, curious. "And Mr. Cates? He is willing to have Ella left behind? To be adopted by us?"

"Don't even think of it!" I shouted at him. "I will not rescue my mother! She never saved me!" I glared at her. "And she could have!" I felt the tears of rage and hurt burn behind my eyes. Joseph reached to calm me, touch my hand. I shook him off, swallowed back my fury.

My mother looked nervously at Ella, back at me, twisted her gloves again.

"I see it," I said, calmer. "It's you who doesn't want her with you. Afraid Mr. Cates might find a young woman more appealing than her older mother. I won't protect you from that!" I felt spent, tired, and my voice reflected it. "Learn to live with the uncertainty of wondering if someone loves you. I did."

"I meant to love you," she said stiffly. "It was forgiveness I found I couldn't give."

"Forgiveness? You should be asking for mine!" My heart pounded in my ears. My mouth was dry and yet I swallowed over and over.

" 'Tis neither of yours to give," Joseph said, stepping over my despair. "But to receive if ye both be willing."

"Well. I'm not there yet, so let's salvage what we can," my mother told him.

"And what's your pleasure, Ella?" Joseph asked. He was always the gentle one, sensed the thread of my need before I could see how to sew it. He knew I lacked time to see the gift my mother had just offered us, and he didn't want me to throw happiness away just to be right.

Ella's answer came to me, not him, and I suspect she'd had enough of being in between.

"Mrs. Herbert has been good to me," she said. I scoffed. Ella glanced quickly at me. She took a deep breath and spoke as though rehearsed. "I'm a good worker. I can clean, cook, ride, milk, read, write, tend the books or the saloon. My temperament is even. I listen and get along with all nature of humanity. I am not demanding. I learn quickly or can be off without a fuss." She sighed.

"I repeat the question," Joseph said. "What's your pleasure?"

Ella looked at him now, a kind of light filling her face as she prepared to risk her wants. "It would please me to come here, to be with you. I know my mother would have wished it." Looking back at me she said, "If you'll both have me."

Joseph had Ella's Saratoga trunk unloaded from the wagon they'd arrived in. My mother left in it without a backward glance or wave.

Ella attended her wedding. I have not spoken to my mother these twenty-one years hence.

Perhaps because I'd been prepared for nothing, I found Ella doubly delightful: she was an unpredictable surprise and the offspring of Francis. So Joseph and I both knew we'd been guided by an angel.

She was light and frothy, full of fun yet on her way to leaving I was sure, as soon as some young man could turn her head. St. Mary's had given her a good education and a better sense of herself than most young women her age.

She volunteered to teach the English classes when she realized Alice M. could neither read nor write. Soon, several of Sunmiet's cousins sent their children and George sent his children too. We were wary of the latter's formal education since there was talk of making it illegal to teach Indians how to read and write. Later, that turned true, but Ella had already made a difference by that time.

Alice M. attached herself to Ella like a pea to honey, the less experienced girl copying the spirited, sweeter one in subtle ways. A tinge of jealousy fluttered in my chest when Alice asked Ella for advice instead of me, but they were sisters, after all. Alice changed the way she combed her hair, took to wearing the red-wine ribbon Ella gave her on the latter's second day here. Alice opened up more, too, in the presence of a sister. She shared with us the way to make sagebrush-twine nets to capture rabbits wrecking havoc on the garden. With the inside of sagebrush, she wove soft leggings she gave to Joseph, to put around his ankles when he walked beside the roads through tall grasses, to protect his pants. She showed us how to capture crickets, grasshoppers, and ants and roast them to crisp. Surprisingly, they proved tasty little bites we served at meals and never once divulged their source, the three of us grinning whenever those tasty "nuts" were mentioned.

Alice never told how she had learned these things—not even to Peter whom she seemed to trust beyond all others, walked often to his and Sumxseet's house, moved now to the same side of the river as our inn. With Ella near, Alice smiled more, and once or twice even looked me in the eye, if only for a moment.

Ella had not done justice to her own list of personal assets identified that fateful day in May. Not only did she do all the things she listed; she did them well. Her ability to cook came at a perfect time, what with Sung-li having made his way rather dramatically to The Dalles and us still needing to feed a bridge crew. Ella pitched in immediately and the men seemed only to notice the addition of a sweet-smelling young woman, not the change in menu. In the weeks before we acquired Tai, our long-term Chinese cook, Ella was a God-sent gift in more ways than one.

Both "A" supports were set for the bridge that day in May, stretching forty feet across the gorge where the river ran more than one hundred feet deep. On following days, cross beams fell into place between the two frames and over the old bridge where possible. Then the planking began, the pounding breaking the morning silence and continuing until the wind came up the canyon as dusk fell.

Within a matter of weeks, the bridge was complete with a solid base and fir side-rails.

James, whose friends had dropped him over the side, told Joseph there were caves back under the rocks and writings on the walls beneath the bridge, carv-ings of a man, animals, figures. "Indian books," he said through Peter, his interpreter, and asked to carve them on the bridge sides, a request Joseph granted warily as he watched James hang out over the water.

We did not have any grand ceremony the afternoon Joseph motioned two heavily weighted freighters across the bridge without a sway or bounce. Several men stood around and nodded their heads appreciatively. The drivers shouted their approval on the other side. "Tell your friends," Joseph yelled to them. "Roads'll look better each time you come!" The drivers waved their hats, slapped the leather on their horse's rumps and headed up the road toward Bakeoven, newly born colts tripping along beside the mares. The freight drivers chatted amiably with the few crew members who understood English as they passed them on their way up the grade.

At dusk on the day I considered the bridge finished, Joseph and I stood at its center, looking over into the swirling turbulence below. The wet muscle of turquoise and white froth twisted beneath us, cutting through the lava rocks. Sea gulls called and swooped at the white water. Men on scaffoldings leaned out over the falls beyond us, arching their long poles with nets into the powerful surf. "We've done it, Janie," Joseph said. "Won't ever have to worry or creak or close your eyes to cross again."

"You've done well," I said, knowing this bridge marked a milestone on my husband's path.

"All of us have," he said. "Been blessed with the best of hands. Yours, and Peter's, James's, Alice's, now Ella's too. Even Benito and Anna and all those who've been with us down this trail." The rush of water, screech of sea gulls and the memories of people and time pushed our voices into silence.

"I can almost see the stagecoaches rumbling down those roads, hear the sheep bleating," I told him after a time. Then thinking of all the work past, I added: "You have visions larger than your hands."

"That's why God gave me yours," he said, taking mine in his. "Gave me a tireless partner. He knew we had much to do. Still do." I felt some irritation with his reminder of what was left undone. I liked savoring completion, liked not always being on the way to somewhere else. Wisely, I did not take the moment to protest. Instead, we savored the rush of water, the pink sunset settling like goose down over the river, reflecting off the red rock walls. For me, the bridge was an ending, a finished piece. For my husband, it was just another beginning, the sign of what could be accomplished with a vision and "mit faith," and mit friends, doing.

In the months and years ahead, Joseph's crews worked the approaches to the bridge until they leveled them with pounded rocks and loads of dirt, making entry from land onto the sturdy frame bridge unnoticeable to passengers but for the change in sound. When the bridge crew finished their work across the Deschutes River, Joseph moved them to Buck Hollow Creek.

"Whatever for?" I asked him. "There's not even a road there, just a trail the Indians use."

"Will be. Someday," he said. And so that bridge, too, rose up to cross the narrow creek, made wide enough and high enough, we hoped, to manage the spring runoff before it poured into the Deschutes. That smaller bridge finished, the men returned to the grade crews, digging and dragging the narrow cutouts being widened up the ridges toward Bakeoven and Canyon City on one side, Fifteen Mile Creek and The Dalles on the other, all linking our remote little family with the world beyond.

Top soil, dug out from the ridges was often loaded into wagons and brought down, across the bridge, to the house. There, other men spread and shoveled, making room for a larger garden we tended vigorously to feed the increased traffic coming down our road.

It was where we buried Bandit.

He'd been missing and Joseph asked if I would ride with him, call, to see if we could find him. I felt a little guilt at having banished Bandit mostly to the outside the year we moved to the river. It wasn't that I didn't care for him. His feet brought in so much dirt, leaving behind him little seeds and piles of fine black sand testifying to his having lain in the river backwater pools then plopped in the dirt.

"Cleaning has become an obsession with you," Joseph accused. "It's fine to not be cluttered, but a place has to be lived in." He was putting on one of the pair of a dozen or more buckskin slippers of varying sizes I kept by the door.

"I can't very well ask all the guests to don Sunmiet's moccasins while they're here and then expose them to a dog's dirt," I said.

"You could make a pair up for him," he said, irritated, trying to find the size tens I kept for him, "since you've such a hankering for variety of size."

The little dog was broader now, not quite as quick as he had been, but his ears were alert and he recognized his name.

"I don't think such tidiness is necessary," my husband finally told me. But he agreed the house was my domain and consented, grudgingly, to my preparing a bed for Bandit in the mud room off the porch.

Joseph hadn't taken Bandit with him much in recent years. The dog moved slowly and couldn't make the leap onto the saddle anymore. He rode fine in the buggy, his tongue dripping onto the leather seat as he surveyed the land he'd so easily adopted.

But when he did not appear at his bed as usual one evening, Joseph and I rode along the river then up into the ravines behind the house, up along the road that had once been a pack trail, up toward the "Y" where we'd once lived. The choke cherries would be ready to pick soon. In the distance stood the roof of our old homestead surrounded by bigger trees, a blacksmith shop, more green besides the lilacs.

"Do you regret it?" he asked me. "Leaving?"

"Not a lilac leaf," I said.

We rode back down and this time walked beside the river, closer to the edge, calling, yelling to the Indians fishing, asking if they had seen the kelpie. No one had. As we were about to quit for the evening, Joseph saw a form he thought earlier had been a rock, lying beside a backwater pool. As swiftly as his bad leg would take him, he descended on the form and found his kelpie.

There were no marks on him. No sign of distress. No injuries. The little dog had simply succumbed to old age, lying there as though sleeping. His face wet with the tears of loss, Joseph picked up the dog and slowly walked toward the garden. So much they'd been through together! So much they had shared. "I'll remind myself he was only a dog," he told me, his lips trembling, "later."

And seeming without notice, despite the changes, gains and losses, my life filled up. Activity swirled around our inn, crews and stagecoaches darting in and out. Chatter of guests exchanging news from the East could be heard three times a day and more often when people stayed over and filled the saloon with laughter. Young men lounged about, pursuing Ella, noticing Alice. And I had seasons to look forward to, Sunmiet's return and the pleasure of old friends sharing memories at the river's edge.

The roads brought fascinating people to our table, a fact which intrigued me. I marveled that we lived so remotely and yet never felt the sense of isolation so many settlers did. We never knew what surprise the roads and bridge now held for us with stages running daily, people traveling, moving east and west.

Sometimes, those who came were not so welcome. Once, while Joseph and I visited Portland, our inn was robbed. An acrid smell seeped through the dining room the morning after when a dazed Ella and Alice and the Fairchilds, our caretakers, awoke. My watch—Joseph's first gift to me—and hard cash were missing along with valuables from Joseph's desk. Seeing that my children and our caretakers were safe, I could become outraged at the violation of it, frightened for those I cared for! Imagine, someone coming into our home, walking where we spent our days, laying cloths of chloroform on the faces of those I loved, then pawing through our things! No one had ever touched Joseph's desk but him. Why, the robber knocked people out with the very thing I used to ease the pain when we pulled someone's tooth! And risked what I most loved besides my Joseph: my Ella and wise Alice.

"Notice anyone unusual?" the sheriff asked the Fairchilds. Neither they nor Ella could recall anything out of the ordinary. The keen eyes of Alice did.

"Large man with pig ears asked about biscuits," she said. "And his eyes got big when Ella says, 'Mr. Sherar likes Mrs. Sherar's better.' Sherar name made him look familiar in his eyes, and far away. Maybe he came back for biscuits."

With a little effort, Joseph pried a better description. Coupled with that picture and the big footprints outside the window, Joseph felt sure the robber arrived from his distant past—Pinky O'Connor, once of San Francisco, last of Canyon City.

His belief was confirmed when the "Pinkish" man was discovered by French Louie at the livery before the week had passed. Seems O'Connor hid his stash in the hills until he thought it safe then came on in to trade his mount. Louie alerted the sheriff. Inside his saddlebags they found most of the valuables, all of the cash. But nothing returned with greater pleasure than my watch, Joseph's special gift to remind me that time stood still when I was with him and did not start again until I went away.

Children, too, came down that road, many brought happily by me.

Sometimes, Sunmiet's people arrived at the river without their children, because the boarding school held them hostage, in session, though the salmon season had begun. It gave me a mission.

Like an untreatable cough, controversy still rattled over the boarding school. Children of the Warm Springs people and the Wascos and eventually the Paiutes were all forced to attend, forced to give up their language and their ways. It became clear to anyone with light in their eyes that the tall brick school set on a wind-swept plain not far from the Warm Springs River was not a place for children.

For many it was only spring they lived for. That time of year, the children waited every weekend in their scratchy brown uniforms, satchels packed at their sides, hoping their families would arrive to take them to the rivers of their pleasure and to familiar open fields. They waited, hoping their families were close enough to fetch them and that they'd not be left in the cavernous building for one moment longer than necessary under the supervision of the matrons.

I could not change the laws that made the children have to go there, but I found my way to touch that place and build my own bridge over disappointment and time. When Sunmiet's people arrived that first spring with only half their families, I began what would become my custom.

At the parents' pleasure, I harnessed a team and set out for the reservation on my own. On those trips, I was thrice blessed.

First, because I found pleasure in my own company without someone always about requiring decision or care. The road I traveled from the river to the reservation was familiar and my mind wandered as I bounced over the rocky roads in the buckboard. Nights, I spent with the Indian agent and his long-suffering wife awaiting my second blessing which came on Friday morning.

It began as I pulled up to the boarding school. There I'd see the looks of cautious joy in the eyes of the children lined up in their little brown uniforms, waiting, to see if anyone they knew would come for them that weekend. Seeing me, they showed no outward emotion. They'd step up into the buckboard, older children helping younger, and stiffly sit, side by side, like wind-dried salmon in the shallow wagon box and we'd start out. I heard only the sound of the hames and the harness and wheels crunching across the rocks until we reached the top of the hill.

With the school out of earshot but still distantly in sight, I'd pull the team up. The children would metamorphose before my very eyes, turning from the brown, closed caterpillars the school had made them into to the butterflies of light and spirit they truly were. Rid of their uniforms, they'd don their buckskins, shake their shoes off, pull wing dresses made of calico from their satchels and on over their heads. To their squeals and laughter, I'd pull from the basket at my side, slabs of cooked or dried venison and thick slices of bread formed into sandwiches washed down with spring water. And they'd talk: of what they planned to do when they reached the river; asked questions about their aunties and their *kásas,* the horses, dogs, and even sheep. We carried on conversations as comfortably as if we were all eating at my table. As we resumed our journey I celebrated inside as from their mouths would come the gentle swoosh and click of Sahaptin and then Wasco and some Paiute, words not allowed all year at school, yet only words their *kásas* could understand. Such a joy to hear them, like squirrels chattering in a language of familiar that I could not understand but knew kept them connected to the things that truly mattered: family.

And then the third blessing, when I delivered my cargo to the river. Like a bouquet of wildflowers, I watched them, tears brimming in my eyes, as the children spilled from the buckboard and scattered themselves along the river's edge to the waiting arms of family; happy, home again. Once or twice a child skipping toward the water's edge or near their family's lodge, would turn and wave at me, blow a kiss. And sometimes, one would run back, with words of thanks disguised as breathless *"kása"* or "auntie." And while their little arms grabbed around my crinolines and squeezed my knees, it was my heart they held in their hands.

Just to watch them was my blessing and my wage.

Filled, I'd lead the team and wagon to the barn where Joseph waited, smiling in his knowing way, to wipe the tears from my cheeks. "You're quite the little mother," he said once.

"Yes, well, I am at that," I told him. With the scent of sweet hay surrounding us, my husband would hold me, and I recognized the fullness of my cup, so filled to overflowing, overflowing with children, overflowing with love.

CHAPTER 30

SPIRITS

"TAKE LADDERS to reach it," Joseph said, "but we wouldn't have to worry over deer or other critters any more."

His voice sounded teasing, but he drew in his sketch book. "Water'll come from the spring up there." He pointed. "Pipe it down. We won't need to always use a ladder to get there, either. When we build the hotel, the third story will be even with the ledge and we'll have a little bridge out to it, from one of the bedrooms."

"The hotel will have a third story?" I asked, incredulous.

"Among other things."

"You can't possibly build something so accurately that you could put a bridge out to a ledge, assuming you could make a ledge in such a place."

Joseph envisioned a garden chipped out of the side of the steep rocks that ran behind the inn. A natural ledge appeared to be there. I thought he brought the subject up to make us laugh at the possibility.

"Why not? We'll hack out the area we want," he said. "Plant the trees now and have a harvest by the time we build the hotel. I'm thinking we should talk with Blivens about sweet grape starts. Make an arbor there along with some peach trees and apples." The man was lost to his dreams.

The "ledge" crew as I soon called them, did begin their work. When they weren't busy tending to roads and bridges, animals and fencing or a hundred other things, they began clearing and carving a space twelve feet wide and three times the length into the cinnamon rocks about twenty feet up above the road, next to the river. As they had time and energy, Peter's crew lifted buckets of dirt and soil onto the finished flat sections, building up the natural soil there, always reminding me that my husband had one more great vision in mind and more work than hands for.

Fortunately, we did not have to feed all these crews at once. Ella, Alice, and I packed lunches in tins for the road crews who left early each morning. In the summer, most came from Sunmiet's band and wisely supplemented their meals with dried fish and eels, roots and huckleberries, and in season, choke cherries from the ravines they dug their roads into. Large breakfasts of eggs and flap-jacks became morning staples along with more house girls and cooks' helpers to tend to the tables.

I found that the more help we hired, well, the more help we hired. And they all needed to be fed.

Feed them we did. So the roads would be built. And later, so the roads and bridges would be maintained. So people would come down them to stay at our inn, pay their toll and two bits for a meal so we could pay the wages of those we hired to help. Sometimes I wondered if we were moving forward with our life or just in a dreamcatcher's circle.

Our life centered on those roads. They were the key to my husband's vision. More than thirty miles in four directions on both sides of that bridge he built on the backs of men and animals. Roads, lifelines to the heart of our community and our future.

And we could not have built the roads without the Indians.

We could not have paid the Indians without the tolls.

Some have said we charged exorbitant fees to the homesteaders and sheep men and freighters and stages that made their way down our roads to the river over the years. We charged $3.75 for each yoke of oxen or team or wagon and a dollar extra for the drivers. We never raised the tolls once we completed the bridge. Cattle crossed at 25¢ a head, sheep for a mere 10¢. These do not seem high when I look at the thousands we have paid to carve the roads out of the sides of reluctant ridges or the work necessary to maintain them and the bridge.

Joseph was very strict about the tolls and required they be put through the slot of a shiny metal bucket kept just for that. In later years, when he had built the calf barn and livery and flour mill and a dozen other structures, and his leg finally slowed him down to using a cane, he would sit at the edge of the bridge in the shade of trees we planted near the hotel. A long-barreled rifle stretched across his knees encouraged ready payment though I never knew him to ever use the gun.

My husband strung a heavy iron chain he had the blacksmith make across both sides of the bridge and no one crossed without dropping their coins into the bucket. He did occasionally negotiate, took pity on some poor family barely making it across the plains let alone across the river. More than once he sent John Suhr to bring flour and beans and coffee from the storehouse for a family barely able to pay their toll. Once he chased a man nearly to The Dalles who cheated him of 10¢, then gave it back plus more when he heard the sad story of his plains crossing. People walking did not pay at all.

He had one other exception in the toll schedule: for the Indians who summered here. Whether they worked for the top wage of 25¢ an hour or not, they never paid to cross. The Chinese he had a different standard for: on foot or not, they paid a dime. I argued with him about that, it seemed unfair. But he insisted, perhaps remembering the sound of a cleaver slicing past his ear.

On paydays, Joseph took me and the huge leather accounts book with him to meet with Peter and pay the men.

My husband still could not pronounce some of their Indian names and so in the books, he gave them names more familiar to him. "This is Patrick," he told me on payday. I knew the slender man looking down at his feet as K'aalas, "Raccoon." "This one's O'Leary," he'd say to the smiling man with an unsavory scar down his cheek, and I would issue coins and a notation in my book beside "O'Leary" though I knew his friends called him Ach'ái, "Magpie," that he was the son of Running Deer and the cousin of Koosh.

The Warm Springs people were tolerant of my husband's poor pronunciation and did not begrudge him his use of his own familiar words because he treated them fairly and as equals. Some even took the names he gave them as their last and use them still.

In fact, they begrudged us little though as I see it now more clearly, we were changing their ways minute by minute, day by day. Our roads brought more and more people into their place of belonging. Along with the government acts for homesteaders and such, gave them more and more reasons to stay.

I sometimes wondered if my husband was the man in Sumxseet's peoples' prophesy, the one Peter shared with Joseph on their first meeting. Perhaps the engineers and builders—not the missionaries as are so often blamed—truly did carry the teaching book that made their world fall to pieces.

Perhaps that's what Standing Tall thought too. It might explain his growing animosity toward us. Oh, he let Sunmiet and me share time together. And he accepted our help of blankets and blood purifier during the typho-malaria epidemic that swept the region killing both Indians and non. Reluctantly, at my urging, he and Sunmiet agreed not to treat the disease with the sweats as was the family custom. His consent surprised me, made me wonder about the depth of his love for his family, his ability to try the white man's way, at least for them. Everyone in Sunmiet's band who did not sweat during the disease lived. Most others did not.

Still, it concerned me that our involvement in their survival seemed ultimately to anger Standing Tall even more.

I considered talking with him about it, but time was an eel that sixth year Ella was with us, and just slipped away.

Spike Crickett wore a fragile temperament he called his "spirit." He landed on our doorstep out of one of Wheeler's Concord "Thoroughrace" stages driven by none other than "Pretty Dick" Barter, as we'd taken to calling him. Several of the passengers that day in 1879 preferred to call them both something entirely unflattering. But then, their whole trip would have taken a heap of flattery to make up for the misery.

It rained that April day and that meant the roads ran like rivers in places, were as slick as eels in a bucket of bear grease in others.

Spike arrived the last few feet on foot despite the weather, well after the others. He carried with him a cage with a gray, long-haired cat named Spirit who whined its distress despite its dry state.

"Hope Barter marries one of those Huots girls soon," snarled one of the regular passengers on the run between The Dalles and Canyon City as he stepped into the dry inn. "Or else stops trying to get down the ridge on time. He waits and waits until the last minute, mooning around her, and then tears down that grade no matter what the weather. Don't dare argue with him. Like a king, he is." As were all stage drivers. The passenger looked weary and worn and he ordered an ale to cheer himself while he took off his boots.

Crickett's arrival did nothing to bolster the other passengers' temperaments. With Spirit howling in the cage, Crickett brushed off the rain as though it hadn't happened and swished his boots in a puddle to clear the mud. Inside, he set the cage on the floor in the saloon and donned the moccasins without complaint, letting his cat do that.

Crickett introduced himself as "Dr. Crickett" which we decided accounted for some of his oddities. His suit pulled against his large frame as though he'd forgotten to buy larger clothes when he grew up; his rust-colored hair had been cut with home shears as a man too busy to barber in town. The cut left an uneven length. He was smooth shaven and loud talking. Still, his nails were pink and clean despite the muddy trip and he knew much about hospitals and medicines and people in distress even if he did only look to be in his mid-twenties. He didn't complain about the rain, simply asked for his trunk so he could change. And when Dick lifted his luggage from beneath the boot in the back of the stage, the valise bore his initial and name preceded by "Dr." pressed into the leather, so we guessed he was.

"Just an eccentric," Ella whispered to me in the kitchen after the noon meal. "Didn't make any friends on the stage, I hear. Guess they were glad the cat got off with him when he found the road too rough to ride on."

"Appetite vely big," Tai, our Chinese cook, noted. "Vely big." He scraped the plates and dipped them in soapy water followed by the required steaming.

"He's bigger than most," I said.

"He has kind eyes," Alice M. volunteered, and both Ella and I raised our eyebrows at each other over her head. "And the cat's mouth was dry. Calmed down with water. He's gentle with it," she added, speaking of Crickett. Alice rarely volunteered information about the travelers, and I hadn't noticed that she had noticed him. It appeared to be a sign that she was growing up, maturing into what must be sixteen years.

"I do wonder if they'll stay a bit," Ella mused, "what with the roads so bad. At least until the rain stops."

I had mixed feelings about them staying. It meant more people would be arriving behind them and we could have twice the number for the supper meal. Waiting would make Joseph's job much easier in the long run, however. Despite his efforts to preserve the roads, rain proved his biggest enemy. It washed out the dirt around the rocks and roots, relentlessly pounded at the packed earth until it wore a tiny hole. Then it washed and washed until the hole became a pit deep enough to sink a wheel, stop a stage. And if that weren't enough to cause repair, any wagon risking the slick, wet road also risked becoming mired in muck or slipping and sliding, loosing its cargo or itself over the steep-pitched sides. Either way, the rain and wagons left the road with deep ruts when it dried out. The crews spent long hours following any storm dragging juniper logs to repair the roads and smooth the ruts.

"Maintenance" Joseph called it. "Never-ending" was my term.

"Looks like Dick's going to risk it," Joseph told me after the meal. We sat at the family table, in the kitchen.

"Was there ever any wonder," I said, checking the larder to determine supplies.

"Says he made up for lost time on the ridge coming down. Had new shoe leather for brakes. Wants to see if he can still get to Bakeoven on time." Joseph pulled his big frame up from the chair, pulled thoughtfully on his long beard. He considered the Cold Shore Cut Plug Tobacco tin; thought better of it. "Best I get the teams ready. Think we'll be pulling him before the afternoon's over. You'll have quite a time making the dance tonight, Ella," he teased as he slipped his boots back on. "Bet your Clayton will be clogged in."

She smiled at him, bantering as she cleared the tables. "He prefers 'Monroe,'" she corrected, "and he knows his way around mud. I suspect he'll get here. Last chance for us to see each other for a while, till round-up's over."

"If he arrives in this muck and weather, you'll probably see him during round-up too," Joseph laughed. "Ah, true love. Carries a bridge over the impossible, right, Mother Sherar?" He winked at me.

"That it does," I said, liking being referred to as "Mother."

April often arrived with the rain. And this year was no exception. The stages rolled, the men rode and repaired. We cooked and served and tended the garden and handled the post office. Together, we plucked chickens, prepared for spring round-up, sheared sheep, planted the garden, and added a peach cutting to the cliff orchard, just as we did every April. The rain made it all take longer, worked us a little harder. The Community Hall at Nansene, where the dances were planned, not far from Fifteen Mile Crossing, promised a respite the young people all made extra effort for, including riding through mud.

Ella especially would. She planned to marry Clayton Monroe Grimes in July and saw this dance as the cool drink of water she needed at least monthly to survive. I had never seen her so happy, her eyes so full of sparkle. Since she'd met Monroe, as he preferred to be called, at the fall round-up, she'd been giddy and taken to day-dreaming. We had no need to wonder of what. At twenty-two, she deserved some day-dreaming time.

We'd hired on extra stockmen that year to handle branding and the several hundred head our herd had grown to. Monroe also did well with sheep and he'd stayed on at the bunkhouse for several weeks, working, and giving the spark of their relationship time to kindle to the flame it became. He'd left in February, marriage proposal secured, to work in the Grass Valley country.

In March, following a month of separation and despite my better judgment, Ella and I rode across the Buck Hollow bridge toward Grass Valley to find him. Wind whipped us along the same route Joseph had taken his first time to the falls, nearly twenty years before. We rode up the ravine and along the ridge past what's now the Buckley place, to intersect with the Dalles Military Road. It wasn't much of a road, compared to Joseph's.

Monroe was said to be working on a ranch near a section of land that bore grass hay on nearly a hundred acres in the middle of dry hills. While I didn't think it proper for a young woman to seek out a young man—even one she was betrothed to—Ella had mooned so, become so sad at not seeing Monroe, I'd decided to throw caution to the wind. We packed a picnic lunch and I made the day's ride with her.

Later, I was always glad I'd done that, taken the risk. First, because it was a quiet time with Ella, one of the last I'd have as she moved on to marriage. She was readier than I had been for that big step though I doubt she could have loved Monroe more than what I'd felt for Joseph. But her caring for him as she did reflected a woman going "to" something rather than "away" from something else. Settled in herself, she carried no animosities, no regrets. She had come to us, given us her sweetness and care and been pleased with whatever we gave in return. Initially, that had not been much, at least from me. I was startled by how selfish was my thinking, how I didn't like to share my personal things, didn't like the attention Joseph, as a doting father, paid to her.

My reservations didn't seem to matter to Ella. Daily, she found something positive to say. She thanked me often for agreeing to adopt her, accept her at Sherar's Bridge. Perhaps that's what I'd miss the most when she and Monroe married—her goodness, gentleness, and the changes in my own reflection I discovered because she was simply in my life.

I had thought that with a child—any child—I would do the molding, that that's what grown-ups did. I had not expected to be changed myself.

Ella had done that, made me softer I think. We laughed together, shared the work, planned surprises for "our" Joseph. She took off some of my hard edges. I even considered contacting my mother, letting her know that despite her ugly reason for giving Ella up, something wonderful had bloomed.

That would have gone too far.

The second reason I was pleased Ella and I shared the trip seeking Monroe is because it's how I found the Finnigan place. My "green river" I called it, even before we ever bought it.

The ground was almost spongy as we rode down a gentle slope and crossed the green that flowed out of the rolling hills just like a wide, meandering river. It was wet, from the springs that must have fed it making the grass come on early and last until first frost. Two old brothers named Finnigan lived in a log house at the edge of the green where we watered our horses. "Put a hundred head a cows on and they can't keep it down," they told us proudly, as though they'd put the water beneath the ground themselves, turned it into never-ending grass.

In the distance, along the green edges, some Indian women and children dug roots—a little early it seemed to me. Their forms looked like Kása's and Bubbles's and her family now grown to five children. Eight spotted ponies grazed at the green. I planned to ask about Sunmiet when we returned, but they had already gone. I couldn't have known then I'd be seeing Sunmiet myself within a month, in circumstances I'd have preferred to avoid.

At the ranch beyond, we found young Grimes. Ella thought after drinking in his face and form, that she could last the spring—if she could see him once a month until they wed in July.

Tonight would be one of those nights if the rain didn't keep him from riding down the hollow, stopping at the falls, picking up Ella on his way. They would drive to Nansene, dance and have a midnight meal, and dance some more. Along with dozens of other couples as was the custom, they'd spend the night and return weary from all that dancing by mid-morning. At the very least, Monroe would spend the night here, at the inn, if the weather worsened. Either way, Ella looked forward to her reunion.

Perhaps it was because of Ella's preoccupation with Monroe that we all failed to see Alice's growing up, her early grieving over her soon-to-be-loss of Ella. Perhaps it was because Ella was so happy in her wedding preparations that Alice took special interest in what marriage was about. Or perhaps it was Dr. Crickett himself who carried the spark that kindled the flame of interest of a sixteen-year-old young woman. Whatever the reason, Alice had noticed Dr. Crickett.

He also noticed her. For though he and the cat left in the rain on the stage, before the afternoon passed, he was back. Cat, cage, and valise in hand, slipping in the rain down the slope Dick's stage had just gone up. As a man on foot, he did not pay any toll as he walked across the bridge. The sun came out briefly as if to put a blessing on their connections. Meadowlarks hopped from rock to rock fluttering their wings of the rain. Water pooled on the bridge lumber, already starting to dry in the sun. Everything smelled as fresh as ripe watermelon. Except for Dr. Crickett, whose wet wool suit in the sunshine released vapors strong enough to make a lady faint.

He walked through the gate of the stone fence we'd built around the inn, stopped at the porch. Alice, Ella, and I all came out, surprised by his presence.

"I decided, don't you know, that since I am on vacation, I can vacation where I am." His voice was higher than his height and girth predicted, giving meaning to the term "high strung." "So often one loses sight of what's important by spending too much time focusing on being somewhere else. One forgets to enjoy getting there, don't you know." His hat didn't fit. It perched on the top of his cantaloupe-shaped head. A cat's breath would topple it. He set the cat cage on the porch next to his valise and caught his hat as it slipped from his rain-slicked hair. "I didn't properly introduce myself earlier. So much was happening, yes, yes it was. I am Dr. Crickett of the Thomas Cricketts of Salem. My name is not Thomas, of course. That's a family name. My mother named me Harrison but that's so stuffy, don't you think? So I go by Spike. You've heard of me?" he asked us, his hazel eyes looking at each face, pausing on Alice's. Seeing our blank expressions overlaid with wonder, he answered his own question. "No, no. Of course not. My work is quite isolated. Being with the unfortunates of that fine city."

I thought he referred to the state's legislators who convened in the capital city, but he continued on, barely taking a breath, and put me straight.

"They come from so many places, with so many pains and miseries. We do our best to put them straight, give them back their strength and courage, send them home, relieved of the demons that possess them, help them instead to behave in marvelous ways, return them to their familiar spirits." He lowered his voice. "We all have spirits, don't you know." Then at full voice added, "We wear troublesome and strange spirits, too, of course. We take them all in. Some get no better." He clucked his tongue in shame, then brightened. "Most do, making one wonder what insanity truly is, where our spirits really emerge from, yes, indeed."

His speech was rapid. His movements jerky. He hadn't given us a moment to respond and I suspected the cat was not the only reason his fellow passengers had encouraged him to walk.

"In my valise is a lovely take-down bamboo rod and your river here, this lovely turquoise water racing through ancient lava rocks—I'm sure it's lava—beneath the Clarno formations—I'm sure it's Clarno—must have some smooth, backwater pools, some places where a red-sided trout could hide and rest in shade and might take up my little flies I've packed along. And so I have returned, sure that I can afford a day or two in your fine establishment. And in your fine company, if you'll allow it." He focused on Alice again, clicked his heels together and bent stiffly at the waist sweeping his hat and arm in a wide arc before his bow.

Alice giggled, charmed. Ella rolled her eyes and I shook my head. A bit dramatic I thought, but said, "You're welcome to stay. Alice, please show Dr. Crickett to the far bedroom, where his cat will have some quiet. While she stays in her cage."

Alice started off with Dr. Crickett following her. She hesitated then said, "I'll show him the backwater holes. I know all the best ones."

Before I could even respond, Dr. Crickett was off and running again. "Delightful!" he crooned. "A natural gift it is to lure a species of the ichthyosis family to the fine line I have prepared to place on my bamboo. It would please me no end to be guided by such a lovely lass." To me he added as though reading my mind, "You've not a worry in your head. I'll take special care of her. Nothing will befall her. We'll be back by dusk I'm sure."

I wasn't sure how he could possibly know how far away Alice might take him, but he was engaging, seemed harmless enough, and I saw no reason not to let Alice enjoy his company, however brief.

Monroe arrived in the late afternoon, coming down the same trail we'd used the month before to visit him. He met the last stage of the day at the bridge, crossed, and with open arms kissed his betrothed who met him before he even stepped afoot his horse. Monroe had an old, serious face that defied his youth and gentleness. He was of medium height, slender. He buried his bearded face briefly against Ella's neck. "Camp on the west side," he said as he walked arm draped around his betrothed's waist into the inn. "Indians must be arriving. They're farther up, toward the White River. Could see them from the ridge."

"Must be Standing Tall and Sunmiet," I said pleased. "They like to camp on this side now that the bridge brings so many. Avoid the traffic downriver and still face the morning east. I'd have thought they would have waited for the Root Feast. I'll be pleased to see her."

When they returned at dusk, Alice and Dr. Crickett confirmed that the

Indian camp up river belonged to Sunmiet and her family. "Her belly is big again," Alice said quietly to me. I nodded. This would be her sixth. "Her eyes, sad."

"Just tired," I reasoned. "Five children and another on the way will do that to you, they say." I said it without a tinge of sadness for myself as I might have in years before. Now, I felt only for my friend.

I introduced Dr. Crickett to Monroe and the good doctor began at once to bubble on about the quality of fishing, the size of the red-sided trout, the risk of the scaffoldings and the wonder of dipping nets into the froth for the big salmon. Monroe bobbed his head trying to keep up with the steady running of Crickett's words and finally managed to mention the dance to Ella.

"A dance! How delightful! It's been years, don't you know, since my residency, that I have spun a lovely lass around the room. Alice," he said as though the thought had just occurred to him—"would you join me?"

Alice blushed. Ella might have wished to have her time alone with Monroe at the dance, but her heart was large, like her natural mother's, and when she saw Alice's delight at being asked, she suggested more. "Mama will pack a lunch for us," she said. "Come with me and we'll fix up together for the occasion."

Alice arrived back in the dining room, lovely. Ella had given her one of her own dresses that flounced blue out over the bustle. A contrasting pale blue bodice rose up tightly to Alice's slender throat. Her hair was swept back, high on her head, exposing her tiny ears. A cascade of curls—one of Ella's own supplements she'd dyed in henna for the occasion—draped from the back. "I planned to have her wear it at my wedding," Ella said. "This seems the perfect occasion to try it out."

She was pretty as a painting.

Off they went, kerosene lamps bouncing from the side posts should they need them. Ella and Monroe in one buggy; Dr. Crickett and Alice—and the cat—in another. Crickett had prattled on about renting the buggy from us for the evening but Joseph had insisted he simply take it, his Alice deserving to arrive in elegance, and we'd settle up whatever the following morning.

So we were alone in the dining room, my husband and I, for the first time in years. Tai brought in two bowls of clabbered milk with corn bread, handed them to Joseph before bowing, backing out. "Maybe I should revive my whittling interest," I said, thinking of the way I once spent my evenings as a child the summer after my sisters and my brother died. The box with special knives was somewhere in the storeroom. It needed cleaning out anyway. Something to put on my list.

"Just sit with me," Joseph said, patting the seat beside him on the horsehair sofa. He handed the bowl up to me. "Eat your sweet milk. Rest a little. You push so hard, always moving. Sunmiet's right, you know. You do rush about like a sandpiper racing the waves to the sea. Slow down a little. Put some meat on your bones."

I settled beside him, ate. Finished, I rested my head on his shoulder, sighed. He smelled of leather and lumber, good smells, of a man doing what he likes. "They'll both be gone before long," I said. "It'll just be you and me, alone all the time." I started to stand, to put the bowls on the sideboard.

He pulled me back. "Alone with a dozen guests, twice the hands." He laughed. Then serious he asked. "Would that be so bad? Time was, before it got stuck under my shirt collar, when just you and me was enough. Sixteen years. Who would have thought it?"

"Sixteen years…week from Tuesday," I said, surprised that it had crept up. "Almost forgot it."

He was thoughtful for a bit, quiet. "What do you say we head out to Nansene, too?"

"This late? What about tomorrow, all the work to do?"

"Tai can handle the morning. We'll be back before midday."

"Think you can dance all night? You're an old man." I punched him gently in his side. No give, solid.

"The one thing I could give ye I haven't yet," he said, thoughtful. "A place big enough to dance in. So I'll borrow Nansene's for a time. Come on. What do you say?"

Why not? I thought. Wouldn't it surprise our girls to have us appear? And we could keep an eye on Crickett at the same time.

"If you bet I wouldn't, you lose," I said. "Just need a minute to freshen up."

He kissed the top of my head, adding as he stood and pulled me to him, "This is one bet I don't mind losing. Let's go. You're fresh enough."

CHAPTER 31

BEGINNINGS AND ENDS

WE BOTH HEARD the commotion at the same time. It came from in front of the inn. A horse, run hard. A woman, crying, screaming almost. Both of us turned with a start, headed out to the rock wall. Joseph grabbed a lantern at the door, night having fallen. He shouted, "Who's there?" and started moving toward the woman before he even heard her answer.

"Sunmiet!" the woman said, sobbing. I saw her slide from the horse, holding her stomach, leaning, steadying herself with the mane of her mount, one arm hanging limp.

"What is it!" I said, reaching her, my heart pounding.

Joseph passed me up. He handed me the lantern and lifted her. Blood oozed down her arm. In the arc of the light, I could see white bone beneath red muscle and I was instantly furious.

"Who did this?" I demanded as I followed them inside. She sobbed again.

"The children...Aswan."

"It was Standing Tall, wasn't it?"

Sunmiet cried, didn't answer.

"Get Tai," I told Joseph. "I'm going after him."

My husband, to his credit, did not attempt to stop me. Tai would tenderly care for Sunmiet. Joseph planned to ride with me, but he had to order up his horse, get John to saddle the big gelding, while I could simply throw myself on Sunmiet's cayuse. I did just that, grabbed my pistol on the way out.

The night air burst cool on my hot face. Rain sleeted in patches. I didn't care. Their camp was on our side of the river and I could ride right to it. My outrage masked my fear. He had finally done it, finally injured Sunmiet so severely she could no longer bend.

The horse responded, moved faster with my knees pressed to his neck. I rode low over him, to speed him, and he made the mile in record time, stopped in a slush of mud in front of Sunmiet's tule lodge. I spun off the horse, cocked my pistol, and opened the flap, willing my eyes to adjust to the pale light I expected before Standing Tall could react.

Both his eyes were droopy, not just the one he was born with. From the dirt floor, both looked up at me, a mixture of anger and confusion. His hand held the dark bottle loosely. Aswan, tall like his father, and Anne, nearly thirteen, sat with arms around Ikauxau and Ikawa and Baby Ida, all huddled in the corner, eyes large. Blood stains darkened a wide swath beside the center fire.

"My mother, she is safe?" Aswan asked. "I stood between them, sent her to you."

"You did well, Aswan."

To Standing Tall I said: "It's over," and remembering my father's instruction long ago, pointed the pistol at his head. He grunted, made an effort to rise. I stepped back, ordered him to stay. I wished, almost hoped, he would lunge for me though my heart pounded against my ribs. I felt sick. Until that moment, I did not know if I could kill another human being. That night I knew I could.

Standing Tall gave me no reason. He settled back, deflated as an empty elk bladder. His hand dropped in resignation.

"Aswan!" I said, my voice in charge. "Take the bottle from your father." The boy stood, did as he was told and I noticed that his once long, shiny hair had the boarding school cut. Standing Tall did not resist. "Go, now," I said. "Take the little ones, to your mother."

"Is she all right?" Anne asked, gathering blankets to drape around them.

I nodded yes. "I'll stay," Aswan said.

"The river's too close. They need you. I'll be fine."

"You white woman, intruder," Standing Tall snarled. He spit other insults at me, but his words were not accompanied by actions. As the children scurried out the flap, he said he did not like my treading on his place as "provider."

"You provide misery for your family," I said, adding nothing more. I learned early on there is no value in arguing with someone who is not present with his mind.

In moments, I heard Joseph's big gelding approach and felt a wave of relief. Together we tied Standing Tall's hands behind his back and walked him in front of the horses past the inn, over the toll bridge where we stopped, pounded on the blacksmith's door.

Teddy, our farrier, roused from his cot, looked startled as he let us in. "What's it to be?" he asked in his thick Boston accent.

Joseph tied Standing Tall, arms forward, around the center post telling Teddy what happened. "I stay awake, watch him," Teddy said though his eyes shifted back and forth and I suspected he gave great power to Standing Tall's height and demeanor.

"Just till we get the sheriff or the tribal elders, whichever might get here faster," I told him. "We'll send someone in the morning."

In the inn, we sent the children off to bed, though Aswan resisted. We relieved Tai of his duties and considered, again, Sunmiet's arm. Tai had cleaned it, held the wound shut so the bleeding stopped. It needed stitches. "I'll do it," Joseph said, and Sunmiet nodded, biting into a linen towel I gave her. She squeezed tight my hand. Her children poked their heads around the corner, eyes large with apprehension. Sunmiet spit the towel from her mouth, gentled her words, reassured them in Sahaptin and Anne herded them, waddling, back to bed.

It did not seem fair to me that she and her children should be the ones to suffer. She who believed in him, stood beside him, bore his children, and then bore the brunt of his frustrations and his pain. "It's always you who hurt," I said. "And it should be him."

"He hurts," Sunmiet said with sadness. "It is why I could not leave him for so long." Her eyes watered, filled with tears, "But now I am afraid to stay."

"You can only bend so much," Joseph said, gentle. I thought of his coping saw, how too much flexibility meant widening a gap.

"A tree does not like to be uprooted," she told him.

"It can be transplanted and be stronger than ever," he said, "but that's for you to decide."

"We'll deal with all that in the morning," I said. "Sew you up now, so you can rest. Joseph will get the sheriff, find out who sells the whiskey."

"I wish it was only the whiskey," Sunmiet said.

She turned down our offer for laudanum yet did not cry out or whimper as Joseph stitched, tied the final knot. Together, we helped her from the chair. "Get some rest," I directed. "We have all had enough for one night." I looked out the window to stars faded by a full moon, thought of the safety of dropping to sleep next to Joseph in our bed; thought of what Sunmiet was missing.

We started down the hall intending to tuck Sunmiet in. Instead, she abruptly stopped. She inhaled her breath in pain and her eyes got wide. "What is it?" I asked, alarmed.

She answered in a tone laced both with fear and wonder. "My water breaks," she said. "We will have a baby."

Joseph's invitation to a dance seemed years not just hours away.

"Is it too soon?" I asked Sunmiet.

She shook her head, her eyelashes fluttering. "No. A little early. Baby is big, so it can come." She sighed. "I did not wish it to happen now, without the father."

"He's drunk," I said, angry once again for her. She didn't deny it or defend him and I set aside my outrage to tend to her.

In one of my trunks, I found a pale nightdress, cooler than Sunmiet's buckskin, not covered with the blood of her wounds. Joseph saw himself in the way and said he'd be in the bedroom if we needed him. He did not sleep. Instead, he said he listened for the creak of the floor where Sunmiet and I walked.

In the ladies' dining room, back and forth, we women walked. Close to the cool spring water available to the kitchen, we walked. Around the dining room table and its benches and chairs, we walked, stopping at each of her contractions, panting, holding. I felt helpless against her grimacing pain, could do nothing but be with her.

Tai stuck his half-shaved head around the corner, wide young-man eyes wondering at the noise. "Go back to bed. This is no place for a boy," I said. He didn't need to be told twice. His braid flipped around his neck as he left.

Sunmiet hung on to me when she stopped, squeezed my hand and squatted, panted, eased her way into the wave graduating to pain, then up and over it, down the other side until the next one, dipping and bending into it like the eagle into wind.

She sipped water in between. I thought of what might make her comfortable: wet a flannel and held it to the back of her neck, dabbed her face of perspiration. I checked the bandage we'd put on her arm. Found a hard candy for her to suck on. She wished a bed on the floor and so with quilts and linen sheets we made a resting place beside the horsehair couch.

"If Kása were here, she would sing to me," she teased, a sparkle in her eye.

"My voice would scare the baby back to Christmas," I said, combing her damp hair from her temples with my fingertips. "Would you like me to send Aswan or Joseph for Kása?"

She shook her head no. "I do not wish to explain my night to her before it is over."

It surprised me that Sunmiet would be calm enough between contractions to just talk. It was not how I imagined my mother bringing children into the world.

Sometimes Sunmiet seemed to doze. Watching her, I thought she could have been my taller, fuller sister, wearing my nightdress, her dark braids pulled over her shoulder. I had never seen her in anything but buckskins; seeing her in my clothes made me warm inside.

Once we heard little whispers and scuffling and turned to see five pairs of eyes at the door. Sunmiet shooed the children back to bed after words of reassurance. "I am well. Your *nana* or *yáiya* comes soon. Go now. Rest. Huckleberry Eyes and I have work to do. You can see the baby in the morning."

Sometimes Sunmiet just sat, ankles crossed, rocking gently. She spoke softly about the baby, pointed when the baby's feet pushed into the wall of her stomach as it turned. She put my hand there to feel the flutter of feet. "It is floating," she said of her baby, preparing its entrance into this outside world. It developed hiccups and we laughed.

Once or twice, following a particularly difficult pain, she reached beneath her gown, withdrew her bloodied hands and said, "Not yet." With great effort, like the wind rising from the depths of a deep ravine reaching for the timbered top, she stood, and we walked and talked once more.

She told me of the argument. Aswan's arrival back from school, his hair having been cut, started it. There had been no choice about his going. All the children were required. Along with being forced to make his way with farming, being pushed back from the Big River, having to use Sunmiet's family's fishing sites here at Sherar's, Standing Tall had been pushed too far, his strong and caring spirit spent. The mean and hopeless part that lives in all of us finally taking over in him. A knife and whiskey both close at hand, he'd struck at Aswan and Anne, then at Sunmiet when she'd intervened. Blade met flesh and pulled to bone.

"Worst," Sunmiet said, "was leaving the children. Aswan said to go, come here, he would keep his father calmer if I left. Could make better time without the babies, but I am glad you brought them here."

Another contraction. This time I could see the pain wash over her face, last a long time. It struck me that even with my mother's last two, Loyal and George, I had been more like the little eyes in the doorway, not there in a privileged placed beside my mother.

And it was a privilege, to be present when new life came. In all my years, I had never asked to be part of someone's birth. Others may have thought it too painful to request me to midwife for them, having had no infants of my own. A reasonable thought. One I'd had myself! No more, not after this!

I knew this was the closest I would come to bringing life into the world. And for the first time, I truly understood what my mother must have felt when she lost the gifts of her womb, understood why she looked for someone to blame. I understood and could finally forgive.

Again Sunmiet squatted, reached beneath her skirt, shook her head. "It is good you stand with me," she said, sweat beading on her forehead. In the lamplight our bodies made bulky shadows on the wainscoting. The Seth Thomas clock struck three. "Not good to have baby reach this world in the company of only its mother. Needs to know at once it has a family."

"Here I am thinking I'm the one getting the gift," I said, "just to be present when you have this baby. Didn't think I was giving a thing."

Sunmiet's smile turned into a grimace of pain and she gritted her teeth, grabbed at my hand, leaned against the table, and cried out. Squatting, she reached again beneath herself, the flounce of the gown draped across her arm. A slurpy sound, then a wad of mucous struck the floor. More liquid. A pungent scent. She squatted lower, her knuckles white in my hand, panting, panting, reaching for the table edge to grip now with the other.

"Do you want to lie down?" I asked, knowing it was close, feeling helpless, wanting to do something, anything, to make it easier.

She shook her head. "Here," she said, and released a long, low moan that rose and fell into a pant. "Be ready," she directed. "To catch it."

Catch it! Good heavens! My heart pounded. I felt my own sweat beneath my arms. This was such a moment! "I'm ready," I said, breathless, and was about to ask her if she was when someone pounded loudly on the front door.

Sunmiet's eyes grew large. "Don't worry," Joseph said rushing past in his undershirt and jeans. He barely glanced in our direction. I heard the blacksmith's voice, heard Joseph shout, heard him stomp his feet into his boots, angrily yell he'd be back and slam the door.

I had to concentrate, not wonder, reassure her with my eyes. Sunmiet moaned again, reached, started panting. My heart beat faster, my fingers ached against her strong grip. Her breath came in short gasps between her gritted teeth. She panted, the pain rising, rising and reaching into pain and then a push and strain before she wailed, "Take it!" I shook loose my hand. She took one deep breath, laid back. "Next push will be the baby!"

And so it was.

With tears I didn't know were hiding there behind my eyes, I reached to catch Sunmiet's child. Into my hands slipped a fine, wet, dark-haired girl with plump and perfect skin of bronze beneath a sheath of water. Somehow my trembling fingers hung on to the warm and fussing form.

"What is it?" Sunmiet asked, her voice weak but excited. "Is it all right?"

"A girl," I said, laughing and crying at the same time. "And she's perfect." I raised and lowered her lightly. "Weight like a silver salmon. Itsa-right," I crooned to baby and mother, "Itsa-right, now." A prayer of thanks rose from my heart; another asked for blessings on this child's life.

Sunmiet sighed, eased back onto the floor-bed. I dabbed gently over the baby's eyes with a piece of soft cotton, laughing, smiling at her and squeezed the mucous from her nose and ran my finger gently inside her mouth. I heard her take in breath. She did not really cry, just sucked at life as I handed her to Sunmiet. "So warm," Sunmiet said, stroking her, eyeing her in wonder as though she'd never seen an infant before.

"Cut the cord," she said. I looked surprised, but of course, someone had to do it. "It is the father's right he gave up as he is not here so it is your privilege." I remembered that my father had been absent at Baby Pauline's arrival. Lodenma must have cut the cord.

My fingers shook. I found my sewing scissors and some flax thread. I tied two places on the cord and clamped them tightly, then cut between them. Blood spurted. It was done. "I will save the cord, and the twist at her belly when it drops off," Sunmiet told me. "And put it with her things. Tie it in a buckskin bag and hang it on her cradleboard when Kása brings the one she made. She will always have something of her time when she and I lived as one, and something of you, for being here at her beginning."

"I'll get a blanket." I remembered that my father had laid out swaddling for the first birth in my memory. His thoughts must have been there with his newborn even if his body wasn't. "Then we'll get you washed up too."

By the time I returned with a swaddling blanket, the infant had coughed and fussed until she settled skin to skin, against her mother. In a peaceful presence, Sunmiet held her daughter to her breast, aided her to nurse and nuzzle, caressed her tiny fingernails.

I put some water on to boil, kept busy, wore a constant smile as I thought about this birthing business. It surprised me, but I did not feel deprived for never having experienced it myself. Instead, I felt blessed to have received the gift of Sunmiet's willingness to share this precious moment of her life. My prayer was one of gratefulness, fullness, not of longing, and I recognized it as something that had eased into my life as I was ready, able to let go of distant dreams and pains and accept just what was.

Sunmiet talked softly as the infant nursed. She winced again, "Must push," she said and for an instant I thought she might have another! She acted as if she had a small contraction, pushed. "Save it," she said of the red moon tissue I held in my hands. "We will bury it tomorrow. In the choke cherry ravine where first we talked of Standing Tall."

Joseph stomped back in, breaking into the pleasant mood. He slammed his rifle down, then calmed when he saw the infant. "Well," he said in wonder. "From the dregs of a miserable night comes something soft and warm. Congratulations, Sunmiet."

"And her father?" Sunmiet asked, eyes wary.

Joseph sighed. "Rattled Teddy with his surly talk. Should have put John to watching him, too. That's why Teddy came to get me. Time we got back," he nodded toward the baby, "her father was gone. I'll wait by the bridge for him. Has to cross to get a horse. We'll get him, don't you worry."

"Unless he goes the other way," Sunmiet said, resigned. "Farther away from the Big River and the reservation." She sighed. "It is already the direction he is going."

Joseph set himself up beside the bridge for the rest of the night, but no one crossed. To my knowledge, Standing Tall has yet to cross it though it's been fourteen years since.

In the morning, Joseph stretched and walked back in to share the day with the infant and Sunmiet's other five who now hovered over the baby, begging to hold it, marveling at its perfect, tiny features. The infant yawned.

"Quite a night," Joseph said.

It was an understatement made even more so when Alice and Dr. Crickett arrived back with Ella and Monroe.

"Bet we can top your evenings," I said to Ella and Alice, leading them to view the baby in Sunmiet's arms, resting now in one of the bedrooms. Monroe and Crickett lounged in the saloon. I could hear Spirit howling.

"She's a wonder," Alice said, "What's her name?"

"Inanuks," Sunmiet said. "It is a Wasco word to honor her father's people. It means 'otter.' She came slippery into this world."

"Such big eyes," Alice said.

"I will think of her," Sunmiet said, smiling at me, "as a young Huckleberry Eyes."

"She is beautiful," Ella said. "But we've a startle of our own. Show her, Alice."

I looked at Alice M., her face ablush, her eyes sparkling with anticipation as she pulled a piece of paper from her wrist purse.

"What is it?" I asked, opened the envelope to read it, then turned to her, astonished. "It's a marriage license!" I said.

"I know!" Alice said, twittering. "Dr. Crickett—Spike—promised he'd take good care of me. And now, he says, we'll be wed within the week."

"I think not!" I exploded. "You barely know him!" I was angry with myself for not seeing this coming. "He has no right to come in here and fill your head. Ella! How could you have gone along with this—this ridiculous thing!"

"She's of age, Mother Sherar. And we have no right, really…I mean, I'm not her sister, nor you her…her mother, really." I knew she hesitated with the word, wanting to walk both sides, comfort each of us yet face the situation.

"Yes. Well," I said, only later realizing why that sounded so familiar. "I'll be having words with Mr. Sherar and then with Dr. Crickett. You, my dear Alice, will stay right here." I lifted my long skirts to move the faster into the men's saloon, annoyed to discover both Ella and Alice right on my heels.

The cat howled in the cage and I dealt with it as the distraction I needed. "Please, retire the cat now or give it water or do something to stop its howling."

"It's quite happy, don't you know," Crickett said brightly. "That's why she sings."

"I'd prefer a miserable cat then, if I'd get silence," I said, spiteful.

Crickett blinked once or twice at my vehemence, rose to lift the cage, and set it just outside. Monroe lounged at the table, arms resting on the arched canes of the chair. He wore a slightly amused look on his face as he stood to offer his arm to Ella, a chair to Alice. Joseph's look was quizzical.

"If it's the marriage you're concerned about," Crickett began as he turned back from the cat, "I know it's quite a rush. Love can be like that sometimes." He had an uncanny ability to anticipate my arguments. "We can visit often. She won't be far away. I'll take the best care of Alice—"

"Alice!" Joseph interrupted.

"I'm not an old man, truly," Crickett pleaded. "Well able to provide." He looked at Alice whose eyes glowed with admiration for him. "It is as though I've found that missing spirit of myself with Alice. Please, don't let it slip away."

Too many events to deal with. Too many people to care about. Too many futures to manage. I could see my life changing minute by minute and knew I couldn't stop it, couldn't control it; at the moment didn't think I would try. I wondered if this was what Mama felt the years after, when she lost what she loved and her world began spinning away.

But I could make a different choice—love my "children"—and let them go.

At least Crickett understood the enormity of what he proposed. And I supposed it was not all that unlike my learning to care for Joseph in an instant though I came to love him in a longer time. I looked to him now when he spoke. "Let's give the idea a few days, Mother, and see where we are by then," my husband wisely counseled.

On the Thursday stage, almost a week after Crickett's arrival and Sunmiet and Inanuks's departure to her people's camp across the river, the letter posting the death of Joseph's brother arrived. Riding right behind the stage came the sheriff. The latter took our attention from the former.

The sheriff thought he was merely stopping for the noon meal.

"Plenty of sage grouse at Chicken Springs," he said. "Always worth the extra here for Tai's peppered steak." The barrel-chested man chewed happily, alone in the dining room having seen the stage off before eating. "And that great tomato sauce you have him make." He smothered the steak with ketchup.

Crickett had spent much of his time with us, fishing. He took evening walks with Alice. Later, I was always grateful that I'd given up my reservations and had joined in with Ella and Alice preparing for the younger's wedding. It would have been a double tragedy if she had not at least had the pleasure of anticipation. Unaware of the hour, Crickett rarely appeared for meals. Instead, he said he "lived on love." At night, he wrote in a little book. "Notes on patients," he said. I assumed at the Salem asylum. Only for Spirit did he seem to have some sense of timing. At noontime, he released the cat to stretch in the shade beneath the rimrocks. The cat's long gray hair fairly frothed around its face as it stood, nose into the gentle breeze. Spirit rolled on its back next to Alice when she and Crickett sat together on a quilt, purring contentedly, rarely howling at all while Alice scratched its belly in the shade of the cinnamon rocks.

It's where the three of them were when the sheriff arrived. Between bites, he mentioned my brother, now eighteen. "George shows some interest in the law," he told me. I was a bit irritated that a stranger should know more of my brother than I. The sheriff went on talking and it was only in passing that he mentioned his mission in coming by the falls. "Looking for an escapee," he said, stuffing potatoes into his mouth, chewing, his black mustache bobbing.

"From the jail?" I asked, pouring more coffee.

He drank, swallowed, wiped his mouth with his palm. "Nope. From the crazy house. Near Salem. Not sure where he was headed. Managed to lift the valise of a doctor going on vacation. Just picked up his things waiting at the hospital. Someone said they sold a man meeting his description a ticket." He took another bite of steak, caught the juice dribbling with his thick tongue. "A gray cat's missing too. One that hung around the asylum, that the escapee took a liking to."

"What's he there for?" I asked in a daze, staring out through the window at a happy couple, the cat's paws jabbing at a long feather Crickett held.

"Didn't kill no one," he said. "Just fits. Of sadness, forgets who he is, where he is. Tried to kill himself a couple a times." He washed his meal down with a large glass of ice tea. "Sure made lots of changes here, Missus. Husband still working the roads?"

"Yes," I said. "He's with the crew now. You say this person never harmed anyone?"

"Nope. But sometimes, he does crazy things. Guess that's why he's in the crazy house!" He laughed at his own lame joke. "Anyway, goes from sadness to laughter and then right on back. Pretends to be what he ain't. Can convince anyone of it, too, he can. Sometimes he's a steamboat captain. Sometimes a musician. Just whatever hits him. I'm supposed to bring him back. Got a family. Not dangerous, though."

I watched in slow motion as Crickett and Alice made motions of leaving their serenity beneath the rimrocks, almost willing them not to come to the house as they approached, hand in hand. Torn by the possibility of danger, the same possibility of safety, I suggested the sheriff walk out the side door, away from the rock wall, toward the river.

Unfortunately, Spirit bounded the same direction, toward the river and she was followed close at hand by Crickett.

The cat startled the sheriff, running straight past him as he did. And I saw something register in the lawman's mind. Perhaps because he knew we kept only the pigs and dogs as pets; perhaps because the cat was so distinctive and would have been described by the hospital staff.

So when Crickett ambled his big frame with his rust hair around the side of the inn, cage in hand, there was little doubt for the sheriff. Though he couldn't have known—none of us could—what would happen when he "Howdy-ed" him.

"You there!" the sheriff said, his arm upraised in greeting. "Is that a Salem cat?"

"Yes, don't you know," Crickett said before he realized his error, "and he loves the country now we're here."

"I thought as much. I'm here to take you and him back, Lonnie." His voice was soft, kind.

Crickett stopped. Alice beside him. "Name's Spike," he insisted. "Spike Crickett."

"You lifted the 'Crickett,'" the sheriff said. "And the doctor's looking for it back. It's time now, Lonnie. No harm'll come to you."

"No," Crickett said, softly. "No!" Louder. He backed up slowly.

"You've had your outing," the sheriff continued. He began to ease toward Crickett who hunched like a cornered animal, shaking his head.

I had followed the sheriff outside and called now to Alice. "Come here, dear," I said. "Just for the moment." I felt numb and agitated at the same time, reaching out to her as I spoke. I wondered how such a peaceful morning could be converted in a heartbeat to the slow motion of a nightmare. Alice saw me, shook her head. She eyed with confusion the man approaching her beloved. "He's the sheriff, Alice. He won't harm either of you," I said, pleading with her to hear me, trust me.

Her eyes were large, moving rapidly from Crickett to me, to the sheriff.

Her thin back stiffened and then with a sinking heart, I saw her reach for Crickett's hand, hang on.

It must have registered with the sheriff at the exact same moment as with me. Crickett looked to take the river, and Alice with him!

"No!" I shouted, walking with lead feet.

The sheriff acted faster. He grabbed for Crickett just seconds before he reached the water, pulled him back away from the cliff ledges, stumbled over Alice, pushed her to the side where she lay sobbing when I reached her.

Crickett scuffled with the sheriff. Helplessly, I watched them wrestle until the lawman tripped his quarry, and with Crickett on the ground, he closed the metal cuffs to hold him.

I heard Crickett sobbing. "No, no, no, no, no." Defeated, he moved his face back and forth, scratching his pink skin on the rocks.

The sheriff decided to wait until the morning stage returned from Canyon City, and arranged for Crickett—or Lonnie Williams as his family knew him—to stay in his room, cuffed to the bed. Crickett turned despondent. The sheriff tried to convince him that going back would not be bad. Crickett sat stony-faced and forlorn upon his bed. Dirt still smudged the front of his tight-fitting vest.

Alice was inconsolable. She spent the better part of the afternoon sitting beneath the rimrock stroking Spirit, crying, her eyes puffed and red.

"It's not the end," Joseph told her when he arrived back from the roads. He folded his long legs beneath himself and leaned back on his elbows beside her on the grass. He did not look at her, honored her, wanted her to know he was there. "Though I expect it doesn't seem so now," he said. "Maybe it's the best place for him."

She looked at him, accusing. "This was the best place for him. Until that man came."

"He's only doing his job, Alice. It'll take you nowhere but to misery to blame another for things the way they are. Not Crickett's fault either. He had to do what he had to do. We all do, I suspect." He reached for her then and I saw through the window that she allowed him to hold her while she cried. It was progress.

Crickett wasn't hungry when I took a tray to him. Even Alice with her handkerchief stuffed up her dress sleeve in case she began to cry again, could not urge him. "Just take a bite," Alice said. Crickett stared straight ahead.

I succumbed to the strangeness of the day and let Spirit spend the night out of her cage with Alice.

In the morning, the stage arrived, three passengers disembarked, donned their moccasins and slipped their feet beneath the table. A pretty woman not much taller than me said she was a photographer from Minnesota, looking to set up a studio in The Dalles or maybe Portland. We talked of Ella's wedding later in the summer and she handed me her card. "Jessie Shep" it read. "I can be reached at this post." She wrote a Portland number on the card. "At least until August." Something about her intrigued me. Perhaps it was talking with someone without having to look up, or enjoying the presence of another independent woman here beside the river.

The male passengers always behaved better when a woman rode with them, so when I met the sheriff and Crickett in the hall, I made a fateful suggestion. "If Crickett wants to eat breakfast, perhaps he could do so without the cuffs? There's a woman passenger." The sheriff shrugged his shoulders, asked a subdued Crickett if he'd like to eat at the table, and Crickett nodded yes.

And Crickett did eat. A bit woodenly but enough to make Alice feel better about him and the long ride ahead. The driver gave the five-minute call, and the men stood to put their boots on. Standing on the porch, they talked of weather, the horses, smoked their rolled cigarettes. Peach blossoms from the upper orchard drifted to the earth in the gentle breeze like snow falling softly. The photographer walked toward the falls and asked if there was sufficient time before they left to take a photo.

"Sure 'nuf," Young Handly, the driver, said. "Got to load the sheriff's passenger yet. Guess we'll tie his horse," he added absently to himself.

The driver lifted the stagecoach boot and handed Jessie her tripod and her camera. She set it up, bent beneath the black cloth and focused, loaded the glass plates and took her shot of the falls. Seeing the men standing on the porch, the inn and the unusual rock wall as a backdrop, the blossoms drifting through the air, she asked if they wouldn't like to pose. A few coughs, lame protests and the men lined up. "You too," she called to Crickett and the sheriff stepping out of the inn. "The men of the meal," she jested. "The tallest—line up in back," which is what Crickett and the sheriff did as she reloaded.

"Got it," she said in a lilting voice after she took her picture. The men moved forward, offered to carry the heavy camera, her tripod. Jessie meandered, seemed to relish the fragrant morning, the roar of the river. Even the sheriff slowed to talk with one of the passengers.

Then into that placid lull before the storm, Crickett made his decision. Our laxness brought opportunity mixed with anticipated loss, and Crickett brushed forward in an instant, past the sheriff, past the photographer, past the stage. He headed for the river.

Crickett's spirit was a good one, though, and while he could not seem to stop himself, when he plunged headlong into the turquoise swirl of the raging Deschutes River, he leaped alone.

UNFOLDING

IT DID NOT SEEM POSSIBLE that in one short week new life should join us and another leave. While we tried to comfort Alice, explain how much Crickett's mind must have suffered to end it as he did, tried to make sense of the craziness of choosing death over the torments of his life, none of it made sense to her. She had lost him just after he was found.

"It's that way, sometimes," I said, holding her while she cried. We sat at the river's edge, Alice's place of belonging.

"Never again!" she said adamantly, pulling back from me. "I will not care so much, never again. Why did that man have to come for him? We should have run from the dance!" A further thought caused more anguish as she said: "If it was not for me, he would never have remained at this river!"

She sat apart from me, resolute. Fearful that she might waste years as I had, I shot an arrow prayer for wisdom and good counsel before I spoke next.

"I know it seems you'll never heal," I said. "And you may not want to. I didn't, a long time ago, when I lost three someones I loved. I thought that I would never want to feel again it hurt so much. Worse, I thought my loving caused it." She was listening though staring straight ahead at the rocks across the river, rocks she loved to fish from, rocks she escaped to. "I waited a long time. I blamed others who blamed me and then myself. I said only one thing could ever fill my empty space. If I had stayed that way," I told her, talking quietly, "I never could have loved you, or Ella when she came." Alice's eyes took on a faraway look. "I would have missed so many moments, from Sunmiet's children, you, Joseph, all the ones I love who softened me up over the years." I thought of my brother, too, wondered if I'd stayed away from him these years not just to avoid my mother but to protect him, afraid my loving him meant I would lose him too. "A hard heart has no room for the good things God gives," I said. She tossed a small rock into the rushing water, watched it sink from sight. "I know your heart feels like a stone now, but please don't let it stay that way. Love did not cause your loss," I said softly. "It gave you your greatest joy."

Alice sat poised like a frightened deer. Almost anything could set her off, make her disappear in fact or form. Then into that taut moment jumped Spirit, springing onto Alice's lap with her fur and purr. Alice startled and patted the cat's arched back, running her hands out to the tip of its tail. The cat put its nose to her chin, pushed, and I saw a small smile through Alice's swollen eyes and knew it would be Spirit who would bring Alice from her deep despair. Spirit, answered prayer, and our unyielding love, which in time gave us back our happy Alice. Spirit, who joined us at Sherar's Bridge that summer and never spent another night inside her cage. Spirit, who some months later, led the real Dr. Crickett and great change to Alice's life.

The letter informing us of James' death back in New York had taken weeks to reach us despite advances in the postal system. Sometime in March he'd died. Eliza penned the letter, said that she and Carrie and Henry would be fine, that she thought James had left them well cared for.

My husband did not grieve, at least not in the way I expected. Or perhaps I didn't notice as I might have. Ella's wedding preparations took my time and energy. That and keeping an eye on Alice. For a brief time we'd been planning two marriages. "We'll have to clean twice as much, mother," Alice had said once, her dark eyes glowing. I had delighted in her new-found consideration of me as mother, was grateful Crickett's death did not take that away.

We prepared for the marriage of our now legally adopted daughter, papers all signed and courthouse sealed. I had thought some great feeling would arise from me the day we signed the papers making Susan Ella Turner become Susan Ella Sherar, but it did not. I suppose I had already accepted her as my own—perhaps even all those years before—so the papers were but the punctuation in a long sentence of our lives.

Every mother imagines her daughter's wedding day. Must be something put into the water of the womb. And while I was deprived of that water, the image did not escape me. So we traveled, Ella and Joseph and I, to Portland to find the loveliest dress that ever fashioned itself over a form.

White lace, layer on layer, flowed from Ella's shoulders out over that bustle right down to her toes. She wore a wide-brimmed hat with a ostrich plume pouring ivory over the side. I couldn't resist purchasing the stuffed silk dove made in Chinatown, though Joseph shook his head like I'd lost mine. We pinned it into Ella's hat, peeking out from under the plume for the occasion. I thought Dr. Hey would have been pleased with my choice of symbolism. After all, I had taken his advice and mixed with the sage wisdom of Sunmiet and Pastor Condon, had found my place in life, found forgiveness and another kind of nesting place, found my family.

Here stood Ella on her wedding day as proud proof.

The dress fit perfectly and was not too hot for July. On her feet, she wore slippers of pure satin. A gold chain draped around her neck, hung down over the tiny tucks in the bodice. Joseph gave it to her along with a locket. Her father from Vale sent her a lovely gold bracelet and I wondered if after all these years of mining, he had finally struck it rich—though he had already given us his greatest treasure. Ella's ash blond hair was swirled on top of her head with a mass of curls and to finish off her modern look, she rubbed real rouge we'd bought in Portland on her dimpled cheeks.

She was as lovely as the white icing on her cake.

I didn't want to think of Ella's leaving. My face must have been speaking up a storm while Alice and I were dressing Ella.

"There'll be grandchildren," Ella said. Then aware beyond her years of how I might take that promise—one I promised my own mother but had not achieved—she added, "And if not, we'll have more time together, Monroe and I. Build a life as you and Father Sherar have, loving other people's children."

Is that how she saw us? Loving other people's children? I guessed that was so. Even Joseph had taken Monroe under his wing, referred to him as one of his boys and I suspected they shared a visionary mind. So Joseph, too, had found a son loaned him from another.

"I don't think a child can get too much, do you? Love, I mean," Ella continued, looking at herself in the mirror. "There are always children enough to go around if you take a little time to find them. You always did."

I marveled that on the biggest day of her life, Ella could find the positive in someone else's life. "And I'll see you, though not like every day, like now." She looked at me in the oak mirror, then at herself, checking her white dress, gloves. "You can come see us, too," she reminded me, sticking the pearl hat pin through the pile of curls, adjusting the brim, the bird peeking out, resting her hands at her side.

She turned from the mirror. "You can ride that same trail we did. Past your 'green river.' Or maybe Father Sherar will work a new grade and you can bring the buggy up it." I nodded, swallowing back tears, not wanting to talk, fearful I might ruin her day. "Change isn't the end," she reminded me, softly, her dress swooshing on the floor as she kneeled beside me. "It's an unfolding, the beginning of something different."

With that bit of wisdom, my bright-eyed, twenty-two-year-old daughter held me, dabbed my eyes with her hankie, adjusted my amethyst watch on my bodice, mothering the mother.

"It's time," she sang, a child again, and she stepped out into the parlor of her future in-laws' home, reached for the arm of her soon-to-be husband, and stood before the justice of the peace to become Mrs. Monroe Grimes.

"It's not the end," I remembered her saying as she took her vows. Beside Joseph, watching the ceremony, I blinked away tears. "It's the beginning of something different," I repeated softly, to which Joseph responded in a whisper: "No doubt."

James's death brought on a new drive for my husband, as though he had not yet challenged himself enough and perhaps that was how he grieved. He began constructing, putting his still firm brawn and muscle into barns. Huge barns, big enough to harbor four stage relief teams at a time; enough to feed fifty calves in winter; enough to nurture twice as many lambs. Along the White River Joseph built a three-story structure—a flour mill—to grind the wheat the rich land gave up to the ever-increasing homesteaders dotting the rolling hills above us. The construction had taken months and my husband had been energized each day he rode the three miles to supervise, consider problems, solve them, and ride back home.

On our river, on the inn side of the bridge, he built storage sheds and from them more than once he ordered flour and salt dispensed to hungry settlers too poor to even pay the toll. But his pride and joy was the calf barn, a huge cavernous structure whose foundation was the river rock. To make walls perfectly straight, he sighted across his gold pan filled with water level to the brim. Then he and the crews stood the fir walls carefully leaving less than six inches from the barn to the precipitous river's edge.

"Why so close?" I asked him. "What's the point of having one side be that tight to the river?"

"Only have to defend three sides?" he proposed.

"Defend from what?"

"It was a joke," he said. "It'll make it easier to build the corral toward the rocks. And be easier to clean it. Into the river." I wondered what that practice might do to the salmon. I suspect that Joseph was driven by the challenge, to see how close his structures could be built to the edge of oblivion, how completely he could make his designs move from paper onto lava rock. I didn't say that. Instead I offered: "You better hope no calves get shoveled out that door. Convenience has its drawbacks." Of course, for some it's the drawbacks that put the fire into life.

When Alice surprised us with a relationship of her own the summer after Ella's wedding, we found ourselves stunned by the irony of it. The real Dr. Crickett (Crickett Two, we called him) arrived with a mild manner, fishing rods, a bald head, and a ring of gray around the back and sides. His clothes fit him better than when squeezed onto the first Crickett. Their odd relationship blossomed into a stunning marriage made more so when Alice chose to remain with us, seeing her husband only infrequently on his rare visits to the inn and the once-yearly trips they made south, to Paiute country in Nevada. We were not privy to their negotiations, only accepting of the spoils they shared with us: Crickett's fresh-caught trout, Alice's sparkling eyes, and Spirit's ever present purr.

When we weren't attending weddings, repairing roads, or serving guests, we were busy simply living. Our life along the river had taken on a rhythm, a giving back to travelers, Indians, children, and all. Accepted more and more by Sunmiet's people, Joseph and I became the local midwives, dentist, and doctor. Along with Alice, we became quite adept at pulling loose teeth or scraping salmon scales from the women's wide hands before binding up their cuts made while cleaning fish. Together, we fought the pesky head lice known to follow children everywhere, replacing kerosene with Sunmiet's more effective bear grease.

Sometimes Sunmiet and I sat near sun-heated water and bathed a young Inanuks, talking. I watched my friend of many years swirl the water so her daughter would not peer at her own reflection. "So she will not spend a lifetime searching for a reflected soul before she is old enough to recognize herself," Sunmiet told me when I asked. I learned something new each day.

And I marveled that it never failed to fill me up each time I held a *yáiya* or a *nana* in a crush of love and laughter, or wiped a child's face of tears—tears from scraped knees or disappointment, tears of anger or of fear.

In the evenings, Joseph and I would often walk arm in arm across the bridge to watch the Indians at their stick games. In the flickering firelight, they sat in teams of four or ten, sometimes even dozens, facing each other as though lining a road. I never grasped the game completely though I watched often, listening to the drumming and singing while the opposite team bet then guessed which hand held the prized sticks, the bleached bones. More than money was exchanged in the gamble. Coins and stones and cloth and personal treasures piled up in little mounds before the players. In the morning, someone would be sporting something new—clothing, beadwork, or a tool, and increased prestige.

Card games persisted in the small barns too, according to Peter. We never tried to stop them. "I've more in common with them in there than not," Joseph said once as a burst of laughter rose from the little shed in the night and I wondered if he missed the weekly games that once consumed his days.

We were invited to the powwows, dances, weddings, and celebrations—George's wedding, Anne's too—and always the glorious meals. Greeted by *"niix máicqi"* we'd repeat the "good morning" phrase, then sit side by side on tule mats to celebrate the salmon's return and the eels. *"Chuus!"* Each would say before we began feasts, holding up a cup containing just a sip. *"Chuus,"* a toast to honor God for giving us first and foremost the liquid of life.

As for the eels, I never acquired a taste for them though roasted they could pass for chicken. Sunmiet said she'd share her roasting secrets with me but I never asked. Joseph hunted and fished with Peter, his men, and son, worked with the crews maintaining the roads. We helped pull soaking deer hides from the river and learned a thing or two about using deer brains to soften them, the art of tanning and smoking them into their distinctive scent.

We were asked to settle simple disputes as outside but interested parties.

It was as though we lived in a world all our own. All we needed was here, here on the edge of the river. And what we had would change. It was the only constant of our lives.

The Bannock War of 1878 took place far from us near the Nevada border on the Paiute's small reservation. Sunmiet worried over her sons and nephews as many Warm Springs and Wascos were conscripted to serve as scouts. Most returned and shaking their heads in dismay, told stories of the innocent Paiutes caught up in the craziness of the war between the white soldiers, white settlers, and the more aggressive band of Nevada Bannocks. Koosh thought he might have seen Standing Tall somewhere in the distance.

When it was over, Paiute men guilty only of their race and being present were imprisoned in Washington and their reservation land given away. Gradually, the Paiutes were released—having never really fought. Many sought permission to come to Warm Springs, to land that once, long ago, had been part of their gathering grounds along the Deschutes River. And the Warm Springs people and the Wascos who once fought with the Paiutes, expanded their large hearts and agreed to let them return to their place of belonging.

It was a good way to end the decade.

The 1880s began with trials. Banks closed and markets fell. Most in the West were hard hit even before the severe winter of 1884 and '85. Because of some premonition Joseph had, we had bought the Finnigan Place before it happened. I never knew how Joseph came up with his ideas, perhaps only fluffy men such as Frederic could really understand. Whatever the reason, I showed him the Finnigan place on our way to visit Monroe and Ella and their little one, Roy. Joseph's eyes scanned the lush green river and marked it for our future.

The grass never seemed to stop growing there. We cut and hauled and piled several hay stacks that lined my green river like a picture frame before we even knew the fierceness of the winter we'd face.

Joseph's other big decision, to buy up sheep in the region, unnerved me. He had a scheme he did not initially share. Instead, he tied up all the cash we had to purchase sheep. He bought up more, actually, than we had cash for, giving notes to those who'd take them, payable in the spring. "Plenty of feed for 'em," he said to my fears. We lugged baskets of peaches and pears from the ledge garden, stored them in one of the sinkholes we'd built a shed over beside the river.

"Feed now, yes," I said, "but if we have a rough winter..."

"Ye've a mind to worry, woman," he said biting into a peach, "This'll work. I know it."

How often I'd heard those words.

The sheep were fed from the Finnigan hay stacks by hardworking Mexican herders who kept the animals clustered in the valley. Snow fell and fell that winter and it was so cold that the herder's camp stoves could barely keep water thawed though sitting on top the flame. An oppressive fog filled the canyon most of January. Even the Canada geese did not call to each other as they rose from the river, silent dark wing tips circling above the ridge through the fog. And what had looked like almost too much hay in late summer soon became rationed, to squeeze enough for the sheep and the cattle and horses and mules who scrounged the crusty, snow-covered hillsides for wispy blades of grass. Though Joseph never admitted it, I saw furrows appear in his wide forehead, his chin jutted out more as he clamped his teeth together even while he read his month-old paper filled with news of the east, something that always used to relax him.

When word came that the cold took human lives as well as cattle, that the reservation was especially hard hit with rotten beef delivered by the agent (all that the unscrupulous contractors had to deliver), we bundled up the sleigh with loads of blankets, foodstuffs from the warehouse, and sides of frozen beef. We reached Simnasho too late to save an aging Kása, but in time to bring some small relief to those who mourned her. Her passing gave an answer to a question that had puzzled me for nearly thirty years.

"At the give-away, for Kása's passing on," Sunmiet told me, "we set aside a basket of hers for you."

"Kása said you were to have it," Bubbles said, the whine still in her voice. "We could not look. So look now." She poked at me with her fat finger. "I want to see what's in it."

Sunmiet gave her a scowl. "You picked up plenty of her things, Bubbles. No need to wish for more." Bubbles snorted a cloud in the cold air of Sunmiet's frame house. I tugged at the lid of the pine needle basket, brittle with age.

Inside was the answer to my question of a day beneath the firs when I first met Sunmiet and her *kása*.

"It's one of Kása's carvings." Bubbles said, disappointed. "A woman, smiling, with a hole in her stomach. So small. You can put it in your hand." She looked for more in the basket. Finding nothing, she lost interest.

My interest increased. For wrapped in the bottom of my dresser drawer, tied into an old lace hankie, was the tiny bead Pauline once held. A bead, painted with the open mouth of a hungry baby. I knew without checking that Pauline's bead would fill the hole in the carved mother, make Kasa's carving complete.

We lost many sheep and cows that winter though we fared better than many. And we did run out of hay—but just before the spring thaw and floods and so we were not ruined. Joseph's bridge held in the heavy snow runoff, a testament to his vision and the men who made it happen. His was the only bridge across the Deschutes that survived the spring.

With snow melted, we bought wool. We bought bundles some ranchers hoarded in years gone by, the fleeces marked by ding balls and rocks, but we took them anyway. We bought sheep from neighbors, loaded diamond-hitched six foot fleece stacks from wherever we could get them. Then onto the Finnigan place, we brought a shearing crew for our own herds that numbered in the thousands. Mostly with Australian sheep dogs and heelers—who brought Bandit fondly to mind—the crews worked for days as other buckaroos scrounged the ravines bringing in the sheep. We women cooked and made stew until the very smell of mutton makes me sick to this day!

Mountains of wool grew on that green river place. Peter suggested we weigh each fleece after shearing, record the weight and mark the ewes so we could breed and cull for heavier fleeces year after year. He wanted to then sort the good fleeces into separate stacks and that way raise our prices. Joseph had looked at him askance, I thought, considering the time such ideas would take. But he laughed his deep, bottom-of-the-belly laugh. "Wish I'd a thought of it myself! Good idea, man!" And so it's been. That year, Joseph had the wool tied in bundle after bundle as was the custom and then stacked. Like a clock I went from side to side, worried first that we'd not have enough to meet our contract; and then to the other side, that the market would drop. Joseph laughed at me. He seemed to spark to life with the uncertainty of it all, the requirement that everything would have to happen as he imagined or he'd be called upon to forge some strange solution if presented with an unplanned challenge. Or perhaps, like so many of our neighbors, we might lose it all.

"It's like a fire," he told me once as we looked over the stacks of wool, patting the thick clumps, picking at twigs stuck in the fluff. He tried to reassure me of this risk. "You've got to take a deep breath, breathe slowly on the flame, add kindling to it but not so much you smother it. I've got the flame; think the kindling's measured too."

I thought I saw a flame reflect inside of him. His was a risky plan I'd finally gone along with: to ship an entire trainload of wool to a Philadelphia market.

On the final days, when our calculations indicated we had sufficient wool for the trainload, I counted as wagon load after wagon load left Finnigan. The double freighters with their teams headed toward the Buckley Place then north, twisting down the steep road west, to the falls. Across Buck Hollow bridge, then Sherar's then up the other side, the wool to be delivered to Moody's Warehouse in The Dalles. Bales of the stuff, some still sporting stickers of sage and weeds that the dogs had pushed the sheep through. Hoisted on board the railroad by brawny men, the piles filled up one entire train which chugged out under heavy steam back East. I sighed relief.

Joseph followed by passenger train which now went all the way to Chicago. From there he transferred and was gone for several weeks. To Alice's utter shock, I cheered and danced around the room when his telegraph reached us. "Arrived safe in Philadelphia. Sale success. Tell Peter. Kindled just right. Home soon. Will bring surprise."

I imagined some new luxury to wear around my neck. Earrings perhaps to flash at the concert in The Dalles. A new hat, maybe, or something to swish through the dining room now seating more than two hundred at the third-time rebuilt Umatilla House. Perhaps a bingo game to play with Ella and Monroe, a new stereopticon to take us around the world, share with Ella's boy, Roy. It didn't really matter. I could relax and anticipate Joseph's return.

I found the separation soothing in a way. I did not need to wonder what time he would want supper, consider what new venture he was into. The road crews took direction well from Peter. John Suhr and Tai and Teddy, the blacksmith, seemed pleased to ask my outline for their days. I didn't need to worry over whether or not I ate even when I wasn't hungry because Joseph was not present to nudge me about "putting meat on my bones."

Alice and I nurtured ourselves at home, keeping things thriving. After we served our guests, Alice often lifted the bamboo fishing rods from their holders, grabbed the willow creel, and followed by Spirit, brought dinner home. I dropped in on the women drying fish, making cradleboards for their nieces and nephews; took a little more time visiting with Sunmiet at their camp across the river. One day we found a way to see each other even more.

Anne, now twenty with children of her own, asked if she might help with laundry or cooking at the inn. "The men work," she said. "We women too."

"And your husband?" I asked. "He will not object?"

"He will not object," Sunmiet answered for her. "He would like to own the cattle, like Peter and Mr. Sherar, not just look after other men's." Peter and George had been developing a herd of their own, taking payment each month not only in cash but in cattle. Apparently the plan was known and coveted. "Unlike her father," Sunmiet said, "she is learning how to make the non-Indian way work for her."

"With money, we can have our own stock," Anne said, her eyes keen, "make decisions about when to sell and buy. Not always have to work the roads. And feed our family not just with roots and fish and berries or the agent's beef, but with ketchup and summer fruit captured in tins." She spoke vigorously, with a hunger.

She gave the same hunger to her work. The tall Anne joined Alice and me to wash and clean the inn, brought her ideas too. Many I adopted but not the striped blankets she wanted. "Warmer," she said. "And made in this land."

"Hudson Bays have done me fine," I told her.

Anne's little ones often came with her, along with Sunmiet whose hands seemed made of leather, always beading some design for this grandchild or that. Occasionally, I allowed myself the luxury of relaxing with her, sitting with active Inanuks, already four. Working or not, I teased and spoiled that little Otter, especially when she warmed my insides by calling me her *kása*.

While Joseph traveled in the East, I had the crews work in the orchards, one beside the inn and the one on the ledge. Both peaches and apples now filled the air with their sweet blossoms every spring. The sweet grapes extended their vines. There was the usual work: milk the cows, make butter, bake bread, keep the larder filled along with sewing and supplying an inn that now had all eight guest beds filled each night. We served three times that number in meals each day as more and more people crossed the river, paid the tolls that John collected in the bucket with Joseph gone. I posted the mail delivered twice daily by stage for the settlers whose small homesteads dotted Joseph's roads twisting up the grades on either side of the river. Their visits caught me up on illnesses, weddings, new births, and trips. We chatted through the window: neighbors picking up their post, telling of their plans. On Tuesdays, the peddler's bell jangled from his cart. We'd stop whatever we were doing to go and finger some new thread or pan or handkerchief or bolt of fresh-dyed cloth. I thought it curious that his Yiddish accent seemed so similar to Sunmiet's speech.

Such everyday "predictable" activities always made me think of Luther when I labeled them as such. Such trivial things made me long for Joseph, too, to share with him the inconsequential events that told of daily form a fascinating fabric, but fray when kept for weeks. I missed his quiet words prayed into my skin.

I didn't really give much more thought to Joseph's "surprise" until the day he stopped the buggy in front of the inn and shouted out, "Mother Sherar! I'm home!"

I left a table full of guests, ran from the ladies' dining room onto the porch and into his waiting arms. He swung me around, kissed me. His beard may have bristled against my lips but I didn't notice so glad was I to see him, smell the scent of leather, hear him whisper my name in his deep, tongue-rolling brogue. He was grayer, little bags nestled beneath his eyes. I hadn't noticed before. His white beard stuck out as though windblown.

"So good to see ye, Janie," he said. "Never know how much I miss ye till I'm gone." He lifted me again and said with a laugh "Have ye not eaten then for weeks? So light ye are!"

Alice joined us and I said to her, "What did I tell you? I'm never good enough just the way I am!"

"Not so!" he defended. "You could be no better."

Just before he set me back down I noticed the buggy. There in it sat what I imagined was my surprise, one I could easily find fault with.

He had not returned alone.

With him was a dust-shrouded, quite exquisite young woman.

CHAPTER 33

PASSIONS

A PERFECT HEART-SHAPED FACE framed by hair the color of obsidian looked out at me from the shadow of her Shako hat. She was the picture of style. Her hat's narrow brim and high, military-like top, was decorated with yellow silk flowers to match the canary of her dress. I saw Joseph's taste in the black silk ascot that flounced at her throat under a jacket cut with narrow lapels pulled into two black buttons at her tiny waist. A pair of black half-gloves covered her hands wrapped around an ebony parasol.

Her eyes matched the obsidian and she met mine straightforward. She blinked long eyelashes, removed her gloves. I thought her some young wealthy, Portland debutante until she took Joseph's hand to help her out and I noted the redness of her knuckles.

And when she said, "Hello, Aunt Jane," I was stunned.

"Caroline?" I asked, mystified. I had only seen her once or twice and then as a child. The photograph we had of her showed a stocky girl with a petulant look, dark sausage curls clustered at her shoulders, a scowl on her face. This person before me was quite different.

"I prefer 'Carrie,'" she said, her voice pleasant. "It seems less formal."

"Isn't she just a jewel?" my husband said, bubbling. "Bet you didn't expect me to bring her back, now did you?"

"I didn't know you'd gone to New York," I said, a little irritated about not being apprised of his change in plans, or something more.

"Well, I wasn't sure I would. But when things went so well and I was already mostly there, I just took the chance I could see everyone."

"Mother sends her regards," Carrie said. "And Henry, too. And all the cousins and aunts and uncles."

"Whole passel of them!" Joseph said. "Henry's already ten and Carrie here is twenty-four. And just a beauty, wouldn't you say?" He grinned at her blushing.

"How long can you stay, dear?" I asked, friendly, yet becoming formal as I did when presented with things I did not control.

"She'll be with us indefinitely," Joseph answered for her. "Just as long as she wants."

"I won't be a burden, Aunt Jane. Honestly."

There was a kind of desperation in her voice which contradicted her stylish outfit, her smooth presentation. It fit more with her knuckles. And the calluses I felt on her hands when I took one and we walked into the inn.

"Of course you won't, dear," I said. "We won't let you."

"Why didn't you just write me?" I said to Joseph later. "It would have been no problem to have known." We were curled together beneath the maple headboard. A picture of my father and one of Joseph's hung on the side wall, staring at us.

"I wasn't sure how you'd take to it."

"How could you even wonder?" I said, thinking of Alice and John and a number of others who had joined us and become like family. "I just don't like surprises of this magnitude. Her being here is fine."

"I hadn't planned to bring her back. Just to see them, make sure they were doing all right. James didn't leave them with as much as he hoped. Or else they've a skill in spending because Eliza's sold their home. She and Henry are living in a small one. And Janie," he paused in remembering, "Carrie wasn't even there. I found her working at this boarding house. Not a place you'd write about. Porch untended. Rats digging about. Workers from the garment facto-ries live there, if you could call it living. She made less than twenty-five dollars a month for cooking and cleaning. Had to pay her room and board out of that. Owner took in mending and ironing and when she wasn't cooking she had Carrie doing that. Girl looked a wreck when I saw her. She's actually put on weight coming across country, if you can imagine that. She was embarrassed to have me see her like that, I think. Her hands are still a mess."

It was a long speech for my husband. "Her hands are red," I said. "That's what I noticed."

"It seemed the thing to do. She wants to work here, fine. At least she'll be with family."

"James would be proud of you," I said. We lay like spoons, me with my back to his chest. He squeezed me gently.

"Truth is, when I saw her I felt this terrible pit in my stomach," he said into my ear. "The same empty well I felt when we reached Canyon City and Ella was already gone. It was like I'd lost something I didn't know I had or even wanted. And I took it as a sign, that if I ever felt it again I would act on it, do what I thought I should however odd it might seem and maybe next time, I wouldn't be too late."

I turned over, looked up at the ceiling. "What did Eliza say about it all?"

"Odd thing. Just that whatever Carrie wanted was fine with her. Said Carrie was old enough to stand on her own, had to when her father died." He paused. "Didn't she write us saying James had left them well off? I'm not sure she even knew what conditions Carrie was living in. Or if she did, she didn't seem to care or be able to do anything about it. Anyway, Eliza said Carrie always got what she wanted and this would be no exception."

"That's what Mama said of me, remember?" I rose up on my elbow, faced him. "That I always got what I wanted. She said it in anger, out of jealousy." I sat, then, hugged my knees. "Papa didn't give me everything I wanted, but it must have seemed that way to her, maybe been more than Mama thought she got. Or needed." I sat awhile, then lay back down, thinking of my life, its richness since I risked my parent's wrath and told J. W. no, said yes to Joseph, all those years before.

"I've had a good life, Joseph, had more bounty than most."

"That's cause you learned to cope, Janie," he said, pulling the covers up to his chin, "being both a strong blade and flexible."

"Yes, and letting faith do the building instead of trying to control it all myself, maybe that's what's made the difference, do you think?"

He yawned. "Too philosophical for my taste," he said. He kissed me gently then turned over to sleep.

Through the window, I watched the moon come up over the rocks, cast a glow onto the river making its route to the sea all shiny and sure. And I believe now as I write this that what made the difference in my life was trusting. Trusting that God took steps beside this river, knew what was coming, and led me here with these people and these challenges to let go of being bitter, to hang on to what is love. Trusting, and letting a man ease into my life.

"It was the right thing to do, Joseph," I said, "bringing Carrie into our family. I suspect the two of us have traveled similar roads." My traveling man was already sound asleep.

Caroline Sherar became a resident of Sherar's Bridge the summer of 1885. And while she was not of my womb, she was my daughter just the same. As much as Ella; more so than Alice who still kept in her private place.

With the Sherar women, Ella and Carrie, came a bond, a closeness though each arrived to live with us relatively late in their young lives.

It struck me, too, as I sat watching Carrie embroider in the lamplight, that both of the young women we claimed as "Sherars" had been brought into my life by Joseph. He had been touched by them first, saw in them their needs and matched them up with mine—ours. He reached beyond what might have been convenient to bring them to our hearts as surely as if he had fathered them himself.

I did have family. Carrie only made it fuller.

She bubbled with interests, her passions. She was dramatic, poured the coffee from a distance making it a game to hit the cup. She cascaded a stream of honey from two feet above the biscuits. When she hit her targets, she bowed to pleased applause. We marveled that she never missed. Visiting children, especially Anne's and Sunmiet's Inanuks, were charmed by her stories.

As with me, Sunmiet's family delighted her, and Carrie relished any part of

Sunmiet's life—being invited to a powwow, name-giving, or a sweathouse. Many is the evening we'd walk to the Indian camp, sit and talk. Or with Sunmiet, be drafted to hold the eel bags, hoping the fat snakes the consistency of liver would stay in them, not slither through holes to wiggle at our feet in the dark. Carrie loved the adventure of it!

While her sense of style, her flair for living, attracted her to others, it was Carrie's diligence and her ability to listen to you fully, without distraction, that most endeared her to me.

Probably the same thing that kept her many suitors coming back. Though she danced with several stockmen and sheepmen at Nansene and at Grange Halls around the area, she was finally won by Samuel Holmes.

A stockman and teamster, Sam drove often through Sherar's Bridge, even worked for us, some. We moved him back and forth across the bridge to the Finnigan Ranch as needed. After Carrie came, he preferred his time at Sherar's, working cows with Peter, helping Joseph on the grades.

Though twenty-five years younger, Sam shared the same visionary qualities as Joseph. And anyone who looked could see the valued way he handled stock. His efforts and good planning on his preemption claim near the Grass Valley area, not too far from Finnigan, would someday put fine wool suits on his muscular frame, make him wealthy.

Carrie saw his kindness and persistence, and when he finally got up his courage to ask her, into his clear blue eyes she said, "Yes! I thought you'd never!"

Her trousseau came from Lipman Wolfe, one of Portland's finest stores. I packed our bags and Carrie, Joseph, and I left in the summer in 1889 for Nicholville, New York. Samuel joined us two months later. On August 15, surrounded by dozens of nieces and nephews, some brothers and sisters and his mother, Joseph and I were witnesses at the wedding of these two young people I knew would be forever in my life.

They honeymooned in Nova Scotia where Sam's people came from, and stayed there, visiting, getting to know them and each other. Then they made their way to the high desert country of Reno. I wondered if they walked some of the same spots as Alice and Crickett when they made their yearly journey there. I never asked, though.

Mabel Jane was born in Reno, just nine months and one week after her parents were married.

Oh, how I missed them! I missed being there when Mabel Jane came. Missed spoiling as a *kása* should. Time with Ella and with Sunmiet and their children eased the distance, but I knew nothing would ever do until Carrie came back home. Here, to Sherar's Bridge or at least close by.

I don't think Carrie liked it much in Reno, living with her husband's brothers, watching him see if he could make a stake by plastering houses in the growing town. So when word came that they planned to travel back, I knew they'd be staying, at least if I had my way.

Just a few months before Carrie came back home, Joseph reminded me of a warning I had given him about his calf barn. While shoveling out the manure one day, out through the open door just six inches from the drop into the river, a curious calf wandered by. Before the stockman could deter it, the calf stepped out. It plunged thirty feet into the twisting water below, and was carried swiftly out of sight.

Joseph was distressed when told of the calf's drowning, more for the animal than for any financial loss we suffered. There'd be no hope for it, as for anything—beast or man—who found itself in the boil of those swift, relentless waters. Lost bodies were rarely ever even recovered. The first Crickett's hadn't been.

So when Peter rode to tell us that a calf had been spotted bellowing from a cave up under the ridge beside the river, Joseph was elated. "Think it's mine?" he asked Peter. "Could be one of yours."

We ran our herds together, Peter and his son's and the Sherar herd, separating them at round-up with the different brands. Ours is a single J, left hip. Peter's is shaped like a wineglass, though I expect it has a different meaning for him. "Can't see the brand on this one," Peter said. "Will help get it, no matter."

"Good!" Joseph said and organized a crew to do just that.

It was an event worth recording though some say it typified my husband's lust for acquisition, counting up the cost of one small calf. I think the event better typifies his need for passion, for taking risks, for that's exactly what it was, what his life has been.

With Peter, Joseph and several of his men crossed the bridge and looked back at the barn. Just below it, not far downstream, up under the cliff but still thirty feet down the side, sat a small red calf at the mouth of a shallow cave. "Sure enough there," Joseph said. "What'd ye think?"

The men pondered the situation, considering this way and that, then returned to the barn side. Several of the Indians noticed the commotion of the gathering and coming away from their scaffoldings, offered their advice. While a mule team was harnessed, others gathered up rawhide and hemp ropes. They secured one rope to a boulder at the base of the rimrock in case the team faltered and the other end to my husband. Then with separate rawhide ropes, they attached Joseph and the team, then lowered him inch by inch over the sheer face side.

"Back! Back!" the handler spoke to the mules. They twisted in their harness, wary about the roaring water and the closeness to the river's edge.

The roar of the water at that site, still rolling and twisting some five hundred feet beyond the falls, made yelling directions difficult. Mist boiled up from the churning. A sea gull screeched. Some men stood on the bridge shouting, waving their arms; several more watched and counseled from the Buck Hollow side.

That's where I stood, fingers to my mouth to keep from shouting, knowing there was nothing I could do. For it was Peter to whom Joseph entrusted his life that day. Peter, who gave the order to lower him over the side and huddled close to the edge, gave encouragement, looked back to the team, signaled, ordered, while his friend was lowered to the mist of the river. It was a mark of their devotion—the way Peter cared for Joseph, how Joseph trusted him—devotion begun when these two men had crossed that river together nearly thirty years before.

They had made a kind of chair for Joseph with the ropes. He carried a coil of rawhide draped over his head and his shoulder. I saw him signal with his arm to the men across from him who relayed the message back to Peter, above him, and his son. Peter's grandsons, Frank and Young Peter, peered over the edge and I found myself worrying almost as much for people's safety at the cliff side as for Joseph's.

He pushed out from the rocks with his feet, the way a mountain climber might. The rocks were sharp and the rope tension severe, but Peter had doubled them, for extra safety, had several men on the ropes in addition to the team. Strapped and swinging like a pendulum, he made his way down the side. A slip, a gasp, caught ropes, a jerky drop, and Joseph stood, to cheers, at the cave's floor. It was a shallow cave and didn't permit my large husband to stand upright in it.

The calf was cold and frightened and did not dart or bound from him as I thought it might. The men on our side signaled Peter who lowered another set of ropes. They tangled once on the knobby edge of a rock, jerked free and dropped down. Still, Joseph had to reach out and grab the lines and I held my breath as his bad leg buckled and he slipped, the rope around his middle holding him, strained against the side, as his legs went into the surging water.

A shout from our side signaled Peter who eased the team forward. The ropes jerked Joseph up like a marionette. "Not too far! He'll hit his head!" someone yelled. We signaled. Peter stopped the team, and Joseph stood bent, head intact, once again.

"Ready!" he shouted when he'd wrapped the calf. He tugged a signal on the rope and those on my side signaled Peter who gave the order to bring the calf on up. It rose, stiff-legged, bawling as it bounced against the side, caught once on the same knobby rock and then was pulled free, settled on solid ground. A cheer rose up as one man carried the calf away from the river's edge, walking it back to the barn.

"One to go!" Peter shouted and again the crews moved to Joseph's line. The team pulled. The men watched the ropes strain and tug. The muscles of the fishermen, familiar with the power needed to lift a sixty-pound salmon from the boiling falls, felt the effort and exertion of lifting four times that weight— were glad the team was there to do it.

Coming up was twice as hard. The rope was slippery and even in that short time, showed signs of fraying from the sharp lava rocks. At the point I knew he was safe—men were cheering and clapping him and each other on the back— relief washed over me, then great joy.

His safety gave me pause as I watched the men peel off his ropes, hand him a blanket. Why would my husband risk his life for something that while dear, did not compare with his worth, his value to me and to so many others?

I asked him that later when I walked with him to the calf barn to check on the other survivor.

"Better than robbing banks," he said.

I missed his meaning. "No," I corrected. "I want to know why you did that today, risked dying, just for a calf."

"Better than robbing banks," he repeated. "Or driving hell-bent down the ridge road on a wagon load of dynamite. Got the same inside push, same flood of energy that those might bring but with less danger, really gaining something for the risk."

I was sorting out his words, keeping quiet for a change. "Would you have me take the risk of driving cattle from here to Utah? Suppose that would gain the feeling." He ran his hands over the calf, checking for bruises, dabbed some liniment on an open wound. "There's something rich," he said holding his stomach, "inside. When you can do it together. Have something to accomplish, a goal, and then put your minds and muscles into one track and everyone gets there, together, at the end. Gets there because you were together and knew where you were going. There's something really good about that feeling."

Swallows nested in the barn pitch. They swooped and dipped, chattered above us. I was aware of warm animal smells, the presence of my husband. He took my hand and we walked out through the massive double doors left open in August to cool the barn. From the doorway we could see the bridge and the inn, the cliff orchard as we called it now, small trees dotting the red rocks with green. Indians were back on their scaffoldings, women off to the side next to their pink salmon halves turning red on the drying racks. The sun set and a pink glow hovered over the canyon.

"Even this," he said. "We could have done none of this alone. Without others."

"Without your energy and vision," I said. "And God's plan and blessing."

"And it's twice the blessing that he would give us this, all the people and resources we need, and then let us have it not just as paupers, barely scraping by, but richly, able to give to others. 'Good measure, pressed down, shaken together, running over.'" His eyes had a far-away look. "Turners gave me that verse and I've hung onto it."

At the bridge he stopped, looked up again at the cliff orchard. Alice still tended the sweetgrape arbor. It had become her favorite haunt when she wasn't fishing. Joseph stared at it. "There's one more thing," he said, "that I promised we would do together. And we can now. No reason not to."

"What?" I asked, not sure I wished to hear the answer. "I already have my family, everything I want."

"Build that house," he said, a catch in his throat. "I want to build a grand house to sleep fifty or more. Solid redwood, porches and gables and all the latest conveniences." I stared at him, shook my head, and smiled. This man with his visions. "Most importantly," he added, looking down at me with that twinkle in his blue eyes so I knew that it would happen, "I want a room large enough to hold a crowd, one for you and me to dance in."

THE DANCE

LIKE *SPI'LYA'S,* "COYOTE'S," winter fur, his hair has grayed. It's thinning, and what he's missing from the top now cascades from his chin, a muffler for his mouth. His eyes droop a bit and his left hand has taken on a shake. But this November, when he turns sixty, I suspect he'll load his new Winchester Model '92 and ride the hills above Tygh Valley or scour the ravines of Buck Hollow and bring home another buck. He does so love to hunt. Still wears his red wool vest and turquoise bola for the occasion. Some things have not changed despite the years since first our paths crossed not far from here, near the reptile pile, just beyond these falls. I still marvel at how he has seeped into my life, like the snowmelt of the mountains, spreading new over old.

Challenge is still his constant companion, the very newest being this house or hotel some call it. "Sherar House" it's known as. It took nearly a year to complete and it stands as a monument to his love of building. Risk, too, times being shaky now, in '93. But mostly, Sherar House is a symbol of a man's great love wrapped up in a promise kept.

Joseph began constructing it for real that very evening of the calf rescue. When we finished our walk, he dusted off his sketch book and began drawing.

He showed me designs of homes he once admired back east, doodles of ideas of his own.

A big home had always been a fantasy for me, one nurtured that one day of closeness with my mother where I danced alone and thought of marriage and my future children. I had never dreamed I'd see a home large enough to sleep one hundred, though after seeing what my husband could accomplish I should have been forewarned.

I wish that I could see as Joseph does, see the lines and angles set against a backdrop of his choosing. I close my eyes, imagine walls, a porch or roof. They never look the same to me as when the structure's finished.

"We'll visit places," Joseph said. "Make a picnic of it." And so before we asked the death-defying dynamite crew to blast the basement from the rocks, before Peter's crew began framing up the walls, we visited other houses in the region. We made an adventure of our search, my husband honoring my need for information, my joy in anticipation almost greater than the thing itself.

A favorite house belonged to John Moore, just north of the Grass Valley country. Californians, they'd sold out an interest in a gold mine and arrived with $100,000 and a wish to stay. They bought land outright, brought their cattle, and built a two-story Italianate home with single bay windows on both stories and gables and a chandelier that would turn an Astor's head. I especially liked the transoms over each door that twisted on a pin to help circulate the air and heat. Painted with sepia brown, they bore a spider web design and made me think immediately of Sunmiet and her dreamcatchers. They are repeated in our home.

They also planted trees about their house. Guess we all do that here, so few natural trees grow. Mrs. Moore had special problems what with her thirty-five cats and had to wrap the trunks in burlap to protect them. Spirit has left our trees alone so we have expanded our orchards.

Joseph wanted a fifty-room house. Fifty was the critical number for nurturing profits he told me. Fifty hardly sounded like a "home" to me. So we settled for a house with a basement under dining rooms and kitchens, laundry rooms and pantries, an office and large saloon and guest rooms all with linen closets numbering thirty-three.

"I'll not have this built as close to the river as your barn," I said, firm.

"The rimrocks limit us," he said, showing me as we walked beside the rope-like lava that had been the backdrop for our life. "And we can't go up much past three stories I don't believe. Guests won't climb those stairs; help neither."

But he agreed, we would not build right at the river's edge though where the house sits there's barely a wagon's width distance from the porch to those turbulent river waters.

It is the largest house between California and the Columbia River, a fact that tickles my husband no end. But then, he does not have to clean it.

I do find pleasure in seeing a building rise from nothing. It is much like watching flowers grow. The ground is cleared, a seed is planted, and we await the push through earth. It appears, fresh with dew each morning, each day having changed it by another leaf or two. Sherar House rose from the flat rocks beside the river in much the same way.

The foundation is of native stones, three feet thick. The basement is the coolest place around on hot summer days though I confess, I always scan it well for reptiles before I step my moccasins on the floor. We keep ice there, under sawdust just as Frederic had, and chip away at it through the year. It serves us well for iced teas, lemonade and the ice-creams we often make. It's almost too cold to store the peaches and apples in but is a good place to scuttle to during thunderstorms. We still keep the melons in the hay barn sunk into the grass from Finnigan and when we pluck them out at Christmas time they're just as pink and fresh as newly pulled.

All the lumber for Sherar House came from Redwood City, California. Joseph ordered horse teams loaded with redwood brought north to build our dream. We encountered our old friend J. W. in the process, passed into his seventies and still traveling, now driving freighters instead of leading mules. "For something to do," he said adjusting his smudged spectacles, "since the wife died."

If we could have constructed the hotel and done nothing else, our life would have been so simple. Why I should have expected such indicates I'm growing older, wanting life to sit beside me on a porch swing instead of pulling me into rough and tumble as it does, like children playing statue on a summer's eve. Even with the means to pay others to perform the work, the building engaged us. Other constructing did too.

At Finnigan, Joseph built a massive hay barn. It also housed a hundred sheep, as many calves, and stood a team and wagon, too. When that was finished, he built a smaller barn across The Dalles Military Highway. It is my favorite of the barns he built. Twenty cows can stand and chew their cuds in stanchions while calves wear barbed blabs forged up by the farrier to keep them from nursing while we milk. I still consider Finnigan mine and do not mind at all the time it takes for me to ride there, check on cows or calves, confer with Jim Dennis, or eat his famous sour dough biscuits while we talk of bulls and calves. And while I would not change my living in the canyon of the falls, I do enjoy the mountains sparkling in the summer heat or watching the weather roll in across the wheatfields from a distance. These are views afforded only when I leave the river canyon of my belonging and travel up the twisting grade, following the ridgetop on the way to my green river.

Because of my traveling back and forth the fourteen miles or so between Sherar's Bridge and Finnigan, Joseph decided that a decent road ought to be built up the grade, one that could still use the Buck Hollow bridge but take people north toward The Dalles Road better, let them use a buggy if they choose. Of course, he didn't expect to be thanking the Lord over that bridge nor rebuilding it either.

Having thought about the road, he began it. A trained engineer from Oregon State came down to see the work my husband did and he was more than complimentary. "As good as with surveying instruments," he said. "Better in some places where you've followed the contours of the ridges but fixed the pitch better for horses and wagons." He rode up the grade in a buggy, amazed that my husband and his crew of Indian workers had made this winding road ease its way up the ridge above Buck Hollow, rising like a lazy snake two thousand feet upward in just a mile or so. "Sure you've had no schooling in surveying?" he asked. My husband beamed.

His schooling has been seeing, walking, watching, learning from the land about him. He looks to work *with* the rocks and hills and natural grasses not against them; ponders why a grade's washed out then fixes it, being always gentle with the land leading to the falls he's come to love.

So when I make my trips to Finnigan and on to visit Ella, I have the finest road. And two fine bridges to go across to reach Sherar House, though after the difficulty we had last spring I wasn't sure if I would ever see again those bridges or our fine hotel.

Joseph oversaw construction even while we collected tolls, served meals and performed those daily drudgeries of living.

Joseph wished the tightest house, so the hotel is held together with fine wood pegs. Redwood glows everywhere. The maids keep it all shiny—inside walls, wainscoting, even the shutters on the dozens of windows, and the porches—of which there are several. During the season, Joseph displays his largest antlers from the second-story porch facing the river. And on the Fourth of July, we shoot flares and Tai's firecrackers out over the river to the delight of all the children.

At the toll paying end are bay windows. It's inviting, I like to think, and folks stop and count their toll in the bucket. Some come inside for a shot of C. J. Stubling's whiskey or a piece of fresh peach pie in season. They all don those buckskin moccasins.

I have weakened in my old age, and now let the setter sleep inside and sweep his tail across the hardwood floors. Spirit has managed to elude the coyotes and still be with us, a cat alone. "We live so far out we need our own tom cat," my husband says.

We will have Tai cooking here until he dies I'm sure, having added the latest cooking range to the large kitchen, boasting inside running water—enough to steam the plates. Two pantries, one dark one, to keep grains and flours in and all the weevils out. And a second dining room to seat all the help. Especially Anne who now directs their labors.

The water is a convenience found in few hotels. Each floor has a bathing room for tubbing privacy. And the latest in commodes. We've moved the outhouse seating in. No more rustling up moccasins for a night walk or creaking about in the dark for a thunder bucket. Most of the guests' rooms are on the second level and the housekeepers and servers that don't come across from the summer camps, sleep on the third.

When Joseph first showed me how the cliff orchard would be connected to the house I was skeptical; but his design is perfect. He's built a small bedroom with a porch facing the lava ledge. And from the porch my husband has created what has become his trademark: a bridge. We can cross from the hotel to our ledge garden, pick peaches and apples, and in the fall, gather sweetgrapes from Alice's flourishing arbor.

That man and his bridges! Who could have known how those bridges would impact our lives, taking us from here to there, across difficult waters. Bridges are a part of us, my husband's dreams, even our hopes for a family. God always provided someone or something along our path to make needed bridges across life's paths.

At Sunmiet's mother's burial not long ago, the elder spoke of bridges, too. At the dressing, Morning Dove's body was draped in white buckskins and wrapped in a colorful blanket. We mourners then each picked up handfuls of earth and dropped them on Morning Dove's body, walking by the gravesite, women first, then men. And when we finished, the elder spoke his prayer. "Death is just a bridge between this world and the next," Indian Peter said. "It is not to fear. We will not be on this bridge for as long as the eagle flies, but only for a moment. Then we will pass over to those waiting on the other side." I could picture Rachel, Pauline, and Loyal, even Papa, arms outstretched, waiting.

I thought of those words earlier this June, too, when J. W. and I stood near the Buck Hollow bridge. I'd been at Finnigan with trusty Bandy, my bay gelding. Patsy, the Irish Setter, panted beside me on the buggy's leather seat, her tongue dripping onto a bouquet of wildflowers that slowly wilted beside me—evidence I'd been dallying along the creek that perfect June day in 1893. High rimrocks lined the river canyon on either side and sliced cleanly into the royal lupine blue sky.

I took a brief mid-day break beneath the cottonwood trees and let my hat lie in the grassy shade. Even worked my knife on a soft wood block, carving. I didn't stay long. Joseph would be coming back from the flour mill or perhaps return early from work on the grade and I could meet him at the house for supper if I hurried.

I met J. W. and his freighter at the Buck Hollow bridge, just before the place where the clear stream joins the river, below the twisting, swirling falls and below our own Sherar's Bridge. Pure coincidence that I should meet him there beside the river. He was ahead of me on the grade. When he saw me behind him, he pulled up, motioned me beside his freighter, and we chatted a bit. He didn't rub his eyes, not once.

I guess I'd forgotten how kind his leathered face was, how broad his smile. He squinted his sun-hardened eyes at me and I wondered if he still saw a sassy girl sitting beside a dog or if his memory had grown older too and so he saw me as the busy, bony matron I've become.

"Good timing, Missus," he said, touching his fingers to his hat in greeting. "Go on ahead. No reason for you to ride drag."

"Why, thank you, J. W.," I said, still somewhat formal as his presence always made me think of Papa, too. "I've done my share of tasting dust today. We could certainly use some rain up the hollow, dry as it is." I shaded my eyes with my hand, aware that the sun prepared to set behind the rimrocks as we spoke.

We chatted for a moment more. His gnarled hands crossed gently over his knees, loosely holding reins. His bulky body covered in patched homespun shifted easily as the team stomped impatiently, rattled singletrees and loose tugs, flicked tails at flies. Bees still hummed in the June heat and the fragrance of late lilacs drifted to us in the light breeze. J. W. eventually got down to check the harness, then tipped his sweat-stained hat at me and waved me on. "Be straight behind you," he said, "in a flash."

I snapped the reins on Bandy's back and started across the bridge, thinking the roar that rose behind me was the wind picking up as it always does in the river canyon at dusk.

J. W. and his team and wagon started across the bridge behind me, I thought, as Buck Hollow passed under me. I heard the clatter at a distance meant not to press me or the horse. And then the rising shout of men's voices, shouting not in anticipation of reaching the inn for a good evening's meal, but men in front of me waving frantically, swinging their arms to hurry me on. Peter ran toward me. Bandy, startled and confused by the running and the roaring, reared backward, stepped sideways.

I worked the reins, my knuckles white, calling to the horse to steady him as we rolled across the bridge. The dog barked close to my ear.

"Patsy! Quiet!" I snapped. She leaped forward, well beyond the frightened horse. I heard J. W.'s voice somewhere behind me, yelling, his words muffled, lifting now above a roar I just could not place. Peter ran, ran toward me. Behind him other wranglers, their faces masks of fright and terror.

I heard the roar and splinter of wood behind me and Patsy's barking as she ran, scaring further my terrified horse charging toward safety at the toll bridge and the barn. Peter and the men stopped the buggy, lifted me out, swirling my skirt at my ankles as my feet touched the rocks.

I turned back to Buck Hollow bridge. A gasp caught in my throat. Instead of the bridge, I watched a wall of water fourteen feet high push the gentle little creek into a massive, rushing flood of roots of trees and logs and twisted shrubs and branches. I stared at the brown legs of J. W.'s team rolling between frothy white and turquoise water, rolling over pots and pans and tiny cans of baking powder swirling up and over and beyond, pushing, pushing on into the Deschutes River, taking with it everything now in its way. It spared not even the splintering bridge I'd just been on.

The twisting, dirty water pulled the animals over and over. I simply stood and watched, spent by the energy of seeing so much loss in just a flash of seconds. J. W. stood forlorn but safely on this side.

A cloudburst and flash flood and his timing for kindness wiped his freighter out. His ability to scramble from his team and up the rocky side saved his life. That, and his over-worked guardian angel.

He made his way to me, asked first about my safety. We shared another bond having stepped just ahead of fate. "Beats swimmin' with bow-legged women," J. W. told me, his eyes sparkling.

"And I'm not even," I said, and laughed as his words telescoped me back all those years to his misplaced toast the day we became engaged.

The men sat for hours with him later in the bar, pouring Stubling's liquid for him, shaking their heads in dismay. They recalled other flash floods they'd seen though none at quite so close a distance.

The fading red and yellow stage from The Dalles arrived; meals were served. I found a brief moment to tell Joseph when he returned with the Bakeoven grade crew. His jaws clenched tightly and he held me close. Then in a rare public expression of affection, he kissed me tenderly before striding to J. W. to thank him expansively at the bar.

During the evening, I caught Joseph's eyes once or twice across the room as he chatted with the men; swimming eyes that spied everything it seemed, then added a softening touch. He lifted a graying eyebrow and sent an "arrow smile" he called them, shot over the heads of others, an expression of comfort when words were not possible to share.

I was anxious for the quiet of our room where I could sort out my thoughts of this day of chance and sweet survival.

"You're like a protective bird," he told me later in our new bedroom, "nesting." I picked a thread from the lace window curtains and tightened the corner on the coverlet before pulling the Hudson Bay blanket smoothly over the down mattress. Sunmiet and Anne still urge me to use Pendleton blankets in the Sherar House, but I have always liked the whiteness of Hudson Bay's and so stand firm. A cobweb had attached itself to the oak picture frame hanging forward from the wall.

"Or that sandpiper Sunmiet called you," Joseph continued, "always managing to stay one trace ahead of the waves they chase while cleaning the beach."

I settled, finally, at the dressing table staring at the dark huckleberry eyes staring back.

A breeze from across the Deschutes River stirred the lacy bedroom window curtains and fluttered the dreamcatcher's feather as it hung on the wainscoted wall. My eye caught the feather's movement. A dreamcatcher: leather and sinew, feather and beads, history and hope: a gift from Sunmiet and Inanuks.

"At least we can still catch dreams," I said, putting an epitaph on the day. Looking up, I caught my husband's gaze in the mirror as he watched me from the bed. My eyes glued to his, I gently tugged on the tortoise shell combs, felt my hair fall like summer rain over my narrow shoulders and pale chemise, stopping just a whisper from the floor.

"A day like this one needs a predictable ending, don't you think?" I said.

"Strength and flexibility too," he added.

"We'll replace J. W.'s outfit?" We'd been at this trail-crossing before.

Joseph nodded agreement, said nothing as he watched me. Like a blind woman untangling loose yarn, I ran my fingers through the dark strands working out the tiny snags, comforted by the nightly ritual. I reached for the silver brush that lay on the dresser cloth next to one of my carved animals. The brush had been an extravagant fifth wedding anniversary present from Joseph. His extravagance worries me less. I find I'm enjoying the spoils of his expansive heart and generous spirit. The silver handle of the brush felt cool and soothing.

As I brushed, hand over hand, I considered: I am not yet forty-five years old, and once again death has slipped its cold shadow beside me and I hadn't even the slightest inkling or premonition that it lurked nearby. It does not bode well for a woman who seeks control, works still on letting Someone larger plan for her life.

"Coulda been cold as a wagon tire," J. W. had told Joseph philosophically at the bar. "We beat the Dutch for sure." I think J. W. knew he'd carry more pounds now; like me, learn that surviving put an extra burden on a soul, came with responsibility saddled on its back. This time, though, we all survived and none of us carries the survivor's guilt of living life fully while someone we loved could not.

"Not sure how ye can look so settled after such an unsettling day," Joseph said. "I know you're resilient, but even strong and solid trees should look a little windblown following a storm!"

"I learned to cope by leanin' into the wind," I said, "just like you told me."

In the mirror I watched him cross his arms behind his head and lean into the maple headboard. Joseph smiled, then became serious. "Ye mean everything to me," he said. "All the dreams, all the things I hope to do yet, hold no value if I lose ye. You're still a huckleberry above a persimmon. Always will be to me."

I'm still learning to accept compliments and did nothing with that one out loud, felt the fullness of belonging, inside.

He watched me a while longer and then I saw this gleam in his eye; an idea, a vision forming in his head.

"What is it?" I said, wary, light. "Don't you have to check corrals, the bridge, or whatever?"

"I've something else in mind," he said, a grin forming.

"We've a houseful coming tomorrow, to celebrate the opening," I protested. "Ella and Carrie and their broods, my brother, George...Sunmiet, her family. The De Moss Family Bards will arrive early to play...no time for anything but work or rest until they get here."

By then, he stood behind me, smiling at my busyness. He lifted me by my shoulders and turned me to him, holding my face like precious crystal in his calloused hands. He kissed my forehead, brushed his gray beard against my skin. In a voice as deep and smooth as a cello, he said "I love you, Janie. Always have, always will. Let them all come tomorrow. Tonight, while it's just the two of us, I want the first dance."

Tears welled up behind my eyes.

"Here?" I asked, my heart pounding like we'd just begun our lives together. The breeze fluttered the dreamcatcher over the bed, separated the lace curtains to reveal the moonless night sky. Through the window I caught the fireflies of the fishermen's fires near the scaffoldings, hoping for salmon and eels through the night. I hoped no one would be injured, lost to the water, wanted no more tragedy to add to this day. I heard a baby cry in its sleep, then quiet, safe for the night.

Joseph brought me back from the outside, into his presence. He touched his fingers to mine and began to hum "Sweet Betsy from Pike" as he pulled me to him. I felt the rough of his vest through my thin gown, the gentle touch of his hands at the small of my back. He curled my fingers in his and curled our hands to his heart, his chin lightly touching my head.

While the lamplight reflected off the mirror of our new bedroom, we danced. While the roar of the Sherar's falls echoed off the rimrocks, we danced. Patsy lay at the foot of the bed, head on her paws, one eyebrow raised in question. The smell of my husband's leather and our home's new lumber rose like a comforting fragrance. Soft light surrounded us as we swept gingerly across the floor.

"I could not be happier in my life than I am at this moment," I told him. Throat tight, I sunk into his chest.

I felt wetness on my cheek, felt him swallow. "And we might have missed it all if we hadn't taken a chance, wanted this dance," he said.

"I love you, too, Joseph Sherar," I told him.

We adjusted a little, he for his leg and me for my height. We adapted, as we had and would need to, traveling the path laid out for us, turning it into our own. Joseph swirled me, lifted me off of my feet.

A hundred things awaited doing for tomorrow; but tonight, I'd take what I'd been given and would cope, supple and strong, thankful, as we danced on into the rest of our very full lives.

EPILOGUE

❧

JULY 1907

Dawn came like a baby's breath: soft and sweet and warm. It blushed the river canyon with its soothing pink then spilled through the starched curtains into the bedroom where Joseph sat. He heard the Seth Thomas clock strike six just as the muted light brushed across his tired eyes and he closed the last of the leather bound books. What a gift she'd left! And such a surprise! Ella had discovered them in the back of Jane's closet while searching for the box holding her amethyst watch. Ella knew Jane would want to wear that watch this day.

Dusting the books off the night before, he'd slid into Jane's leather chair beside the bed intending only to rest a moment before struggling to remove his boots. Instead, he'd read through the night, his boots still on.

Jane's final notebook entry lay now balanced on his bony knees. "She's the one," he said out loud, his words causing the Irish Setter to raise his eyes to the man, cock his head to the voice. "She writes about this old man, his buildings and roads. But they were nothing. Nothing." He shook his head in wonder. "She's what's held the coping saw with a steady hand."

He shook his head again, this time in sadness. With his right hand, Joseph lifted his left and rubbed some of the stiffness from it. His limbs were always

415

stiff in the morning and then they seemed to tremble and shake with a life of their own. She had always massaged his hand at sunrise, kneading it like a yeast dough, helping him ease into the day as they talked. He wondered when she'd found the time to write all those words! "Had no idea how she felt about some of those things, Gus," he told the dog who thumped his tail on the redwood floors at the sound of his name. "The watch, the dances, Sunmiet's sweathouse. Even that old coping saw." He shook his head. "Wonder why she stopped writing in '93?" She had stopped fourteen years too soon, he thought.

Maybe there were other notebooks. "Have to ask her," he said.

Before the words had even left his mouth, he felt the piercing pain of grief rise up to steal his breath, eclipse his heart. His eyes watered. He swallowed, let his head drop back against the chair. Remembering, the tears came, companions to the sobs that followed. He had no way to ask her now, nor ever hear her answer, on this earth. He cried silently, his head sunk into the chair, her chair. Her scent still lingered on the leather.

When he heard the knock on the door, he stopped himself.

"Father? You awake?"

"Awake," he said, clearing his throat, his voice husky. He thumbed his eyes with his right hand.

"You need to come, Father." Ella's voice held urgency.

"I'll get me cane," he said, looking for it. "Be with you." The journal fell from his knees as he struggled awkwardly from the leather chair, wiping his face, drying his hands on the trousers over his knees.

She unlatched the door to the bedroom to help him search. If she noticed he still wore his coat and vest of the night before, or that the bed had not been slept in, she said nothing. She simply located the hickory cane beneath the clutter of journals he'd spent the night reading. She didn't take the time to tidy them up. Enclosed with a hurriedly tied sash, her nightrobe billowed out around her, a single braid dusted the floor as she bent to retrieve his cane.

"Have to keep track of it meself," he said taking it from her, noting the pain in her eyes. "Now, what's the bother?" he said kindly.

"They want to come in."

"Who?"

"The Indians."

"Do they now." His voice held a hint of wonder.

"They're standing outside, waiting. Guess that's what they want. To come in."

"Well, let's go see, then," he said with effort and leaned into his cane.

The two made their way down the stairs of the Sherar House followed by the setter who stopped behind them on the landing. Joseph gazed at the pink dawn pouring out into the canyon, lighting the faces of silent mourners that stretched beyond his sight toward the falls. Their falls. Her falls, too.

"Open 'em," he directed Ella who padded in slippered feet to the doors, letting the new dawn pour in. At the sight of Joseph standing in the doorway behind Ella, a line began forming from the people waiting outside.

Sunmiet led, dressed in her best shell dress, a wide beaded belt tucking in her thickening waist, a woven basket hat on her head. Old women in their buckskins and wing dresses with soft doeskin moccasins on their feet followed her. Then the young women made their way, some with their own toddlers in tow, black hair shining, ermine skins lifted lightly from their braids by the morning breeze. All carried gifts of themselves.

Sunmiet moved up the steps of the house and quietly swayed through the doors of the dining room toward the parlor and her friend, her eyelashes blinking rapidly as she passed by Joseph.

Jane's body lay on a hastily made coffin as it had since arriving from The Dalles hospital the afternoon before. Joseph had coped the coffin's corners, pounded the nails himself.

"They've been out there all night," Ella whispered to him, grabbing her robe tighter around her against the morning cool.

"Have they now," he said. He wrapped his arms around his only daughter.

He had not sent them word. Should have; but he knew that they would know. He never knew how the word went out, but it always did.

"When they started toward the house, at dawn, I wasn't sure what to do. So many..." she said, her voice trailing off.

"Just appreciate it," he told her. "Your mother would."

He watched the gift bearers pass before him, nodding their kerchiefed heads at him, acknowledging his loss, their loss, as they left parts of themselves at her feet: a beaded bag, dried salmon, huckleberries, shells and wampum strings, roots, ivory game sticks, a child's doll. Anne lifted her youngest to lay a dreamcatcher on Jane's pillow. Some left blankets, fine tanned hides, baskets and mats, treasured family heirlooms all set on the reds and browns and rich plaid greens of the Pendleton blankets Sunmiet had spread like royalty out before Jane's casket. He smiled through his tears. She would have Pendleton blankets after all.

When the women and children had laid their gifts they passed back by him, touching his hands like a shadow, looking briefly into his eyes, their faces filled with tenderness, eyes sharing pools of emptiness and loss. The scent of smoked leather lingered on his hands as they passed. Sunmiet and Anne, then Inanucks and her children. They hugged him, their hands free to hold him.

"The eagle has carried her to her place of belonging," Sunmiet told him, her voice thick with grief.

They offered prayers for him and Ella and Carrie and their husbands. Jane's brother, George, who was there now too, had joined them as in a receiving line at a wedding.

If only he could see it as rejoicing. Rejoicing because his wife was finally released from the pain of the infection the doctors could not stop. Such a simple thing, a cut that did not heal. He wished he could see it as rejoicing, knowing he would someday see her once again. Yes, he had that to comfort him.

He didn't want to think now, about not seeing her. He had believed she would survive him. She was the survivor, the strong one. "Men make plans," she'd always said, "but God directs their paths."

"He took you on a different path, Janie," he said out loud, "and you were strong on it, knew when to bend, you did."

He wanted now to just experience these acts of devotion, take inside of him the wealth of the tributes, fill up with the depth of emotion they settled on him like a wool blanket, settled on him from the people she loved and called her family.

When the women finished, the men followed bringing their gifts: dip nets, a salmon freshly caught; arrow heads and hand-tooled scrapes. They laid pieces of their prized regalia, porcupine necklaces, moccasins, ermine skins, a drum. Peter and George and George's sons moved up the steps of the hotel, and Joseph saw that Peter's black hat no longer held his prized eagle feather as he passed by.

Instead, he watched the feather appear at Jane's feet, Peter's hand lifting in farewell like a butterfly in flight.

Joseph could feel the tears begin again as his nose burned. He swallowed, leaned heavily on his cane, overwhelmed by the magnitude of their tribute to her, the gift her life had been, the depth of his loss.

"They must have loved her so," Ella said, a film on her eyes.

"They leave no doubt," Joseph answered.

He let his arm drape around his daughter, pulled her to him and stroked her head at the temple as she put her head on his shoulder. The procession showed no sign of ending.

Watching, Joseph stopped himself each time his thoughts moved too far forward, to when he would have to face the days alone, without her. There would be no one to tell of this moment who would understand as well as she. He shook his head. For now, he would remember this dawn, maybe even write it down as she had. He used to do that, write things in his sketch book. What was that verse he'd taken from his book and shared with her, the one and only poem he'd ever written? *"To be so loved that time stands still when I'm with you, and does not start again until you've gone away, and I am left alone to wonder why the hours move so quickly when you're with me, and so slowly once you've gone."* With her, time had moved so quickly. He was alone, now, time leaving her memory in its tracks. How she had touched him!

"Was she did the touching," he said. Ella nodded. The procession going on before him testified to that, to her strength and caring. And the way she had eased into their lives. How had she put it, her description of their beginnings? *Like the slow rising of the river from an early snowmelt in the mountains, almost without notice, flooding, new over old.*

Gus whined. The dog pushed on his hand, panted. "They loved her, too," Joseph said as he patted the dog. He scratched the setter's ears and watched the procession make its way back toward the turbulent river. An eagle circled, dipping its wings to the wind.

As the man leaned to quiet the animal, he saw the beaded banners he had missed. Someone had draped them across Jane's folded hands, the ends of the banners spilling out over her casket to the floor. With Kása's prized hummingbird designs at the ends, the shiny cut beads spelled out in glorious color: *Mother. Kása. Friend.*

"She was all of those," Joseph said, remembering gratefully the richness she had given to his life and to so many others. "And oh, so very much more."

Author's Note

⚜

JANE AND JOSEPH SHERAR came into my soul with Donald von Borstel's words. Written by a schoolboy as part of a county-wide essay during the Depression, Donald's words drew me to this frontier couple who lived and worked beside the falls in the mid-1800s. *A Sweetness to the Soul* grew from their lives.

These remarkable people did indeed make their mark beside the narrowest section of the Deschutes River, one of Oregon's most wild and scenic rivers, in a remote and rugged canyon. For more than thirty years, they operated an inn renowned for its hospitality and care. They ranched, constructed the famous bridge, and returned their profits to improve the roads, portions of which can still be seen and driven on today as part of Oregon Highway 216 between Tygh Valley and Grass Valley. They built their Sherar House in 1893. The Sherars could not have become known as great road builders and hotel managers without the help of Indians and mulehandlers, housekeepers and buckaroos. Their lives intersected with people of color as portrayed: Latinos, Chinese, Native Americans. Theirs was an interdependent life despite its remoteness.

Theirs was also a devoted life. Evidence exists that Jane and Joseph Sherar shared a love that transcended the difference in their ages. Descendants of Carrie treasure Joseph Sherar's signed valentines and Christmas cards. He did indeed give a gold and amethyst watch to Jane, another gold watch to Carrie.

The characters of Jane Herbert, her parents and siblings are all based on real people. Mr. Herbert lost an eye on the trail and was later elected a Wasco County Commissioner. Elizabeth Herbert was active in the Methodist Church. George Herbert became a sheriff of Baker County in Oregon. The tragedy of Jane's siblings did happen and there is strong evidence that these deaths affected Jane and her mother in the way portrayed. A brief notation in a Wasco County History published in the 1950s, quotes the daughter of Mrs. C. M. Grimes (Ella's daughter) as stating that "the Herbert and Sherar families became enemies" over the adoption of Ella which happened many years after it was begun because Mrs. Herbert would not give Ella up.

Joseph Sherar was known as one of the greatest road builders of the west. A remarkable visionary, he could have met Frederic Tudor who did ship ice from the rivers and lakes of Vermont to New Orleans and beyond, a fact reported by J. C. Furnas in his book *The Americans: A Social History of the United States, 1587-1914*. Furnas also reported the sea slug caper. Someone much like Frederic Tudor very likely influenced the creative genius of Joseph Sherar. Arriving in San Francisco in 1855, Joseph Sherar spent the next years packing with Hispanic handlers and their families into gold fields of California and southern Oregon; ranching and acquiring a fortune. In the 1860s, he arrived in Oregon, packed and farmed again in two different places prior to purchasing the site along the Deschutes. Accounts of his holdings are based on fact.

Several characters did exist and interact with the Sherars. French Louie, "Pretty" Dick Barter, Mr. Crickett, Sam Holmes and Monroe Grimes, John Todd, and O'Brien were all real. Lodenma May and Philamon Lathrope are recorded as witnesses for the Sherar's wedding, April 26, 1863. Alice M. is listed as a "hskpeer" in the 1880 census of Sherar's Falls. J. W. Case was indeed a packer though his influence in the Sherar's lives is strictly fiction. Ella Turner's family did mine for gold in Canyon City; Carrie Sherar joined the Sherars in 1885; their marriages honor historical information, as does Joseph's family in New York.

Indian Peter LaHomesh, his wife Mary, and their son George Peters are an important part of the Sherar story. Margaret Charley, great-granddaughter of Frank Peter, Indian Peter's grandson, provided information about Mary's

Indian name, the family's love of learning, and George's real name. Only non-Indians persisted in calling him "George Washington."

Tribal member Olney Patt related the story of Mr. Sherar's difficulty in pronunciation of Indian names and that his great-grandfather was called "Patrick" when he was paid. The family name, "Patt," shortened from "Patrick," originated from Mr. Sherar. Several tribal members reported stories about their fondness for the Sherars, their integrity and compassion, and remember him as "a great man among my people."

The Sahaptin and Wasco languages have only recently been written down thanks to the Culture and Heritage Department of the Confederated Tribes of the Warm Springs Reservation. The words used by characters are as accurate reflection as was possible for a non-Sahaptin speaker.

The Sherars became affluent. Mr. Sherar was well respected for his integrity and ability to work with people of all races and creeds, though his separate toll charge for Chinese people is also substantiated by family history. He did ship an entire train load of wool to Philadelphia and evidence exists that he made a first fortune shipping a load around the horn to Boston. The Sherars did build the bridge across the Deschutes and did engineer and maintain nearly thirty miles of roads down some of the steepest, most rugged real estate in Oregon. The roads and bridge opened up the vast grasslands for homesteaders in the years ahead. Records of the 1890s show Sherars collecting thirty thousand dollars one year in tolls at the bridge; they spent over seventy-five thousand dollars on the roads in their lifetimes. Amazingly, the Sherars did give their generous gift to a family at risk of losing their children though their name was not Blivens and they replaced the Heppner string and the freighter's outfit as recorded.

Mrs. Sherar was known for her meticulous management, great hotel food and service, her relationship with the Indians, and her compassion. Stories support her request that people don moccasins at the inn. She knew her way around guns, and the incident with the Indian woman and her husband is based on fact, as is the incident with the Chinese cook, the flash flood, and the rescued calf. A news account of her funeral is accurately reflected by the epilogue. As though unable to live without his wife, Joseph Sherar died six months after her.

The John Moore home still stands outside the town of Moro, Oregon. A

Sherar-built barn can be seen along The Old Dalles Military Highway at Finnigan. The spelling of Finnigan is taken from handwritten notes of Joseph Sherar. The description of the Sherar House is factual including the ledge orchard and sweetgrape arbor. Photographs of the Sherar House and their family are displayed at the Sherman County Museum in Moro, Oregon.

Still today, the Confederated Tribes of Warm Springs is composed of Wasco, Warm Springs, and Paiute peoples who continue to live together on the reservation in Central Oregon. True to their history of conciliation, Paiute families were invited to join the Confederation well after the Treaty of Middle Oregon Indians in 1855 and after the Bannock War. Today, the Confederated Tribes operate a number of successful businesses in Oregon including a lumber mill, resort, radio stations, hydroelectric plant, the Museum at Warm Springs, as well as the departments necessary to operate a small city including an early childhood education center licensed to serve more than four hundred children and their families. The generally peaceful history with non-Indian peoples is based on fact. Each year on June 25, the tribes honor the treaty signing with *Pi-um-sha,* a powwow of celebration. The site at Sherar's Falls came back to the care and custody of the Confederated Tribes in 1980.

Today, where the Sherars lived and loved, only the spindly scaffoldings remain. A new, concrete bridge permits crossing. In 1994, because of the decline in the fish population, the Confederated Tribes of Warm Springs took the leadership to halt fishing at Sherar's Falls with the hope the salmon will someday return. Only ceremonial fishing from family fishing sites is currently permitted there.

This is a work of fiction and I, alone, am responsible for the words written to bring this story to life. Some actual events in this story were changed for dramatic effect; others were added in an effort to honor the spirit of the Sherars and the truth as it was recorded and remembered.

Eagles still soar over the cascading falls of the Deschutes, and the natives who stand beside the river of their ancestors still speak of the friendly spirits at Sherar's Bridge. The Dreamcatcher series hopes to keep alive their stories and the stories of other remarkable frontier people who with strength, flexibility, and faith followed their dreams into the future.

All words are Sahaptin (Warm Springs language) unless indicated.

ach'ái—magpie

aswan—boy

Chewana—Columbia River

chuush—water

chchuu txanati—"Please be quiet" said to a group

hehe—happy

ikauxau—owl

ikawa (Wasco)—badger

inanucks (Wasco)—otter

iyái—pregnant

kápn—digging stick

kot-num (Wasco)—long house

k'usi—horse

k'usik'usi—dog

k'aalas—raccoon

kása—grandmother

lukws—round root with white flowers

nana—sister

niix máicqi—"good morning"

páwapaatam—"help me"

piaxi—bittersweet root

pimx—uncle, father's brother

shaptákai—Indian suitcase

spi'lya—coyote

wapas—root bag or sally bag

wilalík—rabbit

yáiya—brother

From *Warm Springs Sahaptin: How the Warm Springs Language Works: A Grammar*. Copyright © 1991 by the Confederated Tribes of the Warm Springs Reservation of Oregon. Used by permission.

ALSO BY JANE KIRKPATRICK...

LOVE TO WATER MY SOUL

A remarkable story of God's constancy and provision
for all lovers of history, romance, and faith...

"I carved and shaped my name, deciding, 'Alice M' did fit me. But it is 'Shell Flower' that I cherish. I received it my third year with the Wadaduka people. I added other names through the years, but 'Shell Flower' pleased me most for it was given as a gift and as a sign that I was loved. It is such love that makes things grow, even yellow shell flowers that bob and weave in the desert spring. And it is the memory of such love that waters my soul..."

Based on historical characters and events, *Love to Water My Soul* recounts the dramatic story of an abandoned white child rescued by Indians. Among Oregon's Paiute people, Shell Flower seeks love and a place of belonging...only to be cast away from her home.

In the years that follow, she faces a new life in the world of the white man—a life filled with both attachment and loss—yet finds that God faithfully unites her with a love that fills all longing in this heart-warming sequel to Jane Kirkpatrick's award-winner, *A Sweetness to the Soul.*